RAFFLES REVISITED

Raffles Revisited

NEW ADVENTURES OF A
FAMOUS GENTLEMAN CROOK

Barry Perowne

INTRODUCTION BY OTTO PENZLER
DRAWINGS BY RICHARD ROSENBLUM

1817

HARPER & ROW, PUBLISHERS
NEW YORK, EVANSTON, SAN FRANCISCO, LONDON

Grateful acknowledgment is made to the following magazines for permission to reprint the stories listed:

Ellery Queen's Mystery Magazine for "The Grace-and-Favor Crime" (originally titled "A Costume Piece"); "Princess Amen" (originally titled "Raffles and the Princess Amen"); "The Birthday Diamonds"; "Six Golden Nymphs"; "The Governor of Gibraltar" (originally titled "Jack of Diamonds").

Saint Magazine for "Kismet and the Dancing Boy" (originally titled "The Rooking of Raffles"); "The Dartmoor Hostage" (originally titled "Raffles and the Silver Dish"); "Man's Meanest Crime" (originally titled "Raffles and the Meanest Thief"); "The Coffee Queen Affair" (originally titled "Raffles and the Coffee Queens"); "The Doctor's Defense" (originally titled "Raffles and the Doctor's Defence"); "The Riddle of Dinah Raffles."

John Bull Magazine for "The Gentle Wrecker" (under the title "Raffles and the Gentle Wrecker"); "An Error in Curfew" (under the title "Raffles and the Banned House"); "Bo-Peep in the Suburbs" (originally titled "Raffles and Little Bo-Peep").

FIRST EDITION

Designed by Lydia Link

Library of Congress Cataloging in Publication Data

Perowne, Barry.
   Raffles revisited; new adventures of a famous gentlemen crook.
   CONTENTS: The grace-and-favor crime.—Princess Amen.—Kismet and the dancing boy. [etc.]
   I. Title.
PZ3.P426Rag3 [PR6031.E54]   823'.8   73–14321
ISBN 0–06–013314–7

TO

Frederic Dannay

AND

Evelyn B. Byrne

AND

The memory of E. W. HORNUNG,
creator of The Amateur Cracksman

Contents

Introduction

There is certainly no criminal ambiance inside the club. A subdued fire is reflected by leather chairs and mahogany tables, enhancing the warm glow brought on by several glasses of old port. The talk is of hunting, King Edward, past military campaigns, India, gout. One of the younger members has slipped away early, with discreet innuendo, and his companions have exchanged smugly knowing glances, chuckling enviously. The lucky devil was off to a rendezvous, and it would not have shocked these respectable gentlemen to learn that his tryst was with a young wife of one of the dozing, chess-playing former colonels in the other room.

It is just past midnight, but most respectable people are already behind locked doors. What transpires behind those doors may be less than strictly respectable, but it is generally carried off in good taste, at any rate.

The hiss of the chilling wind, the clip-clop of a horse and the rattle of the hansom's iron-covered wheels on cobblestone, and the regular tap of the adventurer's footsteps on pavement are the night's only sounds. The yellow fog, billowing visibly under a gas-lamp, effectively muffles the city's usual whispered cacaphony of indistinguishable noises.

The match lighting his Sullivan cigarette reveals eyes blazing with anticipation, but his jaunty steps carry him to a rendezvous that would cause the red faces at his club to bluster and cough if they knew its object was not the sensual pleasure of flesh, but the greater conquest of courage. A few steps more, and he is at the window of a darkened house. In a moment, his fingers will caress, not the warm softness of a woman, but the cold hardness of diamonds. It is over in minutes, the evening clothes remaining unsoiled, unwrinkled. His gait is brisker, perhaps, as he retraces his steps; not because of fear, but of élan. It is the third successful bit of work in as many weeks, and the satisfied smile does not diminish as he cheerily greets a bobby on his nocturnal walk.

Only a handful of universally recognized characters live in the pages of English literature. The authors who created them may be forgotten, the books in which they appeared often remain unread, but the characters are more real and alive than most actual historical entities.

Robinson Crusoe is such a character, and Alice and Peter Pan, perhaps Silas Marner and Tom Jones, and certainly a few of the creations of Shakespeare and Dickens. It is an extraordinary achievement to put words on paper and watch them grow into flesh and bone and soul, instantly recognized on any busy street corner in the world. That sort of creation seems as much a religious event as a literary one.

Ironically, this ultimate literary triumph has been most often achieved by the much-maligned genre of mystery, crime, and detective fiction, and its far-reaching family of shady relations. Some of the most illustrious members of the elite community of fictional giants come from the alleged fringes of "real" literature: Sherlock Holmes, Frankenstein's monster, Dr. Fu Manchu, James Bond, Count Dracula, Dr. Jekyll and, of course, Raffles.

The first adventures of A. J. Raffles, the gentleman jewel thief, appeared in 1899, in a volume of short stories by E. W. Hornung: *The Amateur Cracksman.* This was followed by two more collections: *The Black Mask* (published in the United States as *Raffles: Further Adventures of the Amateur Cracksman,* in 1901) and *A Thief in the Night* (1905), and one novel, *Mr. Justice Raffles* (1909). Although Hornung lived until 1921, he did not write about his cricket-playing rascal again. When Hornung died, it seemed that no more would be known about Raffles, whose fame and popularity rivaled that of Sherlock Holmes in Edwardian England. The original stories were reprinted again and again, motion pictures (starring John Barrymore, Ronald Colman and others in the title role) appeared, but the public thirst for tales of the debonair safe-cracker could not be slaked. New stories were wanted, and in 1932 they arrived, but not without a good deal of intense soul-searching.

Barry Perowne, then a successful twenty-four-year-old crime fiction writer living in Mallorca, received a cable from his agent telling him to return to London at once if convenient; if inconvenient, to come all the same. Born Philip Atkey, Perowne was the nephew of Bertram Atkey, whose many stories about Smiler Bunn, the ingenious crook, enjoyed wide popularity during the first part of the century. Recently married, Perowne had just had his first hardcover book published (with contracts for two more in hand), and he had two series characters running in the best-selling British periodical, *The Thriller.* He was not rusting from inactivity.

Perowne's agent and Montague Haydon, the editor of *The Thriller,* proposed that he revive Raffles for the pages of the magazine. At that time, the adventures of another popular scoundrel, Simon Templar, better known as The Saint, were appearing in *The Thriller.* They had a large readership, and the editors felt that the additional exploits of a similar character would satisfy the public's demand for this type of story. They neglected to tell Perowne that the proposed revival of Raffles had already been offered to The

Saint's creator, Leslie Charteris, and had been declined by him.

Perowne's decision to produce Raffles stories for *The Thriller* was made with reluctance, especially because of the type of story Haydon wanted. The magazine was accurately named, and its huge readership did not expect to find cerebral exercises, or slow-paced mood pieces, between its covers. They wanted action—fast, violent, breathless—and the new Raffles stories were to be no exception.

Unlike Hornung's Edwardian gentleman cracksman, who was comfortable in posh clubs and at weekend cricket parties at country estates, the new Raffles was to be a two-fisted adventurer whose action-filled exploits took place in the contemporary settings of 1932. Arrangements were made with the Hornung estate, and the career of fiction's most illustrious rogue was placed in Perowne's hands.

He had mixed emotions about the situation. "Whether the egg they were putting in my ink-stained mitts would hatch out a bird-of-paradise or a cockatrice, I personally was by no means sure," Perowne said in retrospect. "It seemed to be up to me. So I roosted on the egg, and in far less time—due to deadlines—than I should have preferred, I brought forth, dubiously clucking, the first four 30,000-word stories."

The series was an instant success, and more than a dozen serializations followed in *The Thriller,* later published in book form. But, while the stories were good, they did not involve the genuine Raffles, in spite of such superficial gimmicks as rooms in The Albany, Sullivan cigarettes, and his hero-worshiping companion, Bunny Manders. The stories were pure thrillers in the best pulp magazine tradition: quickly written, quickly read, and quickly forgotten. These action yarns are not read today, to the enhancement of Raffles' stature as a literary figure—and much to Perowne's relief.

In fact, he tried to terminate them himself by getting Raffles married in a long 150,000-word novel, *She Married Raffles,* the motion picture rights to which were purchased by a Hollywood studio in 1939. At this point, although Perowne disclaims any connection, World War II immediately broke out in earnest; among the casualties were *The Thriller* and the Raffles series in it.

Then, in 1950, Perowne was in New York and Frederic Dannay invited him to begin a new series of Raffles stories for *Ellery Queen's Mystery Magazine*—but, this time, setting the adventures in the original period to which they rightly belong: late Victorian and Edwardian England. The challenges involved in this were intriguing, but certain pitfalls had to be avoided. Like Hornung's narratives, these new Raffles stories were to be set around the turn of the century, and they were to have that sense of atmosphere, of spirit, that is indelibly linked with the period. But these were not written for the audience for which Hornung had written, but for a modern audience with more sophisticated attitudes about morality, ethics and social conscience. It was an audience, too, that intimately knew the horde of criminals whose characterizations were borrowed in varying degrees from the original Raffles. No matter what name the crook used, this audience did not want more adventures of The Saint, The Baron, The Lone Wolf, Bulldog Drummond, or Arsene Lupin—all of whom eventually became more detectives than crooks.

If Raffles were to remain distinctly a crook, there was another problem. While it is amusing to read about the romantic escapades of a courageous cracksman, possibly even to admire or envy him, when one is securely ensconced in a well-protected home in a relatively crime-free time and place, such as Edwardian England, it is a different matter entirely when rampant crime presents an authentic, omnipresent threat to the reader, as it has for the past few decades. No matter how charming a fictional criminal may be, one cannot read about endless crimes in the daily newspaper, then be expected to empathize with him, unless he has mitigating motives for his depredations. The new Raffles, therefore, while still a decadent hedonist, generally had a dual motivation for each of his crimes.

Thus, although Raffles and Bunny sometimes profit from their adventures, more often than not they undertake them as a means, peculiar to themselves and sufficiently reprehensible, of resolving a difficult situation, often providing the justice that flaccid laws have no power to administer.

The Raffles in this volume, then, even though a criminal in the legal sense, has a strong sense of social justice and acts according to it. He is slightly ahead—in social perception—of the times in which he actually lived. Hornung's Raffles, an honorable man with a powerful (if unorthodox) code of personal ethics, did not consider his social responsibilities. So Hornung's Raffles and Perowne's Raffles are vastly different. To ensure that his Raffles should have individuality, and also differ from the many fictional descendants of Hornung's character, Perowne looked to real life for a model.

As Sherlock Holmes was patterned after Dr. Joseph Bell, and Father Brown was a fictionalized Rev. John O'Connor, and Dr. Fu Manchu took the shape of a mysterious "Mr. King," so Perowne's Raffles appeared as a representation of C. B. Fry, a prominent figure in English sporting society in the early years of the twentieth century, endowed (strictly fictionally) with an amoral streak.

Charles Fry was, in real life, a handsome man and a celebrated athlete. As an undergraduate at Oxford, he was a member of a brilliant social and intellectual coterie, all of whom subsequently made great names for themselves. One member was F. E. Smith, a distinguished classical scholar (as was Fry) who went on to gain eminence at the Bar, ending up as Lord Birkenhead, Lord Chancellor of England; another was Winston Churchill, who also had a successful career.

Fry's accomplishments were different. At Oxford, he got his "blue" (the highest honor) for cricket, soccer, rugby, and field hockey. After leaving the University, he continued his career in sports, becoming one of England's most famous cricketers, the world record-holder in the long jump, and a member of the Olympic fencing team.

He played cricket with one of the greatest batsmen of all time: Prince Ranjisinjhi. Ranji, as all England called him, was fabulously wealthy, and when he later succeeded to his Indian state, Fry went with him as an aide in the administration of Ranji's principality. When the League of Nations was established, Fry was offered the rulership, the Rajahdom, over another Indian state by the people of that state, but he modestly declined the honor.

Fry was rich. His enormous intellect and varied abilities would almost have ensured success in any field, but he chose to devote himself to sport and the *Life Worth Living* (the title of his autobiography). Today he is remembered mostly as an epicure of life, a great cricketer, and as a brilliant figure of the Golden Age of Amateurism—the Edwardian era.

Raffles, with his charm, his looks, his athletic ability, and his fine intellect, seemed to Perowne to be much like C. B. Fry—but without Fry's independent means.

When Perowne reflected on Fry as a model for Raffles, he asked himself: "Had Charles Fry not been wealthy, might not his innate hedonism and his passion for sport of all kinds have led him into a double life—a clandestine life of crime in order to obtain the money to live his glittering outward life of luxury, sport, and hedonism?" So Raffles became Perowne's idea of what Fry *might* have become if he had not been rich enough to finance the "glorious" life to which he was accustomed.

That left only Bunny Manders, Raffles' idolater, as a major ongoing character to be brought to life. Here, Perowne took as a model a man whom he knew intimately and would fill the role perfectly—himself. Bunny's background of Fleet Street journalism, his entire set of values, his uneasiness in the presence of risk, are Barry Perowne's. And every story in this volume—indeed, every turn-of-the-century Raffles story by Perowne—is based on an experience in the author's own past. Real life provides the setting, a few characters, bits of action, and the flavor, but the stories are not fictionalized accounts of actual historical events. Raffles' operations are purely Perowne's invention.

The opening scene of "The Governor of Gibraltar," for instance, relates the all-too-human incident of Bunny being duped by a pretty girl. Has the young man been born who could resist coming to the aid of a lovely lady in distress? Certainly Perowne is not the man. In a busy railroad station one day when he was about twenty-six years old, he was sitting in a train bound for Tilbury Docks and a ship to Gibraltar. A young woman came along, expertly conned him, as described in the story, out of ten pounds and, in real life, was never seen by Perowne again, causing him equal parts of chagrin and disappointment—but providing the subsequent story.

On another occasion, Perowne was playing cricket for a team in Somerset against another team from Bristol. He went to the scorer's box to see what number he had been placed in the batting order and happened to look at the other team's lineup. To his astonishment, he saw that the surname of every player on the Bristol squad was Robinson. Eleven of them! He learned that they were all members of the same family, and the idea for "Six Golden Nymphs" was born.

When I first learned that Raffles' adventures were based on fact, I suggested that Charles Fry was not the original for the gentleman cracksman after all, but that the prototype was no less than Philip Atkey, alias Barry Perowne, himself. "I wish it were true," replied Perowne. "Alas, I haven't the Raffles kind of nerve. I'm the sort that feels—and probably looks—guilty when he goes through customs . . . even if he has nothing whatever to feel guilty about."

Enough, perhaps too much, of literary antecedents. These stories were written for entertainment and cannot fail to satisfy the reader who wants no more than tales as fascinating as a magician's act. But that is a trifle too simple, and does them an injustice. A bottle of 1961 Chateau Lafite Rothschild can be consumed to quench a thirst, and a pretty little melody can be played on a Stradivarius, but it is criminal to allow the wine and the violin— and the Raffles stories—to be merely functional. Excellence transcends its initial intent. That is why, when you have finished these fourteen tales, Raffles as a character will be even more memorable than these superb stories themselves—individually or collectively. That is why Raffles is immortal.

OTTO PENZLER

". . . thieves break through and steal."
—MATTHEW 6:19

The Grace-and-Favor Crime

Where was Raffles?

The question was urgent in my mind as I stood on the balcony of my club in Carlton House Terrace.

Below, in the flag-hung Mall, twin ranks of the Grenadier Guards, rigid in scarlet tunics and towering bearskins, their naked bayonets glittering in the sunshine, held back a multitude of spectators.

Fanfares, the thud of saluting cannons, and roars of welcome from the crowd greeted the appearance of Europe's kings and princes with their chiefs of staff and debonair aides-de-camp.

Harnesses jingling, the mounted groups passed with a hot flash of spurs, helmets, jeweled orders, gemmed sword hilts.

"Kings' ransoms," I told myself wryly. "A fortune on the hoof!"

Where, then, on such a day of rich prizes as this, was A. J. Raffles, gentleman of prey?

As the successive groups passed on toward Buckingham Palace, where Her Majesty, imperious as ever in her old age, was receiving her august guests to the midsummer military maneuvers due to begin next day, I became aware that the cheers of the crowd were diminishing.

I guessed that this signaled the approach of the monarch whose policies disquieted all Europe.

Sure enough, when he came within my purview, it was to applause that had become scattered and dubious. That he was aware of this, and scorned it, his demeanor showed as he passed along the Mall with his hoof-clattering sovereign's escort.

His face, under his spiked helmet, was a taut mask of hauteur; his jet mustache was twisted up to points under his eyes; his withered arm was thrust into the breast of his tunic.

His passing was the climax of the morning. Spectators on the club balcony here began to drift through the French windows into the dining room for luncheon.

I did not accompany them. My subscription was overdue. My credit was exhausted. Though my Savile Row suit was faultless, its pockets contained only a few paltry coppers.

I was in trouble, and it was my own fault. One of Raffles's ventures in crime had brought us so close to disaster that I had mistaken my aftermath of funk for the small voice of conscience.

"Never again!" I had said. "Never again, Raffles! From here on, I'm going my own way—going straight!"

"A broad and pleasant highway," he had said. "What will you live on, Bunny?"

"My pen!"

"A pleasing accessory to graceful living," Raffles had said, "but a dubious crutch, old boy—as I think you found once before."

"I'll make a go of it this time, Raffles. *I'll* show you! You'll see!"

Famous last words.

Within weeks, I had been obliged to move from my flat in Mayfair to a Knightsbridge garret overlooking Tattersall's stable-yard, where horse auctions were held. And, today, I did not even possess the week's rent for that horse-smelling garret.

Moreover, I was hungry. If only Raffles would let me join forces with him again, I was ready to eat the words I had flung at him. Nobody else wanted my words, anyway—certainly not editors.

I left the balcony, reclaimed my gray top hat in the club lobby, and walked up St. James's Street to The Albany, the secluded residential backwater, just off Piccadilly, where Raffles lived in bachelor chambers. I had called there earlier in the day, without any luck, but I hoped he might have returned.

The porter shook his head.

"Sorry, Mr. Manders. Mr. Raffles hasn't been in all day."

Where the devil was he?

By nine o'clock that night I was in poor shape. I walked back wearily to my garret, thinking up excuses to give my landlord in lieu of rent. On the corner, near Tattersall's, was a baker's shop. It still was open and, with hunger gnawing, I paused to look in the window.

Fingering the coppers in my pocket, I stood wondering if it would look peculiar if a man as well dressed as I was were to buy some halfpenny rolls.

Suddenly a hand fell on my shoulder, and a voice said, "All alone, Bunny?"

I spun round. Tall, impeccably turned out, a pearl in his cravat, his face clean-cut, handsome, his eyes gray and keen, A. J. Raffles stood smiling at me.

I seized his hand. My spirits soared.

"Raffles!" I exclaimed. "At last! I've been hunting for you all day long!"

"Really?"

He gave me a shrewd glance, but made no comment. Instead, he nodded at a dog which he was leading by means of a handkerchief knotted to its collar.

"Recognize him, Bunny?"

The dog, an elderly black spaniel, panted up a sedate welcome at me.

"Surely," I said, "it's old J. Benjamin's dog?"

"The dog he calls Captain," Raffles said. "I had a fancy for a chat with old Benjamin, J., this evening, so I looked in at Florian's for a bite of dinner. They told me Mr. Benjamin had been in earlier, and gone. As I was leaving, I found Captain whining at the door, evidently on the stray. I thought I'd better take him in tow before he got under the wheels of some hansom. They didn't know Mr. Benjamin's address at Florian's, but I thought you might know, so I was coming to your lodgings. You're a particular friend of his—"

This was quite true. I was. But at his first mention of J. Benjamin, there had flashed into my mind a vivid vignette from the day's magnificence—an emperor with a gray face set in a rigor of arrogance, a withered arm thrust into his tunic, a jet mustache twisted up to his eyes, and two ramrod generals for his grim, inseparable shadows.

I looked at Raffles with a sudden, excited conjecture. For between the emperor in the Mall and Florian's Chophouse around the corner there was a link, and a strange one.

Florian's, just opposite Knightsbridge Barracks, was a dim little paneled place with leather-padded settles, a wealth of sporting prints from *Pickwick* and *Jorrocks,* and a pewter-laden sideboard. Since my decline and fall from Mayfair, I had been a frequent diner at this chophouse, for its economy and its convenience to my garret.

Another regular at Florian's was a neat little man with a leathery, snub, wrinkled face, a severe upper lip, mutton-chop whiskers, and very blue eyes under bristly hair brushed down in a bang across his forehead. He wore always a brown bowler hat, a suit of covert cloth cut tight in the leg, and a heavy watch chain embellished with small silver whips.

He always came into Florian's in company with a sedate black spaniel—the very spaniel Raffles was now leading.

The old man and the oldish dog were a self-sufficient couple. Watching them in their booth at Florian's, the spaniel with flopping ears looking up unwinkingly at his master as he divided their joint dinner into two exact parts, to hand down the dog's share on a special plate, I had felt a liking for them.

When the dog had licked the plate clean, groomed his chops with a connoisseur's tongue, and reflected upon the repast with the detached air of a bewigged judge savoring a tidbit of evidence, he always arose and gave the old man a prod of thanks by way of grace after eating.

I had not spoken to them until one night when, running into Raffles soon after our dissolution of partnership, I had taken him into Florian's to demonstrate a spurious solvency in literature by buying him supper. The place chancing to be full, we had shared a booth with the old man and the dog. Perhaps because he was lonely, the old man had been communicative about himself. He had introduced himself as Mr. Benjamin.

"Benjamin, J.," he had said. "I've got a young brother— Benjamin, T."

The difference in age, it had transpired, between himself and his "young" brother was barely a year. And they were as like as "two peas in a pod." This happy circumstance had gained them employment in the stables of a sporting Duke, who, proud of his equipages, liked the touch of uniformity provided by the brothers Benjamin on the jehu's box, in their white whipcord breeches, bottle-green livery coats, white stocks, and gray top hats with yellow cockades.

They had remained in the ducal service until their mutton-chop whiskers had grown as gray as their hats, when a turf miscalculation at Ascot and a baccarat catastrophe at Homburg had obliged the Duke to curtail his stables. Much of his bloodstock, auctioned at Tattersall's, had been bought *en bloc*.

"By order," said Benjamin, J., with a discreet cough as he fingered his watch chain, "of a reigning monarch."

The fraternal coachmen had accompanied the horses on their journey abroad to the imperial stables, where the two diminutive, dignified men had made such a favorable impression that it had been intimated to the Duke that it would be convenient if he would release them to the imperial service.

Settling down in the magnificence of the foreign capital, the Messrs. Benjamin had lodged together near the palace stables; and, as seems often to happen by a kind of fate to small men with severe upper lips, both had conceived a passion for a bosomy blond widow —their landlady.

"We fell out," Mr. Benjamin told us, patting his dog's head laid in sympathy on his knee, "over Frau Emmy."

For a year and more they had been at daggers drawn—until suddenly the capricious widow had bundled them both out of the house and married an interloping farrier-sergeant.

"You'd 'ave thought this would 'ave 'ealed the breach," said Mr. Benjamin, "but not a bit of it. No, gentlemen. We blamed it on each other, and it rankled."

Matters had come to a head in a strange way. Late one snowy night, a landau had been ordered to report to a side door of the palace to take a passenger to the station to catch the St. Petersburg express. Benjamin, J., being on duty, had reported with the landau accordingly, and two men had emerged quickly from the palace.

One of the men, a Russian, was a civilian in a heavy black ulster and black felt hat, wearing pince-nez and carrying a dispatch case; the other, a squat, thickset officer in spiked helmet and military cloak, was known to Mr. Benjamin as Colonel Saxe.

Colonel Saxe had told the coachman to wait a minute, as there was a third person to come; and both men had ducked into the landau.

"The night was still," Mr. Benjamin had told us. "Just the flakes comin' down thick and sizzlin' on the 'ot brass of the coach lamps, an' the 'osses given a thump an' a jingle now an' then. The gentlemen seemed excited and pleased with theirselves. They was talkin' away inside the landau while we waited. As it 'appened, I'd been takin' lessons in the language from Emmy for a year, nigh on, to inwaygle myself. I could 'ear every word the gentlemen said, an' I could understand about 'alf of it."

What he had heard and understood had made Mr. Benjamin's stock feel tight about his throat and his heart-thump sultry as he sat there on the box, a rug over his knees, the flakes whirling gray in the wan shine of the coach lamps.

"You see, sirs," said Mr. Benjamin, "I'm English born— native of Sevenoaks—an' what I 'eard didn't bode no good to them at 'ome, to my way of thinkin', and I felt it ought to be knowed of in London."

So when the third person had emerged from the palace and taken his place in the landau, and Mr. Benjamin had driven through the wide, deserted, snowy streets to the station, then back again—the Russian gentleman with pince-nez having been seen off on the St. Petersburg express—to set down the other two at the palace, Mr. Benjamin had gone on to the stables, put up his horses, and walked off through the night and the snow to the British Embassy.

"They listens to my story," said Mr. Benjamin, "then they ses, 'You're goin' to London, Mr. Benjamin, an' you're goin' quick and secret.' So I ses, 'What about Benjamin, T.?' There was no love lost between us, sirs, not since Emmy. Still, I didn't 'ate him, not the way 'e 'ated me. An' when it got out where the leak come from, I didn't much fancy the idea of their takin' it out on 'im—bein' my brother, all said and done.

"The embassy gent ses, 'Don't worry about 'im,' he ses. 'We'll tip him off an' do as much for 'im as we're doin' for you. 'E won't be to London far be'ind you.' "

"They have ways and means," Raffles had murmured.

"I dessay," said Mr. Benjamin. "None the more for that, I bin back two years, now, an' ain't never 'eard a word from 'im from that day to this."

"What happened?" Raffles had asked, frowning.

"All I know," said Mr. Benjamin, "when I got back and told my story to various official gentlemen, they was uncommon put out by it, but they ses, 'You done right and proper, Mr. Benjamin, an' we'll block that little caper of 'Is Imperial Majesty 'ere an' now,' they ses. An' I reckon they done it, they was that vexed. Further and more, they must 'ave mentioned your 'umble to the Queen 'erself, for the next I know—God bless 'er—I'm awarded a pension an' a lifelong tenancy of one of the Queen's Grace-and-Favor 'ouses, in 'Er Majesty's personal gift."

"And your brother?" Raffles had asked.

"Never a word from 'im, sir. Not a particle. I was told the embassy done like they promised, an' tipped 'im the wink and offered to get 'im 'ome. But no," said Mr. Benjamin, " 'e refused. 'E said 'e wouldn't stoop to soil 'is 'ands with any doings of mine. 'E was like that, sir—after Emmy. Proper 'ated me, 'e did. Anything *I* done that was wrong—an' 'e 'ad to do the opposite.

" 'Let 'im go,' he ses. 'I'm stayin' where I am.' An' 'e stayed. But I've often wondered whatever become of the 'eadstrong feller," Mr. Benjamin had said, shaking his head, his blue eyes guileless under his bang. " 'Is Imperial Majesty was never one to take a hinjury without *somebody* payin' for it."

I thought of that gray, rigid face of hauteur I had seen today in the Mall—and I looked searchingly, now, at Raffles, in the dim light from the baker's window.

"Yes," I said, "Mr. Benjamin is a particular friend of mine. I've often talked to him at Florian's, since that night he told us about himself."

"Has he ever mentioned Colonel Saxe again?" said Raffles.

"Colonel Saxe?" I said. "No. Why?"

"I just wondered," Raffles said. "You know Mr. Benjamin's address, Bunny?"

"Yes. It's a stone's throw from here," I said. "But tell me, Raffles—what made you come looking for him tonight particularly?"

"Just a fancy," he said. "I've been in the Mall today—"

I snapped my fingers. "I knew it!"

"Some pretty baubles, Bunny," he said, chuckling.

"And your fingers itched," I said. "Particularly when His Imperial Majesty rode past, scorning everybody and everything! That's what put you in mind of Mr. Benjamin?"

"I had a fancy," Raffles admitted, "to hear him ramble and reminisce. These retired royal servants know a lot about the habits of the exalted. One never knows when one might pick up a useful hint."

I drew in my breath.

"Raffles," I said tensely, "whatever you're planning—I'm with you!"

He laughed.

"Had enough of the sheepfold, Bunny? Good man! Welcome home to the wolf run! Not," he added, "that I'm planning anything. Just sniffing the air. These purple midsummer nights, Bunny, with a hint of thunder in them and all London *en fête*— they make one tingle. A night of kings and diamonds!"

A thrill fled up my spine.

"Let's take the dog home," I said. "The old man's probably missed him by now. He'll be so relieved to get him back, he'll certainly ask us in. You can talk to him. Come on!"

We passed up a dark alley which brought us out opposite Knightsbridge Barracks, where in rooms behind rows of yellow-lit windows redcoats moved with glint of steel and gleam of brass, preparing to mount guard over the crowned heads of Europe.

Nearby, on the side of the street on which we stood, was the dim little entrance of Florian's. Farther down, to the right and on the opposite side, a bracket lamp burned on the arch above the entrance to a courtyard.

"That's Park Yard," I told Raffles. "Benjamin, J., lives in Number Four."

Crossing the street, we passed under the arch with the bracket lamp into a small, cobbled courtyard enclosed by six narrow little three-story houses, attached and identical—Grace-and-Favor houses.

"These patriots are out seeing the sights," said Raffles. "Only one window has a light."

The light, in one of the two houses across the end, glimmered on a yellow front door with an iron knocker and the number 4.

"That's Mr. Benjamin's," I said, in relief, and I mounted the steps with Raffles behind me leading the dog.

I beat a tattoo with the knocker. The reverberations rang hollow through the dark courtyard. From the far side of the house, which backed on Hyde Park—where the gates remained open late on this special night—came a jingling and clip-clopping from passing carriages.

The dog whined, and Raffles, a step below me, stooped to pat him. The lighted window was close to my elbow; flowers in the window box made a delicate, dark fresco against the primrose glow through the drawn curtains. I heard no sound from within the house.

"Try him again," Raffles said.

But as I raised my hand to the knocker, I heard the bolt shot and the chain rattle. The door opened. Mr. Benjamin's short, erect figure, in shirt sleeves, his watch chain draped across his unbuttoned waistcoat, appeared against the dim light within. He peered at us from under his bang, his jaws moving on a mouthful.

"Good evening, Mr. Benjamin," I said cordially. "I'm afraid we've taken you away from your supper, but—"

Suddenly I felt Raffles's hand on my arm, gripping hard, checking me.

"We were passing, Mr. Benjamin," he said, "and thought you might be lonely and would care to come and see the sights with us. A big night in the West End! But perhaps," he added doubtfully, "it's a bit late for you—past your bedtime?"

"Sirs," said Mr. Benjamin, making valiant efforts to gulp his mouthful, "much appreciate. Unexpected—take it kindly. A bit late, per'aps, though—as you say—"

"Never mind," said Raffles cheerfully. "Some other time. Just a passing thought. Good night, Mr. Benjamin."

"Good night to 'ee, gentlemen." Mr. Benjamin knuckled his bang. "An' thank'ee—honored, I'm sure—"

Raffles's iron grip on my arm drew me down the steps. I heard the door closed and bolted behind us. I was totally bewildered by the transaction.

"But the dog, Raffles," I protested. "What—"

"Just so," said Raffles. "The dog. Didn't you notice?"

"Notice what?"

"That the dog didn't know his master," said Raffles, "and the master didn't know his dog."

I would have stopped dead, but his arm, now linked in mine, hurried me on out under the arch.

"And look at this," he said. "I saw it lying on the steps when I stooped down to pat the dog."

His arm still linked in mine as we crossed the street toward Florian's, he opened his hand. I saw on the palm a section of silver watch chain embellished by miniature coach whips.

"But Mr. Benjamin's chain wasn't broken," I said blankly. "He was wearing it. I saw it. He always wears it. He told me the Duke gave them both a half-hunter and chain when—"

I stopped suddenly.

"Exactly," said Raffles, with a kind of icy vivacity. "The old fox, eh? Coming to the door with his mouth full, to disguise any slight possible discrepancy of intonation—oh, pretty!"

I was thunderstruck. "You mean—that *wasn't* our Mr. Benjamin?"

"Just so," said Raffles. "That, undoubtedly, was Mr. Benjamin, *T.!* Brother Jehu!" His tone was suddenly grim. "I'm afraid *our* Mr. Benjamin is now in alien hands—at the disposal of a monarch who never forgives an injury."

He pushed open the door of Florian's.

At once there was wafted to my nostrils the aroma of Florian's pies, those succulent concoctions of hare, beefsteak, kidneys, and mushrooms, swimming in a rich burgundy sauce and topped with a crisp, golden crust. My knees wavered. I knew that before I could bring my mind to bear on the situation which confronted us I must dine; and I said so.

Raffles looked at me with concern.

"My dear old chap, of course you must dine! I had no idea . . . Here, let's take this booth. Richmond!"

He beckoned the old waiter, who, a napkin over his arm, hobbled up with such alacrity that his stiff dickey burst from his waistcoat.

"The menu, Richmond, and the wine list," Raffles said.

"Yes, sir," said Richmond. "Still got Mr. Benjamin's dog, I see, sir."

"Yes, we're looking after him," said Raffles. "Bring him a bone or something, Richmond. He's a patient old dog."

"That he is," said Richmond, one side of his collar detonating from his stud as he stooped wheezingly to pat the dog. "I like to see them together—Mr. Benjamin and Captain. It does your 'eart good."

I met Raffles's inscrutable glance across the table.

He took out his cigarette case, lighted one of the cigarettes he got from Sullivan's in the Burlington Arcade.

While I ate, he leaned back on the settle, sending adrift at the gas globe on the paneled wall those leisurely smoke rings which were always, with him, the overt evidence of cerebration.

"You know, Bunny," he said, breaking a long silence, "I think I've always half expected something like this might happen—ever since Benjamin, J., told us his story and mentioned Colonel Saxe."

His head, with its crisp dark hair, leaning back against the settle, he narrowed his eyes at the drifting smoke rings.

"As you know," he said, "I've always made it my business to keep informed as to who's who at the various embassies. About eighteen months ago, one Colonel Saxe appeared in London as an officer on the staff of the military attaché at the embassy of His Imperial Majesty. In actual fact, Colonel Saxe's real function—as it is the function of some official or other in all embassies—is clandestine intelligence. In short, he's in charge of the dirty work.

"When I heard Mr. Benjamin mention him as having been working at the palace, at the fountainhead, I wondered whether the Colonel's banishment to an embassy might not be due to the leak through Mr. Benjamin. One of His Imperial Majesty's moves on the European chessboard was spoiled by that leak, and he'd want someone's head on a charger for it. I fancy the Colonel may have paid the price—and the Colonel, like his imperial master, is no man to forgive an injury!"

He relapsed into thought. Richmond brought a ripe, napkin-wrapped Stilton cheese. He set it down with a slight snapping sound as he shed a rear trouser button. Raffles crushed out his cigarette, called for ink and paper. He dipped a pen in the ink bottle, began to write.

His pen scratched swiftly in the quiet.

It was eleven o'clock by the ticking wall clock, too early for the late-supper trade, and Florian's was almost empty. Monsieur Florian was clinking sovereigns in the cash-cage. Richmond, imperfectly concealed by the frosted-glass screen before the service hatch, was patiently holding up his coattails while Madame Florian sewed on his button. Captain rasped at his bone.

Raffles folded the letter, tucked it into an envelope, and glanced at me as he flicked the gummed edge along his tongue tip.

"Feeling better, Bunny?"

"Ready for anything!"

He nodded, started on a second letter. He sealed this one, addressed both envelopes, untied Captain from the leg of the settle. He walked up to the cash-cage, gave the envelopes to Monsieur Florian, together with some earnest instructions. Florian nodded his shock of grizzled hair.

"You there, Reeclimou!"

"Sir?" said Richmond, with a start that caused his bow tie to come unclipped and dangle.

Raffles handed over Captain to him, and the old dog trotted off obligingly with Richmond to the kitchen. Raffles came back, our hats in his hand.

"Where are we going?" I asked, rising.

"To the Imperial Embassy," said A. J. Raffles.

In the hansom, bowling up toward Hyde Park Corner, he explained.

"You can see what happened, Bunny. When it was realized that Benjamin, J., was responsible for the leak, Colonel Saxe would have had Benjamin, T., up on the carpet. Benjamin, T., would have denied any hand in the business, and he'd have revealed his hatred for his brother. Now, the Colonel's a clever man. He'd have docketed that hatred, and the physical likeness between the brothers, for reference. And he'd have had Benjamin, T., put aside to simmer till he could see how best to make use of him."

"And then?" I said.

"The Colonel is banished to an embassy job," Raffles said. "Meantime, he hears how well Benjamin, J.—*our* Mr. Benjamin—has come off. A pension, a lifelong tenancy under the Queen's Grace and Favor. How His Imperial Majesty and the Colonel must have gritted their teeth over that! And then, Bunny, this imperial visit comes up, and the Colonel sees his chance. He arranges for

Benjamin, T., to be brought over as a groom with the horses of the imperial suite. Then he puts his scheme to Benjamin, T.—that he take his brother's place, draw the Queen's pension, and live rent-free for the rest of his life under the Queen's Grace and Favor, while his brother is shipped back in his place to face whatever punishment His Imperial Majesty may order privily meted out. Probably life imprisonment."

He shook his head.

"The poetry of it, Bunny! Benjamin, T., spending the rest of his life as the Queen's pensioner, and Benjamin, J., the rest of *his* incarcerated secretly at His Imperial Majesty's pleasure! And no one the wiser. The imperial suite has diplomatic immunity. I doubt whether *our* Mr. Benjamin has ever been able to put more than X —his mark—as a receipt for his pension. Can't you see them chortling, rubbing their hands—the Emperor, the Colonel, and the Vengeful Coachman? It's a score over the Queen. It's one in the eye for England. By Jove," said Raffles, "they really were deuced unlucky to trip up over the dog!"

"How do you fathom that?" I asked.

"Pretty obvious," said Raffles. "We know Mr. Benjamin and Captain went to Florian's for their dinner, as usual. When they came ambling back, the dog at Mr. Benjamin's heel, I fancy there must have been a four-wheeler drawn up in Park Yard. Our Mr. Benjamin walks up his steps and is promptly seized by the Colonel's men. The little chap must have put up a fight, to judge from that bit of broken watch chain. But they bundle him into the four-wheeler and away with him. Unluckily for them, nobody notices the dog, which is probably scared and bolts back to the only place it knows where it has friends, the place where I find him sniffing forlornly round the door—Florian's."

The hansom bowled round a corner just then, and there, ahead, between the jogging ears of the horse, was a shine of lights from the lofty windows of the Imperial Embassy.

The trap in the roof of our hansom opened. The cabbie

screwed a purple face into the orifice to breathe down on us a reminiscence of breweries.

"Right up to the hentrance, sir?" he said.

"Right up to the entrance," affirmed Raffles, and he handed up a coin. "There's another half-bar for you if you wait for us."

"You're a toff," said the cabbie.

He dropped the trap, his whip cracked, and we went past the waiting carriages at a jingling trot, to pull up with a flourish at the red carpet laid across the sidewalk under a canopy.

A flunky gorgeous in white gloves and knee breeches hastened forward to hand us down. The fellow seemed taken aback by our morning dress. The occasion was formal. From the open windows of the second floor came the strains of an orchestra. A ball was in progress.

"Kindly inform Colonel Saxe," Raffles requested the flunky, "that two gentlemen who prefer to be nameless are here to see him in the matter of the coachman's dog."

"The coachman's dog, sir?" echoed the flunky.

"Just so," said Raffles.

The flunky hesitated for only a moment. Then, probably because he was not wholly unaccustomed to the receipt of somewhat cryptic messages for Colonel Saxe, he motioned us to follow him. We mounted the steps, crossed a vast hall, and were ushered into a spacious morning room.

I turned quickly to Raffles as the door closed upon us. "What are you planning?" I said. I was uneasy. It seemed to me that we had thrust our heads gratuitously into the lion's den.

He put a warning finger to his lips.

"An admirable likeness, Bunny," he said conversationally and nodded toward a huge portrait in a gilt frame above the lofty marble mantelpiece.

From the frame His Imperial Majesty regarded us malevolently over the spikes of his mustache.

The crystal doorknob rattled. The door opened and a squat,

broad-shouldered man strode in. He had a jutting, ivory-hard jaw, heavily-pouched and stony eyes, and thin hair brushed straight back from a massive forehead. He wore a dark blue uniform, the skin-tight trousers strapped under patent-leather shoes. Behind him was a tall, pale-faced, aquiline man, younger, with sleek black hair and a contemptuous expression, wearing a more striking uniform glittering with jeweled orders.

Raffles addressed the shorter man.

"Good evening, Colonel Saxe."

The Colonel stood with legs straddled, his hands behind him, his battering-ram jaw jutting pugnaciously.

"You have the advantage of me, sir," he said harshly.

"Precisely, sir," said Raffles, "and I propose to use it. Colonel, I give you two minutes to produce the person of Her Majesty's subject, Mr. J. Benjamin."

The squat Colonel stood as though rooted. I did not breathe. So still was the great room that the ticking of the marble clock on the mantelpiece and strains of music from the floor above were clearly audible.

The Colonel spoke with a seeming effort.

"Sir," he said thickly, "you talk in riddles."

"A riddle of two coachmen, Colonel," Raffles said. "You're unlucky in your agents. They bungled their job. They substituted T. Benjamin for J. Benjamin, but they overlooked J. Benjamin's dog. The dog unmasked the impostor. Unfortunate for you, Colonel. The dog is now in safe hands, for delivery to Scotland Yard, together with a letter exposing your maneuver, in the event that my friend here and I do not report back, bringing Mr. J. Benjamin, by midnight exactly."

A vein swelled, throbbing, on the Colonel's massive brow.

"Who are you?" he said hoarsely.

"Two gentlemen of London," Raffles said, "and, I trust, sportsmen. You've played and lost, Colonel. We've no desire to make trouble. Whether a certain august personage"—he glanced fleetingly at the portrait above the mantelpiece—"is privy to your maneuver, or whether it's a brilliant bit of initiative designed to procure your own advancement, you know better than I. You are also in a better position to judge of the possible repercussions, at this delicate political juncture, if an affair of this disgraceful nature should become known to the public."

The Colonel opened his mouth. He closed it. His neck thickened, flushing darkly, above the tight, gold-crusted collar of his uniform. Suddenly he turned on his gorgeous lieutenant with an epithet so bitter and insulting that it struck the younger man white to the lips.

"Your bungling," snarled Colonel Saxe. "Your mismanagement, you titled nincompoop! This is what happens when they send me high-well-born halfwits as recruits to Intelligence! Get out! Get the man. Bring him here."

The blue, close-set eyes of the younger man glittered as icily as the gemmed orders on his breast. Mute with rage, he clicked his heels and strode from the room.

Colonel Saxe walked across the parquet floor, his heavy shoulders hunched, his hands clasping and unclasping behind his back. He turned on the hearth rug, his pouched, stony eyes on Raffles.

"As you have said, sir," observed Colonel Saxe, speaking with difficulty, "I have played and lost. I am prepared"—he breathed hard through his nose—"I am prepared, in order that this affair be not bruited about, to meet any reasonable monetary claim you may—"

"Sir," Raffles said dangerously, "do you take us for common adventurers? I have the honor to inform you that this matter will go no farther, except in one event."

"And that event?"

"Any interference hereafter," Raffles said, "with the private life of Mr. J. Benjamin, retired under the Queen's Grace and Favor."

The Colonel ground his teeth. "You have my word, sir."

"Then you have mine, sir," said Raffles. "As to Benjamin, T., he is your responsibility. It would seem advisable to remove him from Park Yard without delay."

"He will be removed," said the Colonel.

I was astonished at Raffles's remark about Benjamin, T. But I had no time to reflect upon it, for the door opened, and there—with the Colonel's glittering and furious lieutenant behind him—stood our Mr. Benjamin, with his respectable mutton-chop whiskers, turning his brown bowler round and round in his gnarled coachman's hands.

Except for the dangling end of his broken watch chain, and for the fact that an extensive area round his left eye was turning rapidly black, he seemed none the worse for his misadventure.

"Gentlemen!" he exclaimed when he recognized us. "You here!"

Colonel Saxe gave a savage jerk at a bellpull to the right of the mantelpiece.

"I need detain you no further," he said, grinding his teeth.

With Mr. Benjamin between us, we followed the flunky back across the hall, out on to the red carpet. Our hansom, with the purple-faced old reprobate in the debauched topper on the box, jingled up promptly. We mounted, Mr. Benjamin squeezed in between us, and, as the horse clip-clopped off, the cabbie lifted the trap in the roof to treat us to a blast of malted vapors.

"Where to, sir?"

"Through Hyde Park," said Raffles. "Pull up at the back of Park Yard, near the barracks. *And drive like fury!*"

The cabbie cracked his whip. For a moment I was at a loss to understand Raffles's sudden air of urgency. He was glancing back, now, through the rear oval window of the hansom.

"Gentlemen," said Mr. Benjamin, "I ain't altogether clear about what's bin 'appenin'—except that my brother, Benjamin, T., seems to be in the jiggery-pokery some way. None the more for that, whatever 'e may feel about me, sirs, and whatever 'e's been up to, I wouldn't like for 'im to come to grief."

"That's all right, Mr. Benjamin," said Raffles. "Don't you worry about a thing."

The reason for Raffles's haste now dawned upon me. It was not that he thought we might be followed, but that he had made a mistake in reminding Colonel Saxe that Benjamin, T., was at Park Yard. He was anxious, now, to warn Benjamin, T., before the Colonel's men came for him.

Sure enough, Raffles said, "Have you got a back door, Mr. Benjamin—a door on the park side?"

"Yessir."

"Got a key to it?"

"Yessir."

"Trust me with it, will you?" Raffles said. "Capital!" He lifted the trap. "Driver, when we get out at Park Yard, you'll drive the other gentleman here round to Florian's Chophouse." He dropped the trap. "You hear, Mr. Benjamin? You're to wait for us at Florian's. You'll find Captain there."

The hansom swung to the right, round the Achilles statue. A sudden lilac flare in the sky westward lit the trees in the park to brief, black silhouette. A roll of thunder trundled across the sky and was bombarding overhead as the hansom reined in at the back of Park Yard. Raffles leaped out, with myself close behind him.

The hansom moved off at once, and Raffles darted across a strip of lawn to the railing at the back of Mr. Benjamin's house. A gate in the railing gave on to a short flight of steps leading down to a back door. Thunder was squeezing the first fat raindrops down on us as Raffles unlocked the door.

He stepped in, struck a match, held it aloft. We were in a narrow passage leading to a short flight of stairs. Raffles led the way up the stairs, dropped the spent match, struck another. Its reflection glimmered redly in the glass of many photographs, in Oxford frames, of the Benjamin brothers on the boxes of phaetons, dogcarts, traps, landaus, victorias, shooting brakes. The walls of this tiny hall were covered with them.

I had expected Raffles to wake and warn T. Benjamin at once, but he did nothing of the kind. Instead, I saw a triangle of lightning, electric-blue, where Raffles, having dropped the spent match, was holding the window curtain aside to peer out into the courtyard.

"Here they come," he said. "Bunny, feel for the bolt of the door. When the knock comes, open instantly!"

I was at a loss to divine his intentions, but I felt for the door, found it, slipped the bolt and chain. I waited tensely, my hand on the knob, and listened.

The thunder reverberated heavily over the Queen's Grace-and-Favor house. A fierce deluge now was slashing down in the courtyard. Then I heard the clop of hooves on cobbles, the rumble of a four-wheeler. Footsteps ran up to the door; the knocker was furiously pounded. I jerked the door wide.

Against the dim glow from the four-wheeler's lamps, swimming in the downpour, I saw a tall figure in a military ulster.

"Benjamin?" a voice said peremptorily.

Raffles's hand shot out, clamped on the ulster, jerked the man in.

"For Mr. Benjamin's black eye," said Raffles, and I heard the thud of his fist as he struck. "Bolt that door, Bunny!"

I had it bolted in an instant.

"Strike a match!"

I struck one. Raffles was down on one knee beside the sprawled figure of the aquiline, pale-faced, contemptuous man with the sleek black hair who had been present at our interview with Colonel Saxe.

"I fancied the Colonel would send this johnnie," said Raffles —"and that he'd lose no time about it if I jogged his memory a little!"

He threw open the unconscious man's cloak, and jeweled orders on the breast of his tunic caught the match flame with a faceted, dazzling radiance. I saw the sheen of Raffles's silk hat as he glanced up at me with the smile I knew so well.

"It would have been gross neglect," he said, "not to provide this walking jeweler's window with a little reception committee!"

His hands moved deftly over the glittering tunic. The match burned my fingers. I dropped it. Simultaneously, above the detonations of the thunder overhead and the lash of the downpour, a shout rang out from the courtyard. Feet stomped up the steps. The doorknob rattled. The knocker was pounded violently.

"His men must have noticed something," said Raffles, and I heard his chuckle ironic in the darkness. "All right, Bunny, it's a clean sweep and a useful haul. Come on! Out the back way!"

Even as shoulders were hurled with dislocating vigor against the front door, we regained the park by way of the back. The thunder rumbled in reluctant retreat across the sky, taking with it the night's heat. Through the slackening rain and the refreshed foliage, the globes of the gas lamps shone white and clear. I felt braced and uplifted, alike by the cleansed air, by the sense of a sterile rectitude irrevocably shed, by the resumption of a felonious alliance with my friend, and—not least—by the thought of what he carried in his impeccable pockets.

I trod the London asphalt with a step more buoyant than for months past. And it was not until, after a circuitous walk, we were approaching Florian's, where Mr. Benjamin and his spaniel awaited us, that a monstrous omission occurred to me. In my consternation, I stopped dead.

"Raffles! What about Benjamin, T.?"

Raffles's gesture dismissed an irrelevance.

"Miles away by now," he said. "He was warned earlier in the evening, not that he deserved it. But that was the second letter I wrote—for Richmond to pop round and push under the door of the Queen's Grace-and-Favor house while we were at the embassy."

I drew in my deep breath, deeply.

"Raffles," I said, suiting the action to the word, "I raise my hat to you."

"As to that, Bunny," he said, "thank you. But I can tell you one thing—"

"Yes?"

"I was devilish annoyed when Colonel Saxe offered us his disgusting bribe. He may be an officer," added A. J. Raffles, as he pushed open the door of Florian's, "but he doesn't know a gentleman when he sees one."

Princess Amen

"I've never realized before," Raffles remarked thoughtfully, "that there are quite so many banks in Kensington."

It was an evening toward the end of summer and, in a hansom jingling westward through the lavender twilight of the London streets, we were bound for a dinner engagement.

We were in evening dress, and Raffles, as he offered me a Sullivan from his cigarette case, asked, "Have you an account in this neighborhood, Bunny?"

Now, in the days before my abortive attempt to cut loose from involvement in the double life he lived, I had had accounts in various names at half a dozen banks scattered about London, as he had himself. It was a matter of mere prudence for men who lived on their wits.

"As it happens," I said, "there's a branch, just ahead, of the County and Continental. I still have an account there that dates back a good four years. It's in the name of Lesage."

"Lesage?" said Raffles.

"A man of slight build," I said, "with a scholarly stoop,

rimless eyeglasses, and prematurely white hair. The bank has never had an English address for him, as he's an Egyptologist and is abroad a good deal, delving beside the Nile."

"That romantic literary mind of yours!" said Raffles, amused.

"My romantic literary mind," I said, "has been shown the way out by practically every editor in Fleet Street."

"Where banks are concerned," said Raffles, "I'm more interested in the way in. What prompted you to choose Egyptology as a cover?"

"The number of museums in this neighborhood," I said. "It struck me that they'd provide—by implication—a background to the character."

"Good idea, Bunny," said Raffles.

"I'm glad you approve," I said, pleased. "As a matter of fact, the County and Continental manager, a Mr. Purkiss, believes Lesage to be a frequent member of field expeditions sent out by one or other of the museums. Purkiss thinks the occupation an intriguing one, and though Lesage has never had much of a balance in his account, he's quite one of the bank's favorite customers. Purkiss never fails to have a personal word with him when he drops in at the bank—which isn't often, I may say, because of the nuisance of having to whiten my hair."

I indicated a building which the hansom now was passing.

"That's the place," I said.

Raffles looked at it. From the windows, with their lower panes of frosted glass protected by grilles of spiked iron, the white light of gas globes shone out into the deepening dusk.

"A snug little bank," said Raffles. "Working late tonight, aren't they?"

"Getting out quarterly balances, no doubt," I said.

"Very interesting," said Raffles.

He drew meditatively at his cigarette as our hansom swung to the left, into the quiet square where we were to dine at the home of a friend.

Dick Farr was waiting on the steps of his house to greet us as our hansom jingled to a standstill. He was a big, sandy-haired chap with a blunt face and rather solemn blue eyes. He was a good all-round games player. He and his brother Frank had been at school with us.

As so often happens with the children of a rakehell father, both Dick and Frank Farr took a serious, idealistic view of life. Frank, in fact, had become a missionary and was out in West Africa. As for Dick, he had a vocation for medicine, and that he should have been eating his heart out in a clerking job on a high stool in a Threadneedle Street office, instead of studying to qualify as a doctor, was entirely the fault of his sire.

Old Ferdinand Farr, in his heyday, had been a country squire, a famous steeplechase rider, a renowned port drinker, and a notorious gambler. Horses, wine, and cards had been the ruin of him. He was no longer a country squire. Estates that had been in the possession of his family for centuries were gone forever.

Mortgaged up to his purple nose and bushy eyebrows, he lived now in this Kensington Square. And about the only relic of past glory which remained to him was a gem-crusted scimitar, of great historic and intrinsic value, that dated from the days of an ancestor who had crusaded with Coeur-de-Lion. I once had seen a photograph of it—"Courtesy of Ferdinand Farr, Esq."—in an illustrated magazine.

"The guv'nor's superstitious about that scimitar," Dick had told us once. "He's convinced that if it went out of the family, after all these centuries, by any act of his, he'd be struck dead or something. A typical gambler's quirk. But for that, he'd sell it like a shot and invest the proceeds in things that my sister Josie and my brother Frank want to do—and in my medical studies, too, perhaps. It's a pity really. He feels he *ought* to sell it, for our sake, but he just can't bring himself to do it. Because of us, he tortures himself with the thought of all he's chucked away in the past. Nothing we can say makes any difference. To the good, I mean.

Sometimes the most innocent remark one of us may make he'll take as a reproach, and that'll start him drinking; then he just doesn't care what happens, poor old coot!"

There was an incident at dinner that very evening which started the poor old coot drinking. It was something his daughter said—or, rather, nearly said.

Josephine was twenty, with fair hair, very clear blue eyes, and great beauty and character in her face. Her brother Frank, the missionary out in West Africa, was her hero. She glowed when she spoke of him.

"Frank's doing wonderful things. I'd give anything in the world to be able to go out there and work with him." She turned to her mother. "Truly, Mama," she said, "women *are* doing things like that nowadays. You simply don't know! And Frank has all kinds of plans I could help him in, if only he could get them started. It's just a question of—"

She checked suddenly, biting her lip. But the unspoken word, the hideous word "money," seemed to clang horribly across the room. The family stared at her aghast. Raffles and I pretended to notice nothing amiss as Josephine, with a blush of remorse, glanced covertly at her father. I saw the stricken look on the old man's purple face; he was cut to the quick.

Raffles, in his easy way, steered the conversation into channels less treacherous. But the damage was done, and old Ferdy, when the ladies had withdrawn, was pretty hard on the port—merciless, in fact.

To wean him away from it before the poor old profligate subsided under the table, Raffles asked if we might see the celebrated scimitar.

"Damned thing," the old man muttered. "I keep it at the bank—only place for the damned thing. Pass the port, Dick."

Dick held on to the decanter.

"We'd better go, guv'nor," he said. "Mother's expecting us in the drawing room for coffee."

"Damned women," said old Ferdy.

He was well away. We had not been long in the drawing room before he must needs want to play cards—and poker, at that. The ladies gave him up as a bad job and, with resigned expressions, went off to bed.

Raffles, closing the door on them, gave me a meaning glance. I took it to signify that we must be easy on the old boy. Accordingly, I discarded the constituents of several promising hands; and it was some time before it dawned upon me that Raffles, an impeccable figure opposite the increasingly flushed and tousled ex-squire, was playing a razor-edged game.

The chip values, at Dick's insistence, had been set low. Even so, when it came to squaring up, Raffles had over ten pounds to come from Ferdy. The old man, mumbling, fished a meager handful of gold and silver from his pocket.

"Please don't run yourself short of cash," said Raffles considerately. "A check will do just as well, sir."

Old Ferdy scrawled a check.

"A pleasant evening," said Raffles, as Dick accompanied us out to the steps to see us off. "I was disappointed not to see your family heirloom, Dick. Still, I imagine the insurance premiums would come heavier if it weren't kept at a bank?"

"They're heavy enough, as it is," Dick said.

It struck me that his tone was standoffish, his "good night" distinctly curt. I had to admit to myself that I could understand why. And when we had picked up a hansom and were clip-clopping back along the way we had come, under a horned moon hung silver in the sky, I could not resist a comment on Raffles's behavior.

"Granted we can do with a bit of grist to the mill," I said, "but really, Raffles, are we so far gone that it was necessary to take that tenner off poor old Ferdy?"

He seemed not to hear my question.

"We're just passing the bank again," he said. "I see the lights are off. They must have got their balances out." He took a slip of paper from his pocket. "I also see, from Ferdy's check, that he banks at the same branch of the County and Continental as Lesage, the noted Egyptologist—"

My heart gave a sudden hard thud.

"So *that's* what you wanted to find out—where Ferdy banks, where he keeps that scimitar. But, man alive, you can't be quixotic enough to think of—"

"Trying to crack a bank vault?" said Raffles. He put a cigarette between his lips. "In order to steal a scimitar from a deposit box, and so put a packet of insurance money in the hands of a ruined old gambler, to enable him to get square with his conscience by giving his kids a fair start in life?"

He struck a match. The light gleamed on his opera hat as he touched the flame to old Ferdy's check. The horse's hooves clip-clopped.

"Trying to crack a bank vault," said Raffles, "is a mug's game, Bunny!"

But I saw his odd smile, and the gray glint of his eyes, as he dipped his cigarette to the flame in his cupped hands.

I was uneasy for weeks afterwards.

However, nothing untoward developed and, as time passed, our evening *en famille* at the Farrs' faded from my mind.

Summer turned into autumn, and one misty night in November he took me to dinner at an Italian restaurant in Soho. It was one of those places of romantic assignation that have a mezzanine balcony divided into stuffily curtained cubicles, like theater boxes; and in one of these, with the curtains closed, we dined by the light of candles with seductive pink shades.

The place was not my style, and I said, rather peevishly, "Why did we have to come here?"

"What's the matter, Bunny?" said Raffles. "Don't you like spaghetti?"

As he spoke, he slightly parted the curtains so that he could peer down into the main salon of the restaurant, from which rose stridently a din of voices, a plinking of mandolins, a jingling of Neapolitan tambourines.

"To tell the truth," he said, dropping the curtain into place, "we came here to see a certain lady without being seen by her. I thought we ought at least to know her by sight, as she's on the eve of playing a significant part in our affairs. She mustn't know us, though. Look discreetly, and you'll see her down there across the salon, at the table backed by the mural of Tiberius's villa. Red-haired woman with a champagne glass in her hand, talking to a cauliflower-eared man who looks like an ex-pugilist."

I made a chink in the curtains, put my eye to it, and, through a floating haze of cigar smoke, saw the woman at once. She was strikingly handsome, though rather loudly dressed, with rust-colored hair elaborately coiffured.

"Who is she?" I said, turning back to Raffles. "What on earth has she to do with us?"

"Her name's Birdie Minton. That, I understand, is her real name. She has a number of aliases." He poured Chianti into our glasses. "She was recommended to me, for a role in a small venture I have in mind, by one of the few people in London who know the regrettable truth about me—Ivor Kern, the receiver I do business with, whom you've not yet met, but soon will."

He looked at me over his wineglass.

"You recall our snug little family evening with the Farrs, Bunny? Well, a day or two after that evening, Birdie Minton called at the County and Continental Bank, Kensington branch."

I laid down my fork. My appetite had deserted me.

"Calling herself 'Mrs. Randolph,' " said Raffles, "and saying she'd recently returned from India and was house-hunting in London, she opened an account with a hundred pounds—advanced by Ivor Kern, who's always ready to invest modestly in my modest enterprises.

"She also deposited with the bank, for safe keeping till she found a house, a large packing case containing allegedly valuable silver and carpets. It's lain there in the bank's vault ever since. . . . Now, then! The day after tomorrow, 'Mrs. Randolph' will call at the bank. She'll explain that she's now found a house to her liking, and she'll take her packing case away. She'll deliver it to Ivor Kern's place, and that'll conclude her part in the affair. Foolproof, as you see."

"But what on earth's the point of it?" I said, puzzled.

"The point of it," said Raffles, "is that when she withdraws her packing case, *I* shall be in it!"

He tossed aside his napkin.

"Now, if you're not going to eat any more of your spaghetti, Bunny," he said, "we'll take a little ride in a cab."

My mind was in a turmoil as the cab carried us through the wet streets, where the lamps glimmered through the mist, to a small shop in the King's Road, Chelsea. The shop, closely shuttered, bore the legend: ANTIQUES—IVOR KERN—OBJETS D'ART. As the cab trundled away, Raffles jerked a bellpull in the dark doorway. I heard the bell jangling remotely within.

Suddenly the flap of the letter slot, set vertically at eye level in the door, was poked up. I saw the yellow glimmer of candlelight. Raffles spoke softly through the slot. Bolts and chains rattled, the door opened a crack, we slipped inside.

Rebolting the door, a thin, tall young-old man in a frock coat turned to us. He held up his candlestick. His pale face and high forehead were unlined; his dark eyes rested on me with a quizzical intelligence.

"The Egyptologist, I presume?" he said, in a dry, cynical voice. "Princess Amen is awaiting him."

He motioned us to follow. Shapes of furniture bulked darkly about us in the littered shop, shadows loomed and shifted, innumerable clocks ticked.

Bewildered, I whispered to Raffles, "Princess Amen?"

"An old flame," he said.

Kern opened the door of a rear room. It seemed to be a kind

of workshop for a craftsman in woods and metals. He nodded to a long, coffinlike box which lay on the floor.

"Her Highness," he said.

The box was of some time-blackened wood, with a dim red diamond shape painted on each side, and here and there squares of hieroglyphs crudely painted in faded yellow, after this style:

Shipping labels stood out in sharp relief on the box: LESAGE —ALEXANDRIA TO TILBURY; BAGGAGE HOLD; NOT WANTED ON VOYAGE; FRAGILE—THIS SIDE UP.

"The box," Kern said, "has a lock that can be worked from the inside. The squares of hieroglyphs placed here and there have the object of helping to conceal the presence of breathing holes."

Raffles, stooping, opened the lid. The hair stirred on my scalp. The candlelight cast its flicker on a mummy case. Its mask of carven wood, though worn and defaced by forty centuries in desert sands, yet conveyed a haunting sense of serenity and wisdom.

I was astounded to hear Kern say, "It took me the whole of last week to fabricate Princess Amen. She's nothing but a lid, well pierced for breathing. Underneath are shavings—"

"On which," Raffles said, "I shall recline at ease. The mask slips off easily, Bunny, and our good friend Ivor here has so arranged things that I can get my right hand to the inside of the lock."

The light hollowed his eyes under the slanted brim of his opera hat as he lighted a cigarette at the flame of Kern's candle.

Inhaling, his eyes on me, he said smoothly, "Just before the bank closes for business tomorrow afternoon, Bunny, you'll deposit Princess Amen, for safe keeping, with your friend Mr. Purkiss, the manager."

My heart thumped like a hammer. "But, Raffles—"

"When the vault's locked after the day's business," he went on imperturbably, "I shall emerge from Princess Amen. I shall have my bulls-eye, my skeleton keys, and the run of the vault for the rest of the night. It's a pity that I shan't dare meddle with their bullion or specie, but any defalcations of that kind would be spotted as soon as the staff arrives in the morning. No, reluctantly I shall confine myself to getting old Ferdy Farr's scimitar from his deposit box—and to mulcting any other boxes which strike me, on examination, as being grossly overstuffed with hoarded gems and negotiable bonds. About an hour before the staff is due to arrive in the morning, I shall get—with my plunder—into Mrs. Randolph's packing case."

I seized on a flaw. "But isn't that already crammed with stuff?"

"Tarnished electroplate and threadbare carpets," he said. "I shall transfer them to Princess Amen's box. The point is, Bunny, if you were to deposit Princess Amen just before close of business tomorrow and remove her just after the opening of business next day, it might look a bit fishy. I don't say it would, mind you, if you had a good excuse, seeing that your bank account is of four years' standing. Still, it might. So we play a deeper game—for safety. I go *in* inside Princess Amen, but I come *out* in Mrs. Randolph's packing case. She'll call for it ten minutes after the bank opens on Saturday—the morning after next."

I stared at him. I felt cold beads on my brow. Even so, I could not but feel that there was in the very simplicity of the plan a dreadful feasibility.

Raffles flicked ash from his cigarette.

"Princess Amen," he said, "together with Lesage's and Mrs. Randolph's trifling current balances, we shall write off to running expenses. The Farr heirloom Ivor here will hold for us for a few years. Later, when Miss Josephine and Dick and Frank have their lives soundly established on the basis of the insurance indemnity, we'll find out from them, subtly, whether the recovery of the heirloom will make them—or old Ferdy—any happier. If this proves to be the case, then we'll contrive for the police to 'recover' it, and the Farrs can come to terms at their convenience with the insurance company. Naturally, anything *else* we may glean from the vault is entirely our own business. We have to live, too, you know."

He smiled at my expression, pressed my shoulder with an encouraging hand.

"Cheer up, Bunny," he said. "All *you* have to do is entrust Princess Amen to your old acquaintance Mr. Purkiss."

It seemed simple enough.

A November drizzle was falling, and raucous newsboys were shouting "Latest race results! All the winners!" when the driver provided by Ivor Kern reined in his neat brougham before the County and Continental Bank a few minutes before closing time next afternoon.

In the gloom of the brougham, I was cramped by the great box, which was placed obliquely across the facing seats, from corner to corner. I tapped lightly on the box, heard Raffles's answering tap from within it, and, drawing in my breath deeply to steel my resolution, stepped from the brougham and walked into the bank.

The cashier at the counter, shoveling gold sovereigns into a canvas sack, while behind him the clerks at their high desks posted the daybooks in their beautiful copperplate, glanced at me in my guise as Lesage, and at once smiled in recognition.

"Why, good afternoon, Mr. Lesage! Back in England again?"

I admitted the self-evident fact and, summoning a smile, asked if Mr. Purkiss were busy.

"He's only signing his letters, sir," said the cashier. "He's quite alone. Perhaps you'd care just to tap on his door there?"

I tapped, was bade enter, and the manager, a sturdy, gray-bearded man in a cutaway coat, rose with outstretched hand and came toward me.

"Mr. Lesage! Quite a stranger! Where have you dropped from this time?"

He pushed forward a chair for me and, after an exchange of civilities, I broached the matter of the mummy.

"Normally," I explained, "I should have left it with the museum authorities, but I'm sorry to say I've just had a rather disagreeable half-hour with them. I feel they've treated me parsimoniously, and I don't intend they shall have what I've brought back with me this time. I shall negotiate elsewhere. In the meantime, I should like to entrust it to your vault—provided, that is, that you can assure me that the vault is quite dry and warm?"

"I can do so without reserve," he declared heartily, and, jerking a bellpull, said to the burly man who answered the summons, "Ah, porter, Mr. Lesage has a box outside. Ask Mr. Andrews to be good enough to help you bring it down to the vault. Now, Mr. Lesage, if you would care to step this way—"

He opened an inner door. I followed him down a short flight of steps to a gaslit stone passage.

"Warm and dry, you notice," he observed smugly. "Now, here is the vault."

The immense door, as thick as that of a casemate and armed with a formidable great engine of a lock, stood half open. As we entered, a rather dandified young man, who was checking some documents on top of a safe which stood in the center of the vault, shuffled them together hastily.

"You may go, Mr. Dacres," Purkiss said curtly, and the fop, thrusting the papers into a deed box, locked it, replaced it on one of the iron racks which lined the walls, and made himself scarce.

Purkiss waved a hand.

"A roomy and secure vault, Mr. Lesage—"

It was certainly roomy. The wall racks were laden with japanned deed boxes and steel deposit boxes, large and small. Crates, domed trunks, even gun cases, stood here and there about the concrete floor. Each was labeled, and a yellow line painted on the floor marked out neatly the space it occupied. The blood throbbed in my temples as I noticed a large packing case labeled MRS. RANDOLPH.

"Ah," said Purkiss, "here comes your box. We'll have it just here, Mr. Andrews, if you please. Gently now, porter. Thank you, that will do."

He stood looking down at the box, shaking his head, as the two men left us.

"The strangest treasure our humdrum vault has ever housed," he said. "Might I—"

"Of course!" Taking the key from my pocket, I unlocked the box, raised the lid. He gazed down reverently on the worn, serene mask of Princess Amen.

"Three thousand—nay, four thousand years?" he said, his voice hushed. "It is a sobering thought, Mr. Lesage."

Sobered indeed, I relocked the box, we went back upstairs to his office, he wrote me out a deposit receipt. The bank by now having closed for business, he ushered me off the premises himself. And with the closing of the door on me, the sound of bolts being irrevocably shot, my part in the affair was finished. The die was cast. Raffles was in the vault.

It had been even easier than he had predicted.

Reaction to tension left me feeling drained and unreal as I stood there in the rain, gazing through my rimless spectacles at the closed doors.

Kern's coachman drove me to my flat in Mount Street. I let myself in unobtrusively, to avoid any neighbors who might spot my unwonted garb and whitened hair, and locked the door.

Lighting the gas in my sitting room, I poured myself a strong whisky and soda and sank into a chair before the fire. The coals glowed cozily behind the wire guard, but my thoughts were with Raffles.

The clock on the mantelpiece ticked steadily. Glancing up at it, I judged that by now the massive door of the vault would have been swung into place, the lock and burglar alarms set, Purkiss and his staff dispersed in the direction of their various homes, the bank in darkness.

I slumped lower in my chair, chewing at my lip.

Suddenly the doorbell rang. I straightened, rigid, listening.

Again, urgently, sounded the clangor of the bell. It jerked me to the hall. Above the front door, the bell on its spring was aquiver with diminishing tremors, but even as I peered up at it, it was convulsed by a renewed and violent agitation.

Fearing I knew not what, and clean forgetting my whitened hair, I unlocked the door, opened it, glimpsed a tall, black-clad figure. It was Ivor Kern. He thrust past me, strode on into the lighted sitting room. I locked the door, went after him.

"What is it?" I said. "Why are you here? What's wrong, man?"

He stared at me, his eyes jet black, a sheen of moisture on the pallor of his face.

"Manders," he said, "the game's up!"

I swallowed with a dry throat. "What do you mean?"

"Here," he said. "Look!"

He thrust an evening paper at me, pointing to a headline: £500 CONFIDENCE TRICK—AMERICAN VISITOR VICTIMIZED— WOMAN SOUGHT—BELIEVED FLED COUNTRY.

"Birdie," he said. "Birdie Minton! I gave her her instructions yesterday about collecting the packing case as soon as the bank opens tomorrow. It was all clear, all fixed. But now . . . Manders, she's fled, all right. She's *gone!* The instant I spotted this in the paper, I got in touch with a crony of hers—ex-bruiser she goes about with. I've just come from him. It's true, Manders! She's bolted. Got clean away on the Dover-Calais boat this morning. She's in Paris by now."

We stared at each other.

"You realize what it means?" he said. "Raffles is trapped! *There's no Birdie Minton—alias Mrs. Randolph—to collect that packing case from the bank tomorrow!*"

I did not breathe. The clock ticked loudly. The gas mantle made a soft, insistent roaring in the room; the light seemed to shine with a nightmare brilliance. Like a stunned man, I watched Kern go to my bookcase. He took up the decanter from the brass tray, splashed whisky into a glass. He tossed off the drink, passed a hand over his high, white forehead, and looked across at me.

"Clever devil," he said. "He got *in* there, all right. But, by heaven, it'll puzzle him to get *out!* Listen, Manders. Tomorrow's Saturday. Assume the fact that the deed boxes have been looted is not discovered during the course of the morning. The vault won't be opened again till Monday morning—a further forty-eight hours, on top of the twenty-odd he'll already have been in there. Stale air, thirst, starvation, panic—Manders, by Monday morning he'll probably be unconscious, possibly dead."

He poured more whisky, drank it, shrugged.

"Well," he said cynically, "that's the way it goes. It comes to every crook—their luck runs out. They're too clever by half, they try it once too often, and"—he snapped his fingers—"finish!"

"Don't," I burst out. "Don't talk like that! Damn you, Kern, we've got to do something—"

"Do what?" he said. "What *can* we do? I know no man in London who can crack a bank vault—not even Raffles himself, one of the best, though he *does* pose as just a gentlemanly amateur. As to trying to get some other woman to impersonate 'Mrs. Randolph,' it's out of the question. It wouldn't work for a minute— not with a *bank*, Manders. Apart from anything else, Birdie holds their receipt for the packing case. They wouldn't dream of giving it up without getting their receipt back. This is a *bank* we're dealing with, Manders! No, I tell you, we've got to face it. This is the end of Raffles!"

"Never!" I paced the floor in agony, gnawing at my knuckle. "There must be some way—some way we can help him—"

"Talk sense," said Kern. "This is the finish."

"Not if I know it," I said. "Not without—" I turned on him. I was shaking with excitement, with desperation—with the germ of an idea. "Kern, it's not the finish—not yet. Lend me a tin of varnish and a paintbrush from your shop—and we'll see!"

It was the thinnest of thin chances that sheer anguish had incubated in my mind.

In the cold light of morning, after the most dreadful night of my life, I was shown into Purkiss's office at the bank.

My thin chance seemed, then, scarcely a chance at all. The only item on the credit side was the fact that neither the clerks and cashiers outside nor Purkiss himself showed any sign of perturbation, as surely they would have done had they discovered as yet anything amiss in the vault.

Steeled to a greater resolution than I had known was in me, I played my gambit.

"I'm so sorry to bother you," I said to Purkiss, "but, you know, I'd hardly left here yesterday when it dawned on me that I'd entirely omitted what the museum people would have seen to at once. Quite vitally important. That is, to give the mummy case a light coat of preservative varnish before storing. If you wouldn't mind—really, I've spent a sleepless night thinking about it—I've brought the stuff along with me—"

He glanced with a frown at the tin and brush I held.

"Will it take you long, Mr. Lesage? It really is rather inconvenient. Saturday morning, as you must know, is a very busy time."

"A matter of minutes only, Mr. Purkiss," I said earnestly.

He fingered his watch chain, his bearded lips pursed. I could see he was irritated. It was touch and go. I seemed to hear the thin ice cracking under me in all directions. Abruptly, he nodded. I breathed again. He rose and led the way down to the vault.

I dreaded what I might see there, but all appeared to be in order. The boxes on the racks looked undisturbed. There on the floor, in their yellow-painted squares, stood the domed trunks, the gun cases, the Egyptian box—and Mrs. Randolph's packing case. Perspiration started out on me at the sight of that ill-omened object.

"Kindly," said Purkiss, "be as quick as you can, Mr. Lesage."

Naturally, he had no intention of leaving me. I had not hoped for such an impossibility. Raffles was in the packing case. I knew he must be listening with every nerve in his body, expecting at every second to feel the packing case lifted and borne out.

The most I hoped to do was to convey to him, in some form of words addressed ostensibly to Purkiss, that things had gone wrong, that some time over the weekend he must get back into the mummy case, and that on Monday I would come and withdraw Princess Amen. How in the world I was to convey all this without betraying my ulterior motive, I could not for the moment imagine.

I groped desperately for a revealing—yet not *too* revealing— formula of words. Never before had I so realized the poverty of the English language.

"A most inconvenient thing to have happened," I said loudly —then dropped my voice to add, "my having to bother you like this, Mr. Purkiss."

I knelt down by the Egyptian box and fumbled in my pocket for the key.

"Hurry, if you please," Purkiss said testily.

I felt his impatient regard on the back of my neck as I found the key and inserted it in the lock of the Egyptian box. And suddenly, belatedly, with a sense of utter despair, I realized an appalling thing. I realized that I dared not open the box. For Raffles probably had stuffed into it, *on top of the mummy case,* the tarnished electroplate and threadbare carpets from Mrs. Randolph's packing case. And Purkiss would see them.

My head swam. I felt physically sick. There was surging like surf in my ears. I was cornered, trapped, done for. It was the finish.

I knelt there paralyzed, staring down at the box, not daring to turn the key. And dimly, in that nightmare moment, I became aware of something on the box which certainly had not been there before—new yellow paint on the faded yellow of the most prominent of the squares of hieroglyphs.

Additions had been made to the hieroglyphs!

My heart was pounding so that I could scarcely breathe. I bent lower over the box, pretending to have difficulty in turning the key in the lock, and I slid a covert glance round the vault.

On one of the wall racks was a tin of paint with a yellow-dabbed brush in it—the paint used for outlining on the floor the storage space taken up by the various articles on deposit.

I looked again, narrowly, at the additions to the hieroglyphs: a pair of sails, a policeman's helmet, a pair of long ears (rabbit's ears—Bunny!), three arrowheads, an opera hat and a diamond shape and a pair of legs, a pointing arm. Thus:

I knelt there, rigid. It seemed utterly impossible that Raffles, locked all night in this vault, could have learned of Birdie Minton's flight. Yet there, clearly, was Birdie, pursued by a policeman, boarding a ship. Equally clear were the instructions to me, Bunny: namely, that Raffles was in the Egyptian box, the box with the diamond shape painted on the side, and that I was to carry it away.

I was so stunned that I had forgotten to keep up my pretense of difficulty with the key in the lock.

"Mr. Lesage!" Purkiss said sharply. He came to my side. I saw that he had a great silver turnip of a watch in his hand. "I do beg you to hurry, sir!"

I rose. My knees felt weak under me.

"I must apologize," I said. "I—I was thinking."

I drew in my breath.

"You know, Mr. Purkiss," I said, "I—I really fear I shall have no peace until this valuable mummy is in the care of experts. I don't think I could endure another night like last night—tossing, turning, worrying all the time. It just isn't worth it, Mr. Purkiss. I've come to the conclusion that I'd rather eat crow and let the museum authorities have the mummy on their own terms, stingy as they are. I'll take it to them right away, I think. I've a four-wheeler outside."

Purkiss rasped at his beard. He was thoroughly vexed.

"Well, really, Mr. Lesage!" he said.

But he called for the porter and Mr. Andrews and, leaving them to deal with the box, escorted me back up the steps to his office. I surrendered the bank's receipt and, with a very cursory handshake, he closed—practically slammed—his door on me.

There were a good many people at the cash counter. As I walked past them toward the street door, I heard a voice I knew speak to one of the cashiers.

"Might as well have a look at my damned mortgage agreement while I'm here," the voice said. "I'll trouble you to have up my blasted deposit box."

I stole a glance at the speaker and saw the back of a purplish neck topped by a rakish gray topper. It was Ferdy Farr!

I fairly shot out of the bank, passing the porter and Mr. Andrews, who had just put the box in Ivor Kern's brougham. Barely troubling to return their salutes, I told Kern's driver to drive like the devil to his boss's place. I ducked into the brougham as he cracked his whip. The great box, placed obliquely across the seats, squeezed me into a corner. Breathing hard, I rapped on the box with my knuckles.

"Raffles?" I said hoarsely.

The weight of the world seemed to lift from me as I heard his voice.

"Pretty work, Bunny! Pretty work!"

The clopping of the horse's hooves broke from a fast trot into a canter. I looked back anxiously through the oval peephole, watching for any sign of pursuit. I still had seen none when I felt his hand on my shoulder. He was out of the box. He wedged himself into the space beside me, massaging his thighs, smiling.

"A tighter fit than I'd thought," he said. "But, Bunny, you did marvels. I couldn't have a better partner! Mind you, I never doubted you'd come as soon as you heard about Birdie's flitting. That'll teach us to rely on a woman, by Jove!"

"Never again," I said.

"Never again," he agreed. "Still, my main fear was that you wouldn't spot my little hieroglyphic code."

He took out his cigarette case.

"You know," he said, I quite enjoyed myself in that vault—up till the moment when, as I was going through the deed boxes, I came across that very afternoon's paper in one of them. I wondered what the devil it was doing there, took a look at it—and, Bunny, I saw that story about Birdie Minton! From then on, my night in the vault was as vivid an experience of hell as ever I want! Would you see the report? Would Ivor see it? What would one or both of you do? Would you come to try to get a warning to me? If so, could I contrive some message for *you?*"

He shook his head.

"Bunny, that newspaper saved my skin! But how, in the name of heaven, did it get into a deed box in the vault?"

The solution flashed on me instantly. I snapped my fingers.

"Dacres!" I exclaimed. "Raffles, when I arrived at the bank

with Princess Amen yesterday afternoon, the newsboys were shouting the latest race results. This Dacres, a dandified young chap, was down in the vault when Purkiss and I entered it. Dacres shuffled some documents a bit hastily into a deed box he had open. I'll bet you anything he was checking the racing results on the sly, didn't want his manager to see him with a newspaper in his hand, so when Purkiss told him to buzz along, just shoved the newspaper into the deed box along with the documents, and didn't get a chance to retrieve it."

I drew in my breath, marveling.

"And Ivor Kern imagined your luck had run out!" I said. "Ye gods!"

Raffles laughed aloud.

"Fortune favors the wicked, Bunny. And Josephine now, there's a girl to restore our faith in women, after our experience with Birdie—Josephine and Dick and Frank are running in pretty good luck, too, because old Ferdy's due to have a good, ripe insurance indemnity fall into his lap shortly!"

He lighted a Sullivan.

"Well, let's rummage in Princess Amen's box and have a look at the rest of the swag—*our* share, as you might say—if it's all right behind, Bunny?"

I glanced back again through the oval peephole. The horse's hooves were clopping in a brisk, inspiriting trot. I could see no sign of pursuit. In the gray light of the November morning, the good old London drizzle was falling. Never had it looked so delightful to me.

"All right behind," I said.

Kismet and the Dancing Boy

Against the limpid sky of a London springtime evening, insignia projecting above the doors of great business houses, in the silent streets east of St. Paul's, stood out with curious effect. Raffles and I had had occasion to call on a friend in the City Office and were walking now in quest of a cab.

It was seldom that we found ourselves in this financial quarter, and we were struck by the romance of such pendant objects as a totem pole denoting a company trading into the Far West, and a gilded centipede which distinguished a bank trading, on the other hand, into the Far East.

Suddenly Raffles paused.

"Bunny," he said, "where have we seen those elephants before?"

The pachyderms in question, which were of lacquered wood, one ivory in color, the other coral-red, hung side by side above a doorway. Each bore on its back a howdah in the shape of a crenellated tower from which flew a carven pennon.

"Chessmen of the Indies," Raffles said. "The elephants stand for Castles or, as we say, Rooks. But they ring some other kind of bell in my memory. What *is* this place?"

We walked forward a few paces, looking up at the lacquered chessmen. They swayed a little, creaking, in the evening airs. Down the long street not a soul was in sight. In the distance the dome of St. Paul's, soared about by the restless specks of pigeons, floated in the sky.

The house of the chessmen was old, even a bit askew. It was narrow, six stories in height, with leaded casement windows, the frames and sills of which were of carved teak. Behind the diamond-shaped windowpanes were what looked like closed shutters of iron.

Two steps led up to narrow double doors, also of carved teak, with a chessboard inlaid in each upper panel. On the right-hand lower panel was a brass plate, so worn by long polishing that we were obliged to peer closely to read the legend:

JOSEPH CAVENDER & SON
The Chess House

EAST INDIA MERCHANTS   MING TAN CONCESSIONAIRES

"Cavender!" I exclaimed. "Raffles, you remember! At school! The mystery man—Roy Cavender!"

"Who always wore a watch chain with two elephant Rooks on it," Raffles said, "miniatures of those hanging there. Yes, of course. He was a form or two ahead of us, and left before us. A prefect. Queer, haunted kind of chap—long, gangling, stoop-shouldered as though he carried the weight of the world on him. Harassed expression. Aloof, miserable kind of johnnie."

"He used to be excused from games," I recalled.

"Yes, and had special coaching in chess, instead," said Raffles. "He was so good that he used to be asked to play in the Masters' Common Room."

He offered me a Sullivan from his cigarette case as he looked up thoughtfully at the building.

"Obviously, Bunny, we've stumbled on a bit of that chap's family background. I was always curious about him, and I'm still more curious, now, as to why chess should mean so much to a family of—what do they call themselves? 'East India Merchants— Ming Tan Concessionaires.' "

He struck a match, holding it first to my cigarette, then to his own.

"Ming Tan!" he said suddenly, as he flicked away the match. "Bunny, I've just thought of somebody who could give us some information. And, by Jove, here comes a hansom!"

The horse's hooves sounded hollowly in the stillness as the hansom came swaying out of a side street and, at Raffles's hail, was reined in with a jingle of harness.

"Where to, sir?" asked the cabbie.

"Clifford's Inn," Raffles said.

As The Chess House receded behind us into the maze of streets east of St. Paul's, he told me that the man who had sprung to his mind was a venerable lawyer of the name of Orde Gilmer, who was a member of a club to which we belonged.

"I'm certain I've heard him speak of Ming Tan," Raffles said.

"What is Ming Tan, exactly?" I asked.

"It's an island somewhere in the vicinity of Java and Bali," said Raffles. "Gilmer's the man to give us chapter and verse on it. I've a notion he's done some law work in connection with the place. Let's hope we can run him to earth."

In a twilit, stone-walled passage in the ancient confines of Clifford's Inn, we found that the lawyer had not sported his oak; the door stood open. Raffles tapped on the baize-covered inner door, and we went in, to find old Gilmer in the act of decanting sherry.

He cocked an eye sidelong at us over his spectacles. "A. J.

Raffles and Bunny Manders?" he said. "Well met, my dear fellows! You shall give me an opinion on this wine."

He was a sturdy old boy with the noble white head like Judge Blackstone's and a long, clean-shaven, legal upper lip which stretched with gusto as he sampled his sherry.

"Ming Tan?" he said, when Raffles had broached the purpose of our call. "H'm! At school with Roy Cavender, were you? Thought him a bit of a mystery? No doubt, no doubt."

He waved us to saddlebag chairs, sank into one himself.

"Ever hear of Lyndon Smith?" he asked.

We confessed our ignorance, and the old lawyer explained to us that the administration of the independent island of Ming Tan had been vested for a century and more in a dynasty founded by an Englishman called Lyndon Smith.

"Grand old chap he must have been," said Orde Gilmer. "A naturalist and a medical man. He was a widower, and he and a son of his made their home in Ming Tan. They loved the gay, sweet-natured people of the place, and did a great deal for them in medical and other ways.

"The upshot was, the people became attached to the Smiths, and relied on them, and they made the old man their leader, with the title of Hanahmi—which in the Tanee language is Prince—with succession vested in his descendants. In that simple way, the dynasty of the Smiths of Ming Tan was founded. And now, where do the Cavenders come into the picture, you ask?"

He took a sip at his sherry.

"The only trader to call regularly at Ming Tan in those days," he went on, "was one Joe Cavender, master and owner of the barque *Sundown*. Now, old Hanahmi Smith was a chess devotee. In recognition of that, the people of the island had made him a gift of a set of chessmen carved in Ming Tan in very ancient days. I've seen it, and it's the most beautiful thing I ever saw in my life.

"Unfortunately, though chess is a great game with the people of Ming Tan, as with so many peoples of the East, old Smith was too good a player for the local opposition. The only time he could get a real game was when Joe Cavender dropped anchor. He could always beat Joe, but still, Joe could make him think sometimes. He used to look forward to Joe's coming, but there was one fly in the ointment.

"Joe was a man with a gimlet eye to the main chance. He had most of Ming Tan's trade, but he foresaw growing competition and he was always nagging at Hanahmi Smith to give him an exclusive concession. Old Smith didn't see it, and one day he got so sick of listening to Joe's eternal importunities, when he'd much rather have been playing chess, that he was goaded into trying to put a stop to them once and for all, and he threw down a challenge."

Orde Gilmer looked at us over his spectacles.

"Mind you," he said, "old Smith knew very well he had Joe's number at chess. So he said, 'Now, look here, Joe—the first time you win a game of chess from me, I'll grant you this exclusive concession you keep harping about. And, by heaven, I'll make my Ming Tan chessmen here the seal and token of the bargain. The day you win a game, the concession, and the chessmen as token of it, shall become yours—until such time as I challenge and defeat you in a return game.

" 'Should you win a game, and something happen to us before we play a return game, then the concession and the chessmen shall remain in the possession of your descendants until such time as a descendant of mine shall challenge and defeat, in a single game, your family's chosen best player, when the concession shall be forfeit and the chessmen returned to Ming Tan. Mark you, no challenge from a Smith can ever be refused, and the game must be played within forty-eight hours of the challenge.

" 'If you should win a game from me, and the chessmen pass into your possession, their safety shall become your responsibility. I or any descendant of mine shall have the right to view the chessmen on demand, and failure to produce them will involve immediate forfeit of the concession. All games resulting from challenges from a Smith to a Cavender, should it ever come to that, shall be played with the Ming Tan chessmen in the presence of a man-of-law and two witnesses from either side. There you are, Joe! Now, I don't want to hear another word about a concession. Play chess!' "

"The very existence," Raffles said, "of the building we saw just now—"

"Implies that Joe ultimately won a game?" said Gilmer. "He did. After eight years of trying, eight years of study, with the games between them getting steadily keener, one day when he dropped anchor off Ming Tan and had himself rowed ashore, he found Hanahmi Smith in bed on the verandah of his bungalow palace overlooking that wonderful bay. The old man was dying.

"Joe Cavender was a hard nut. He saw that it was now or never for him. He lured Hanahmi Smith into a final, a farewell, game. And Joe won.

"Hanahmi Smith was inflexibly a man of his word—as his descendants have proved to be. He lived long enough to put his signature to an agreement drawn up in approximately the terms I've outlined to you. I'm the London lawyer for the Hanahmi Smith of Ming Tan, as was my father before me, and I've seen that agreement. Whatever its legal merits, the simple fact is that the Smiths regard themselves as morally bound by it. And that's the position to this day."

"I think," Raffles said slowly, "that I begin to understand Roy Cavender's peculiarities at school—"

"The Cavenders," said Orde Gilmer, "have lived for a century in dread of challenge and defeat by a Smith at a single game of chess. They've made a great fortune out of their exclusive concession; but the greater that fortune grows, the greater is their dread of losing the plank it's founded on.

"Every Cavender boy, generation after generation, is dragooned into chess, whether he has aptitude for it or not. As kids, they're haunted by the sense of carrying on their shoulders a load of responsibility to the family. One Cavender schoolboy, fifty years ago, actually drowned himself because of it. I imagine it's much the same with the young Smiths of Ming Tan, because the Cavenders have become leeches on the island economy; their exclusive concession has become, in changed conditions, an incubus. Since the early days, the Smiths have sent five challengers—all unsuccessful."

Orde Gilmer reached for the decanter.

"In each generation," he said, "when a Cavender proves himself currently the family's best player, he's elected automatically, regardless of age, chairman of the family concern. The present incumbent is your old schoolfellow, Roy. He defeated his father, Norris, who thereupon stepped down from the nominal direction of affairs but is still the real driving force of the firm—a clutch-fisted old fanatic, soured in youth by the need to master a game for which he had no talent.

"There are some very strange stories behind some of the insignia you see over doorways in the square mile or so of the City here. And that's the story of the elephant Rooks of Joseph Cavender and Son.

"And now," said the old lawyer, "I'll give you a bit of current news. There's a new Smith challenger on the sea at this moment, bound for London."

He refilled our glasses, cocking an eye at us.

"You play chess, either of you?"

"Both of us," Raffles said, "though indifferently."

"H'm," mused Gilmer. "You were at school with Roy Cavender but you weren't friends of his? Quite so. Well, now, I wonder if you would care to be present at the coming challenge game, as the two witnesses for our side, that of the Smiths?"

"With the utmost pleasure," Raffles said instantly, and I nodded agreement.

"In that case," said the old lawyer, "I'll ask you to raise your glasses to our twenty-one-year-old challenger, Miss Ann Lyndon Smith—otherwise, the Hanahma Kismet, the Princess Kismet, of Ming Tan!"

Naturally, we were eager to know what kind of girl our champion would prove to be. The time passed all too slowly for us. At long last, the P. & O. liner docked, and there came to us from Orde Gilmer an invitation to luncheon, to meet his interesting client.

Through all London, now, the spring was singing, and tulips were tall in the window boxes against the gray walls of Clifford's Inn when we alighted from our hansom.

Again, Gilmer's oak was unsported, and as we pushed through the baize-covered inner door into the tobacco-ey old sunlit room, I saw a slender figure standing framed against the open casement.

She turned at our entrance. She was not tall, and, though she was dressed in the charming springtime mode of any English girl, I saw in the magnolia of her complexion, the subtlety of her dark eyes, and the raven sheen of her hair, intimations of a more exotic clime.

Old Gilmer presented us. Miss Ann, he called her, for she did not use her title outside her island.

Over a glass of his finest sherry, we talked for a few minutes, looking down on the occasional bewigged barrister who hurried in the sunshine across the courtyard below, and I was enchanted by the music of her calm, clear voice.

We sat down to luncheon a small party, just the four of us, waited on by a pantry boy in white jacket and striped waistcoat. And when the pleasant interlude came to an end, Gilmer consulted his watch.

"Miss Ann," he said, "our appointment with the Cavenders, to convey your challenge and arrange the details, is for three-thirty. We've still an hour or so to spare. I wonder if you would so far indulge an old buffer, himself a humble devotee of the pastime of philosophers, as to grant him the honor of being the first in this country to play chess with you?"

I guessed at once that he was curious to gauge the strength of her game.

"With pleasure," she said, smiling. "Where is your board?"

He produced it with alacrity, and a shabby old thing it was to set before a Princess.

Highly expectant, Raffles and I stood one each side of the table, looking on at the game.

Her hands were delicate and graceful. She used only her right hand in play, I noticed, the fingers of her left toying meanwhile with an ivory figurine of a turbaned East Indian boy, which conveyed an astonishing effect of vivacity and mischief, dancing at her white throat on a thin gold chain.

She lost little time in reflecting upon her moves, her strategy seeming rather to be dictated by a swift divination. However, very soon I saw that Raffles was frowning at the board as though puzzled, and that Orde Gilmer's legal lip was visibly lengthening.

At last, as though compelled to it, he ventured a remonstrance.

"Are you *sure,* Miss Ann?" he said. "Are you *sure* you want to make that move? The threat to your King developing here at—"

Her attractive brows knitted as she appraised what even I could now see was a distressing predicament.

"Oh, dear!" she said. "How silly of me!"

The old lawyer gave us over his spectacles a look of the most dismal significance. Simply, the tragic truth was, the girl was very poor at chess.

"Miss Ann," said Gilmer heavily, "shall we leave it? A lovely spring afternoon is no time for young ladies to agonize over chessboards. Come, let us show you London—"

"But our appointment?" she said. "My challenge?"

"Miss Ann," said Gilmer sadly, "this Roy Cavender is a formidable player."

"And you think I'm no match for him?" she said. "Oh, I know I'm not good. I have no illusions. Only, you see, I was *sent.*"

"What in the world," marveled old Gilmer, "were your father and brothers thinking of?"

"It wasn't they who sent me," said Ann Smith, and her fingers went to the tiny, mocking figurine at her throat. "It was the little, forgotten god who gives his name to our island, the little god Ming Tan, who whispered to me, over and over, 'Go! Go to London and make your challenge. Something to all our good will happen there. Go to London, Hanahma Kismet!'"

She looked round at us, smiling a little.

"So, please," she said, "my dear friends, don't look so unhappy. It isn't *this* game that matters, but the game with the Ming Tan chessmen."

She pushed aside the board and rose.

"Isn't it time to go now?" she said.

I was touched by her faith in her superstition, her feminine intuition, whatever will-o'-the-wisp it was that had brought her so long a voyage. We all three were. We were reluctant to let her expose herself to the humiliation of defeat at Cavender's hands in a few moves.

But we had no choice in the matter and, deeply depressed—except for Ann herself—we rode to The Chess House in an open four-wheeler.

We were received by the Cavenders, father and son, in a lofty hall with a chessboard floor, lacquered walls inlaid with a chess motif, and huge, intricately wrought Balinese chandeliers.

Norris Cavender, the father, was a gaunt, frock-coated man with a massive, bony forehead, a hard mouth, and deeply sunken eyes. His son was even more gangling and bowed than he had been at school; he was haggard, hollow-cheeked, nervous. I noticed that he still wore the elephant Rooks on his watch chain; and on the father's chain was a similar device, with the addition of what looked like a clock key.

Roy said that he remembered Raffles and myself very well from schooldays; but his brown, uneasy eyes kept sliding to Ann. Plainly, both men were tense, fearful as to the degree of the threat she might represent as a possible chess prodigy. They little knew!

We were conducted up a curving staircase to Roy's office. Here again was a chessboard floor; here again were lacquered, checker-inlaid walls. And here tea was served to us, a pale, fragrant tea in delicate little dove-blue bowls.

"The tea of Ming Tan, Princess," said Norris Cavender, giving her her title with grim punctilio.

"It's good," said Ann, sipping from the bowl which she held in both slim hands; she gave him a long, level, contemplative look.

"I wonder, Mr. Cavender," she said, "why, in all the years you were head of your firm, you never once came to Ming Tan to see the tea in flush?"

I saw Roy Cavender raise his head and look at her strangely.

But his harsh father said, "I've always been a busy man, Princess. In these days, here in the City of London, it's hard for a man to hold his own."

"Hard, too," said Ann, in her calm, clear voice, "for a man to distinguish at all times what is, in justice and humanity—his own?"

The room was utterly silent. Through the diamond-paned windows, I could see in the distance the dome of St. Paul's, a poem in stone against the cloudless blue.

"Well, well," said Orde Gilmer abruptly, "we're here for a purpose. First, I would see produced for my client, as is her right on demand, the Ming Tan chessmen."

"Of course," said Norris Cavender and he rose at once and stalked into an adjoining room, closing the door behind him.

Gilmer polished his spectacles. Raffles's face was impassive.

Roy Cavender glanced with shy unease at Ann, serenely sipping her tea. In the stillness, the measured ticking of a clock became audible from the adjoining room.

Finally, the door opened and Norris rejoined us, carrying a gold-hinged ivory board and a large box, also of ancient ivory, miraculously carved.

He opened the board on the desk.

Together, he and Roy, neither with hands quite steady, set out on their appointed squares the chessmen of parchment-hued ivory and those of ivory coral-red—the magnificent, tall Kings in the tailed turbans of majesty, each with a ruby diadem; the splendid Queens in their *kains* or sarongs, with short shoulder capes and bared, proud breasts; the sage and stooping holy men, with staves and rice bowls, who stood for Bishops; the mounted Knights in gold-disked armor, with swords upflung; the elephant Rooks, with tight-curled trunks, bearing patiently their gold-tower howdahs; the foot-warrior Pawns with *kris* and buckler.

In the stillness a sun ray, mote-filled, slanted down from the windows upon the chessmen of Ming Tan.

"All my life," Ann said, scarcely above a whisper, "I've wanted to see them—and take them back to the people to whom they belong."

"They belong in this building," Norris said grimly, "in the safe in my room there—until a certain eventuality. As you know very well, Princess."

Raffles took out his cigarette case.

Ann looked at Roy Cavender across the board.

"It's you whom I have to defeat, I understand?" she said. Her fingers went to the figurine at her throat. "Shall we play, then?" she said.

"Play?" Roy looked blank. "Play now?" Bewildered, his brow beaded, he glanced at his father, then stammered, "If—if you wish it, Princess, why, then, of course—"

"No!" Norris said sharply. "This is too precipitate. Our own man-of-law is not present. Mr. Gilmer, I must remind you of the terms of the agreement—game to follow challenge at *any* time within forty-eight hours. I do sincerely feel—"

"Your son seems discomposed," said Orde Gilmer dryly. "You want to give him time to steel himself, is that it?"

"Father," Roy said, "I—"

"Tomorrow, then, at this hour?" Ann suggested. "It really won't take long."

"Not long?" said Norris.

He was visibly jolted. The idea seemed to make him feel ill. He stared at the girl as at some sphinx seen in the fevers of nightmare. He passed a finger round inside his collar.

"So be it, then," he said hoarsely. "Tomorrow, at this hour, in this office."

Orde Gilmer was smiling wryly as we drove away in the four-wheeler.

"They sense disaster in your very name, Princess *Kismet!*" he said. "If they only knew! Four moves—four moves, I tell you—will be enough to dispel their terrors. Raffles, Manders, what irony! Ah, Miss Ann, Miss Ann, what in the world are we to do about you? Your tranquil confidence has no—no rationale. What miracle is it that you hope will happen? What—"

"I don't know," said Ann. "I just feel that *something* will happen. I was sent."

I looked hopelessly at Raffles, sitting facing me. We were going up Fleet Street. He was taking a Sullivan from his cigarette case. A queer half-smile lurked about his lips. And my heart gave a sudden great thud. For, in a flash, the challenge which the girl had flung down, not only to the Cavenders, but, all unknowing, to A. J. Raffles, was staring me in the face.

As I met his gray eyes, grown curiously expressionless, I knew beyond doubt what was going to happen. Tonight. After dark.

Sure enough, about midnight, a neat brougham belonging to our friend Ivor Kern, antique dealer and receiver of stolen property, with Kern's loyal and discreet coachman, Jem Stoker, on the box, passed over Holborn Viaduct with the horse at a rapid trot, to approach The Chess House by a maze of side streets.

In the darkness of the brougham, the red dot of Raffles's cigarette alternately kindled and faded.

"This'll be a hard crib to crack, Bunny," he said, "but we've never had a more worthwhile one. It's obvious that the only way the Cavenders' exclusive concession is likely to be broken is through the provision for its automatic forfeiture if they should be unable to at any time produce the chessmen. I intend to get them. I have on me every safebreaking tool I possess. With those iron window shutters, and no approachable back or side entrances, the place looks pretty impregnable. But as we were leaving this afternoon, I spotted what might, with luck, prove a weak point."

My palms were clammy as, having left the brougham in a side street and appointed a rendezvous with Jem, we made the final approach on foot. We were in evening dress, with capes and opera hats, as though returning belated from some Livery Company banquet.

Each way, the street stretched vacant, silent, shuttered, the streetlamps glimmering at intervals. When we reached The Chess House, Raffles moved at once to the left of the two front steps. In the angle here, he stamped with his heel on the pavement. It gave off a hollow, wooden sound.

"A double-leaf trapdoor with external iron hinges," he said, "just like the ones that taverns have over their cellars. It's probably for the ingress of tea chests. This kind of sidewalk trapdoor is usually secured by an iron bar across underneath. Same thing here, as I can tell by the sound."

He dropped on one knee. A thin ripsaw gleamed in his hand.

"As I thought," he said, "this saw fits nicely into the crack where the two leaves meet. Now, keep cave, Bunny!"

I peered each way along the street.

The sudden rasping of the sawteeth on the iron bar, a sound hollowly exaggerated by the wooden trapdoor, set the perspiration streaming from me. I thought the dreadful din never would cease, but at last it did; and with a jemmy Raffles forced up one leaf of the trapdoor, got his gloved fingers under the edge, pulled it up.

"Hold it up, Bunny!"

While I held the door at the vertical, Raffles struck a phosphor match, dropped it into the black aperture. The match fell on flagstones beneath, sputtered bluely there for a moment, lighting a vacant space confined between a stone wall and a wooden door. The match went out abruptly.

Raffles sat on the pavement with his legs dangling in the aperture. He gave himself a hitch forward with his hands, dropped from sight; and his voice came up, sepulchral, from the depths.

"Sit on the pavement with your legs dangling," he said.

With a quick glance each way along the street, I obeyed, balancing the trapdoor with one hand. I felt his strong grip on my ankles.

"I've got you," his voice came up to me. "Hold yourself rigid, letting the trap down gently."

Again I obeyed, and he took my weight, lowering me slowly, so that the trapdoor closed down over us without the frightful report which otherwise would have wakened the echoes in the empty street.

The confined blackness under the pavement here was a relief to me after the stark feeling of exposure on the surface.

"A damned solid door to get through here, by the feel of it," Raffles muttered.

I heard him striking the door, sounding it, with the edge of his hand.

"No lock, but bolts on the inside, top and bottom. Now, then, brace and bit—a good big bit. I'm going to drill through an inch above each bolt, close up to its socket, put a penknife saw through the drilled holes, saw down enough to make a slot for the ripsaw, then cut down through wood and bolts together. A good shoulder shove should do the rest. Keep your ears pricked for a bobby's footsteps above our heads."

But all I could hear, as I perspired in the close darkness, was the steady bite of the greased bit into the wood. It was the longest hour of my life, getting through that door; but, at last, we were groping into the dry, warm darkness of a basement redolent of tea, nutmeg, cinnamon, and sandalwood.

Raffles lit our bulls-eye lantern, shone its oily ray round over stacks of chests bearing Tanee script. From the basement a short flight of steps led up to a door. It was locked, but Raffles with a picklock made short work of it, and we stepped through to find ourselves in the lofty hall with the chessboard floor.

The bulls-eye threw our shadows hugely aslant as we mounted the stairs swiftly to Roy Cavender's office.

"Question, now," Raffles muttered, "is how tough a nut the safe is going to be."

We went into the adjoining room, Norris Cavender's office, almost the twin of Roy's, except that a square, medium-sized safe stood flush against the left-hand wall. I held the light while Raffles went down on one knee to examine the safe.

"Ordinary office safe," he said. "Standard-type combination lock. I feared something more elaborate."

He went to work on the cylinder with his sensitive fingertips and acute hearing. But after a minute, he stopped and looked up at the lacquered wall above the safe.

"That damned ticking," he said. "It puts me off."

I shone the light up on to the clock, a wall clock in a frame of gilded sun rays. It ticked softly, its hands pointing to twenty-five minutes to two.

"Shall I stop it?" I asked.

He shook his head. "No need. I've a gadget here that I've never tried before. Now's the time."

He took a binaural stethoscope from his pocket, adjusted the earpieces, went to work again. In a few minutes, he put a hand on the door lever, depressed it, pulled. Slowly, the heavy door swung open and, with an exclamation of triumph, I shone the ray of the bulls-eye into the safe.

It was stacked with letter files, pink-taped bundles of documents. No ivory-and-gold chessboard! No large ivory box of chessmen! I stared, in stupefaction. I could not believe my eyes.

"But he *said*," I exclaimed, "Norris Cavender *said*, to Ann, 'They belong in this building, in the safe in my room.' Raffles, could they possibly have taken the chessmen home with them—to play —to work out some strategy for the game tomorrow?"

Still kneeling there on one knee, gazing into the safe, he shook his head slowly.

"It's improbable, Bunny," he said. "For a century, they've kept the chessmen safely in this building, with its safeguards of iron shutters and so on. Why should they take the chessmen home all of a sudden? If they want to play, they'd have half a dozen sets at home; they're chess—"

He broke off for an instant, then said in an odd tone, as he pocketed the stethoscope, "They're chess people. With chess minds. Masters of the tactic of deception, the hidden defense—"

In the silence, the clock ticked softly.

Suddenly he looked up at it. A gleam came into his eyes.

"Bunny," he said, "when Norris Cavender came in here to get the chessmen, did you hear this clock ticking—although he'd closed the door?"

"Why, yes," I said, mystified.

"So did I," said Raffles. "But, man alive, it's impossible! No one in Roy's office, with the door closed, could possibly hear the quiet ticking of this clock!"

He pushed shut the door of the safe, rose swiftly.

"Two other odd things! This clock was audible *only* while Norris was in the room here. And, he wears a clock key on his watch chain! Almost always, a clock key is kept in, behind, or under the clock to which it belongs. Why wear a *clock* key on your *watch* chain?" He stepped up on top of the safe. He opened the clock glass.

"And why," he said softly, "why a third keyhole? One for ordinary winding, one for winding the striker. But will you kindly tell me, why a third, by itself, just above the figure six?"

My heart thumped.

"I'm going to try an experiment," Raffles said abruptly. "For all I know, it may set off a whole hive of alarm bells, but we must chance it."

He took from his pocket a jeweler's pliers with a long, thin pincer. He inserted this into the third keyhole, gripped the pliers hard, gave them a turn to the right, the winding direction.

Instantly, the ticking of the clock was drowned by a synchronized ticking that seemed to come from behind the lacquered wall itself, an altogether louder and heavier ticking. With an exclamation, Raffles leaped down from the safe.

"Damned thing's rising!" he said.

He shone the circle of the bulls-eye on it, and slowly, before our eyes, the safe rose, in a series of scarcely perceptible jerks, vertically, to its own height above the floor, then stopped. And, for the first time, we were seeing the *whole* of the safe, instead of just the upper half of it.

I heard Raffles draw in his breath.

"The chess-playing foxes!" he said. "Bunny, this deserves to be known as the Cavender Ming Tan Defense! A double safe! Two doors, upper and lower. Lever and combination cylinder external on the upper door, recessed in the lower door. A flange between upper half and lower half, the flange overlapping the parquet when the safe is lowered, so giving the appearance of a perfectly ordinary safe, flush on a solid parquet floor. Ninety-nine times out of a hundred, any cracksman who cracked the visible half of this safe would go away empty-handed and discouraged, never dreaming there was an *in*visible half!"

He chuckled.

"Defense by deception—a discovered check!"

He dropped on one knee to examine the combination.

"Same type as the upper door," he said. "Bunny, we'll be out of here, up through the sidewalk by the way we came, in half an hour—with the Ming Tan chessmen. Combinations reset, everything left just as we found it, except for two sawn bolts and a sawn iron bar—which, as those iron hinges of the sidewalk trapdoor will hold it quite firmly if anyone should walk on it, may not be discovered for quite a while."

And presently, as he drew open the lower door of the safe and took out the Ming Tan chess set, he added wickedly, "I can't tell you how I'm looking forward to three-thirty tomorrow afternoon!"

It was an afternoon glorious with all the promise of summer. After a pleasant luncheon in Orde Gilmer's chambers in Clifford's Inn, the old solicitor and Ann—neither of whom so much as dreamed of our overnight exertions—arrived with Raffles and myself at The Chess House.

Never had I seen A. J. Raffles so blandly genial, and I was myself hard put to it to conceal my secret jubilation.

As before, the Cavenders, harsh father and haggard son, received us in the chessboard hall. Though both were as men on hot bricks, I had a strong impression that they suspected nothing as yet of what had transpired in their queer old building during the night.

The situation was ironic. As we sat in Roy's office, sipping the subtle tea of Ming Tan and exchanging hypocritical civilities, I knew that what restrained Orde Gilmer from suggesting getting on with the game was his dread of Ann's humiliation, and that what restrained Norris Cavender from making the suggestion was his dread of her triumph.

It was Ann herself who put a period to this harrowing interlude.

"Shall we," she said pleasantly, "do what we're here to do?" Norris rose, granite-faced.

"I'll bring in the chessmen," he said. "But, first—the man-of-law and the other witnesses for our side."

He went to the landing door and, on opening it, disclosed a meek individual in the act of raising a hand to knock.

"Ah, Tonkin," said Norris curtly, "run along and tell Mr. Crouch, the solicitor, and Mr. Grope, from the countinghouse, to come in, now."

"Very good, sir," said Tonkin, who seemed in the grip of some strong emotion. "But, sir, I came to say we've just found out that down in the basement, sir—"

My scalp suddenly tingled. From the corner of my eye, I saw Raffles pat a yawn and take a Sullivan from his cigarette case.

"I cannot talk to you about the basement *now*, Tonkin," said Norris impatiently. "Do as I tell you."

"Yes, sir," quavered poor Tonkin, a hand trembling at his mouth. "But, Mr. Cavender, down in the basement—"

"*Will* you do as I say?" snarled Norris, and he slammed the door, crossed to the door of the adjoining office, went in, and slammed that door, too.

The surge of the pulse in my head was such that it made it difficult for me to catch the sound for which I listened, that of augmented clock-ticking from the next room.

Just as I heard it, the landing door opened and two frock-coated men, the Cavenders' solicitor and their accountant, came in. There was some byplay of introductions all round by Roy. Into the midst of this to-do there penetrated from the adjoining room an uncanny sound.

It was like no sound, whether human or animal, that I ever had heard before. My very hair stood on end at it. And it struck the company mute, staring at the closed door.

Raffles, crossing his legs gracefully, leaned back in his chair with an expression of courteous interest.

The door was jerked open. Norris Cavender appeared. He looked as though he had been struck by lightning. His eyes seemed to have receded into their sockets. His jaw jutted like a crag. His voice was so thick-tongued as scarcely to be comprehensible.

"The Ming Tan chessmen," I understood him to say. *"Gone!"*

In the electric silence, Mr. Crouch cleared his throat.

"I did hear," he mentioned mildly, "some rumor downstairs about a robbery—"

"Rumor?" Norris Cavender shouted. "I tell you, they're gone!"

Ann's fingertips went suddenly to the tiny ivory figurine of the dancing boy at her throat, and into her dark eyes came a shining wonder. But into the aged eyes of her lawyer, Orde Gilmer, peering at Norris over his spectacles, came an unholy glee. However, before he could claim forfeit of the concession on the spot, Roy Cavender cut in.

"Is this really true, Father?" he said, in awe.

His father did not deign to answer. Not once had he taken his eyes from Ann. There was shrewdness, cunning, hatred in them, and now he spoke to her directly.

"You!" he said. *"You're* behind this, of course! You may or may not be capable of beating my son at chess. You couldn't be sure, could you? So you made certain of your forfeit in another way. *You're* behind this! You hired some skillful, wicked scoundrel of a cracksman—"

"That's demonstrably untrue," Roy said sharply. "Princess Kismet was ready and willing to play me yesterday afternoon. It was *we* who backed out. You've made a vile suggestion, Father, and I apologize humbly for you to the Princess. I apologize in my capacity as chairman of this firm."

He was standing straighter than I ever had seen him before. He was thoroughly roused. He looked a different man.

"I've never before reminded you that *I* am chairman, have I, Father?" he said. "As such, I tell you now that I made *my* decision, in the course of a sleepless night, about this game that was to have been played here today. For a century, in this family, fathers have ground down the faces of their sons into chessboards from the time the poor little toads could toddle.

"The only game permitted—chess, chess, chess! And why? To hold on for dear life to this concession that's already enriched us out of all reason. It's blinded us to every other value in life. I've never really understood what we've been losing—until Princess Kismet, yesterday afternoon, sat there in that chair where she's sitting now.

"When I saw her, when I heard what she said to you—about the tea in flush—then, by heaven, my eyes were opened for the first time in my life. And I lay awake all night—seeing her, hearing her voice—and I came to a decision, I tell you."

"A decision?" Norris said hoarsely.

"I decided," Roy said, "that if I should see that she could beat me on her merits, well and good. But if I were to see that she couldn't, then I was determined to play for self-mate—that is, *compel* her to win!"

He turned to Ann, who was sitting very still, her eyes on him.

"I'm ashamed to have said all this before you, Princess," he said, "but it's the simple truth. So, you see, this astounding coincidence of the theft of the chessmen affects the issue in no way whatever."

I did not breathe. I felt as though I had been stabbed in the back. I glanced at Raffles. Never had I seen on his face so extraordinary an expression.

"The issue," Roy said, "was decided yesterday. It was decided at the moment, I do truly believe, when you spoke, Princess, of the tea in flush. I bitterly regret the loss of the chessmen. Not for *our* sake—we've held them for a century—but because, if you and I had sat down to our game of chess together, they certainly would have gone back to Ming Tan with you, where they belong. It would have made no difference if you were the worst chessplayer in the world, and I should, most deeply, like you to believe that."

They looked at each other. The rest of us might have been nowhere within a mile radius. And I had a feeling that what was coming into being here between these two, in this strange room of Chess and the Indies, with the dome of old St. Paul's visible from the windows, was something high and most enviable, the greatest good fortune that could come to any two people, anywhere, at any time. And when Ann spoke, her voice, to me, was as a quiet bell in some temple of Ming Tan, though all she said was:

"I feel sure I should always believe anything you told me, Mr. Cavender."

I felt Raffles's hand on my arm. Very unobtrusively, we went from the room.

All the way down Ludgate Hill in a hansom, up Fleet Street, along the sunlit Strand, we had not a word to say. Only when the horse was clip-clopping up Haymarket did Raffles break the silence between us.

"I think we can take it for granted," he said, "that from here on Ann will call the tune."

My mood was grim.

"Raffles," I said, "those chessmen must be returned!"

"What do you take me for?" he said. "Of course they must. Without wishing to rush the fences in any way, I rather think wedding presents will be in order before long. We'd better make ours, the chessmen, strictly anonymous. If it'd been *we* who broke the Cavender concession, in the way we'd planned, then we could have hung on to the chessmen—for services rendered—and a small fortune Ivor would have got us for them! But we were rooked, old boy. We were taken in flank by one of the Cavender rooks.

"Who'd have dreamed Roy had it in him to turn round like that? When he revealed that he was determined to sacrifice that game, why, then—as gentlemen, after all, dammit—we were beaten! In chess parlance, Bunny, we were mated. The truth is, of course, we were mated by the springtime—and by the little god Ming Tan, who sent Ann, against all reason, half across the world to London."

His tone lightened.

"Incidentally, Bunny," he said, "I begin to suspect that the little god Ann calls Ming Tan is a less obscure character than one might think. I fancy he's known also, though under another name, in our western world—known, in fact, as the very god of mating."

He chuckled, pointing with his stick as the hansom swung to the left out of Haymarket into Piccadilly Circus. And there ahead, above the jogging ears of the horse, I saw against the blue sky a recently erected statue of a winged boy, poised on one foot upon his pedestal, leveling bow and arrow at the unsuspecting passers-by —Eros, god of love.

The Birthday Diamonds

With clip-clop of horses' hooves, and glimmer of candlelamps through a chilly mist, innumerable carriages were passing up and down the Champs Élysées. Inconspicuous among them was a fiacre carrying Raffles and myself to, of all things, the Annual Dinner of the Antique Dealers of Paris.

"This may not prove a terribly exciting function, Bunny," said Raffles, as he offered me his cigarette case. "Still, since Ivor Kern couldn't use the two invitation cards sent to him and gave them to us, since we were coming to Paris, it seems a pity to waste them. We've nothing better to do."

"Personally," I said, as I took one of the profered Sullivan cigarettes, "I can think of a lot better things to do, on the first night of a visit to Paris, than dine in the company of several hundred antique dealers."

I looked at the twin lines of misty gas lamps converging up the slope before us to the massive, brooding shadow of the Arc de Triomphe. I looked, between the bare trees passing on either side, at the snug red glow of great coke braziers in the glassed-in terraces of cafés. Above all, I looked at the ladies of Paris gliding by in their

71

carriages to mysterious rendezvous, and I felt a yearning for an adventure of a kind unlikely to be found among antique dealers.

I said as much.

"Now, there," said Raffles, "one never knows. In Paris, anything can happen."

He struck a match, holding it first to my cigarette, then to his own, then before the face of the gold half-hunter which he took from the pocket of his white waistcoat.

"We're going to be late, I'm afraid," he said.

Our fiacre swung out of the stream of carriages circling the Place de l'Étoile, entered the darker Avenue Victor Hugo. Here the horse came jingling to a standstill before a large but somber hotel, the Hotel des Réunions, which specialized in catering to just such formal functions as that to which I had by now resigned myself.

Anything more tedious than the foyer we entered, with its red rep and red plush, its gilt-framed pier glasses, ponderous chandeliers, and groups of droning habitués, it would have been hard to imagine.

My gloom was deep, as having deposited our dress capes and opera hats, we approached a notice board which stood on an easel, between potted palms, at the head of two wide, shallow steps leading to a higher level of the foyer. This notice board indicated in which rooms were to be found that evening's banquets.

There were two only, spelled out in wooden letters slid into grooves of the board. I spotted ours at a glance, for it was the topmost:

ANNUAL DINNER: ANTIQUE DEALERS OF PARIS———>

I was about to turn to the right accordingly, toward the lofty double doors indicated by the arrow, when Raffles's hand on my arm checked me. He pointed to the second announcement on the board:

"You wanted an adventure?" he said softly. "You shall have
one, my boy!"

He glanced back over his shoulder toward the lower, more
populous level of the foyer.

"Stand a bit closer to me," he muttered. "That's it. Just to
cover my hands while I slip these wooden arrows out of their
grooves. So! And slip them back in so that they indicate the opposite rooms from what they did before. So!"

My heart gave a great thump.

"What's the meaning of this tomfoolery?"

"Not tomfoolery," said Raffles. "Prudence. Should a need for
explanations presently arise, we've only to point to this notice
board for it to be seen that we're the mere innocent dupes of some
passing humorist. It's our alibi."

"Our alibi for what?" I gasped.

"For participating, I hope," said Raffles, "at the Social Banquet of the International Congress of Police Officials."

As he spoke, he was steering me firmly toward the doors on
the left. Perspiration prickled out all over me. I tried to hang back.

"Are you out of your mind?" I panted. "This—"

"Note, first," said Raffles, "that an international congress
implies a gathering of people who're strangers to each other. Note,
second, that the doors of both banqueting rooms are closed. That
means that the dinners have got under way, and that the men who
just now doubtless were at the respective doors, collecting invitation cards, have been withdrawn. I see no reason why we shouldn't
get in quite easily, and among an international assortment of several hundred policemen we might hear some stimulating things.
Just one point, though—"

He checked. We were a bare couple of paces from the lofty

doors with their panels after Winterhalter. From the look on his keen face, the vivacity which danced in his gray eyes, I knew he was resolved on this risky escapade.

"A word of warning," he said. "Whatever happens, don't lie. Be evasive. Be specious. Or be dense. But don't tell a direct lie. It could be dangerous. Right? Then let's hope these rather florid doors don't prove to be locked. Pull yourself together. Now, then —here we go."

He stepped forward, turned one of the great crystal doorknobs. The door opened a crack. He pushed it wider. Cupping a compelling hand under my elbow, he steered me forward into a polyglot roar of voices, a clatter of cutlery, a scurrying to and fro of bedeviled waiters.

Open-mouthed, I gazed on a fabulous sight—the stiff shirtfronts and shining faces of several hundred of Europe's leading police personalities in convivial mood.

Under dazzling chandeliers, they were seated on either side of four tables which ran the length of the banqueting room to an elevated, crosswise table from which presided what I could only assume to be the elect, or super, policemen of the continent.

Raffles's hand was urging me forward. At this end, the least distinguished, of the table nearest the door, were a number of vacant places. Putting his other hand on the back of the chair next to that of the endmost diner, Raffles addressed him in excellent French.

"*Si vous permettez, monsieur?*" Raffles said.

"*Je vous en prie,*" said the diner, with a cordial gesture.

We sat down. As in a dream, I took up the napkin before me, shook out its starched folds. Raffles's neighbor, now no longer the endmost diner, turned to us. He was a man of about fifty, of an agreeable appearance, big and broad-shouldered, with a trim beard but rather rumpled hair, both quite gray, though his eyes were blue and bright, disconcerting in their alertness and intelligence. His smile was pleasant.

"Less from your accent than from your appearance," he said, "I take you to be Englishmen. May I introduce myself? My name is Louis Tral."

"I," said Raffles, advancing a cue for aliases while yet adhering to the truth, "am called A. J. This is my friend Bunny. We're inexcusably late, I'm afraid."

"You've missed nothing, Mr. Ajay, Mr. Bunny," said Tral, kindly bestowing upon us the aliases angled for. "A soup without distinction. Still, the wine is palatable and this salmon not bad. You must start with this. *Garçon!*"

Dish succeeded dish before me. I scarcely knew what I ate; it might have been so much cardboard that my teeth were crunching. I could not credit in what fearful company we were dining and wining.

In the uproar, I could hear little of what Raffles and Tral were talking about, though they seemed to be finding each other congenial to the point of affinity.

On my left I had no neighbor. Thus I became aware, as the roar of talk swelled louder and looser and from the high table the signal to smoke was given, of the stealthy opening of the door to my left and a bit behind me. I glanced over my shoulder in that direction, to see a cloaked gendarme peering into the room.

I instantly thought of the notice board, so flagrantly tampered with, and my insides felt peculiar.

The gendarme stepped in. His eyes searched the tables, then he tiptoed up behind Louis Tral, handed him a note. Tral nodded, and the gendarme, still tiptoeing despite the din in the room, withdrew.

Tral lighted a pipe, sucking at it. When the tobacco was burning to his satisfaction, he opened the note and studied it, frowning, puffing.

My collar felt tight. I eased a finger round inside it. My misgiving deepened as Tral turned and spoke quietly to Raffles. Raffles nodded, turned to me.

His eyes warned me, This may be awkward—keep your head, but his voice was easy as he said, "Bunny, Mr. Tral suggests we slip out before the speeches start."

I did not like the sound of this. If someone had seen our finagling of the notice board and had sent out for a gendarme, who had scribbled a warning to Tral, it would be no good our trying to pretend that we had got into the banquet by accident.

As we followed Tral from the room, and the closing of the doors behind us shut off the noise, I fully expected to see the gendarme waiting, primed with denunciations. But there was no sign of him, and I exchanged an uneasy glance with Raffles as we followed behind Tral to the *vestiaire*.

We withdrew our things. Tral slung a cape over his evening dress, donned a widebrimmed black felt hat of rather bohemian appearance and, tossing pipesmoke over his shoulder, led us out to a neat brougham waiting in front of the hotel.

The gendarme also was waiting there. He touched his kepi to Tral, opened the door of the brougham for us, closed it on us, mounted to the box beside the driver, and the horse set off at a brisk trot.

"Bunny," Raffles said, "our friend, Mr. Tral here, is a divisional police inspector. His headquarters is in the Rue de la Pompe, nearby. He's suggested that, instead of listening to after-dinner speeches, we might like to see a typical Paris police station from the inside."

Seeing any police station, Parisian or otherwise, from the inside was just what I was afraid of. But I forced myself to say brightly, "Oh, really?"

"I suggested it, Mr. Bunny," said Tral, "as I've just been called to a case that promises to be piquant. I should like to give you and Mr. Ajay an insight into our actual work here, and my assistant wouldn't have sent for me had the matter been commonplace."

He sounded genuine enough. But I hardly knew what to think. If the gendarme really had come from the police station with a note, then surely, I thought—and I knew Raffles must be thinking —the wretched man, misled by the notice board, must first have intruded upon the antique dealers at their repast? Surely he would mention the fallacious board to Tral?

"You are very kind, Mr. Tral," I said, but my smile felt like localized rigor mortis in the darkness of the brougham.

I could only hope that the gendarme had inquired at the desk as to the whereabouts of the police banquet and, the door being pointed out to him, had had no occasion to consult the notice board. This seemed a possibility, though hardly one to bank on. I ground my teeth over Raffles's initial recklessness, as the horse turned into a quiet, narrow street of tall, old, gray buildings, Rue de la Pompe, and jingled to a standstill.

The blue lamp of a police station shone wanly through the mist.

The gendarme sprang down from the box, opened the door of the brougham for us. He did not address Tral, nor accompany us into the police station; and I exchanged with Raffles a brief glance of relief. Luck was with us; it was obvious that the gendarme must have inquired at the desk and not looked at the notice board at all.

For all that, I devoutly wished myself elsewhere as Tral, beckoning us to follow, strode ahead into his office, an almost bare room lit by a naked gas mantle, with whitewashed walls lined with shelves holding dusty pink dossiers.

A bald man sitting at the desk, and a young woman sitting before it, both jumped up as though they had been impatiently awaiting Tral's arrival.

The woman was about twenty-two, elegantly dressed, of a glowing brunet beauty, with slender, eloquent hands, and angry brown eyes that sparkled.

"Inspector," said the bald man, "this lady is Madame Colette

Guyomar. She reports that she's been robbed. As I said in my note to you, there are features of the case which made me think you might wish to handle it personally."

"Of a necklace," she said vehemently, "a necklace of twenty-one diamonds given to me by my father on my twenty-first birthday. But this is not a matter of the sentimental or intrinsic value of the necklace. My father is a dying man, monsieur, and this is a matter of the bearing the necklace has upon his testamentary intentions."

Tral waved Raffles and me to a row of hard wooden chairs. He himself took the desk chair respectfully quit by the bald man, his assistant, who remained standing.

"Your father, madame," Tral said, "is—"

"Lucien D'Arzac, the jeweler, of the Rue de la Paix."

Resuming her seat in the chair before the desk, she explained to Tral that though Lucien D'Arzac, one of the most eminent of Rue de la Paix jewelers, had devoted his life to the adorning of feminine beauty, he was at heart a woman-hater.

This eccentricity had its origin in the fact that years ago his wife, a lovely, flighty, willfully extravagant woman much younger than he, had fallen in love with another man and run off with him, deserting not only her husband but her daughters, Denise and Colette, then aged eleven and nine respectively.

For the two little girls life had been made miserable thereafter by the behavior of their father.

To the beautiful women who frequented his treasure house in the Rue de la Paix he had dissembled the bitter disillusion he had conceived for their sex. But at his home in the Avenue Montmorency he had not scrupled to show his true feelings for everything female, and the girls had grown up in the knowledge that he detested the very sight of them, a sentiment which inevitably they had come to reciprocate.

The one alleviating influence in their lives had been the care and affection of their elderly nurse, Hélène. This woman had shielded the girls as far as possible from their father's harsh treatment and mordant tongue, and it was thanks entirely to her nagging that he had made a gesture of sorts when first Denise and later Colette had attained their twenty-first birthdays.

Grudgingly, he had presented to each of them a necklace of twenty-one diamonds—one diamond for each year of the lives he had done his best to make unhappy for them.

"Call the necklace your dowry," he had said brutally to each of them. "You need look for no more from me. And I predict that within a year you'll have started selling the stones one by one and frittering away the proceeds, just as your ineffable mother frittered away everything I ever gave her."

Within a year of her twenty-first birthday, each girl had married.

"Denise three years ago," said Colette. "And I've been married eighteen months. My husband, André Guyomar, is the soul of honor. But Paul Bechtel, Denise's husband, is a low, lying, degraded, semi-bankrupt waster. He—"

She checked her startling flash of passion.

"You'll see soon enough," she said grimly.

And she went on, "About four o'clock this afternoon, our old nurse, Hélène, came to see me. She stayed on with Father, you understand, after Denise and I left home. At this moment, she's nursing *him*. She came to tell me that he was fatally ill. Oh, no, he didn't want to see me. His deathbed hasn't softened him. What she'd come to tell me was that she'd learned by chance of his testamentary intentions, which are, she says, that Denise and I shall share his entire estate—provided we've each preserved our twenty-first birthday necklaces intact."

She raised a hand quickly as Tral made to speak.

"If only one of us should have her necklace intact," Colette continued, "she's to get everything. If neither of us should have her necklace intact, everything's to go to some unheard-of charitable organization.

"And *there*, monsieur, you have his real intention! He believes implicitly in his cynical prediction and is convinced we'll have behaved extravagantly, as our mother would have done, and frittered our necklaces away. Hélène told me that the clauses touching ourselves are conceived in a spirit of pure malice, pure mockery. She was most anxious to know whether I had my necklace intact. Fortunately, I was able to assure her that I had, that my husband André would never dream of letting me sell a single stone. But now here, monsieur, is the damning thing: what Hélène confided to me she'd already confided, since she never favors one of us above the other, earlier in the afternoon to Denise."

She rose from her chair.

"*Now* do you see why my necklace has been stolen? Denise and her vile husband have frittered her necklace away long ago. This afternoon, Hélène can scarcely have left their house, to come to me, than they conferred and decided there was only one thing to be done—and done quickly, while the iron was hot—and that was to possess themselves of *my* necklace! They *had* to, don't you see? So I am here to demand that their house be searched and the necklace found and returned to me instantly!"

She was imperious. She looked magnificent. I glanced at Raffles. He was watching her with an impassive face.

"Please sit down again, madame," said Tral, "and tell me: are, or were, these necklaces identical?"

"Virtually so," said Colette. "What of it? I tell you, only one necklace now exists intact, and that one is therefore mine."

"That no doubt," said Tral soothingly. "Now, when did you first miss your necklace?"

"This evening, of course," she said. "My husband went away yesterday on a business trip. I was alone. After Hélène's visit, I sat for some time in my salon, thinking over what she'd told me. Then, as I hadn't worn my necklace for several nights, I had a fancy to take it out and look at it.

"Figure yourself, monsieur, it had become of certain significance! I keep the necklace, in its case, in a drawer of my dressing table. Monsieur, when I went into the bedroom and lighted the gas, I got the shock of my life. I tell you, my heart stopped! The window was standing open to the fire escape, mist was creeping into the room, the drawer of my dressing table was open, necklace and case were gone.

"In a flash I realized that, either at the very time when Hélène was talking to me in my salon, or perhaps afterwards as I sat there alone thinking of what she had told me, Denise—or, more probably, her reptile husband Paul, with Denise's connivance—had forced my bedroom window and taken the necklace!"

"Your sister visits you frequently?" Tral asked.

"Never! We haven't been on speaking terms for nearly three years. But that's not to say," declared Colette, "that she wouldn't guess perfectly well where to tell Paul to look for my necklace."

Tral rubbed his bearded cheek with his pipestem, studying her with his blue, lively, disconcerting eyes.

"*Bon!*" he said abruptly. "I see here, from the notes made by my assistant, that your apartment is on floor seven of a house in the Avenue Mozart. Your sister, Madame Paul Bechtel, lives in the Rue Chalgrin. Both quite close."

He rose.

"You will please return to your home, Madame Guyomar. Leave everything in the bedroom just as you found it. I shall call upon you shortly."

As the bald assistant ushered her out, Tral turned to us.

"You find it not without *chic,* my friends, this little affair of the jeweler's daughters? More so, I fancy, than after-dinner speeches now in progress! Burglary is in your line, I hope?"

"I've devoted some attention to it," Raffles admitted.

"So much the better, Mr. Ajay," said Tral heartily. "Now, there is a little bird that whispers in my ear to approach this affair with circumspection. So next, I think, a word with the person who best knows these contentious daughters of D'Arzac the jeweler. The nurse Hélène."

Mist haloed the streetlamps, and the horse's clip-clop woke lonely echoes in the quiet streets of this most respectable neighborhood, as the brougham, with the gendarme no longer on the box, bore us to the nearby Avenue Montmorency and the mansion of the expiring woman-hater.

In an imposing but ill-lit and ice-cold hall we interviewed Hélène, a tall, worn woman in a black dress, with scraped-back hair under a starched cap, her apron, collar, and cuffs also stiffly starched. She at once admitted having told the sisters of their father's testamentary intentions.

"I acted in accord with my conscience," she said. "They're the intentions of a bitter and cynical man. My poor girls, their young lives were made very unhappy by him. The loyalty I feel is to *them*. The husbands they married aren't wealthy men. So I was anxious for the girls' prospects, anxious to know whether their necklaces were intact. They both set my mind at rest. And I said, 'It is well that you have your necklaces intact,' and indeed, monsieur, it lifted a load from my mind and made it easier for me to sit at the bedside of a very wicked man."

"Madame Hélène," said Tral, "you better than anyone else know these girls. In your opinion, is it in the character of Denise to have connived at the theft of Colette's necklace?"

"It's not for me to uphold one girl against the other," said Hélène. "I have affection for them both. But after this news you bring me, I begin to wish I'd kept my mouth shut. It seems I said too much this afternoon. Too much. I'll say no more."

In the brougham again, bound now for the Rue Chalgrin, it was some time before the scrape of a match broke our own silence. The fitful flame cast a glow on the bearded face of the detective, sitting opposite Raffles and me, as he sucked his pipe alight.

"My friends," he said, between puffs, "you'll be thinking, as

I am, that this affair tends in a certain direction. Namely, should Denise prove to be in possession of a necklace of twenty-one diamonds, how are we to prove whether it's rightfully hers or rightfully Colette's?"

"Just so," said Raffles.

"In that connection," said Tral, "you'll also be meditating, as I am, on the possible significance of Hélène's use of the plural."

"The plural?" Raffles said.

"You missed that?" said Tral. "You surprise me. I refer to Hélène's remark, 'It is well that you have your necklaces intact.' "

I was startled. So far had I entered into the unfamiliar situation in which Raffles and I found ourselves—seeing an actual problem as it presented itself to a detective—that I almost had begun to think of ourselves as the detectives Tral believed us to be.

The fact that I did not now see quite what he was getting at, and the further fact that he seemed to have picked up—what we had missed—some significance in one poor little lonely consonant, came as a rude reminder as to who was the trained detective in this case and who were the impostors.

"I foresee," said Tral, "that much may hinge on that remark of Hélène's. But here we are," he added, as the horse jingled again to a standstill, "at the Rue Chalgrin. Now for sister Denise and her —in the trenchant words of Colette—'low, lying, degraded, semibankrupt waster' of a husband, Paul."

His pluck at the bellpull set up a clangor within and brought to the door a tall, singularly pleasant-faced young man wearing a smoking jacket.

"Yes, I am Paul Bechtel," he said. "Yes, my wife is here. Please come in."

In marked contrast to the hall in which we had interviewed Hélène, the one into which we now stepped was warm, cozy, homely, lighted by a fringed standard lamp. Between draped portieres framing the open door of an unpretentious parlor, a fair-haired young woman appeared.

"Who is it, Paul dear?" she asked.

Her husband glanced at the card Tral had handed him, and said, in some surprise, "Divisional Inspector Louis Tral, Rue de la Pompe."

"Indeed?"

In her blue eyes was no sign of perturbation, only of polite inquiry. Though the elder, she was smaller than her sister, more simply dressed, and her whole appearance suggested, to me at least, the sweetness, gentleness, and placidity of a woman happy in her marriage.

"What can we do for Inspector Tral?" she asked.

"I'm told," said Tral, "that you possess a necklace of twenty-one diamonds. I've reason to ask, madame, whether I may see it, if you please."

"You're seeing it," she said.

She moved forward into the hall, and the light kindled a sudden sparkle at her throat.

"I put it on this evening," she said, "because my father, who gave it to me, is a dying man, and whatever his feelings toward me —I'm afraid they're not kindly—I can't help my thoughts dwelling on him tonight, and I feel sorry for him, and I wish him well."

"Correct me," said Tral, "if my eyes deceive me, but I seem to count in the necklace you're wearing fifteen diamonds only."

Denise glanced up at her husband with a little smile, and she put a hand in his.

"Inspector," she said, "we've had rather a struggle during the three years we've been married. Now and then, to help out, I've *insisted* on selling a diamond from my necklace."

"Just as your father predicted!" Tral exclaimed. "Oh, yes, madame, I know all about that. I also know that, unless your necklace is intact, you can't qualify for participation in his estate."

"Oh, no," she said, "I'm totally disqualified, I'm afraid. I only hope that my sister Colette isn't."

"A sentiment, if I may say so," said Tral, "of remarkable

generosity, in view of the fact that, according to my information, you've not been on speaking terms with her for the past three years."

Her face clouded.

"That's true, I'm sorry to say. As children, we were allies in a difficult home. We were everything to each other. But later—well, frankly, Colette was in love with Paul here. He married me. And I'm afraid Colette's a little like Father—she doesn't forgive very easily."

Tral's eyes probed her.

"This afternoon your old nurse Hélène called on you. She asked if your necklace were intact. Why did you lie to her?"

Paul Bechtel flushed angrily. But Denise in her calm voice said, "For the simple reason, Inspector, that if Hélène knew I was disqualified from all participation in my father's estate, she'd feel even more bitter toward him than she does already. The knowledge might easily have made her—the only person who can do anything whatever with him—walk out of his house and leave him to his fate. So when she told me of these testamentary intentions so peculiarly characteristic of him, and asked if my necklace were intact, I just patted her hand and said, 'Yes, of course.' Later will be quite soon enough for her to learn the truth."

There was a moment of silence, then Tral said, "Thank you. That will be all—for the present."

Back in the brougham, bound for Colette's home in the Avenue Mozart, Tral said, "Well, my friends, was that a truthful, generous-hearted, and charming young woman? Or was she lying and was that necklace really Colette's and had Denise and her husband removed six diamonds from it, and hidden them, because our visit was expected and we were to be thereby hoodwinked?"

"It seems a tricky point," said Raffles, and I agreed with him.

"Oh, come," said Tral, "hardly that! Obviously, Denise wouldn't dare produce a necklace of fifteen diamonds to me, then produce afterwards a necklace of twenty-one to her father's executors! No, she was telling the truth. The one who's lying is Colette. She lied when she told Hélène her necklace was intact. Knowing how much depended on it, she'd have lied—to give herself time to think—had the Archangel Gabriel himself put the question to her.

"My English friends, it will grieve you, as it grieves me, to have to admit that the woman-hating jeweler was right in his cynical prediction, but he was, you know. *Neither* girl has kept her necklace intact! When Denise told Hélène she had done so, that was a so-called white lie. On it, this whole case turns. As I foresaw, Hélène's use of the plural is significant. 'It is well,' remarked that good woman, 'that you have your necklaces intact.'

"To whom was this remark addressed? Obviously not to Denise, since Hélène visited Denise first. It was, then, addressed to Colette. What did it tell Colette? It told her that Denise had her necklace intact. The idea that Hélène's remark embodied a white lie never entered Colette's head. She took the remark at its face value, and the thought that Denise had her necklace intact made Colette desperate.

"What did she do? She promptly ran to the police station with a tale that she had been robbed. What was her object? I've no doubt it was to try to create, right at the outset, at least enough shadow of doubt as to the ownership of the one intact necklace she *erroneously* believed to exist as to make possible a subsequent litigation over the will.

"I shall now, therefore, set about finding a way to break her down, show her up—compel her to withdraw her charge before she lies her way to the witness bar and a perjury indictment."

I still was thinking over this very able analysis when the horse jingled to a standstill in the Avenue Mozart. The house was a large one.

"Guyomar?" said the concierge who answered Tral's ring. "Seventh floor left."

Though each landing was lighted by a gas jet pulsing bluely in a wire cage, the carpeted staircases were in almost total darkness. We groped our way up on Tral's heels, and in response to his tattoo on the knocker of the seventh floor left, the door was flung open.

"At last!" exclaimed Colette in her vivid, fiery way, so different from the placid manner of her sister. "Why so long? Come in, come in!"

The salon into which she led us was furnished with far greater splendor than the simple parlor of Denise and Paul Bechtel. Impressive oil paintings in gilded frames hung on the walls.

"Well?" she demanded, her fine eyes sparkling. "My necklace! You've recovered it?"

"Madame," said Tral, "is it your intention formally to charge your sister and her husband with the theft of a necklace of twenty-one diamonds?"

"Yes, yes! I'll drag them through every court in the land!"

"That evidently," said Tral. "First, then, I'll examine the bedroom."

"In here," she said eagerly. "The light's already on."

She threw open a door to the right.

"There! You see? Everything is just as I found it—the window wide open to the fire escape, the mist stealing in, the drawer of the dressing table open, the necklace in its case gone!"

Tral pointed his pipestem at her. His voice was hard.

"Why keep a diamond necklace in a flimsy drawer when there's a safe in the other room? Answer me that, madame!"

The question came as a shock to her. I saw her eyes widen, the color drain from her face. Personally, I had seen no sign whatever of a safe in the other room. I glanced at Raffles. He was looking at Tral with such deep respect that I knew he, too, had seen no sign of a safe in the salon.

Hastily, breathlessly, Colette said, "It's nothing to do with me, that safe. It's my husband's for his business papers. It has no bearing on this matter. He—"

"Let me explain my thought," said Tral. "It occurs to me that you may have suffered all your anxiety needlessly—that, in fact, the person who broke into this room was an ordinary burglar and that he went away empty-handed. No, wait, please! Where there is a safe in a house, and a wife possesses diamonds, then a husband often is insistent that those diamonds be kept in that safe.

"Further," said Tral implacably, "should he come upon those diamonds in an insecure place, then he is quite apt to snatch them up with a curse and put them in the safe himself. Believe me, madame, I speak from experience. I've known this very thing to happen. Many times.

"No, no, wait! You mentioned, I recall, that it was some nights since you'd had occasion to wear your necklace. Also, that your husband went away yesterday on business. To satisfy ourselves, therefore, before we proceed further, that it wasn't an ordinary burglar who broke in here and went away empty-handed, I must ask if you've looked to make sure that your necklace isn't in the safe, placed there by your husband in a moment of marital vexation?"

"No, no," she said. "Impossible!"

She was very pale. She was badly shaken. So used were Raffles and I to being in the position of the hare, rather than of the hounds with whom we were now so strangely leashed, that, for myself, I was beginning to perspire from sympathy with her.

I had to admire the spirit with which she shouted at Tral, "Your whole suggestion is imbecile!"

"Merci," said Tral. "Nevertheless, have you checked? If not, we'd better do so at once."

He strode back into the salon. In great distress, she followed him almost at a run. Exchanging a glance, Raffles and I followed, too.

Tral looked at us.

"You'll note, Mr. Ajay, Mr. Bunny," he said, "that all the pictures in this room are suspended by long wires from a high picture rail. With one exception. I refer to this medium-sized 'Courtiers at the Tuileries,' after Delacroix, above the escritoire here. This particular painting is suspended by a short wire from a nail. Why the exception unless for convenience in removing and replacing this particular painting? The obvious deduction is that this picture conceals one of the wall safes now coming into common usage."

He lifted down the picture.

"*Et voilà!*" he said. "A recent model of a keyless combination-lock lever wall safe. Now, if you will please open it, madame, and check that—"

"Impossible!" she said breathlessly. "Only my husband knows the combination. He's away. He can't be reached. He's gone a long distance. He won't be back. It's—"

"A predicament," agreed Tral, and he scratched his bearded cheek with his pipestem.

I could not help feeling sorry for Colette. She looked really dreadful. I understood, now, the extraordinary skill and cunning of this Paris detective. He had judged from Colette's reaction to his mention of the safe, the presence of which his ratiocinative power had revealed to him, that, just as Denise had done, so, too, had Colette sold *some* of the diamonds from her necklace, and that what remained were in the safe—to give the lie to her entire story that her intact necklace had been stolen.

Suddenly Tral pointed his pipestem at Raffles.

"Now, here, Mr. Ajay," said Tral, "is where your presence is fortunate. Madame, Mr. Ajay here is an English expert on burglary and safes. With your permission, Mr. Ajay will see if his study of the subject is equal to fathoming out this combination for us. Mr. Ajay—"

Poor Colette swayed. She put out a trembling hand to a chair back. I saw Tral's left eyelid flicker at Raffles in a shadow of a wink. I understood. Raffles was being recruited to go through the motions of cracking the combination, in the hope that the sight of him at it would bring Colette to such a pitch of strain that she would break down and confess.

Slowly, Raffles walked forward to the safe. Thus to lend himself to a trap set for a misguided young woman must have gone bitterly against the grain with him. Yet he could not do otherwise. Tral believed him a colleague, a detective. He had no choice but to play the part through.

Never in all our felonious experience had I known a stranger situation. There, before the very eyes of the Paris detective, certainly a detective of exceptional ability, was Raffles, the neatest of London cracksmen, manipulating the combination of a safe.

There was not a sound in the room.

After an almost careless twist or two of the small cylinder of the combination, Raffles seemed to settle to the task. He brought an ear close to the cylinder. His face was keen, his hair dark and crisp, his evening black-and-white immaculate. His brown, lithe fingers moved with a surgeon's delicacy.

I dared not look at Colette. I was acutely conscious of her beside me, of the fern fragrance of the perfume she used, of her slim, clenched hands, of her pent breath.

Raffles's gray eyes roamed over us sidelong. They seemed not to see us. We might not have been there. His expression was remote, withdrawn, abstracted. He was biting at his lip, as in a concentration akin almost to pain. Then, suddenly, his face cleared, the tension of his posture relaxed. He nodded, put a hand on the lever.

Colette sprang like a cat. She caught him by the wrist.

"No!" she blazed. "You shan't, you shan't! You shall not open my husband's safe! I won't have it! I won't *have* it, d'you hear?"

She hurled his hand from her. She was raging. She was beside herself.

"Get out!" she shouted. "All of you! Out! Get out! Get out of my home!"

"Madame," said Tral blandly, "what does this mean? Am I to take it that you wish to withdraw your charge against your sister and her husband?"

"All *right,*" she panted, "all *right,* all *right!* I withdraw it! Now, go! Get out, damn you! And damn my father's money! I won't lower myself—I don't want it—I wouldn't touch it—I don't care—" Her voice broke. "Get *out,* will you? Get out and *leave me alone!*"

Her voice rose in a wail. She pressed her hands to her face. She rushed into the bedroom. The slam of the door behind her made the windows rattle. There was an outcry of springs as she flung herself on the bed.

This time it was Raffles who winked. He winked at Tral. He gave the lever of the safe a jerk. The safe door remained solidly immovable. He and Tral grinned broadly at each other. Raffles took up the picture and replaced it on its nail.

"Good enough," said Tral. "*En avant!*"

He clapped on his hat, and I followed him from the apartment, Raffles bringing up the rear. There was little sense of triumph in me. On the other hand, I could hear Tral, as I groped after him down those seven flights of dark stairs, chuckling to himself.

"No need for Denise to know anything about Colette's 'burglary' charge," Tral's voice came up to me. It sounded hollow in the dark stairwell. "I found a pretty neat way to break her down, *hein?* Better than to let the silly girl go on to the point of perjury. I must say, Mr. Ajay, you backed my hand superbly. Why, do you know what?"

Raffles made no reply. Surprised by his silence, I peered round. The hair rose up erect on my head. I could see no shadow of him, hear no sound of his footsteps.

Raffles was not with us.

"Do you know what, Mr. Ajay?" Tral's voice came up to me again.

"What?" I said, trying with parched lips to sound as much like Raffles as possible.

"Why, you did it so well at the safe," came Tral's voice, "that for a second, absurd as it sounds, an odd, worried feeling came over me. You know, you really should have been an actor, Mr. Ajay!"

I forced a laugh, trying to make it sound like Raffles feeling gratified at a compliment. My head was a tumult of surmises. I kept peering back up, with the result that I precious near tripped and descended the rest of the way headlong.

Perspiration soaked me. I was getting desperate. Tral, with me making as much noise as possible just behind him, almost had reached the ground-floor lobby.

Suddenly I caught a sound from far above. I knew it was Raffles coming. He was coming down from the top of this tall, dark house, racing down the seven flights of black staircases, recklessly, risking his neck to overtake us.

I felt him check himself just behind me, and I heard his quickened breathing, at the very instant Tral stepped down into the lobby and the concierge emerged, scratching, from his cubbyhole to let us forth into the night.

Never had the phantom, cool touch of mist felt so comforting on my burning face.

"It's very late," said Tral, turning to us as he opened the door of the brougham. "Still, we really must have one small drink before we part. I insist!"

"Delighted," said Raffles. "In you get, Bunny."

I ducked into the brougham, but, had I been able, would instantly have backed out again when I heard Tral's direction to the coachman.

"Hotel des Réunions, Avenue Victor Hugo," Tral said.

He was chuckling as he joined us in the brougham, pulling the door shut by its strap.

"We may find one or two of our colleagues still at the hotel," he said. "It is *chic*, this little affair of the jeweler's daughters. It might divert our colleagues."

To my intense relief, however, we found the huge foyer deserted and looking gloomier than ever with most of its lights turned out. Sitting at one of the occasional tables on the lower level, we had a couple of brandies apiece, brought to us by the night porter, then Tral excused himself.

"I really must let my coachman go off duty," he said.

He looked at us with his blue, shrewd, disconcerting eyes.

"Well, Mr. Ajay and Mr. Bunny, I hope you don't regret missing the after-dinner speeches. And that we'll meet again sometime—in your bailiwick or mine. *À bientôt, hein?*"

"*À bientôt!*" we echoed warmly.

And with a final handshake off strode Louis Tral in his vigorous way, cape swinging, bohemian black felt hat atilt, the pipesmoke of achievement tossing back over his shoulder.

"Damned clever chap," said Raffles admiringly, as we sank back with sighs of relief into our chairs. "There's more to this detection business than I'd been led to believe. He showed us our limitations, Bunny. He simply ran rings round us. Why, I don't think we made a single contribution to the detection, did we? Inevitable, I suppose. It's his line. Trained man."

"Raffles," I said tensely, "you cracked that combination right under his nose!"

"Now, there again," said Raffles, "we see that the cobbler shines brightest when he sticks to his last. Of course I cracked it, old boy. Quite a nice job. It was a bit of a twister. And, of course, I left the front door ajar when we came out. All I had to do was see you two started down the stairs, then nip back in and—this time not omitting the formality of *turning* the lever before pulling it—open the safe door. Poor Colette was crying buckets in the bedroom."

"And the diamonds?" I demanded.

"She had nine left in the safe. So I scribbled her a note—unsigned, needless to say—telling her Denise had fifteen, and they'd better liaise and make up one complete necklace. That'll qualify one of them to inherit, and they really must work it out for themselves which it's to be and how they're to share. I can't be bothered."

"Fifteen plus nine," I said, staring at him, "is twenty-four."

"Just so," said Raffles. "And, you know, Bunny, it's damned odd to think that because those two girls weren't on speaking terms neither would be qualified for a single franc from their father's estate, and you and I wouldn't be the richer by three superfluous diamonds, if it hadn't been for—"

He nodded across the foyer. The night porter was standing before the easel, between the potted palms. He had a wooden box in his hand. Something seemed to be puzzling him. He glanced toward the doors on the left, then toward the doors on the right.

He looked at the notice board again. He scratched his head. He shrugged.

He slid the wooden letters out of their grooves into the box he carried, took up the easel and notice board under his arm, and walked off with them.

I heard a chuckle, beside me.

"Shall we go now, Bunny?" said Raffles.

We went.

The Dartmoor Hostage

"You know, Bunny," said A. J. Raffles, "it's a pity that this beautiful moor should be renowned chiefly for a prison."

It was a perfect afternoon toward the end of summer, and we were in a dogcart clattering briskly along an unfrequented, dust-white road. With our portmanteaus and cricket bags, we were sitting behind a poker-faced young groom who held the horse's reins.

After the stuffiness of the train which had brought us down from London, it was a joy to see the wide, blue sky and to breathe an air redolent of the lonely heaths which rolled away on all sides.

"As a matter of fact, Raffles," I said, lowering my voice so as not to be heard by the groom, "I was just thanking our lucky stars that it's not that confounded prison we're bound for."

He smiled. "It hasn't come to that yet."

"Touch wood," I said, knocking hastily on the side of the dogcart.

He had no superstitions himself, whereas I liked to be on the safe side.

"Don't worry," he said. "A prison may be one kind of cram-mer's establishment, but not the kind we're bound for. I think you'll like Henry and Cassie Standish, Bunny."

Henry Standish, M.A., and his young wife, Cassie, were friends of Raffles. Standish ran one of those places to which fellows went when, plowed in exams for their chosen professions, they were obliged to seek intensive tuition in their vacations. According to Raffles, the presence of Cassie was enough in itself to ensure the popularity of even the severest kind of crammer's establishment.

"What sort of a cricket team has Standish got?" I asked.

I spoke a bit uneasily. Months ago, Raffles had promised that, when his serious cricket was over for the season, he would come down and turn out in a game or two for the Crammer's Eleven, and bring someone along with him. He had persuaded me to come, rather against my better judgment, for I was well aware that the view taken of my cricket, in most circles, was that it was pretty contemptible.

"These crammer teams vary a lot, Bunny," Raffles said. "Their strength depends on who they happen to have studying there. It's impossible to guess what kind of a crowd one'll find in residence at a crammer's." He added, "That must be Standish's, just come into sight ahead there."

The poker-faced groom had turned the dogcart off the road on to a rutted, heathery sidetrack that meandered across the heath to a big, old, rambling house in the distance. The place seemed to me ideally situated for a crammer's establishment. In all directions, as far as the eye could reach, there were no visible distractions to tempt the students from conning their books.

Our approach must have been seen, for, as the dogcart jingled and crunched up a graveled drive, two men came down the steps of the house to greet us.

Henry Standish, M.A., who looked to be not much more than thirty, was a tall, fair-haired, haggardly handsome man wearing a suit of academic pepper-and-salt. He had worried-looking blue eyes. He shook hands with us, introduced the other man as Captain Gordon.

"Gordon's helping me with the Army Class fellows," Standish explained.

The military usher was a big, bald, brick-red man of forty or so, in point-to-point tweeds and a canary waistcoat. He had an air of boisterous bonhomie, which quite swamped Standish, who seemed by comparison hesitant and introspective.

Telling the poker-faced groom to take our portmanteaus and cricket bags to the Blue Room, Captain Gordon led us through a large, cool hall to a small lobby, where we had a quick hand-wash, after which he shouted cordially, "Now for a drink to swill the moorland dust down! You must be gasping. Damned hot. This way—"

Raffles frowned slightly. I heard him murmur to Standish, "Everything all right, Henry?"

"Of course, of course," said the crammer, with a sudden flush.

Through a doorway at the back of the house, Captain Gordon led us out on to a sunlit lawn. "Attention, everybody," he shouted, in his hearty, military way. "Here they are, the two acquisitions for our cricket team—Mr. Raffles and Mr. Manders!"

I never had been at a crammer's establishment before, and I looked about me with interest. Four white-flanneled, blazered fellows were playing croquet on the lawn. Beyond the lawn was a small cricket ground, with some chaps practicing at the nets. In the shade of two monkey-puzzle trees, to the right of the lawn, was a group of flanneled and blazered men, about a dozen of them, with their backs to us.

Nobody seemed to be doing any studying. As the group under the trees turned to look at us, I noticed that it was not books they held in their hands, but drinks. Nor was it a blackboard to which they had been clustered like bees at a honeypot, but two women.

Clearly, we had reached the crammer's at a recreative hour.

I realized at a glance that the taller woman was hardly the honeypot, for she was a steely blonde of a certain age, with an acid smile. Beside her, the other seemed little more than a girl. She rose. Her dress was summery. In the flicker of sun and shade under the trees, as she came forward between the blazered crammees, her soft hair had a blue-black sheen. She was lovely, but seemed pale, and her eyes were darkly violet. Approaching quickly across the lawn, she held out a hand to Raffles.

"I'm so happy to see you again," she said.

"And I to see you," said Raffles. And holding her hand in both of his, he asked, "Is all quite well with you here, Cassie?"

It was not so much what he said as the way he said it. His even and pointed tone seemed to give a curious significance to the simple question. It seemed, oddly, to isolate Raffles and the crammer's young wife, there on the sunny lawn. I had an impression that a stillness fell on the blazered figures all about.

But Cassie Standish gently withdrew her hand.

"We're all very well here," she said, and she went to her tall husband's side, and the haggard crammer put an arm about her.

The croquet players resumed their game. The balls knocked together with a hollow sound.

"Well, well," said Captain Gordon. He mopped his palms, tucked the handkerchief back into his cuff, military style. "Agnes, my dear," he said, to the gimlet-eyed blond woman on the rustic seat, "may I present Mr. A. J. Raffles? Mr. Raffles—my wife."

Raffles bowed, and Agnes Gordon said, with an acid simper, "It's a great honor, Mr. Raffles, that so celebrated a cricketer should condescend to play for a Crammer's Eleven in a simple country cricket match against a Warders' Eleven on a prison ground."

My scalp suddenly tingled. I had a fleeting impression that some nudging and whispering was going on among the students, but I paid no attention to it, I was too taken back by what Agnes Gordon had said.

"It'll be a pleasure, Mrs. Gordon," Raffles said blandly, "to play anywhere for Henry Standish's team. We're old friends, aren't we, Henry?"

Knowing him as I did, I knew that he was as startled as I was at this news of a match to be played at the prison; but he showed nothing of it as he glanced with a smile at Standish.

Again I saw that quick flush in the crammer's haggard, handsome face.

"I arranged the match with the Prison Governor only about a fortnight ago, Raffles," he said. "That was well after you and I had fixed the date when you'd be coming down with Manders, to play a game or two for us. The prison match is tomorrow. They've quite a nice little ground, in a hollow just outside the walls. I told the Governor I'd probably have you and Manders in my side. He was delighted. He said he knew you, Raffles; had played with you in Marylebone Cricket Club teams."

"Indeed?" Raffles said, frowning. "What's his name?"

"Colonel Tucker."

"Old 'Friar' Tucker?" Raffles exclaimed. "Good Lord! Is he a Prison Governor now? He was soldiering when I knew him."

"Well, well," said Captain Gordon, mopping his palms again, "I'm sure we're all looking forward keenly, most keenly, to our visit to the prison tomorrow. As you see, Raffles, some of our fellows are hard at it practicing in the nets. They're all eager, I'm sure, to rout the Warders." He tucked his handkerchief back into his cuff. "But we're being remiss, Standish, my dear fellow. Raffles, Manders—brandy-and-soda? Or whisky? Or tea?"

Decanters and tea tray stood on a table at Agnes Gordon's end of the rustic seat. I plumped for brandy myself. I needed it. Not an hour ago, Raffles and I had been congratulating ourselves on having no truck with the prison. Now, here we were, doomed to play cricket under the very walls of the place. The mere thought cast a damper on my spirits.

I drank my brandy. I wished we were back in London, never had come to the crammer's.

I looked about me at the students. It struck me, in my darkened mood, that they would have been doing themselves more good by studying than by idling about in shiftless groups, muttering among themselves.

I was not much taken by them. Though mostly in their twenties, they seemed to me a more experienced-looking lot than I had thought to find at a crammer's. Some of them, in fact, had such a dissolute and reckless look that I did not greatly marvel at their having failed their exams. It was just what I would have expected.

One of them, in particular, I did not like the look of at all. He was lolling with his hip propped on the arm of the rustic seat. Cassie Standish had resumed her place there, beside Agnes Gordon, who now was knitting. With acute embarrassment, I saw that the arm of the fellow was sliding stealthily along the back of the seat, behind Cassie's slender shoulders. He was smirking down at the parting, straight and white, in her pretty hair.

I thought at first that she was unaware of him. She seemed to be listening to the conversation of her husband and Raffles and Captain Gordon. But she was tense. Her hands were clasped tightly together in her lap. I caught the expression in her eyes, and it was one of such acute unhappiness, and even fear, that a shock went through me.

At that moment, Raffles turned rather sharply. His elbow caught the loose-lipped lout full in the mouth and knocked him flying off the seat arm on to the grass.

Raffles seemed oblivious of the fellow and of the sudden silence which had fallen.

"Cassie," he said, with a smile, "could I take a splash more soda?"

He stepped to the table. The siphon hissed in the hush. I saw the fellow sitting on the grass dash the back of a hand across his mouth. He looked at the smear of blood on the hand, from his cut lips. He looked up at Raffles, who had his back turned. The fellow's hand flashed to his blazer pocket. He sprang to his feet. He held a revolver, leveled at Raffles's back.

Before I could shout a warning, Captain Gordon roared, "Put that away!" His jowled face and bald head were brick-red with rage. His eyes were hard as agate. "All right," he said, "time to end the farce."

Raffles turned, glass in hand.

"High time, I should think," he said. "Henry, what *is* this choice company you have here?"

"Tell him," said the military usher.

"Raffles," Henry Standish said, "for a week this house has been in the hands of criminals—lock, stock, and barrel."

"Waiting," said the military usher, with a hard grin, "for Mr. A. J. Raffles to lead our cricket team in a Trojan-horse raid to liberate a convict from the prison across the moor."

Cassie buried her face in her hands.

Raffles looked about him. I followed his glance. My heart hammered. In the shade of the monkey-puzzle trees, under the blue moorland sky, we were ringed round by the blazered youths, hard-eyed, all with their right hands in their pockets.

"There are twenty-five of them here," Henry Standish said, "posing as 'pupils,' 'grooms,' 'domestics.' For a week, that woman there has never left Cassie's side, night or day. My own domestic staff have been living as prisoners in the stables."

"Henry, Cassie, you've been in hell," Raffles said. "I saw that, from the first. With our military friend here, Captain Gordon, as resident bully chucking his weight about?"

"Not Gordon, Raffles," the big, bald man said. "The name is Sime. That rings a bell? You've heard of the Sime cousins, perhaps —Rodney and Walter? We were described by the newspapers, at the time of my cousin Rodney's trial early in the year, as 'swell mobsmen.' Rodney was sentenced to twelve years. Luckily, *I* wasn't caught, nor were most of the efficient little organization of young men we'd built up and led. The lady there is not Agnes Gordon. She's my cousin Rodney's wife, Agnes Sime. Rodney's in the prison across the moor there. As I say, we plan to raid that prison and get him out."

I felt as though I were dreaming. From the cricket nets sounded the thud of ball against bat. Pigeons were crooning peacefully somewhere. The tree shadows were growing longer, slanting across the croquet lawn. Hands slapped my pockets.

"They've nothing on 'em, Walter," reported one of the bogus crammer pupils.

"Naturally not," said the big, tweeded man in the canary waistcoat. "Who ever heard of cricketers going about armed? Yet what better articles in which to conceal rifles, revolvers, and rope ladders fitted with grappling hooks, than cricket bags? Eleven cricket bags. Enough to carry an arsenal. You begin to see the color of my Trojan horse, Raffles? Dark, my dear sir. Damned dark."

His laughter had a brassy heartiness, but his green eyes were cold, crafty.

"Faced by the problem of how to muster on the moor, not too far from the prison," said Walter Sime, "a force of twenty-four active young men, strangers in the area, without exciting attention, I made a preliminary reconnaissance. You can imagine my delight, Raffles, when I chanced not only on the perfect solution of the problem, but the perfect base for operations—a crammer's establishment."

Raffles took a Sullivan thoughtfully from his cigarette case.

"I took the place over," Sime said. "I compelled Standish to write out telegrams of cancellation to all the students and tutorial help he was expecting. I had those telegrams sent from various offices well away from the moor. I then had my own lively lads arrive in small groups by train—like you and Manders—and met by Standish's dogcart. Since there's always an influx of young men for Standish's at this time of year, naturally no comment was aroused. But that wasn't all."

Again his laughter brayed.

"Would you believe it?" he said. "I'll be damned if I didn't discover that our crammer friend here actually had arranged a cricket fixture against the Warders' Eleven, on *their* ground. Right at the prison! And that A. J. Raffles, one of the best-known amateur players in England, a man above all conceivable suspicion, would be coming down, with his friend Manders, to play for the Crammer's team. And you know the Prison Governor personally, have played with him before!"

Exultantly, the big man mopped his palms, his bald head. He tucked the handkerchief back into his cuff.

"The job's handed to me on a silver dish," he said. "When I give my signal—as late in the day as possible, so as to have failing light when we make our withdrawal across the moor—those screws'll never know what hit them. Their team, ten of 'em and their Head Turnkey, this Colonel Tucker, will be blackjacked and laid out cold in the pavilion. And when the alarm sounds, where will the reinforcements, the rest of the off-duty warders, be?

"I'll tell you. A few, due for night duty, may be asleep in their houses. But by far the most part will be sitting unarmed on the grass round the boundary, as spectators of the game, all ripe and ready to be rounded up at rifle point. They'll be there, all right. They won't want to miss seeing the celebrated A. J. Raffles playing on their little ground under the prison walls."

Raffles said quietly, "You've really thought this out, Sime, haven't you?"

"I have," Sime said. "And I advise you to think, too. Because your friend Standish will unfortunately pull a muscle and be unable to play tomorrow. He'll be present, though—he and his charming young wife. We shall travel in two shooting brakes. One will carry the 'Crammer's Eleven,' with you as captain and me as the visiting umpire. I'm glad to say I bear no physical resemblance to my cousin Rodney.

"In the second brake will be your dear friends, Henry and Cassie, surrounded by the rest of my lads, as 'crammer students' come to see the game. Henry and Cassie Standish are hostages. One move, one word, one whisper out of place tomorrow, Raffles—or tonight, come to that—and you'll see just how short will be your dear friends' days in the land. To say nothing of your own."

His stony stare moved from Raffles to myself.

"Understand, both of you?" he said. "Right, then that clears the air, and we all know where we are. Now, we've an evening to get through. Always a bit of a strain, the eve of action. Still, dinner will be at seven, and after that—billiards, cards. Simple, country house pleasures. We live a quiet life, here at the crammer's. Eh, Standish? Cassie? Come, what about another drink?"

A stranger dropping in at the crammer's that evening after dinner probably would have noticed nothing out of the way. In the drawing room, Cassie and the steely blond woman Agnes Sime sat side by side on a sofa, a fringed standard lamp giving light for their knitting, the coffee things on a small table nearby.

It would not have occurred to a stranger that Agnes Sime was Cassie's jailer. Or that the alleged crammer pupils, still flanneled and blazered, were lascivious young swine whose prowlings and eyeings gave Cassie not one moment's peace. Or that Agnes Sime, with her thin, acid smile, found some malicious satisfaction in Cassie's ordeal. Yet it was the Sime woman who ended it, at last, putting away her knitting and rising to her feet.

Cassie rose, too. Ignoring the fellows standing about, and the others at the two or three card tables, she came to Raffles and me. She gave us, in turn, her hand.

"Henry and I," she said. "This is our home. We so much wanted you to come. And we've brought you to *this*. What can we say to you?"

I could not meet her eyes.

"Cassie," Henry said gently, and he put an arm about her and walked with her to the door.

He did not kiss her. I knew why. I saw the watching eyes on her, the lip-licking grins all round the room. Agnes Sime stood waiting with her acid smile. Cassie went with her, and the tall crammer, closing the door on them, turned and looked haggardly at Raffles and me.

Walter Sime's laugh brayed out.

He was full of little pleasantries. One of them was the "Blue Room" to which he grandiloquently had instructed the groom from the dogcart to take our luggage. That must have amused Sime, for, when at last we were conducted to the room, it turned out to be no more than a boxroom. I saw at once why it had been chosen for our occupation. It had no window. Moreover, obviously for our special benefit, strong bolts had been fitted to the outside of the door. I heard them rammed home.

There was nothing in the room but a couple of camp beds with a folded blanket apiece, and our own gear dumped on the beds. Not that I cared. All I could think of was the look in the eyes of Henry's young wife, her horrible ordeal of the whole of the past week.

"Poor Cassie," I said.

Raffles did not answer. I glanced at him. He was standing there holding the candlestick with its single candle. He was looking at our portmanteaus and cricket bags, gaping open on the beds.

"They've been searched, Bunny," he said.

Suddenly he thrust the candlestick into my hand. He went to his cricket bag, rummaged in it under the bats and pads. His expression lightened extraordinarily. He took something from the bag. He stepped to the door, listened at it for a moment, turned to me.

"Keep your voice low," he said. "There are a couple of 'em out on the landing—our night guard." There was a gray gleam in his eyes. "Bunny, they've searched our gear here. They searched us, too, out on the lawn. They're not likely to search us again. Old boy, I think they've made a little mistake."

"Mistake?" I whispered.

"Of the fifteen men present on a cricket pitch when play's in progress," Raffles said, "which two are least likely to have occasion to touch the ball with hand or bat?"

"The umpires," I said. I felt a sudden, prickling excitement. I stared at him. "Walter Sime will be the visiting umpire tomorrow—"

"Just so," said Raffles.

He spun up, and caught, the red leather cricket ball he had taken from his bag.

"Sime and his mob want to get inside a prison," he said. "It's an unusual ambition. Still, we must do all we can to help them gratify it."

He sat down on one of the beds.

"Bring the candle closer, Bunny," he said.

He took a penknife from his pocket.

The ball was burning a hole in the right-hand pocket of my blazer as I sat next morning in a yellow-wheeled shooting brake crowded with the Criminals' Eleven on the way to play the Warders' Eleven. We all were in cricket gear.

The lout whose lips Raffles had split yesterday was driving the brake. Next to him, on the high driving seat, was Raffles himself, bareheaded, wearing an I Zingari cricket club blazer and muffler. Beside him sat Walter Sime, in a floppy white linen hat and an umpire's white coat. Under the feet of the rest of us, sitting in the back, were eleven cricket bags containing a minimum of cricket tackle and a maximum of rifles, revolvers, rope ladders fitted with grappling hooks.

It was a glorious morning. The sun blazed down on the wide reaches of the lonely moor. Not a breath of air stirred. Already, heat currents were beginning to shimmer over the heaths. The two shooting brakes from the crammer's establishment, clattering along steadily on their dangerous errand, were the only moving things on the winding, dust-white road.

I looked back at the second brake. The reins were in the hands of the poker-faced young groom with the neat white stock and square-set bowler who had met us off the London train yesterday. Beside him sat Cassie Standish, her dress summery, her dark hair uncovered, her face very pale. On Cassie's other side sat her sinister chaperone, the blond, hard-bitten Agnes Sime, holding an open parasol.

Behind them, the brake was loaded with the rest of Sime's men, wearing ordinary summer suits and boaters, with the other hostage, Henry Standish, in their midst.

As I looked back at Cassie and thought of the weight of responsibility which Raffles had imposed on me, I felt hollow inside. The message he had gouged with his penknife in the leather of the ball in my pocket seemed to burn through my blazer into the very skin of my hip: *Sime mob's team. Walter umpire. Raid planned. Standishes held hostage. Act warily. A.J.R.*

The match was due to begin at eleven-thirty. When our brake clattered into Princetown, the village of prison staff houses in the heart of the lonely moorland, the clock of the small church was pointing to eleven-thirty exactly.

The horses were reined in, jingling, alongside a low, drystone wall to the right of the road. To the left was a long, low-eaved inn. On the other side of the drystone wall, the rough ground fell away steeply to a treeless hollow. In the hollow, towered over by the outer wall of the great prison on the opposite slope, was the level green of a cricket ground with a small pavilion, in the far left-hand corner, standing at an oblique angle with its back to the prison wall.

In front of the pavilion, the Warders' team, white-flanneled, were having a knock-up. Other off-duty warders, with their wives, children, and picnic baskets, were beginning to gather. All round the boundary line, the little family groups settled down on the grass.

The sight of the women and children there, and the grimly significant weight of my cricket bag as I lifted it from the brake, added to my consciousness of the frightening seriousness of the situation.

I glanced toward Raffles. He was shaking hands with a short, thickset, powerful man with a blunt face and grizzled sideburns, who wore flannels and an M.C.C. cap, and whom I guessed to be the Prison Governor, Colonel Tucker.

"Standish hurt?" I heard him saying, in a booming, hearty voice. "So you'll be skippering the Crammer boys, eh? Well, delighted to see you here at the prison, Raffles. And you've brought an umpire along, I see. Well done. And isn't that Standish himself and his charming young wife in the other brake just pulling in? Brought the rest of his pupils over to cheer you on, eh? The more, the merrier!"

He waved as the horses of the second brake jingled to a standstill behind our own.

"Sorry to hear you're hurt, Standish," he called. "Nice of you to bring your party, though. Hope we give the ladies a game worth watching. Well, now, Raffles, what d'you say—shall we make a start?"

Sime, in his floppy hat, his right hand constantly in the pocket of his umpire's coat, kept close behind Raffles and the Governor as they walked together, followed by the rest of us carrying our heavy cricket bags, down a dusty track alongside the ground.

The track curved on round to the left, to a pair of gigantic doors, massive and iron-studded, in the prison wall. A blue-uniformed warder with slung rifle was on duty before the doors. But our party turned to the right, moving round to the front of the pavilion.

We tramped into the small, woodenly echoing building. It had one large room, the front and rear walls of which consisted of broad flap-shutters. The shutters facing the ground were propped up, lean-to fashion, but the rear shutters were bolted down. At each end of the room was a wooden partition, doorless, one marked STAFF, the other VISITORS.

Raffles and the Prison Governor, with Sime trailing close behind them, walked on out to the wicket. Sime fiddled with the stumps while Raffles and the Governor took a look at the turf. All the time, Sime's right hand was in his pocket. I knew that the slightest sign of a whisper from Raffles, or an attempt to pass anything—even a coin to toss with, a coin on which a message might have been scratched—to the Prison Governor, would bring Raffles a bullet.

The shot would serve as Sime's signal. It would bring death to Cassie and Henry. It would bring the rifles out of the cricket bags. It would bring the bogus crammer students, up there in the brake acting as a miniature grandstand above the drystone wall, pouring down the slope.

The ball burned in my blazer pocket. Raffles was right. The ball was our hope. It was our only hope.

I saw the Governor, out at the wicket, take a coin from his pocket. He spun it up. It flashed silver in the burning sunshine trapped here in the hollow. Raffles called. They stooped to look at the coin. The Governor picked it up. They started back to the pavilion, Sime at their heels.

I was standing in the midst of the other criminal players. One of them gave me a nudge. We carried the heavy cricket bags behind the partition marked VISITORS.

"It'll shorten the agony if we win the toss, Bunny," Raffles had said. "We know Sime wants to act as late in the day as possible. And at a time when all the Warders' team are in the pavilion. That means the tea interval. If the Warders bat first, and we can't get 'em out, they'll probably declare their innings closed at about three-thirty. Our plan will still hold good, but it'll be hell to wait that long."

My throat was dry as Raffles and Sime came behind the Visitors' partition. Sime took a bit of paper from his pocket.

"It's a good wicket out there," he said sardonically, "and our captain's won the toss for us. Here's our batting order. I've put our captain Number One, and you"—he looked at me—"Number Six. The rest of you can see where you are for yourselves. Our scorer has a copy."

As he went out, I saw that at the scorers' table, before the raised ground-side flaps in the main room, a man in shirtsleeves and warder's trousers was sitting with one of the bogus crammer students. Raffles was putting on his pads. As he stooped over the straps, his gray eyes gave me a single glance that told me, clearly as words, "So far, so good. Now for it."

He had played cricket for England. Now, he was playing for the life of the crammer's young wife, and perhaps for many lives, and, if he were to lose his wicket, all would be lost.

With the rest of the criminal team, of which with such appropriate irony Raffles had been appointed captain, I sat on a bench before the pavilion. One only of them stayed behind the Visitors' partition to keep an eye on the lethal cricket bags.

"Sime's team'll behave as normally as possible," Raffles had predicted. "They'll sit in front of the pavilion, like any other country match batting side. Try to get as near the end of the bench as possible, Bunny."

I was next but one to the left-hand end of the bench, facing down the wicket, almost in an exact line with mid-off, who was the Prison Governor, Colonel Tucker. The bowler from the pavilion end was a huge, brawny young warder with a shock of tow-colored hair. He had a long run. He was very fast but wildly erratic, bowling mostly down the leg side. Three times in his first over, Raffles glanced him to the fine leg boundary. It was no manner of use to us.

I started violently at a sudden metallic rattle to my left. I slid my glance in that direction. The scoreboard was there. It was just a post to which was nailed a square board with hooks on it. Another shirtsleeved man in warder's trousers had cast down an armful of numberplates on the grass. He hooked a couple on the board: 10. Behind the scoreboard, and to the left of it, the grass was ankle-deep. A big roller stood there. The grass was perfect for our purpose, if only—

A clatter of stumps sent my heart into my mouth. An outbreak of clapping came from the little family groups sitting all round the boundary. The sweat of relief poured from me as I saw that it was the other opening batsman, not Raffles, who was returning to the pavilion. The numberplates rattled: 15—1—3.

The man on my right on the bench had his pads on. He rose. He walked out to the wicket. Another man went into the pavilion to put his pads on. Up in the village, the church clock peacefully chimed twelve.

Raffles was contriving to keep himself mostly at the far end, facing me. I cursed and blasted that tow-headed Warder for slinging them down on the leg. When twelve-thirty struck, the scoreboard read: 30—2—0. The man on my left went into the pavilion to pad up. There now was nobody on my left at all.

At last, the thing I had been praying for happened. The Governor took the tow-head off. Then I saw that the Governor himself was rolling his sleeves higher. He took off his M.C.C. cap, handed it to Sime, umpiring at the pavilion end, his back to me.

I saw now why the Governor was called "Friar" Tucker. He had a grizzled tonsure, and he windmilled his arms, loosening up, as though he were whirling a singlestick. He trotted up to the wicket and bowled Raffles the very ball I had dreamed of and prayed for—a half-volley outside the off stump.

The ball came off Raffles's bat like a bullet. It arced high in my direction, but a bit to my left. It soared over the boundary and landed full pitch on the roller, which gave off a deep note like a gong.

I already was running to retrieve the ball as it fell in the long grass. I saw the ball lying there. I stooped as though snatching it up, but I did not touch it. As I stooped, I jerked the other ball from my blazer pocket. And as I turned and threw in, hard and high—"Straight to the Governor, wherever he's fielding," Raffles had said —it was the ball with the message that I threw.

Leaving the match ball lying pretty well concealed in the grass, I ran back to the bench. I resumed my seat. I saw the Governor take the throw-in on the first bounce.

"Old Friar Tucker'll feel those gouges on the ball," Raffles had said. "He'll wonder what the devil and take a glance at it—"

The Governor was walking back to start his run. I did not breathe. He was looking at the ball in his hand. He walked slowly. He seemed to be meditating what kind of spin to put on the ball for his next delivery. He reached his run mark. He turned. He trotted up to the wicket, bowled again.

"Whatever fielders handle it after the Governor," Raffles had said, "will feel the gouges and take a glance at it before throwing in. They'll read the message, but they'll all know old Friar Tucker's seen it first and they'll take their cue from him. They're *warders,* Bunny."

Sure enough, the game went on. By the time the clock struck one, almost every man on the pitch had handled the substituted ball except for two batsmen—*and the two umpires.*

As the bails came off for lunch, the Governor caught the ball, tossed to him casually by the wicketkeeper, and himself tossed it as casually to the Warders' umpire. They came walking in together, with all the rest, Walter Sime keeping close behind Raffles. The Warders' umpire went off somewhere, but the Governor, coming into the pavilion where the rest of us were now foregathered, exclaimed, "Ah, I see these kind ladies have been busy!"

A number of pleasant-faced matrons, whom I assumed to be warders' wives, had set up a long table, with a row of chairs each side of it, in the main room. However the gentry on the other side of the prison walls might fare, visitors on the outside seemed to be done pretty handsomely, for great jugs of cider and ale stood down the middle of the table, while before each place was a heaped plateful of ham, beef, tongue, and pickles.

"Thank you, ladies," the Governor said cheerfully. "We mustn't keep you from your own lunches any longer, you kind souls."

As the beaming matrons withdrew, Friar Tucker rubbed his hands together with tremendous relish.

"Well, now," he said, "let's see. I'd better take the head of the table, I suppose. Raffles, will you sit on my left, and the rest of your Crammer boys down *that* side? Umpires here on my right, and our staff team down *that* side. Good, good. Well, now, all of you, do please just carry on. Raffles—and our visiting umpire here—let me help you to cider. We're rather proud of our cider, at the good old prison here."

He was still talking, keeping everybody happy as a good host should, when the Warders' umpire came tramping in.

"Come along, Shinn," said the Governor. "You're all behind with your lunch, man."

"Yes, sir," said Shinn remorsefully. "Sorry, sir."

He was about to take the vacant chair adjoining Sime's when the Governor said, "Anyone find it hot in here? I do. Let's let the breeze blow through, if there *is* any breeze. Shinn, before you sit down, just shove up the flap-shutters on the rear side, there's a good fellow. Johnson, give him a hand."

Behind me, the flap-shutters were unbolted, pushed up on their supports.

"That's better," said the genial penologist. His tone suddenly changed, and his great voice boomed formidably in the pavilion. "Now, if all visitors, except Mr. Raffles, have their hands flat on the table in one split second, they may be lucky enough not to get their heads blown off by the twelve rifles leveled at them through the apertures just opened. *That's* the style."

I was rigid, my palms flat on the table. Across from me, Walter Sime was sitting similarly, his jaw dropped, his greenish eyes protruding in stunned incredulity as they stared past me at the rifles I could not see.

"Right," said Governor Tucker. "Now, you staff players, your colleagues outside will pass the bracelets in to you. Clap 'em on our visitors. Hold them here till I give you different orders. If any one of 'em opens his mouth, club him." He rose. "Raffles, a word with you—"

Raffles stood up, putting a hand on my shoulder. "This is Bunny Manders, sir, friend of mine. Very good thrower-in."

"Ah," said the Governor. "Come along, too, Manders."

He led us behind the partition marked STAFF. The flap-shutter there was up, on the ground side. He turned to us.

"When Shinn, our umpire, nipped into the prison," he said, "to bring out that rifle squad, he also dispatched a messenger to rout out the night-duty men asleep in their houses up in the village and muster them behind the inn. He has his instructions. Those crooks up in the shooting brake, in the glare of the sun, can't see what's happening down here inside the pavilion, and they can't see the riflemen at the back there. But *we* can see just what happens up there at the shooting brake. And here comes action, I think—"

We watched tensely. Above the drystone wall edging the road, up there across the ground, there had come into view a single file of flat-topped blue uniform caps, the up-pointing muzzles of a dozen slung rifles. At a marching rhythm, as of a squad going on duty, the caps came on along the road.

The bogus crammer boarders in the brake, eating sandwiches, turned their heads to look at the squad marching past. Suddenly the hand of the tail-end marcher shot up and jerked Agnes Sime clean off the driving seat. The steely chaperone's pink parasol fell like a struck flag. In an instant, the flat caps were all round the brake, their rifles covering the occupants. The hands of the bogus students shot aloft. Cassie buried her face in her hands.

The Governor turned to us.

"Raffles," he said, "Manders, I can't part with that ball. After it's been offered in evidence, I want you both to autograph it, and I'm going to have it mounted and kept in our staff clubroom here at the prison. But I'm sure I speak for the Prison Commissioner when I say we'd like you each to have a little memento of today, a gift from us all here at the old place—bit of silver, dish or something, with a suitable inscription. And remember, we'll always be delighted to welcome you both any time here at the prison."

Raffles chuckled as we were driving back together in the yellow-wheeled shooting brake to the crammer's place, which had been left with only the imprisoned domestic staff in it. The other brake was a little ahead of us, empty except for Henry and Cassie on the driving seat.

"Well, Bunny," Raffles said, "no need to be overmodest about your cricket any more, now that you'll have an authentic trophy to show for it. I never saw a faster retrieve and throw-in. Sime and his mob wanted to get inside that prison—and you've certainly put them there."

"We," I said.

He nodded absently. The reins in his brown, strong hands, he looked above the jogging ears of the horses at Henry and Cassie in the brake ahead, on the lonely moorland road under the blue sky. The tall crammer had an arm about Cassie's slender waist, and her head rested on his shoulder.

"You know, Bunny," Raffles said, "Sime bragged that the whole job had been handed to him on a silver dish. After what he did to Cassie, it's good to know that it's you and I who steal away with the dish."

The Doctor's Defense

"An act of simple civility, Bunny," Raffles said, "can sometimes result in something to one's advantage."

To escape the winter, we were visiting Madeira, and on this, our fourth day in Funchal, Raffles had thought it politic for us to leave our cards at the British Consulate. After our brief call there, we strolled away, white-suited and straw-hatted, along the narrow, animated street.

Except for fluffy, mid-afternoon clouds hanging over the high summit inland, the sky was blue. Pink and white quintas, or villas, dotted the mountainside, the Desertas Islands lay low and purple on the horizon, and into the tranquil bay a white liner was slowly steaming.

"A beguiling scene, Raffles," I remarked. "On the other hand, I wonder whether there's really much chance of some lucrative adventure among the wealthy English winter colony here, or whether we've merely marooned ourselves? I—"

"Surely," a voice interrupted, "it's Raffles and Manders?"

A passing *carro,* a canvas-canopied carriage on sled runners, drawn by a pair of yoked oxen, trundled to a standstill on the

cobblestones, and from between the side curtains a slender, gray-haired man alighted with twinkling eyes and outstretched hand.

"Albany Bryce!" Raffles said. "Well, well! Are you wintering here, too?"

"Wintering?" said Bryce, a member of a club we belonged to in London. "My dear fellows, I'm the British Consul here! What a coincidence running into you! Do you recall a fellow club member—young Hal Nares?"

"Very well," said Raffles. "Decent chap. Medical man, isn't he?"

"He's the ship's doctor on that liner just coming in—the *Karroo Star*, from Capetown for Tilbury, calling at Funchal here and Lisbon. She'll be here for a couple of days."

Bryce smiled.

"Poor Nares, I may say, is in love. He looked me up here, on the outward voyage, and it was quite touching to hear him rhapsodize about a pretty stewardess aboard called Ellen Ames. A romance fraught with difficulties—ship's doctor and stewardess—as the captain takes a stern line on affairs of that nature among his ship's people."

He took out his watch and glanced at it.

"I'm due down at the Pontinha mole when the ship drops her hook," he said. "I've things to see to aboard her, and I'm curious to know how young Nares's affair has developed. Look here, are you doing anything tonight? Where are you staying? Ah, good. Then I'll call for you and we'll dine together at the Cava Costa and drop in at the Casino afterwards, quite the focus point of our winter colony. I'll try to bring young Nares with me. Forgive me now, I really must rush along to the office."

He resumed his seat and, with the picturesque *carroceiro* walking at their heads, the oxen moved off.

"Decent old stick, Albany Bryce," Raffles said, as we walked on. "His invitation suits our book very well, Bunny. We'll pump him for chapter and verse on the whole winter colony. This shows how it pays to observe the conventions. If we hadn't bothered to leave our cards at the Consulate, we shouldn't have run into Bryce."

The agreeable Consul turned up that evening without the doctor of the *Karroo Star.*

"I gathered," Bryce told us, "that he hardly likes to come ashore, enjoying himself, unless Stewardess Ames can get liberty, too. Circumstances remain very tiresome for them aboard, I'm afraid. They have to be so discreet, you know."

In the Casino, the evening's gaming was at its height. Patrons were gathered two-deep about the roulette and baccarat tables as Raffles and I strolled with Bryce through the opulent rooms. As we had hoped, the Consul pointed out to us various persons of consequence in the winter colony.

"Take particular note of the bald fellow there," he said, lowering his voice as we paused at one of the roulette tables. "That's Lord Ivor Skene, social arbiter of our sunshine exiles. An invitation to his town house nearby, the Quinta Skene, is the accolade. Oh, absolutely!"

He added, with a twinkle, "Skene's a bachelor, but I've often noticed he has a nice taste for the feminine."

A parchment-faced man in his fifties, with a cordless eyeglass glittering in his left eye, Lord Ivor Skene had certainly a most striking companion seated beside him. Her tawny hair, her faintly sun-gilded complexion, her shapely shoulders glimmering through a foam of chiffon, her light, vivid eyes, the diamond-blue sparkle of her earrings, all made her a figure of unusual brilliance.

Skene was whispering to her. Evidently he was giving her roulette counsel, for she was placing small towers of gold here and there about the squared green baize.

"A Mrs. Gilbert," Bryce confided to us. "Casilda Gilbert. Not a resident here. Came in on the *Karroo Star* and going on to Tilbury. That's her husband on her other side, a Major Glyn Gilbert."

The husband, a tanned man in his thirties, with sleek, pale hair, had a mouth that turned downward rather mirthlessly. He lacked his wife's brilliance.

"*Nada vai mais,*" intoned the croupier. "Nothing else goes."

He spun the wheel, deftly flicked the ball into it.

"I believe the Gilberts dined at the Quinta Skene this evening," Bryce whispered. "An uncommon honor, for transients." He added, "Some worthy residents sitting yonder keep catching my eye. They have some grievance to air, I suppose. I must go and dispense consular balm. Won't you come and meet them?"

"If you don't mind," Raffles said, as he spilled some of our all too few gold coins carelessly from one hand to the other, "I'd like to take a flutter at this table. I feel the mood coming on. What d'you say, Bunny?"

I nodded and smiled, but the blood began to pound in my temples as I spotted what had prompted the mood Raffles had mentioned. In the heat of suspense, as the wheel slowed and the ball hopped capriciously from slot to slot, Casilda Gilbert had put back her chiffon scarf, disclosing a dazzle of fine blue diamonds set in a necklace of delicate gold filigree.

The winning hazards were called next moment, and I was surprised by Mrs. Gilbert's exhibition of rapacity. Her slim fingers positively seized on the stacks of specie pushed deftly across the baize to her by the black rakes of the croupiers.

"*Fazem sous jogos,*" begged the man at the wheel. "Make your games, please."

His eyes were on Mrs. Gilbert, but she would have none of his blandishments. Having won, she tucked the bank's money away exultantly in her evening bag, rose to her feet. She did not even, as a winner should, put a gratuity in the slot for the personnel. Only a woman of brilliance could have afforded to indulge in such a breach.

As for Major Gilbert, he had won nothing, and his thin smile turned downward more mirthlessly than ever. It was Lord Skene who slightly redeemed the situation by dropping some paltry contribution in the slot. He took a cigar from his case as he gauntly accompanied the Gilberts from the table.

Raffles glanced across the room.

"Bryce seems occupied, Bunny," he said. "What d'you think, shall we get a breath of air?"

The Casino gardens were a widespread jigsaw of starlight and tree shadow. The night was mild, fragrant from many flowers, and there was a seething of crickets about us as we strolled along the path taken by Skene and the Gilbert couple.

"Not a gracious woman, that, Raffles," I remarked.

"Bunny," he said, "if she and her husband aren't wrong 'uns, my instinct is not what it used to be. I think we owe it to ourselves to find out something about them, because if they're wrong 'uns they might—with diamonds like that—be worth our attention. Are the Gilberts staying ashore as Skene's guests while the liner's at anchor? If so, what's the lay of the land at this Quinta Skene? This seems a good opportunity to inform ourselves on those points."

Not far from the Casino gardens, the trio ahead of us paused before massive doors set in a white wall. Skene unlocked the doors and the trio passed within. We strolled on by. A fine old mansion showed, looming, above the wall. From covered balconies trailed the starlit blossom of creepers. At the angle of the outer wall was a black opening. It was an alley. With a quick glance each way, we faded into the darkness.

The alley was cobblestoned, sloping steeply upward. Beneath our feet, water tinkled musically in some covered runnel. A narrow door showed blackly in the white wall to our right.

"Side door to the Quinta Skene garden," Raffles whispered. "Might as well have a look round."

The door, iron-studded, with a heavy iron ring for a handle, was locked, but with an implement from his pocket Raffles soon turned the wards back. He tried the door again.

"Not bolted," he said. "Good. Come on."

We slipped inside.

We were in a narrow strip of garden at the side of the house. Foliage rioted, the air was heavy with scent. Close at hand, I heard the flutter and chirp of canaries, restless in the aviary inevitable in any Funchal garden. I felt Raffles's hand on my arm. He pointed upward at a lighted first-floor window.

The fretted ironwork of a balcony showed against lines of lamplight shining out through the slats of a venetian blind. There was a tall shadow on the blind, Lord Ivor Skene's shadow. His voice was inaudible to us, but he seemed to be talking, gesturing with his cigar.

A second shadow appeared, facing him. Casilda Gilbert's shadow. The shadows seemed larger than life-size. The woman's hands were raised to her nape. She took off her necklace, handed it to Skene. He seemed to be examining it. He moved from view with it.

"Carried it to the lamp for a closer look," Raffles hazarded, in a whisper. "What the devil, Bunny? Are the Gilberts trying to sell it to him? Just as well we followed our instinct. This is interesting. Hullo, here comes Gilbert . . ."

The Major's shadow was handing a glass to his wife's. Both shadows stood sipping, evidently watching Skene. Fascinated, we peered up. Skene's shadow returned to view.

"Giving her the necklace back," Raffles whispered. "No sale. Telling 'em a thing or two, by the look of it. What's it all about?"

The woman's hands were at her nape as she put on her necklace again. She took her glass back from her husband's shadow. Skene's shadow raised a glass. The glasses of the other two went up. All three shadows, quite obviously, were drinking a toast.

"To *what?*" Raffles breathed. "Bunny, I'd give a lot to know!"

As he spoke, the shadows moved from view, and light wheeled over the blind slats, as though someone had picked up the lamp. The slats seemed to revolve like spokes, then the light was gone, the creeper-hung window left to the star glimmer.

With the garden door relocked behind us, we were watching from the corner of the alley when the trio emerged from the massive doors at the front. The woman between the two men, they walked down to the nearby waterfront, the Estrada da Pontinha.

The clap of Lord Skene's hands rang like a pistol shot. From one of the small craft rocking gently alongside the mole, a boatman roused himself, holding up a lantern with one hand as with the other he helped Mrs. Gilbert embark from the steps. Her husband followed. Oars dipped up faint phosphorescence as the boatman rowed out toward the *Karroo Star* at anchor, a cluster of lights on the dark water.

Skene walked away. The smoke of his cigar floated back to us in the tree shadow where we stood.

"We'd better return to the Casino, Bunny," Raffles murmured, "before Bryce starts wondering."

All next day we kept an eye on the boats which brought shore-excursioning passengers in from the liner, but we saw nothing of the brilliant Mrs. Gilbert and her husband. By evening, it was pretty clear that they had no intention of coming ashore again, and over dinner at the Cava Costa we discussed the situation.

"On reflection, Bunny," Raffles said, "how do you construe that odd little shadow play we saw last night?"

"Why, as you suggested," I said. "Casilda Gilbert was trying to sell Skene her necklace, but he turned it down."

Raffles poured Madeira into my glass. We had the Cava Costa, a fine old place with a flagstoned floor, whitewashed arches and pillars, candles in sconces, racked wine casks all round the walls, pretty much to ourselves.

"It won't wash, Bunny," Raffles said. "I've been thinking about it. She'd just had a thumping good win in the Casino. Why, then, try to sell her necklace? Furthermore, what the devil were they toasting? That's what intrigues me. D'you know the notion I can't get out of my mind? The notion that we saw the shadow of *two* necklaces on that blind last night, not one."

I stared at him. The candlelight flickered on his keen face, his crisp dark hair. His gray eyes gleamed.

"I've wondered," he said, "whether it's possible they knew they were followed last night and staged that shadow play for our benefit. But, going over it in my mind, I'm confident that that's not so. No, what we saw, Bunny, we were not meant to see. The problem is to construe what we saw. Now, it was Lord Skene, you noticed, who was doing all the talking—laying down the law, or giving orders, or something."

I nodded.

"But *two* necklaces, Raffles?" I said. "How . . ."

"Casilda Gilbert," he said, "took off her necklace, gave it to Skene. Skene examined it, moved from our view with it. The other two stood watching him. What were they watching him do? I can't rid myself of the notion that they were watching him open a safe, put the necklace in it, take out a duplicate necklace, which we then saw him hand to Casilda Gilbert, who put it on and covered it with her chiffon scarf. After which, they all three drank a toast together. A toast to what? Surely to some enterprise in which they're mutually engaged."

"But if the Gilberts are wrong 'uns, as you suspect," I said, "and Skene was giving them orders, that'd make him the boss wrong 'un! A man in his position? A peer of the realm? No, really!"

"Bunny," Raffles said softly, "can you imagine a more perfect cover for some imaginative and masterly criminal than that of social arbiter of the winter colony in this Eden of Madeira? Such a man could sit here and move his agents like pawns about the world. It warms my heart to think of it."

He refilled our glasses.

"If my notion has anything in it," he said, "Casilda Gilbert's necklace of very fine diamonds is in Lord Ivor Skene's safe. To get hold of it would in no way give us the truth about Lord Ivor Skene. On the other hand, if the Gilberts are two of his agents and are acting under his instructions, to follow the necklace now about

Casilda Gilbert's lovely throat might prove very illuminating indeed."

I was aware of the slow thump of my heart as I met his eyes in the candlelight.

"Are you game to sail in the *Karroo Star* tomorrow?" said A. J. Raffles.

We sailed accordingly. And long before the cloud-topped mountains of Madeira had fallen from sight astern, we sought out Dr. Hal Nares. We found him in a cabin, with a rolltop desk littered with stethoscopes and pillboxes, far aft on the promenade deck.

Having heard from Albany Bryce that we were in Funchal, Nares greeted us without surprise, but very cordially. He was a big, good-looking young chap, blue-uniformed, with candid blue eyes and a golden beard.

"I grew it since I joined the ship," he told us, with a grin. "It gives the women patients confidence, you know. Aboard a liner, you have to cater to the women."

"Talking of women," said Raffles, availing himself of the opening, "what a brilliant creature Casilda Gilbert is. Bryce pointed her out to us in the Casino."

The young doctor's face darkened.

"Don't talk to me about that hellcat," he said. "I detest the very sight of her. Flashing her damned diamonds about! Yelling for her stewardess every other minute! 'Ames, Ames, where *are* you, Ames? Ames, do this. Ames, do that. Do you *hear* me, Ames?' I could cheerfully strangle her for the way she's treated Ellen Ames, the whole way from Cape Town."

Very decently, Nares got us places at the table he himself presided over in the dining saloon. The Gilberts were at the Captain's table. I saw the flash and sparkle of Casilda Gilbert's earrings, as she made her entrance that evening, but she did not put back her chiffon scarf and I could only just detect that she was wearing her necklace.

Next morning Raffles and I were sunning ourselves at the rail when Hal Nares came striding toward us along the promenade deck with his black bag in his hand and his beard split from ear to ear by a broad grin.

"What d'you think?" he said. "I've just come from treating Mrs. Gilbert."

"What did you treat her to?" said Raffles. "Something fatal?"

"Only a harmless sedative," Hal said. "She thinks she picked up a touch of Madeira fever while ashore in Funchal. Pure imagination. Still, I've got to look in on her again after lunch."

"Bunny," said Raffles, as the young physician strode off, "if Mrs. Gilbert's been given a sedative, we'll allow time for it to put her to sleep, then we'll sort of drift below for a wash before lunch. Major Gilbert hasn't stirred from his steamer chair, along the deck there, since breakfast time. There might be half a chance, if Mrs. Gilbert's asleep, for a closer look at that necklace."

Unfortunately, when presently we drifted down the stairs to the A deck vestibule, it was no sleeping beauty that we found. The Gilberts' cabin, as we already had been at pains to ascertain, was an inside cabin in a beamships alleyway opening into the vestibule. From the stairs we could see the cabin door, which was on the hook.

"Ames! Ames!" Casilda Gilbert's voice was clamoring bad-temperedly. "Where's my tea? Ames, do you *hear* me?"

In the break of the stairs was a recess containing laundry hampers. From our point of view, it was inconveniently placed, for almost always there was some steward or stewardess sitting on it for a bit of a rest. A motherly, gray-haired stewardess was sitting there now, massaging one stockinged foot. She replaced her shoe, and the hamper creaked as she rose from it and, shaking her head in despair, went to the door of the Gilberts' cabin.

"Your stewardess is bringing your tea directly, Mrs. Gilbert," she said placatingly through the crack.

"Well, tell her to hurry," said Casilda Gilbert's voice waspishly. "I get no service from her at all. I shall complain to the Chief Steward."

At that moment, a young stewardess came hurrying into the vestibule carrying a tea tray. In her fresh, frilled apron, with her dark gray eyes and her amber hair curling about her little starched cap with the ship's anchor insignia on it, she looked as pretty as a picture, and all the more so for her fluster of haste.

"You're for it, Ellen," said the motherly stewardess. "She hasn't half been creating."

"Well, honestly, Mattie," said Ellen Ames, "what does she expect? Asking for tea and biscuits just when the galley's dishing up luncheon!"

"Tell her you hope it chokes her, my dear," said Mattie.

"All right," said Ellen, "so I will!"

Raffles and I, pausing unobserved on the stairs, naturally hoped she would. She obviously had plenty of spirit. But she also had her job to consider and, as she unhooked the cabin door with a smile and a wink at Mattie, I was disappointed to see her assume a demure expression before going inside with the tray.

That afternoon we were reclining in steamer chairs on the promenade deck when a sudden jar and tremor went through the ship.

"What was that, Raffles?" I asked.

"I don't know, Bunny," he said. "Engines seem to be slowing down."

Running footsteps thudded along the boat deck above us, orders were shouted, davits swung a boat outboard. Joining the passengers thronging the rail, we watched the manned boat lowered to the water. Beside the coxswain in the stern sheets sat young Dr. Nares with his golden beard and his black bag.

"Portuguese sardiner out there," volunteered a man beside us at the rail. "Flying the signal 'Request medical assistance.' An officer just told us."

Oar blades dipped and lifted in flashing unison as the liner's emergency boat drew away steadily toward the sardiner, a lonely little craft with a high wheelhouse like a sentry box, rising and falling on the slow Atlantic swell.

We watched the boat go alongside the sardiner and Dr. Nares scramble aboard. It was the best part of half an hour before he climbed into the boat again and was pulled back to the *Karroo Star*.

As the liner resumed her course, and the lonely sardiner receded astern into the illimitable blue dazzle, all the passengers were agog to hear what the trouble had been.

"We'll ask Hal at dinner time, Bunny," Raffles said.

At dinner, however, the doctor's chair at the head of our table remained conspicuously unoccupied. Raffles's eyes were speculative as he glanced round the saloon.

"Captain, Purser, Doctor," he murmured, "all absent from their tables tonight. Something queer going on, Bunny. We'll drop along after dinner and see if Hal's in his cabin. Might learn something."

There was a light in the doctor's cabin when we knocked on the door.

"Come in," his voice called.

He was sitting at his rolltop desk in a cloud of pipesmoke. His bronzed forehead was furrowed, but his eyes lightened as he saw us.

"I'm glad you chaps came along," he said. "I need someone to discuss this with. I'm in a hell of a hole, and so's Ellen Ames. That troublemaking hellcat Casilda Gilbert. Her diamonds have been stolen, and she's accusing Ellen and me."

I was about to sit down. I checked. I felt the blood rush into my head. I stole a glance at Raffles. He sat down and took a Sullivan from his cigarette case. His keen face was impassive.

Hal Nares rumpled his hair and beard distractedly.

"You know I gave Casilda Gilbert a sedative this morning," he said. "I left a second dose, to be taken an hour later, and was to look in on her again after lunch. I did so, and I found her asleep.

I took her pulse—not her diamonds, dammit—and I left her.

"About six this evening, an old stewardess called Mattie came to fetch me to the Gilberts' cabin. Seems Mrs. Gilbert had woken up and started yelling for Ellen. The infernal woman was in hysterics, Mattie said, and accusing Ellen of stealing her diamonds.

"I went down with Mattie, and no sooner had I set foot inside the cabin than Mrs. Gilbert rounded on me and accused me of being in league with Ellen. Said we'd been seen whispering, thick as thieves, in dark corners all the way from Cape Town, and she said that not a living soul but Ellen and me had been in or out of her cabin all day. She was beside herself. She brandished the chain of the necklace in our faces, and the diamonds were gone, sure enough, gouged out of their soft gold setting."

"What did you do?" Raffles asked quietly.

"I sent at once for the Purser, Chief Steward, and Master-at-Arms," Hal said. "The whole thing was flogged out there and then. She had her necklace at mid-morning. She's a vain, brilliant kind of woman and, when she sent Ellen to fetch me, it seems she was primping up a bit in her bunk and putting on her earrings, as the doctor was coming, and her jewel case was open and Ellen admits she caught a glimpse of the necklace in it then."

His hands shook as he relighted his pipe.

"There's always a steward or stewardess hanging about in that recess where they keep the A deck laundry hampers," he said. "They've been questioned, and the whole day's covered.

"Mrs. Gilbert never once left the cabin, and Major Gilbert—they don't get on too well—never went near it from the time he left it for breakfast. Only Ellen and I entered the damned cabin.

"The worst of it is, we both were in there after lunch, when she was asleep. I took her pulse, as I've said. Just after, Ellen went in to tidy up a bit, quietly—the woman throws her things all over the shop—and take away the tea tray she'd had in lieu of lunch."

"Has the cabin been searched?" Raffles asked.

"By experts," Hal said. "The Purser, Chief Steward, and Master-at-Arms went over every inch of it. It's an inside cabin. No porthole. The ventilator has a fine-mesh grille, and the paint on the screws shows it can't possibly have been tampered with. This is an old ship. Every drop of water is fetched and carried by the stewards and stewardesses. The cupboard slop pails under the turn-up basins are emptied by them.

"Mrs. Gilbert insisted on being searched herself, by Mattie. No diamonds. Her earrings are all right. She claims that that's because Ellen or I were afraid to touch them because she'd dropped off to sleep with them on."

"Hal," Raffles said, "what was the trouble aboard the sardiner this afternoon?"

Hal stared at the tangential question.

"That?" he said. "That was nothing. Fisherman with a bit of a skin rash. Nothing to signify."

He rumpled his wild hair and beard again.

"I'm at my wit's end," he said. "Ellen and her things have been searched. Nothing found, but she's confined to her quarters. Captain's orders. I insisted on my own person and quarters being searched. Nothing found, of course. But if Ellen and I are innocent —and we *are*—then what in creation has happened to those diamonds?"

As he asked the question, a knock sounded on the door. It opened and a steward looked in.

"Captain's compliments, Doctor," he said, "and he'd be obliged if you could spare him a moment."

Raffles rose, offering his hand.

"Hal," he said, "I want you to look on Manders and me as counsel for the defense. We'll put our heads together."

He smiled reassuringly, but there was no smile on his face when we reached our own cabin. He dropped on his bunk, took out his cigarette case.

"Now we know, Bunny," he said. "There he sits—Lord Ivor Skene, with his arrogant eyeglass and his taste for young women of brilliance. Social arbiter of the wealthy winter colony in Funchal. And what else? A crafty weaver of insurance swindles that deliberately involve innocent people."

"Insurance?" I said.

"What else can this be?"

Raffles lighted his cigarette.

"Back there in Funchal, you and I, Bunny, because we're what we are—amateurs in crime—saw what we saw. Its meaning's now obvious. At some time, Skene provided the Gilberts with that very fine necklace, for them to insure heavily, then travel with from Cape Town, with Casilda flashing it on the ship for everyone to see. At Funchal, Skene took back the necklace and provided a duplicate. The duplicate stones have now been 'stolen,' and the Gilberts will claim as for the real ones. And because of one very cunning incident, Bunny, the insurance company will have no option but to pay up."

"What incident?" I said.

"The incident," said Raffles, "of the distressed sardiner. You see, one or two small points—notably that of the 'thief' bothering to remove the stones from their setting—might make the insurance people uneasy about the Gilberts' claim. But consider. *After* Hal Nares was in Casilda's cabin, and took her pulse but could just as easily have taken her diamonds, *he left this ship.*"

I snapped my fingers.

"Just so," said Raffles. "When the insurance inquiries start, that point will come up. Who entered Casilda's cabin while she was asleep? Dr. Nares. Who goes regularly to and fro on this run and therefore could have confederates in any port of call? Dr. Nares. Who therefore could have arranged for the sardiner to appear where it did at the time it did? Dr. Nares. Whose sole word is there for the presence of a man with an ambiguous skin rash on the sardiner? Dr. Nares's. Who could have stolen the diamonds and conveyed them to confederates aboard the sardiner? Dr. Nares."

"Ye gods!" I said.

"To anyone but you and me, Bunny," Raffles said, "who saw a shadow play and know of Lord Ivor Skene, the case against Hal is so plausible—the men aboard the sardiner will be quite untraceable later on, of course—that the insurance company, even if it should have mental reservations about the Gilberts' claim, will be obliged to settle. Which'll put Hal Nares in the criminal dock."

"Without a leg to stand on!" I exclaimed.

He gave me a strange look.

"With two legs to stand on," he corrected. "You and I. Counsel for the doctor's defense. *We* can guess who planned this conspiracy and who put the sardiner on the liner's course. Bunny, this whole thing has been admirably conceived, planned, and carried out. I've no doubt Lord Ivor Skene, sitting there in Funchal, has agents—like the Gilberts—carrying out ingenious variations all over the world's liner routes. He fishes with deep-sea hooks."

"What are we going to do?" I whispered.

"In Hal's defense, Bunny," he said, "we've got to find a way to demonstrate how the stones from Casilda Gilbert's necklace really vanished from her cabin."

I could not get another word out of him. He still was sitting on his bunk, smoking, when I fell asleep.

I woke to an empty cabin flooded with sunshine. Raffles was not at breakfast. The ship, close in to the rockbound coast of Portugal, was approaching the Tagus.

In growing distraction, I hunted all over the ship, but it was not until mid-morning that I felt a touch on my arm.

"Been looking for me?" said Raffles. "Sorry, Bunny. I've been busy in the ship's laundry, making an experiment. Look here, the Gilberts are in their cabin at the moment. Care to come down and help me interview them? Try to look a bit grim."

His own face was expressionless as he tapped on the door of the Gilbert couple's cabin. The door was opened by Glyn Gilbert.

"Morning, Major," Raffles said. "We've some information concerning your wife's unfortunate loss. Would it be convenient to receive us?"

Gilbert's eyes flickered. He hesitated. His thin, downturned mouth tightened. He motioned us to enter. Casilda Gilbert, fully dressed and looking her most brilliant, was seated with rigid hauteur on one of the bunks.

"What *is* this information?" she demanded.

"It would be best discussed," Raffles said, "over a quiet cup of tea. I've taken the liberty of ordering . . ."

A knock sounded on the door.

"Permit me," said Raffles. Opening the door, he took a tray from the motherly stewardess. "Tea and biscuits," he said. "Thank you very much, Mattie."

Never had I seen such expressions as those on the faces of Casilda and Glyn Gilbert as Raffles set down the tray on the small dressing table.

"We'll get straight to business," he said.

His tone was cold, even, impersonal.

"Yesterday, Mrs. Gilbert, you ordered Ellen Ames to bring you a tea tray in lieu of luncheon. When Ellen had gone, you removed the stones from your necklace—the substitute necklace handed to you at Funchal by Lord Ivor Skene."

I saw Gilbert go white. Casilda's light, vivid eyes opened suddenly wide.

"You dropped the stones," Raffles said, "into the hot-water jug on your tea tray. I now take from my pocket a handful of faintly blue, somewhat diamondlike, faceted stones—similar to those of which you permitted Ellen only the most fleeting glimpse in your jewel case yesterday morning. I'll take two of these stones, quite enough for the present demonstration, and do with them what you did with all of yours, Mrs. Gilbert."

He lifted the lid of the hot-water jug. He dropped in the two stones. I heard the slight rattle as they struck bottom. My heart thumped.

"Having dropped your stones into the hot-water jug, Mrs. Gilbert," Raffles said, "you took the second dose of sedative left for you by Dr. Nares, and you went peacefully to sleep."

"Who *are* you?" Gilbert said hoarsely.

"It's of no consequence," Raffles said. "It's enough for you to know that, most fortunately for yourselves, our brief from the principal for whom we act concerns one man only—Lord Ivor Skene. Our principal is not interested in the immediate prosecution of small fry employed by Skene."

He picked up the hot-water jug, gave it a slight swirl.

"When Stewardess Ames carried away your tea tray yesterday, Mrs. Gilbert," he said, "she naturally emptied the teapot and hot-water jug into the appropriate receptacle in the first-class galley. I shall make use of your washstand, instead."

He lifted the lid of the boxed-in washstand, turned the jug upside down over it. The steaming water gushed into the bowl. No stones gushed with it. Raffles gave the jug a shake. It was empty.

"*That,* Mrs. Gilbert," said Raffles, "is what really happened to your 'stolen diamonds.' They dissolved! . . . Now, take careful note. Lord Ivor Skene will shortly be the subject of extradition proceedings instituted by Scotland Yard. In your own interests, you would be well advised to have no further communication whatever with him."

He took out his watch, glanced at it.

"The ship is now entering Tagus roads," he said. "When the anchor goes down off Lisbon, you will go ashore by the first tender. What's happened in this cabin is totally irrelevant to the brief held by my associate and myself. But because of the position in which you've placed two innocent people—Stewardess Ames and Dr. Nares—you brought our intervention upon yourselves. You will be given four clear hours. At the end of that time, this demonstration will be repeated in the cabin of the Captain of this liner."

We walked out. Raffles closed the door on the brilliant Mrs. Gilbert and her husband.

"Come on, old boy," said Raffles. "Writing room. Quick!"

The writing room proved to be deserted, as everyone was watching the Tagus shores gliding by, high and green with verdure, dotted with red roofs.

"We'll sit at this desk," said Raffles. "Now, while I write a note, here are four more of those stones. Put 'em in an envelope for me. Touch one of 'em to your tongue, if you like."

Gingerly, I did so. The hair stirred on my scalp.

"Soda!" I exclaimed.

"I spent a lot of time in the laundry," said Raffles, as his pen scratched busily, "making these stones. I dropped some crystals of soda into lukewarm water with a blue bag. When the crystals had become very slightly tinted with blue, I fished them out, filed them down to shape and faceted them with a nail file, and worked up quite a high shine on them with a bit of velvet.

"I don't know exactly what the false stones in Casilda Gilbert's necklace were made of, but I felt it had to be something of the kind, because of the fact that the alleged 'thief' had gouged them from their setting. Gold doesn't dissolve in hot water. My stones aren't too bad, are they? As you saw, there's not enough blue in such stones to tint the water in the hot-water jug."

With a plunge, a roar, a prolonged clattering that sounded through the ship, the anchor went down.

"We must hurry," said Raffles. "I'm writing the Captain. I'm saying that, investigating on Hal Nares's behalf, we stumbled on a theory. We tackled the Gilberts, but they fenced too cleverly for us. We were investigating further when we found they'd left the ship, so we've gone after them, as we want to nobble them off our own bat. Meantime, I tell him, here are four of the stones we concocted, to test our theory under experimental conditions, and will he please drop 'em in some near-boiling water."

He chuckled as his pen flew over the paper.

"Finally," he said, "I add that we shall give this note to a messenger ashore, with instructions to bring it out on the last tender to the ship before she sails. And that's that."

He tucked the letter into the envelope with the stones, sealed the envelope.

"The note and the stones," he said, "coupled with the confession of guilt implicit in the Gilberts' flight, will clear Hal and Ellen."

He pocketed the envelope, rose from his chair.

"I think we can now safely say, Bunny, that the defense rests. We'll see that the Gilberts get off on the first tender. We'll then ourselves," said Raffles, "go ashore on the second tender."

The *Karroo Star* must just about have been arriving at Tilbury, three days later, when Raffles and myself, aboard a quite different liner, a Portuguese liner from Lisbon, saw once more the lights of Funchal dotting the mountainsides of Madeira.

It was just on midnight, but we went ashore at once by bumboat. We were in evening dress. We went straight to the Casino. The evening's play was at its height as we strolled casually through the opulent rooms.

At his favorite roulette table sat Lord Ivor Skene. His head shone parchment-hued under the glittering chandeliers. He had a cigar in his hand. His cordless eyeglass was screwed arrogantly into his left eye. He was whispering confidentially into the ear of a young woman of brilliant appearance—but *not* Casilda Gilbert— who sat beside him.

"Off we go, Bunny," Raffles murmured.

We entered the garden of the Quinta Skene by the door from the alley. While Raffles climbed to the first-floor window of the room, now dark, where we had witnessed the shadow play which had proved to be the key to the whole Funchal conspiracy, I kept watch in the garden.

There was a new moon. It jigsawed the garden with light and

shadow. My palms were moist. The crickets seethed. From the unseen aviary came the restless flutter and chirp of the canaries.

It was perhaps twenty minutes before Raffles dropped soundlessly from the balcony and rejoined me.

"Very satisfactory, Bunny," he said, as we walked through the narrow, moonlit streets to the Cava Costa for supper. "I hope you agree that we were fully justified in coming back here to collect the true blue diamonds. I have the swag in my pocket. There were also one or two other items in the safe. Our best haul for years. And the beauty of it is, this master insurance swindler will be in no position either to inform the police or claim any insurance!"

I had to laugh.

"I'd like to see his face," I said, "when he finds his safe empty."

"Not quite empty, Bunny," said Raffles. "I left something in the safe for him to think about."

"You left something?" I said, mystified.

"Certainly," said Raffles, as we entered the candlelit cavern of the Cava Costa. "I left him the rest of my home-made blue diamonds."

The Gentle Wrecker

"Tell me frankly, Raffles," I said. "Have you any ulterior motive for joining this party?"

The party in question was a weekend junket being given by the managing director of a shipping line to celebrate the maiden voyage of his company's new liner.

Our invitation had come from the director's son, Gareth, a chap with whom Raffles had played a good deal of racquets; and we caught an early train down from London on Friday to the West Country port from which the liner was due to sail on Monday for Boston, Massachusetts.

We had a compartment to ourselves, and Raffles, wearing tweeds, a pearl in his cravat, raised his brows at me over the newspaper he was reading.

"As amateurs in crime, Bunny," he said, "don't we always observe certain self-imposed rules? As, for instance, never to let an innocent person bear the onus of a crime committed by us? And, again, never to rob a house in which we're guests?"

Reassured, I changed the subject.

"Anything interesting in the paper?"

"I was just reading an article," he said, "about the claims of various country houses to possess the original chest that figures in the ballad of 'The Mistletoe Bough.'

"You remember? A game of hide-and-seek took place during a house party, and one of the guests, a lovely girl, hid in a great chest or coffer. The lock caught, and the party was so noisy that she could make nobody hear, and she fainted. They hunted high and low for her, but nobody thought to look in the chest."

"She was found ultimately as a skeleton," I said. "Does the owner of the house we're going to claim to possess this dismal coffer?"

"I doubt it," said Raffles. "He's not mentioned in this article. No, Bunny, this is more in his line."

He picked up from the seat another paper he had bought, a shipping paper.

"Here's an item about one of his ships: 'Bristol, Jan. 12. Salvage Association report on *Sir Sagramor*, Round Table Lines. Studs renew, shaft draw, bilge keels shell bars repair.'

"And here's another. 'SIR DINADAN. Rangoon, Jan. 8. Round Table Lines steamer *Sir Dinadan*, Calcutta for Rangoon, general cargo, shipped a heavy sea on the port side on Jan. 6th., which caused damage to port bulwarks, second engineer's room and port fiddley casing.' "

"My sympathy is with the second engineer," I said. "Damp beds cause rheumatism. Are all the ships of our host's company named for Arthurian knights?"

"All their cargo vessels are," Raffles said, "and always have been. It's a tradition of our host's family, an old shipowning family. But their two largest vessels are always, traditionally, named *King Arthur* and *Queen Guinevere*, in honor of the two little trading brigs that the family first started in business with, generations ago. The present *King* and *Queen*—this new *Queen* due to sail on her maiden voyage on Monday—are passenger liners operating on the North Atlantic run to Boston."

Raffles offered me a Sullivan from his cigarette case.

"A curious thing about our host's family," he said, "is that its members, like its ships, are always, traditionally, given Christian names in the Arthurian canon. Our Gareth, for instance. And his father's Christian name is Magus. A branch of the family settled long ago in Boston, to look after the firm's interests on that side of the Atlantic, and the Christian name of Magus's opposite number over there is Uriens. Magus and Uriens, working hand in glove, have steered the firm through many a shipping depression."

The train roared along through a countryside that sparkled white with frost in the morning sunshine.

"In any old family with a hardheaded business tradition," Raffles said, "an exception is apt to crop up from time to time. There's one in our host's family, I believe. I've heard there used to be a third partner in the firm. His Christian name was Bedivere. He was a dreamy sort of chap, I've been told, with some bee in his bonnet about such of the family's ships as had been wrecked in long bygone days.

"He was always roaming the seas of the world, trying to find traces of those wrecks. A queer quest. It made him an outrageous truant from his desk, of course, and I'm told that in self-defense Magus and Uriens had finally no option but to ease him out of the firm before his fecklessness made a wreck of that, too. I never heard what became of him."

It was getting on for noon when the train steamed into our station, which was right in the docks. All round us were warehouses, cranes, shunted wagons, and screaming gulls.

Our friend Gareth, a tall young chap with wiry blond hair and, it struck me, a more haggard, worried look than the last time I had seen him, was waiting for us on the platform.

"Glad to see you both," Gareth said. "The rest of the party have already arrived and my father's taken them on to the ship. That's her over there."

Sparkling with new paint, the superstructure, funnels, and

raised derricks of a liner towered above a warehouse roof.

"My father's showing the party over her before a luncheon he's giving on board today—sort of shipwarming luncheon," said Gareth, "so we'll join them there."

The liner's berth was a scene of activity. Provisions were going aboard. Swarms of purveyors' vans were alongside. A group of about forty powerful men were heaving on an enormous rope, under the direction of a giant of a fellow with his cap pushed to the back of a shock of red hair. He exchanged a greeting with Gareth.

"That's our Shore Bosun," Gareth told us as we went up the gangway. "Good chap, but he and his gang stumbled on an object buried in the mud, when they were doing a job up the estuary a couple of weeks ago, and the damned thing looks like ruining my life."

He stepped into the ship, Raffles and I following him.

"This is the main-deck foyer," Gareth said. "You aren't seeing it at its best, I'm afraid, with all these laundry hampers piled everywhere. Leave your bags here. I think I hear the voices of the party. My father's entertaining them in the first-class galley. This way."

He led us through the dining saloon, where sunshine through the portholes shone on the carnations and maidenhair fern that decorated the one large round table laid for luncheon, all the others having chairs standing upside down on them; and we stepped into a gabble of voices.

The house party was well away. Everybody, including the cooks in their high, starched caps, had a champagne glass either in his hand or handy. And our host, Gareth's father, Magus, a thickset, bald man with bushy eyebrows, was personally opening another bottle. But Gareth checked, staring at a couple who stood somewhat apart from the rest. He turned to us. He looked even more haggard than before.

"That girl over there," he said, in a low voice. "Dark-haired girl—green eyes. Standing with a long, thin wand of a fellow with gray hair. See 'em? I want you to meet them, but I must warn you. They aren't house-party guests. The man's a sort of distant cousin of my father's—Cousin Bedivere. The girl's his daughter Maulfry. They live about a mile up the estuary from our house. I'm crazy about Maulfry, was practically engaged to her, but not any more. I'm in trouble with her about that object that was found in the mud. I'm surprised they've come aboard for the luncheon. Anyway, remember, if they seem cold, it's meant for me, not you."

I was grateful for the information. For as the girl spotted Gareth approaching, her manner turned not merely cold, but positively arctic; and all Raffles and I got from her, when Gareth introduced us, was a subzero nod, then she pointedly turned and walked away.

Her father, however, seemed not so much cold as vague.

I realized that he must be the one-time partner in the firm, of whom Raffles had told me—the one who had been an incorrigible absentee from his desk and had wasted his life roaming the world in impractical quest of wrecks. There was indeed something subtly bizarre in his appearance, as of a kindly but rather careworn knight-errant, as he blinked mildly upon us from his great height.

"That was very rude of Maulfry," he said. "I'm sorry, Gareth."

Gareth shrugged wretchedly.

"She thinks I ought to do something about this find of the Shore Bosun's," he said. "But beyond arguing my head off with my father—which I've done—what else can I do, sir?"

"It's a pity the Shore Bosun took his find to your father, instead of bringing it to me," Cousin Bedivere said pensively. "It was natural enough, I suppose, since he works for your father—and, besides, your father could give him more for it than I could. No, I can't blame the Shore Bosun. It's your father who's doing the moral wrong, Gareth, by proposing to send the find on to Uriens, in Boston, instead of handing it over to me."

"My father'll use any lever that comes to hand," Gareth said, "if he thinks it'll help him arrange some relation's affairs in what *he* thinks the relation's best interests."

"How true!" said Bedivere. "How often I've heard his favorite phrases—'for your own good,' 'it hurts me more than it hurts you'! How often I've had to swallow them from him in the past, when I'd been naughty and absented myself from business. Still, I suppose that if it weren't for men like Cousin Magus, the firm—the nation's whole shipping business, come to that—would have gone under long ago. A great man in his way. And Uriens, of Boston, is just such another."

He shook his head sadly.

"I'm not the man to tackle Magus," he said. "I just seem to exasperate him. I don't *mean* to wreck his peace of mind, but I'm afraid I do. Indeed, I know I do. I always have. But I've got to tackle him again, Gareth. I came to the luncheon for that express purpose. I can't bear the thought of that marvelous find going to Uriens, of Boston—and going in this, of all ships, on her maiden voyage. What irony! No, I must steel myself to tackle your father again—come what may. But first I must have a good deal more of his champagne. If you'll excuse me . . ."

He drifted away through the crowd, like the tall mast of a yacht through a shoal of sailing dinghies, carrying his champagne glass.

"There'll be a hell of a row in a minute," said Gareth. "My father looks as though *he's* had a few drinks, too. . . . Well, we can't stand here, I suppose. We'd better circulate a bit. I'll introduce you to some of the other guests. They're mostly relatives, or key people in the firm—our Commodore, one or two captains and their wives or daughters, and some of the chief of our office staff. It's pretty much a family affair."

Having circulated a bit round the spacious galley, Raffles and I were drawn to a group who were watching the pastrycook demonstrate his virtuosity. A sudden bark of laughter made everyone look round. It was a bark more exasperated than mirthful, and it had come from our host, who was standing with Bedivere near the service doors, wide open to the dining saloon.

The burly shipowner and his elongated cousin made a strange contrast, and I saw people beginning to smile; evidently the effect Bedivere had on the head of the firm was a byword among them. They knew all about it.

"Dammit, Bedivere!" said Magus. And seeing that everybody was looking at him, he said to us all, "Here, listen to this. This is good. Come on, Bedivere, tell us again—*what* was that you just said?"

"What I said, Magus," Bedivere replied mildly, "was that it seems my only chance of getting the Bosun's find from you would be to steal it."

"Steal it," said our host. "Hear that, everybody?" His laugh strangely mingled amusement, affection, and irritable impatience. "Why, Bedivere," he said, "there's not a manjack here who doesn't know you're the most impractical fellow who ever lived. You admit it yourself. *You* trying to crack a crib, eh? That'd be the day!"

"I could hire someone, perhaps," Bedivere murmured musingly, "some skilled—"

"Hear him?" said our host. "Now, Bedivere—ask yourself, dammit! Where would you find your skilled criminal? What would you do—advertise for him? Or d'you think fellows like that go around handing out their business cards?"

I began to feel a hot embarrassment creeping over me. I stole a glance at A. J. Raffles. Glass in hand, he was listening to the conversation with a half-smile of indolent courtesy.

Bedivere looked nonplussed.

And Magus said, "You see, man? You aren't practical. You're always in the clouds. Believe me, anything you could manage to steal from me, or organize to get stolen for you, I give you my heartiest permission to keep, you have my word for it. Why, man—"

He was cut short by Maulfry, who moved forward quickly.

"I think there's been just about enough of this," she said in a taut voice and took Bedivere's glass from him. "Come along, Father."

"Now, Maulfry, no need to get in a huff," said our host, huffily.

"Maulfry!" begged Gareth, in a panic. "Please don't go like that—please!"

She gave him a look that promised him a slapped face if he stirred hand or foot to stop her. And taking her father's arm, she steered the long man firmly away across the dining saloon. There was a momentary, uncomfortable silence.

"Damnation!" said our host, breaking it. He pulled himself together. "Well, well," he said, "we all know Cousin Bedivere. He'd wreck the whole party, if we let him. Steward, what the devil —can't we get luncheon started?"

"It's ready when you are, sir," said the steward.

"Come on, then!" said our host. "Come along, everybody!"

Not a word was said at luncheon about the incident. But I sensed that, while sympathy was about evenly divided between our host and Bedivere, the incident itself was generally regretted.

However, the luncheon went on, at any rate superficially gay enough, far into the afternoon; and the winter dusk was closing in over the docks when at last we all streamed down the gangway from the *Queen Guinevere's* main-deck foyer for the drive to our host's home.

It was a palatial place overlooking the estuary. Lights shone hospitably from the mullioned windows, and a butler, footman, and maid took our coats and things from us, amid the general chatter, and placed them temporarily on one of a number of large coffers which stood around the hall.

It was a huge hall, lofty and paneled, with a gallery landing and, high up, a big sort of dome or cupola of colored glass in which were set small ventilator windows that could be opened on ratchets worked from below by long cords.

"Bunny," Raffles murmured, "I may be wrong, but I rather think I spy the object that was found in the mud."

Startled, I followed his glance.

Across the hall, and opposite the main doorway by which we had entered, there leaned gracefully from the landing banisters a carven image. Of timeworn wood, with a scoured, defaced appearance, still there lingered about it a sort of serene beauty. It was the life-size image of a woman, so carved as to suggest the folds of her simple robe, her sandaled feet closely together, her arms crossed over the long braids of her hair, a crown upon her brow.

"Surely," I said, puzzled, "that's too lovely a thing to have come out of mud?"

"Oh, no," said Raffles. "That may very well have been found in estuarial mud. It's a ship's figurehead, Bunny. And d'you recognize who it is? Queen Guinevere!"

Gareth joined us.

"I see you've spotted her," he said. "Yes, there she is—the queen from the mud. Now, *she's* up there—and I'm in the mud. You see how I stand with Maulfry. Yet, the very day our Shore Bosun made his find, I was looking round our garden with nothing more on my mind than to find the first snowdrop of the year for Maulfry. It's sort of"—he flushed slightly—" 'our' flower—snowdrops. You know? Good Lord, I hadn't the faintest notion what the Shore Bosun was unearthing that day, to mess up my life for me!"

"I take it, of course," Raffles said, "that this is the figurehead of one of those two little trading brigs with which your family originally started in the shipowning business?"

Gareth nodded gloomily, "Cousin Bedivere's spent his life getting together a collection of the figureheads of the family's firsts. He's combed the world for them. He already has the figurehead of our first *King Arthur,* also the figureheads of most of the first of our ships to bear the names of the various knights. He's hunted high and low for the figurehead of the first *Queen Guinevere*—vital to his collection, of course. And she's found by chance in the mud up the estuary, almost on his own doorstep!"

"And handed over to your father," Raffles said. "And your father's sending her to Boston—on the maiden voyage of her modern namesake! It really does seem hard on Bedivere. What's your father's motive, Gareth?"

"Bedivere's own good—in my father's opinion," Gareth said wryly. "It's always troubled him that at the time Bedivere left the firm after a row about his absences there was a shipping depression on and the value of his holdings was at rock bottom. What money he got out with he's spent on his collection. He hasn't got a bean today. It doesn't trouble *him*—he's not the type. He wouldn't take any kind of subsidy from my father when the firm got out of the depression. And Maulfry wouldn't hear of it. She teaches drawing at a school, earns her own living."

Gareth looked up gloomily at the figurehead.

"Uriens, over in Boston," he said, "has a few of the knight figureheads that Bedivere lacks. Uriens would like to have the whole collection. He's a rich man and has offered Bedivere a thumping price for it. My father likes to see everybody in the family decently fixed. He hates this collection that Bedivere's beggared himself over, and it absolutely maddens my father that Bedivere won't take this whacking price Uriens is offering for it but intends just to give the whole lot away—to some maritime museum, when he dies."

"I think I see," Raffles murmured. "Your father—"

"He's shrewd," said Gareth. "Bedivere's dream is to get the collection of firsts *complete.* This queen figurehead is a key piece. If it goes to Uriens, in Boston, Uriens'll be encouraged not to part with the few knights he has, and my father thinks that when

Bedivere realizes that he never can hope to complete the circle of the Round Table—king, queen, and knights—he'll chuck up the sponge and accept Uriens's offer. My father's convinced that once Bedivere gets a good solid chunk of money in his hands he'll be glad he did it. Of course, my father's tragically wrong, but you just can't make him see it. He always thinks he knows what's best for other people."

A footman came into the hall, sounded a gong. The sound swelled up hollowly under the glass dome. All the other guests had gone upstairs.

"Dressing gong," Gareth said. "I'll show you your rooms."

We had adjoining rooms at the end of the gallery landing and, when I was dressed, I went into Raffles's room to get his views on the figurehead situation.

"In Arthurian terms, Bunny," Raffles said, as he tied his white tie, "it's obvious that our host, however worthy his motives may be, is playing the role of Merlin—the omniscient wizard, the crafty manipulator. True, he opened a loophole when he told Bedivere that if he could steal the figurehead, or get it stolen for him, he could keep it. But you and I can't help Bedivere. We can't rob a house in which we're guests. It'd be too unsporting. The odds would be all in our favor."

"Quite," I said, relieved.

But, during dinner, in a quite astonishing way the entire picture altered. The butler came to our host, murmured something to him.

"Shore Bosun?" Magus said. "How many of his gang has he brought? All forty volunteered, have they? Right! Tell him I'll be out in a minute."

"What on earth's the Shore Bosun's gang doing here?" Gareth asked.

"I made a fool of myself this morning," his father said grimly.

"I admit it. Thinking it over afterwards, a nasty idea struck me. Dock thieves!"

A vein swelled on his forehead. Dock thieves were plainly a sore point with the shipowner.

"Cleverest thieves alive," he said. "Now, then. Bedivere's always poking about the docks, hobnobbing with every manjack. He may know someone who could put him in touch with dock thieves."

"But you can't really believe that Bedivere will take up your challenge?" Gareth exclaimed. "Why, Maulfry would never allow it!"

"I'm taking no chances," said his father. "I was a fool, but what I said, I said. Now, for safety, I might have the figurehead crated up this minute and taken aboard ship and put in the strong room. But before that scene in the galley today, I'd decided to let the figurehead stay in my hall over the weekend, because I thought Bedivere would chuck up the sponge and come and tell me he'd decided to sell out to Uriens, when I'd have the whole lot—his as well as the queen—crated up together and taken aboard first thing Monday, and good riddance! That was my intention, before the scene in the galley today, and I'm not altering my plans one iota."

He pointed belligerently at the door to the hall.

"There's the figurehead," he said. "There it stays till Monday morning—as I'd planned. Bedivere knows exactly where it is. If he, or any crook he gets to act for him, thinks he can get it, let him try! I'm having our Shore Bosun and his forty good, hard chaps put a tight cordon round this house tonight, tomorrow night, and Sunday night.

"Daytime's no danger—too many people about the house. The Bosun's forty are armed with cudgels and are free to use 'em. I have no mercy for dock thieves. I'm giving the Bosun's gang double overtime pay, with a reward of a hundred pounds for the man who collars anybody whatever trying to get into the house—or get out of it with that figurehead in the hall."

I glanced cautiously at Raffles. His face was impassive, but I had a sudden premonition that made my heart thump, sultry.

When we all went up to bed, I waited until the house was quiet, then nipped into his room. It was in darkness, but I heard his whisper.

"I'm over here by the window," he said. "Well, Bunny? I think you'll agree that the odds are now so long against us—forty-one to two—that we can break our rule, for once, and try to rob a house in which we're guests?"

"I don't like it, Raffles," I said. "That figurehead's life-size. True, it's wood, but it's teak or oak and it'll take both of us to carry it. If we're caught, it'd mean not only a manhandling from the Bosun's gang, it'd mean absolute social ruin. Raffles, why risk it? After all, mightn't there be something in this dock thieves notion of our host?"

"I think not," he said. "I agree with Gareth. Maulfry'd never let her father attempt anything of this kind in any shape or form. For that very reason, Bunny, I don't think Gareth himself will dare attempt anything. He'll be far too uncertain as to what Maulfry's reaction might be. A man in love, Bunny, lacks the detachment necessary for an understanding of the feminine mind."

He chuckled in the darkness.

"The figurehead was found almost on Bedivere's own doorstep," he said. "It's going to reappear on his actual doorstep, for him to find himself this time!"

"How?" I said.

He slightly parted the curtains, peered from the window. The night was black and cold. Not a sound came from the forty men prowling the grounds, but I knew they were there. They wanted the hundred pounds' reward. A ship boomed desolately, far off in the estuary.

Raffles closed the curtains.

"Yes," he said, "a very interesting crib. I'll give you a tip, Bunny. Remember the ballad we talked about, coming down in the train—the sad ballad of the girl who played hide-and-seek at a house party and tragically hid in a place where nobody thought to look for her?"

A match, flaring like a tiny bomb, gleamed gray in his eyes as he lighted a cigarette.

"I've a feeling that ballad might be useful to us," he said. "Sleep on it for tonight, Bunny. We've two more nights."

Our host, Magus, was in the hall when I went down in the morning.

"Well, Manders," he chuckled—he was looking up at the figurehead—"she's still safe and sound, you see."

My laugh was a bit forced. I was thinking of what Raffles had said about the ballad of the girl who had hid in a great chest and not been found till she was a skeleton. I slid a glance round at those large oaken coffers which stood about the hall. My throat went dry. One of the coffers stood directly below the figurehead.

I accompanied our host into the dining room, where several guests were breakfasting.

"What d'you all want to do today?" said Magus. "It's Saturday. I suggest the races. There's a steeplechase meeting on this afternoon."

"Races?" said Raffles. He turned with alacrity from the sideboard, where he was helping himself to kidneys and bacon. "Splendid idea!"

I sensed that the mention of races was good news to him for some reason; and when we got to the races, I saw his keen glance roving everywhere, and I asked him what he was looking for.

"Some of those secretive folk that any race meeting seems to draw like a magnet," he said. "Yes, there are a few—away over there. Bunny, I'm going to get my palm read. See you later."

In a corner of the field on the far side of the paddock, there stood, with tin chimneys wisping smoke into the winter air, the three caravans of a band of gypsies.

That night, when I had dressed for dinner, I went into Raffles's room.

"Now, look here," I said, "granted that gypsies are the cleverest poachers alive, move like shadows at night, not even gypsies could get through that cordon of forty men prowling the grounds this minute."

"I wouldn't dream of asking them to try," said Raffles. "They might get hurt. Still, I bought a very good long rope from them, had it wound round me under my coat when we came back from the races. It's in my bag there—locked."

He took a clean handkerchief from his dressing-table drawer.

"I took a prowl through the house after you left me last night, Bunny," he said. "At the end of the gallery landing, there's a baize-covered door. Behind it is a narrow staircase leading up to another door—a small one, bolted. Shoot the bolts and you step out on to the roof, right alongside the great bulge of the glass dome over the hall."

He looked at me with a dancing vivacity in his eyes.

"Now, as to the fastenings of the queen's figurehead," he said. "A rod screwed to the foot of one of the landing banisters holds the shoulders of the figure by a simple hook, and another hook holds the feet. One has only to *raise* the figure a little, Bunny, as though one were lifting off an inn sign, and it's free."

The dinner gong sounded just then.

"We'd better go down," he said. "I'll join you in your room tonight when the people in the house are all asleep."

It was not the people in the house I was worried about. It was the forty men outside in the grounds.

Just on one A.M., Raffles slipped silently into my room.

"Ready, Bunny?" he whispered. "Right. Phase One. We stand on the coffer under the figurehead. We lift the queen off her hooks. We hide her where the girl in the ballad hid—in the coffer. Off we go. Not a sound."

It went without a hitch. We worked in the hall in pitch darkness. The only sound we made was a slight creak as Raffles raised the heavy, hinged lid of the coffer. When we stole back upstairs to my room, the queen was in the coffer.

"So far, so good," Raffles whispered. "Now to deal with the men outside—Phase Two. Round my waist I have the rope I got from the gypsies. I'm now going on to the roof by way I told you of. While I'm gone, off with your clothes and into your dressing gown."

I tore off my clothes in the dark. I could not imagine what he was doing on the roof. Those little ratchet windows in the dome could be opened only a few inches by the long cords that hung down.

Suddenly there was an almighty crash of glass.

It frightened the wits out of me. I stood there hardly able to breathe, let alone move. I heard a gabble of voices on the landing, shouts from outside in the grounds. I heard our host, Magus, down in the hall, bawling for lights.

When at last I broke through the nightmare inhibition that held me, and threw open my door, there were candles everywhere, guests in their nightclothes. I stepped to the landing banister, looked down into the hall, certain that I should see A. J. Raffles lying there, that he had fallen through the dome. But there was only broken glass in the middle of the hall floor, and Magus, our host, unbolting the front door, on which someone was pounding.

It was the huge, red-haired Shore Bosun. The shipowner gripped his jerseyed arm, pulling him in, and pointed up at the dome.

Looking up, I saw that there was a great forked-lightning-shaped hole in it, with a length of rope with a noose in it, like a hangman's rope, hanging down through the hole.

"See that, Bosun?" said the shipowner. "Dock thieves! They got one of the small windows in the dome open, shone a light down through it on to the figurehead. They let down a rope, noosed the figurehead, pulled it up to the dome and jerked it right through the glass."

"That's a dock thieves' trick, all right," the Shore Bosun said grimly. "They fish like that, with a rope, through warehouse skylights. They'll never get the figurehead away, though, sir. My men are all round the house. I set two of 'em climbing up on to the roof immediately."

A face appeared in the jagged hole in the dome.

"Bose!" the face shouted. "Not a sign of 'em, Bose. Just their rope up here."

I felt Raffles beside me. He was in his dressing gown. He looked up gravely at the hole in the dome.

"Appalling thing, that, Bunny," he said.

"Now, listen to me, Bosun," said our host, down in the hall. "Divide your men into two sections. One section is to search every inch of the grounds here. Send the other section at the double to Mr. Bedivere's house, throw a cordon round it. If these dock thieves try to reach him with the figurehead, grab 'em. But mark this—none of your men is to enter Mr. Bedivere's actual garden or premises. If that figurehead reaches his premises, then I concede —and I'll admit I never dreamed he had it in him. Now, off you go!"

The butler, imperturbable except that he was wearing a scarf instead of a boiled shirt, came into the hall bearing a large tray loaded with decanters and glasses. Skirting the broken glass, he set the tray down on the very coffer where the queen's figurehead lay serene and safe under the oaken lid.

"Good butler, that, Bunny," said Raffles. "I can do with a drink."

We went down the stairs and joined the other guests all crowding, chattering, round the coffer to be served drinks.

Soon the excellent butler conjured forth hot coffee and sandwiches; and, toward three A.M., our host threw in the sponge.

He called in the Shore Bosun. "No point in beating about out there any longer, Bosun," said our host.

"Mr. Bedivere's thieves have pulled it off, that's obvious, dammit! You and your men had better get along to your homes and get some sleep. Busy day, Monday, with the liner sailing."

He looked round at the rest of us.

"We'd *all* better get some sleep," he said.

When the house was once more dark and silent, Raffles slipped again into my room.

"Phase Three, Bunny," he whispered. "Now that the Shore Bosun's gang have all gone, our friends will have crept in and will be waiting under the big windows of the east wing."

"Friends?" I breathed. "What friends?"

"Couple of gypsies," said Raffles, "who're going to carry the figurehead to Bedivere's house for us, and leave it on his doorstep —with a message. Come on, now. Quietly."

As we crept down the stairs, the hall seemed icy cold because of the broken dome. In the darkness, we lifted the queen out of the coffer, carried her into the dining room. Raffles unlatched one of the tall windows. We lifted the queen over the sill. Invisible hands bore her away from us. Raffles latched the window and, quietly, we went up to bed.

The job was done.

On the Monday morning, the fine new liner, the *Queen Guinevere,* dressed over all and saluted by a chorus of ships' sirens, moved with proud majesty down the estuary, bound for Boston, Massachusetts, on her maiden voyage.

On the way to the station afterwards, Gareth driving us, Raffles said that he would be sorry to go back to London without seeing Bedivere's collection.

Gareth, who had seemed to be in a daze ever since the robbery, demurred a little, appearing nervous about his reception by Maulfry; but finally he took us to the house, a modest red-brick villa up the estuary road. The elongated Bedivere himself opened the door to us.

"Ah, Gareth," he said. "I was rather expecting your father, but he hasn't been near me yet. He'll never believe, of course, that the figurehead just materialized on my doorstep in the night. Quite uncanny! Maulfry has some theory about it, but she won't tell me what it is. She has no Monday drawing class at the school till this afternoon, so she's helping me. I rely on her very much in my rehabilitation work. But Mr. Raffles and Mr. Manders might like to see my Noble Circle. This way—"

The first person I saw, in a large, circular room apparently built on at the back of the villa, was Maulfry. A palette in one hand, a paintbrush in the other, she was standing on a stepladder.

Raffles and I both bowed, but she seemed hardly to notice us. She was gazing with an unfathomable expression at Gareth. Embarrassed, I gave my attention to the room.

From all round the walls, at a height of about eight feet, the ring of figureheads leaned as though breasting invisible seas. The paint and gilding worn away by time and the waves had been renewed, and the figureheads in their fresh pigment shone again with their ancient splendor.

Maulfry had been in the act of rehabilitating Queen Guinevere. With eyes of painted blue gazing serenely on ocean horizons, and the long braids of her hair now gold, the immortal queen was restored to her youth, to her royal place at the right hand of her king, in the circle of her trusty knights.

Under each figurehead was a wooden shield with the name painted in gilt: Sir Lancelot, Sir Brian des Isles, Sir Sagramor-le-Desirous (whose modern namesake recently had had its studs renewed, shaft drawn, bilge keels shell bars repaired), Sir Turquine, Sir Dinadan (whose modern namesake had shipped a heavy sea on the port side in the Bay of Bengal on Jan. 6th., causing damage to second engineer's room and port fiddley casing), Sir Aglovale-de-Galis. But over some of the shields were gaps. Sir Pertelope was missing, Sir Kay, Sir Bleobaris, to say nothing of the incomparable Sir Galahad himself.

"Uriens, of Boston, has some of them," said Bedivere. "But when he hears that I now have Queen Guinevere as well as King Arthur, I'm sure he'll give me best and send me what he has—like the good fellow he is at heart." His tone changed. "Why, Maulfry!" he said, vaguely astonished.

His daughter, putting aside her palette and brush, had stepped down suddenly from the ladder, gripped Gareth's shoulders, and kissed him long and hard on the lips.

Linking arms with him, she turned to us with a radiant smile. "What were you saying, Father?" she asked.

Gareth wore an air of stunned delight, as though he had been transported unexpectedly to paradise.

I remarked on this to Raffles, in the compartment we had to ourselves in the train returning to London.

Raffles grinned.

"The fact is, Bunny," he said, "we didn't break just one of our self-imposed rules this weekend—the one about never robbing a house in which we're guests. We also broke our rule never to let an innocent person bear the responsibility for a crime committed by us. What Gareth fails to understand about the feminine mind, Bunny, is that it always responds to a *fait accompli*. Still, I hope he'll have enough sense to understand his position and keep his own counsel—at least, until after they're married. Then, if he feels he must make a clean breast of it, he can break his denial to her gently."

"His denial of what?" I said, staring.

Raffles took out his cigarette case.

"As I told you," he said, "I instructed our two gypsy friends to leave a message on the figurehead when they laid it by night on Bedivere's doorstep, sounded the knocker, and slipped away. The message wasn't in written form."

"In what form was it, then?" I said.

"In the form of a small bouquet of 'their' flower—Gareth's and Maulfry's. Remember, Bunny?" said Raffles. His gray eyes danced. "Snowdrops!"

Six Golden Nymphs

The telegram read:

A. J. RAFFLES, THE ALBANY, PICCADILLY. COULD YOU FILL GAP OUR TEAM AGAINST THE DENMANS ON EIGHTH AND NINTH AT FALLOAK? WIRE URGENT. JOHN FURNEY.

Attached to the telegram, when I myself first saw it, was a note from Raffles:

Bunny, this'll be the strangest country house cricket match ever played. I've scratched from the County match and wired Furney, accepting, and saying I'm bringing you down with me in case a scorer should be needed. Meet me 10:15 Waterloo Station, tomorrow morning.

I had found the note and telegram lying on the doormat when I had returned to my flat in Mount Street late overnight from a somewhat convivial dinner party. I reread them for about the twentieth time as my hansom, with the horse stepping out smartly, threaded its way through the procession of brewers' drays and crowded two-horse 'buses lumbering across Waterloo Bridge.

With an uneasy feeling, I tucked the note and telegram back into the pocket of my light flannel suit. My head was tender from my overnight potations, and I tilted my boater further forward over my eyes against the midsummer sun-dazzle reflected from the wide river.

Children's voices rising shrilly from the awninged deck of a Margate-bound pleasure steamer, and an earsplitting blast from the whistle of a tug thrusting upstream with a tow of barges, did nothing to mend my neuralgia. And I cursed Raffles for having involved me, without a by-your-leave, in this extraordinary and damnable cricket match between the West Country neighbors, the Furneys and the Denmans.

To me, it was incredible that the match was to be played at all.

Raffles and I had been at school with some of the Furneys. Both they and the Denmans were good old families, somewhere between the prosperous yeoman and the squirearchy. They farmed their land, hunted, played cricket with passionate devotion, and begot sons. In this latter respect, old Matthew Furney of Falloak and old Nevil Denman of Knightswade, the present heads of the families, were exceptionally prolific.

Though no great cricketer myself, a glum fact from which my nickname derived, I could easily imagine the view Raffles would have taken of the Furneys' invitation.

"I've had most kinds of cricket experience in a misspent life to date," he would have said, "but I've never yet filled the one vacancy in a team composed of a father and nine sons in a match against a team composed of a father and ten sons!"

The attraction which this encounter would have for him did not end there. The date for the match had been set many years ago when Matthew Furney and Nevil Denman, then in their prime, had been close cronies and, having each already a fair brood of sons, friendly rivals in the Fatherhood Stakes. They had set the date for the match arbitrarily, as one by which each was confident that he would be able to fulfill a long-standing ambition and lead on to the cricket field a team composed entirely of his own sons. So sure were they of their philoprogenitive prowess that they even had tossed a coin to decide on which of their grounds the match was to be played.

From the Furneys, who had been at school with us, I long had known of the fixture. It had been the talk of the sporting West Country for years. Heavy bets had been laid on the outcome, for both families included some notable smiters of a cricket ball. But, just three years ago, Fate had shattered the plans of the overconfident fathers. The unforeseeable had happened.

One of the Furney sons—Dennis, aged twenty at the time—had got into a ferocious and sanguinary fight with one of the Denman sons, Bob, of the same age, and his inseparable friend. How it had started nobody ever had learned, but the scene of the fight had been a cliff near their respective homes, and the struggle had ended in Dennis pitching Bob over the cliff edge.

Though there had been one or two yachts winking their sails out at sea on that blue summer day, the only actual witness had been an old shepherd scything thistles on a distant hillside. By the time he had been able to fetch help from the village and reach the scene, Bob Denman had been drowned, and Dennis Furney had taken to his heels. He had remained a fugitive, uncaught and unheard-of, from that day to this.

I frowned at the horse's jogging back, the glint and gleam of the harness in the sunshine. I could not understand why, now that the date arranged for the match so long ago had rolled round at last, the game actually was to be played. For the tragedy had hit both families hard; I had been told that there had been no communication whatever between them from the day it had happened.

Moreover, there seemed no longer any point in the match. For though each father had achieved in all eleven children—and with Bob Denman dead, and Dennis Furney a fugitive, each had lost one

—there remained a disequilibrium between them. Old Denman's children were all sons, so that he still could lead a full team on to the field tomorrow; but old Furney could not, for one of his children was a daughter. Hence the vacancy in the Furney side, and the co-opting of A. J. Raffles.

There came back to my mind a recollection of Lady Mendawe's description of Raffles as "a fallen gentleman," and I could not help wondering if there were not, perhaps, a grain of truth in her remark. For I could hear Raffles's voice, now, as clearly as if he had been in the hansom with me:

"Miss this, Bunny? Not on your life! Here cricket and crime, the two pursuits which have given me my keenest and subtlest sensations in life, overlap in a unique way. How will it feel, I wonder, to turn out, in so strange a match as this, in the shoes, figuratively speaking, of a wanted murderer?"

The hansom swung to the right, into Waterloo Station, and the horse's hooves, sounding suddenly hollow under the domed roof, clip-clopped to a standstill.

I spotted Raffles at once. He was standing near the departure platform, talking to a girl. As I approached, carrying my gladstone bag, I glanced curiously at her attractive profile, her soft hair in which the sunshine mellowed by the grimed glass overhead brought out gold-dust lights. I admired her little straw hat and simple traveling costume.

Raffles glanced round and saw me.

"Ah, here he is!" he said. "Mr. Extras himself!" Hatless, his keen face tanned by the summer's cricket, he was casual in a summer suit and an M.C.C. tie. His green baize cricket bag lay at his feet. Putting a friendly hand on my shoulder, he presented me to the girl. "Miss Jane, this is Bunny Manders, our volunteer scorer. Bunny, Miss Jane Furney."

I had not dreamed of meeting here at Waterloo this only daughter of old Matthew Furney. Unprepared, I was embarrassed by the thought of the violent episode in the background of a family otherwise well-regulated, and I felt myself flush as I met her vividly blue eyes and the clasp of her small, firm hand. I could have kicked myself.

Raffles, in his easy way, came to my rescue.

"Shall we find our seats?" he suggested. "I fancy I see the guard unfurling his little banner." He shifted the magazines under his arm, took up his cricket bag. "A pleasant surprise, meeting Miss Jane here, Bunny. She's been spending a few weeks in London, but is going home for the match. She's kindly invited us to share her compartment."

Cupping a hand under her arm, he moved off with her along the platform. I followed and, still feeling embarrassed, stood waiting as Raffles settled her in a corner seat of a First Class compartment. Her labeled suitcase was already in the rack, and a man in tweeds and dusty boots, with rough sandy hair and a beard, sat partially obliterated by the *Times* which he was reading in a far corner.

"Right-oh, Bunny," Raffles said, turning to me, "let's have our traps, now."

I handed him the gladstone and the cricket bag, but at that moment, as he stood there in the doorway, I saw his gray eyes harden to a sudden intentness. I followed his glance to two burly men of dignified presence, wearing blue serge suits and hard hats and carrying carpetbags, who walked past majestically along the platform and got into the train two compartments along.

"Know 'em, Bunny?" Raffles said softly, as he took our gear from me.

I shook my head.

"Yard men," he said, "Inspector Kortright, Sergeant Ellis."

My mouth went dry.

"Food for thought," Raffles murmured significantly.

It was, indeed, and as the train, with ponderous reverberations under the station roof, steamed out into the full glare of the morning sun, I devoutly wished myself elsewhere.

I sat beside Raffles, who had the corner seat facing the girl. At first, he tried to make conversation, but Jane Furney was unresponsive. She seemed preoccupied and troubled, and I was in no better case, though I no longer was thinking about the cricket match. I was thinking about the affair of the debutantes, back in the winter, which had raised more noise and a more protracted hue and cry than any previous exploit of ours; and I was wondering whether the disquieting presence of detectives on the train meant that we had come at last under suspicion. I was far from happy.

Raffles, after a while, gave us both up as a bad job and began to turn the pages of one of his magazines. Jane gazed from the window, and so did I.

The countryside, basking under a visible heat tremor, fled smoothly past. Cows ate their placid cuds and swished their tails in the shade of great oaks, and the hedges were pink with the wild rose.

Unfortunately, the thought of detectives on the train quite prevented me from drawing any sense of peace from the passing scene. In fact, gladly would I have given every penny of loot our felonies had brought us to change places with the yokel out there among the buttercups, watching with vacant mien the passing of the train as he unhurriedly stoned his sickle.

Raffles, laying down his magazine on his knee, broke a long silence.

"By the by, Miss Jane," he said, "it's dawned on me that Bunny and I have been remiss. Am I mistaken in thinking that congratulations are in order?"

She turned her gaze from the window. "Congratulations?"

He motioned to the magazine on his knee. I saw that the magazine lay open at a full-page photograph of a Palladian mansion, with a small photograph, inset, of a middle-aged man with a stern face and tight lips. The caption read:

A Stately Home. Houndsleep Hall, situate between the villages of Falloak and Knightswade, in the romantic *Lorna Doone* country, is the home of Sir Gregory Markis, Bart. Sir Gregory is a distinguished connoisseur and collector. For his six gold coins of ancient Syracuse, bearing the image of Arethusa, Nymph of the Springs, numismatists all over the world have vainly offered record sums.

"Surely," said Raffles, "it must be nearly a year, now, since I saw the announcement of your engagement to Sir Gregory's son, Walter? I know Walter slightly, a good all-round sportsman—sailing, cricket. To tell the truth, I'm rather wondering why he wasn't called on, in preference to me, for this match tomorrow, he being a neighbor of yours and—almost one of the family," he added, smiling.

She bit her lip.

"He wasn't asked," she said. "I broke off the engagement months ago." Impulsively, she added, "It was my fault entirely. I ought never to have got engaged. I—" She checked herself. She studied her hands for a moment, clasped tightly in her lap. Then, looking up, she said simply, "You're friends of my brothers. I can tell you. I shan't ever marry. I loved Bob Denman. I thought I could forget him. I got engaged to Walter, but it was no good. If you'd known Bob—" Her lips trembled. "And now, this match," she said, "this frightful, hideous cricket match—"

She turned her head abruptly and looked from the window.

I met Raffles's eyes. I never had dreamed of this poignant twist in the story of the Furneys and the Denmans—that she had loved the young man her brother had killed. I could see that Raffles was as shaken as I was. He took a Sullivan from his case, but, instead of lighting the cigarette, sat turning it over and over between his fingers, glancing now and then in a troubled way at the girl.

"Miss Jane," he said slowly, at last, "do you think it altogether wise to go home for this match? Surely it will be very painful for you. We're barely halfway, and in a few minutes the train makes a halt. Wouldn't it, perhaps, be better to leave it and return to London—until the match is all over?"

"How can I?" she said. "As friends of my brothers, surely you can understand! Old Mr. Denman sent a note to Father—and let the whole countryside know he'd sent it—saying he expected the fixture to be kept. It's his *revenge,* don't you see? In spite of Bob's death, Mr. Denman still can lead ten sons on to the field—a full team. Father can't, because Dennis is a fugitive, skulking heaven knows where, who dare not show his face. With all our neighbors present tomorrow, from miles around, Dennis's absence, with everyone knowing the reason for it, will be underlined, emphasized, glaring—a terrible, humiliating thing for my father and brothers. Can't you imagine what they will be feeling? Yet how cowardly and shameful and despicable it would be if they didn't keep the fixture? They've no choice. And neither have I. I must be there, to face it out with them, to share whatever happens. I must! I love them all."

The abrupt rustle of a newspaper drew my glance, startled, to the man in the far corner, on Jane's side. He had been so silent, for so long, that I had forgotten his presence; no doubt, we all had. His heavy tweeds and dusty boots, his rough sandy hair, his beard, somehow had given me the impression of a middle-aged man; but now that he had cast aside his newspaper, I saw that, despite the lines in his sunburned forehead, he was young. His eyes, as vividly blue as Jane's own, were fixed on her. He passed his tongue along his bearded lips, and I heard the strain in his voice.

"All of them, Janie?" he said. "All but me? Dennis?"

She sat as still as though death had touched her. The color drained from her face. She gazed at him. And Dennis Furney made a slight, explanatory gesture toward her suitcase in the rack.

"I noticed the label as I walked along the platform at Waterloo," he said. "So I got in here. I didn't know there'd be anyone with you."

Oblivious of us, they gazed at each other across a gulf of three years. The train rattled noisily over switchpoints. The girl did not stir.

"Janie, I couldn't have saved him," Dennis Furney said. "I couldn't—even if I'd climbed down the cliff after him. But I wish I'd tried, instead of losing my head and bolting. Janie, I swear I didn't know, till this minute, how you felt about him. I never dreamed of that. D'you see?" He looked at her desperately, but she did not move or speak to him. He said, in a low voice, "How you must hate me—"

Suddenly he turned to us.

"Raffles, what could I do?" he begged. "You see that I've come back. I had to. I kept thinking about this damned cricket match, wondering what would happen, what it would mean to them, Father and the rest of them. I was in Australia. I started drifting back. I hardly knew why. Only, the nearer the date of the match drew, the nearer I drew to England. I couldn't seem to help myself. I was in Calais night before last. I sat in a café, drinking red wine and staring across the Channel in the direction of Dover, and I tell you I could feel the rope around my neck and the damned great knot of it squeezing my ear. But finally I thought, Oh, the devil, let Father lead ten sons on to the field just once in his life, if it means so much to him! Let him lead us on to the field, and hand me straight over there himself, to old Denman, and let old Denman shout for the police, and there'll be an end of it!"

He appealed again to the girl.

"See what I mean, Janie?" he said. "End the whole miserable business, clear up the mess and uncertainty for you all—pay the piper. See what I mean? That was my idea—get it over with. Only, Janie—try not to hate me too much. I've been in hell. I didn't mean to kill him."

She moved, at last. She put out both her hands to her brother, and her voice was a whisper: "Poor Dennis—"

I felt Raffles's grip on my arm. He jerked his head at the door, and I awoke to the realization that the train was standing in a station. Never had I felt such relief; in my embarrassment, I scarcely had known where to look.

I ducked out of the train after Raffles. Sunshine over banks of flowers, where blue lobelias spelled out the name of the station in a border of oyster shells, dazzled my eyes. Along the platform, milk churns from neighboring farms were being clangingly loaded. Broad West Country accents sounded. And my scalp tingled to a chilling thought.

"Raffles! Those Yard men—"

"Just so," he said grimly. "They're not interested in *us*. There's not much doubt who they're after, I'm afraid. They must have had information." He pushed open the door of the Refreshment Room. "Get a couple of beers, Bunny," he said, and turned quickly to peer from the window.

When I carried two foaming tankards across to him, he took one and gave me a queer look.

"Neither Kortright nor Ellis," he said, "has so much as glanced from the window of their compartment. You'd think that, if they'd had a tip that Dennis Furney crossed yesterday from Calais and may be on this train, they'd take a stroll along the platform at every opportunity, to glance in at the other compartments. Yet there they are, look—sitting in there, peacefully reading."

I peered from the window, and it was true; I could see the two men there in their sunny little compartment. I was puzzled. "What do you make of it?" I asked Raffles.

He raised his tankard to his lips, diminished its contents by a good two-thirds, and said, "Taken and wanted!"

And he went on thoughtfully, "Bunny, I don't believe those two have the faintest suspicion that Dennis Furney's in England. Know what I begin to think? As you're aware, I've always made it my business to keep fairly well informed as to who's who at Scotland Yard. Now, Kortright and Ellis are both West Countrymen. And I'm beginning seriously to think that they're on this train for no other reason than that, like the whole sporting West Country, they're curious to see this cricket match and are treating themselves to a little holiday for the purpose."

"If you're right," I said, "it'll be a lucky holiday for them. They'll pick up Dennis Furney the minute they see him walk on to that field tomorrow."

He seemed scarcely to hear me.

"They say revenge is sweet," he said musingly. "I wonder. For the normal person, the *anticipation* of revenge can be sweet. But when it's in his grasp, when he actually has the whip hand, it's surprising how often the savor departs and the gesture of magnanimity seems more satisfying. Old Nevil Denman has brooded, yes, or this match wouldn't be on tomorrow. But at heart he's a perfectly normal old country gentleman. I know his kind."

"What are you driving at?" I said.

"This," said Raffles. "Picture old Furney walking up to old Denman on that field tomorrow and saying, 'Here's my boy Dennis. In a fight that sprang up between two hotheaded young fools, he killed your boy Bob. He's suffered for it. He'll suffer all his life. Now, here he is. He's come back of his own accord to take his medicine. Take him and do what you like with him.' Now, then, Bunny—would you be prepared to bet your shirt that old Denman's instant reaction will be to shout for the police? Or is it just about equally likely that his instant reaction will be to snarl, 'Get him out of sight, quick, you blockheaded old fool!'?"

I considered the point, and for the life of me I could not have predicted with confidence which way old Denman would be most likely to react.

"Raffles," I said, with rising excitement, "I swear it looks to me just about an even chance. Do you think Dennis realizes it?"

"Not for a second," Raffles said. "He's obsessed with this idea that his father, just once in his lifetime, must lead ten sons on to the cricket field—then hand him over. He sees it as the end for

himself. But, by heaven, Bunny, I think it's just about—as you say
—an even chance that it could be a new beginning. He has his
sister's forgiveness—we saw that. And if tomorrow he should, by
implication, have old Denman's— You follow me? The forgiveness
of the girl who loved Bob, the forgiveness of Bob's father? He'll
never have his *own* forgiveness, of course; he'll never again be a
happy man. But if he could be got out of England once more, I
really think he'd have a hope, this time, of working out some kind
of salvation for himself. Better than swinging by the neck or rotting
out an interminable sentence in Dartmoor!"

"True," I said. "But what's the use of talking? If Kortright
and Ellis are on that cricket field when the match starts at eleven
o'clock tomorrow morning, where's Dennis Furney's even
chance?"

"*We're* going to give it to him," Raffles said. An icy vivacity
danced in his eyes. "By a diversionary action that'll keep Kortright
and Ellis away from the Furney cricket ground for at least the first
hour or so of the match tomorrow."

A thrill went through me. "What kind of diversionary action?"

"Robbery!"

"But of what?"

"Of the golden nymphs of Sir Gregory Markis!" said A. J.
Raffles.

As he spoke, the guard's whistle shrilled. We clapped down
our tankards on the window ledge. Sprinting across the platform,
we flung ourselves back into the compartment just as the train
began to move.

What might have passed between Jane and Dennis Furney in
our absence I had no idea; and I heard precious little of what few
words were spoken between then and the time of the train's arrival
at the small market town which was the station for the village of
Falloak. My mind was racing with this conception of Raffles's—
a diversionary action.

John, who had sent Raffles the telegram, and Peter, another Furney brother, met the train. They had a dogcart waiting for us. They were big chaps, in flannels and blazers, with the same kind of rough, sandy hair as Dennis, but no beards.

Just how they looked when they recognized Dennis, I simply did not see. I was too busy watching the Yard men. Carrying their carpetbags, they walked in their deliberate, dignified way across the little cattle market before the station. They went into an ivied, thatched-eaved inn, The Markis Arms. Not far off was a red-brick villa with a notice board in its front garden. It was the police station, and I guessed that Raffles was counting on their looking in there in the course of the evening for a courtesy call on the local inspector.

Falloak was about five miles out from the little town. We were a silent party in the dogcart. White dust smoked up under the trotting hooves of the sturdy cob between the shafts. John was driving. Both he and Peter seemed stunned by Dennis's arrival. They, and Jane, too, and Dennis himself, no doubt were haunted by the thought of what their father was going to say—or do.

It was a worrying ride, though the air was sweet with the scent of new-made haystacks, and honeysuckle breathed its fragrance from the hedgerows. The sky ahead, luminous with sunset and cawed over by a straggle of homing rooks, seemed the more vast for the presence of the sea, glimpsed now and then away to our left.

We passed a long, high wall of weathered brick in which was set a pair of lofty, wrought-iron gates between stone pillars surmounted by griffons. I felt Raffles's elbow in my side. It was the estate of Sir Gregory Markis.

Presently, there rose up, dark against the fading radiance of the sky, the furze-grown hump of a cliff top—the cliff, I guessed, that had played so tragic a part in the lives of the Furneys and the Denmans. The dogcart, swinging then to the right, passed through a gateway, with a five-barred gate standing open, on to a rutted farm track.

Fields of rustling grain either side gave way to an orchard on the right and a pretty little cricket ground on the left. There was a sizable thatched pavilion with a verandah; in the dusk, a home-made-looking sightscreen glimmered white, and half a dozen big chaps—Furney brothers—were lugging a heavy roller in silence up and down the wicket. From the terraces of lawn between which the ground was sunk came now and then the strident cry of a peacock.

As the dogcart came to a standstill before a rambling old gray stone house overlooking the cricket ground, the twilight bats were flickering soundlessly above our heads. We got out. I saw Jane look steadily at Dennis for a moment, then she took his hand and they went into the house together—to find their father.

"I'll put the horse up," John Furney said awkwardly.

Raffles dumped his cricket bag on the gravel. "We'll come and help you."

In the cool of the evening, we loitered, forcing conversation, in the stables. We all dreaded the thought of going into the house. At last, we had to. We found it filled with a hush, a sense of tension, which were both, I was sure, unusual there. Even the rosy-faced maidservants, in their starched caps and aprons, seemed oppressed by a consciousness of drama. Several times I caught the name, whispered in awe and excitement, "Mr. Dennis—"

Jane did not appear at dinner. She was with her mother, who, we were told, had been deeply affected by Dennis's return. We sat down, round the big table under the low, beamed ceiling of the dining room, without old Matthew Furney, either, and without Dennis. There were just Raffles and myself, the other Furney brothers—who ranged in age from eighteen to thirty-five—and the nice, wholesome-looking wives of the two or three of them who were married.

In the tense silences which kept falling during the meal, the murmuring voices of old Furney and Dennis were audible from the old man's den, nearby. As though fearful of what the sound might portend, somebody or other would make a hasty attempt at conversation. But it soon would wither and fade and that fateful murmuring become audible again—until suddenly, toward the end of dinner, it ceased.

We all were aware of it. And round the table, lit by candles in sconces of the solid old Furney silver, we exchanged glances. No one spoke. Footsteps approached across the oaken floor of the hall. Old Furney came in. He was tall, gaunt; his broad shoulders stooped; his mutton-chop whiskers and bristly hair were gray; his square, mahogany face looked down.

We men rose instinctively. Old Furney's faded blue eyes traveled over us. Dennis stood behind him in the doorway. Old Furney singled out Raffles and moved toward him, offering his hand.

"Mr. Raffles? I owe you an apology," he said. "I have a request to put to you that I find awkward in view of the long journey you've made—a request that, if you grant it, will mean you won't get an opportunity to bat or bowl in this match, though you will be called upon to substitute in the field."

"Twelfth man, sir?" Raffles said.

"Twelfth man," said old Furney grimly.

"Certainly," said Raffles.

Then I knew what was going to happen tomorrow. I knew that Dennis Furney had forced his father's agreement to the gesture that obsessed him, and that tomorrow, for the first and last time in his life, Matthew Furney of Falloak would lead on to his little cricket ground a team of his own ten sons.

Meantime, there remained tonight.

The little cricket ground lay peaceful in the moon-glimmer when Raffles and myself, hugging the tree shadow, walked swiftly and silently past it along the farm track at a little before one A.M. Behind us, the Furneys' windows showed no lights, though I was pretty sure a good many of the family lay sleepless in their beds, thinking of the morrow, and we had had to exercise the utmost caution in dropping from the window of the room we shared.

A half-hour of fast walking brought us to the high wall surrounding the Markis estate. We tied dark handkerchiefs over our faces. I gave Raffles a shoulder. He pulled himself to the top of the wall, reached down a hand to me. We dropped silently to the ground on the other side.

The soft air of the summer night was drenched with the scent of roses. The little ground owls were calling. Before us, mysterious in the moonlight, stretched formal gardens of sunk flagstoned paths, sculptured figures in white marble, black yews tortured by clippers into the likenesses of heraldic beasts.

Crouched in the shadow of a Venus de Milo, we studied the facade of the house, with its tall windows, all dark, looking out over a broad terrace with a stone balustrade.

"Pity we haven't had a chance to case the crib," Raffles muttered. "If we can pull this off, Bunny, and get away with those six gold coins, they're of such importance that it's long odds the local police, knowing two Yard men are handy, will call them in when the robbery's discovered in the morning. So long as Kortright and Ellis aren't present on the cricket ground when the match starts, Dennis'll have his fifty-fifty chance. Well, we can but try it. Come on, old lad!"

Swiftly, hugging the shadows, we crossed the gardens, darted up the steps to the terrace. The shadow of the house fell upon us. Raffles climbed to the broad sill of one of the lofty windows. There was a slow, heavy thump in my chest as I kept my eyes, above the masking handkerchief, watchfully roving the gardens and the upper windows.

Raffles had only a pocketknife by way of jemmy, but he was a craftsman. I heard no sound from him. It was the light touch of his hand on my shoulder that told me he had the window open. I turned. A shadow on the sill above me, he beckoned me to follow —and stepped down into the room.

In a moment, I was at his side. We stood listening, our breath held. All was still. The curtains of the windows were looped back.

Faintly, I could make out the shapes of massive furniture, the crystal sheen of pendant chandeliers.

"A drawing room," Raffles said, his murmur muffled. "More likely to find his safe or showcases in a library or study."

I nodded. As unerringly as if he could see in the dark, he moved forward. I followed closely, till his hand reached back to stay me. We had come to double-leaf doors, one leaf standing open. And I saw why he had paused. Before us, across the wide, dark space of what evidently was a hall, a line of light showed under a door. I heard voices.

In the same moment, another light appeared—faint, reddish, flickering.

Raffles drew back slightly, peering upward.

A candle had come into view, up on a gallery landing. The candle was in a candlestick held in the hand of a man. With his other hand, he shielded the flame as he leaned forward over the banister, as though listening. The light flickered on his face—the narrow, stern face I had seen in the magazine photograph, Sir Gregory Markis.

After a moment, he moved. His dressing-gowned figure passed from view briefly, then reappeared on our level, crossing the hall quickly and quietly, not toward us, but to the door beneath which light showed. He stood there, quite still, holding the candlestick, his head cocked in a listening attitude. His free hand went slowly to the doorknob. Suddenly he turned it, flung the door wide open.

Two young men at a table in the lamplit room sprang to their feet.

"Walter," Sir Gregory said peremptorily, "who is this fellow?"

One of the young men—he held a sheet of notepaper in his hand—said, "Father, I beg you to leave us. This matter—"

"Answer my question!"

"Very well," Walter Markis said, "if you *must* have it. He's Bob Denman!" He shouted suddenly, "*Bob Denman!* Do you understand? He landed at Plymouth today. He reached this house at eleven this morning, but I had to keep him waiting in this room till you'd gone to bed, so that I could talk to him privately. I hoped to spare you— But you leave me no choice. I'd better read you this document I've written for Bob."

"Read it," Sir Gregory said.

Walter Markis read, in a shaking voice, " 'This is a truthful and voluntary confession. I witnessed the fight between Bob Denman and Dennis Furney from the deck of my yacht *Sprite,* in which I was sailing alone. I put in in search of Bob and picked him up half-drowned and unconscious. I was, and am, deeply in love with Jane Furney. She had no use for anyone but Bob. Nobody had seen me pull him out of the sea, and the idea flashed into my mind that here was a chance to get him out of my way. I put straight out to sea. When he recovered consciousness, I told him that Dennis Furney had gone over the cliff with him, and was dead, and that if it became known that he, Bob, had survived, he would be charged with manslaughter, possibly murder. He had no idea of my feelings for Jane and, believing my story, thought that for her sake it would be better if he remained "dead," since he believed he had killed her brother. I landed Bob on the French coast, near Quimper, where I subsequently sent him, in the name he had assumed, money with which to make his way to South America.' "

Walter Markis glanced for a moment at his father, then read on quickly.

" 'After more than two years, I succeeded in persuading Jane to become engaged to me. But gradually I was forced to realize that it was an empty triumph, that she loved Bob and always would. When finally she broke our engagement, my feeling for her remained such that I determined to repair, at whatever cost to myself, the ruination I had brought to her happiness and that of so many others. I knew Bob's whereabouts. I wrote to him telling him that the situation had changed and sent him a draft to finance his return to England. I asked him to come direct to me first. On his arrival, I shall hand him this document, for him to take such action upon as he may decide. I am sorry for the great harm I have done. Walter Markis.' "

The silence was electric. Sir Gregory was the first to speak. "Remain here," he said grimly. "Both of you."

The shadows wheeled over the gallery landing above as, carrying the candlestick, he moved to another room. Walter and Bob stood silent, motionless. Again the shadows wheeled as the tall, stern, tight-lipped man reappeared. He put the candlestick on the hall table.

"Come here!"

They moved to his side. The candlelight flickered over their faces.

"Denman," Sir Gregory said, "I am a man most bitterly ashamed. There's not much I can do, I'm afraid, by way of compensation for my son's appalling act. I can only say to you"—he set down upon the table a small, flat, oblong case, leather-covered—"that here is the most precious thing I own in this world." He opened the case. "There it is. Take it, Denman. It's yours."

Bob Denman reached out a hand. But what he took was the sheet of notepaper which Walter Markis still held. Bob put a corner of the paper to the candle flame.

"Jane is still free," he said, as the paper curled and blackened. "For me, sir, that knowledge is enough to wipe out the last three years. My story will be simply that I hit my head when I went over that cliff, and that I remember nothing between then and about one hour from now, when I'm going to find myself walking up the drive to our home at Knightswade. Good night to you both."

He strode from view. I heard the rattle of a door bolt shot back, then the slam of the door. In the silence that followed, Sir Gregory's hard breathing was audible. He turned slowly to his son.

"As for you," he said, "I have a thing or two to say to *you*. Come with me."

He walked into the room where the lamp burned. Walter

followed. His face was white. The door closed. On the hall table, the candle in the tall candlestick burned serenely. Raffles moved. He walked swiftly, silently, to the hall table. I followed.

We stood looking down at the open case. It was lined with purple velvet. On the velvet lay six golden coins, thin with the wear of centuries, each coin limned, scarcely perceptibly, with an image from the morning of the world—Arethusa, Nymph of the Springs.

My heart beat stiflingly. I glanced at Raffles. Above the handkerchief that masked his face, I saw the gray gleam of his eyes, fixed on the golden nymphs.

The moment was one which would remain forever stamped upon my mind. It haunted me even in the full blaze of the morning sunshine, as I stood on one of the grassy terraces that surrounded the little cricket ground of the Furney family. All down the farm track, to the five-barred gate, stood rows of traps, flys, gigs, dogcarts, wagonettes, governess carts, phaetons. More were arriving every minute. Nearest the house stood the big shooting brake in which the Denman family, of Knightswade, had driven up about an hour ago.

All the sporting West Country, the country of *Lorna Doone,* was here today. Never before had the little cricket ground presented such a sight. The lawnlike terraces were brilliant with the parasols and bustled gowns of the ladies, the blazers and straw hats of the men. Out in the center, fresh whitewash marked the popping crease, and the stumps cast slanting shadows across the emerald turf. The bails were on. The umpires, one of them preserving the shine on the bright red ball by smoothing it lovingly up and down his white coat, already were at the wicket.

Raffles, as twelfth man, had changed into white flannels. He wore the cap of the I Zingari cricket club, as he lounged in a deck chair on one of the terraces. Standing beside him, I was expecting at every minute a summons co-opting me to the scorer's box.

In the strange hush which lay over the crowded terraces, one of the Furney peacocks, spreading its iridescent tail as it pecked the turf before the sightscreen, emitted an alien scream. A smocked old gaffer stepped out to prod the gaudy fowl from the ground with his stick.

At that moment, a kind of sigh of expectancy seemed to rustle round the terraces. The gaunt, stooped, white-flanneled figure of old Matthew Furney, wearing a faded blue cricket cap, had appeared at the head of the pavilion steps. For a moment, he stood surveying the thronged terraces. Then, visibly squaring his shoulders, he walked slowly down the steps, out on to the field, and one by one his ten tall sons came sauntering after him.

The umpire tossed the ball to old Furney. In such a silence as I never had known, old Furney, in turn, lobbed the ball to one of his sons, who was capless and clean-shaven. Old Furney's voice was clearly audible, supremely casual.

"Open the bowling from the pavilion end, Dennis," he said.

Every person around the little ground must have heard it. And a sudden buzz of whispers swept in sibilant incredulity round the sweltering terraces: "Dennis? *Dennis?*"

Behind and above me, a voice said sharply, "It's him! By heaven, it *is* him!"

I glanced round and, with a shock, recognized the big, hard-faced Inspector Kortright. With Sergeant Ellis, he was standing on the next grassy step up. I put a hand quickly on Raffles's shoulder. He glanced round and up, and saw them.

Sergeant Ellis said, "It *can't* be, sir. He wouldn't—"

"It's him, I tell you," said Kortright. Both men were staring over our heads at the ground. Excitement clogged Kortright's voice. "It's the man, all right, Ellis! Dennis Furney! Wanted for murder!"

Raffles raised his voice courteously. "Whose murder?" he asked.

Neither of the detectives so much as glanced at us; they had eyes only for the field. But Kortright said impatiently, "The murder of young Bob Denman!"

"You mean," said Raffles, in a bland tone, "that fellow just coming out from the pavilion to bat?"

I saw Kortright's mouth fall open. I saw his eyes start from his head. Next second, he was thrusting headlong through the crowd, elbowing his way in the direction of the pavilion, with Sergeant Ellis hastening after him.

"It's to be hoped," said Raffles, "that they don't have the bad taste to delay the opening of the game with their fatuous investigations. Too bad we couldn't have pursued our plan to provide them with something worthwhile to investigate! Never again in our lives, probably, shall we have such swag to our hand for the taking as we had last night in Sir Gregory Markis's hall! Six golden nymphs—"

He shook his head.

"You know, Bunny," he said, "there are times when it's ridiculously easy to be a burglar—and damned hard," he added, as he leaned back in the deck chair and pulled his I Zingari cap lower over his eyes against the sun-dazzle, "to remember that one also, after all, plays cricket!"

Man's Meanest Crime

Toward six o'clock on a foggy evening, my hansom jingled out of Piccadilly into the courtyard before The Albany. Near the foot of the steps stood a roast-chestnut vendor's barrow. Its brazier glowed red, and I saw A. J. Raffles, in evening dress, cape, and opera hat, chatting with the vendor and warming his hands.

As the hansom was reined in he came forward quickly.

"That you, Bunny?" he said. "Good man! I've been waiting for you."

He gave the cabbie the address of one of the clubs to which we belonged and took his seat beside me.

"I thought we were going to dine at the Capoulade before going to the opera," I said. "What's this club nonsense?"

I spoke a bit testily. I did not like Raffles's sudden changes of plan; I never knew what they might portend.

"There's a matter I feel obliged to look into, Bunny," he said. "It involves an old friend of mine—and two remarkably pretty sisters."

I said nothing. Raffles struck a match and dipped his Sullivan to the flame.

183

"Remember Bill Foster?" he said. "Young barrister just beginning to make a name."

He drew deeply on his cigarette.

"Last week Bill was the victim of a robbery. It was the eve of the first anniversary of his wedding. Bill had a present for Kathy, his wife, in his pocket, a gift of love—a ruby bracelet.

"A shadow was waiting for him when he arrived home that night. A blackjack smashed down on his head. When he came to, lying on the porch, the shadow was gone. So was Kathy's anniversary gift."

"A nasty sort of trick," I observed.

"It was," Raffles said, "and I felt particularly badly about it because it happened to friends of mine. What's more, it rang a faint bell in my mind. I've been combing back through newspaper files.

"Within the past year or so there have been a number of cases of young professional and business men who've been blackjacked and robbed while returning from their offices to their homes on the eve of the first anniversary of their marriage."

"A system?" I asked, intrigued.

"I'm certain of it," Raffles said. "Weddings, with presents on display, always have been apt to attract thieves. Hence, nowadays, there's often a plainclothesman about at such happy functions. So this ingenious unknown has worked out, I fancy, a bright variation.

"A day or two before the anniversary of a marriage he's selected he probably begins to shadow the young husband, note his habits, and so on. You see? He knows it's almost a sure thing that the young husband, when he hurries home on his anniversary eve, will have a gift in his pocket—probably jewelry of some kind.

"The happy husband goes tearing home with his mind full of love and gratitude and thoughts of the happy surprise he's got in his pocket for his young wife—and waiting for him in his porch, or some other carefully chosen corner along his road home, is this unknown man with the blackjack, the Anniversary Thief."

"It's the meanest crime I ever heard of," I exclaimed.

"I agree," said Raffles. "Are you with me in an attempt to hamstring this chap?"

"It's rather out of our line," I objected.

The hansom was just jingling round into Pall Mall. The fog was deepening; I scarcely could see two streetlamps ahead. I was conscious of the vastness and mystery of London.

"Besides," I said, "finding this chap would be about as likely as finding a needle in a haystack."

"As to that," said Raffles, "I have a notion. In the past year or so, you and I have had invitations to quite a few weddings of the very type this Anniversary Thief seems to pick on. Does any particular wedding stick out in your mind?"

I said, "The wedding that sticks out in my mind is the only double wedding I ever atten—" I broke off. "The pretty sisters you mentioned!" I exclaimed. "Of course! The Kenyon girls!"

"Christine and Carolyn," Raffles said. "Exactly! In point of fact, Bunny, tonight is the eve of the first anniversary of that double wedding. Now, another thing. Christine married Toby Lucas. A fine, storming rugger forward, Toby! You know his job?"

"He's in his family firm. Old-established City concern—something to do with Hudson Bay. Fur importers or something, aren't they?" I said.

"Right," Raffles said. "And Carolyn married Roy Norcott. Remember Roy's job?"

"He's the youngest of the sons," I said, "of Norcott and Sons . . ."

Again I broke off. My scalp tingled as I began to see what he was driving at.

I said, "Diamond merchants, of Hatton Garden."

"And there we have it," said Raffles. "Bunny, old cock, if there's one young husband whom our Anniversary Thief is likely to have noted as being apt to carry home to his wife tonight a gift worth having, surely it must be Roy Norcott—a diamond merchant!"

He flicked his cigarette end into the fog.

"Now, why we've come to this particular club is that I happen to know that on cold nights, with a longish way home before him, Roy usually looks in here for a quick one to warm him up.

"My feeling is that if we pick up Roy's trail tonight and keep close behind him, we stand a first-rate chance of collaring the meanest criminal in London."

As he spoke, the horse clip-clopped to a standstill. Raffles gave the cabbie a half-sovereign. We walked up the steps into the club.

Yielding up our outdoor things, we looked first into a room off the hall. Popular at this hour, the room was hazed with tobacco smoke and thronged with men standing about with glasses and tankards in their hands.

"We're in luck," Raffles murmured.

Sure enough, the very man we were seeking was having a drink at the bar with a couple of men we knew slightly.

One of the men, Philip Henge, was a velvet-jacketed, bow-tied, classically handsome fellow, a fashionable photographer. The other was a gray-haired, dapper chap with an eyeglass and a look of dissipated distinction. His name was Chastayne.

Roy Norcott was in evening dress, and, as we went over to the bar, Raffles said casually, "Evening, Roy. Going to the opera?"

"Hallo, you two!" said the young diamond merchant cordially. "Don't often see you here, you poor, benighted bachelors!"

"Why this superiority?" Raffles asked. He snapped his fingers. "But of course! Time flies. Can it really be a whole year since you and Carolyn . . ."

"A whole year," Roy grinned. "Charles here remembered at once. Never forget an anniversary, do you, Charles? How the devil do you do it? You go to so many weddings."

"I know so many people," said Chastayne. "The perennial wedding guest but never the groom. It's the usual fate of the aging man-about-town."

"If Charles had all the money he's spent on wedding presents in his time," said Henge, "he'd be a rich man today, wouldn't you, Charles?"

Chastayne's eyeglass glittered rather coldly, and, indeed, I myself thought the remark tasteless.

Raffles, intervening in his easy way, asked, "How is Carolyn, Roy?"

"Wonderful!" replied the poor, enamored devil. "We're celebrating tonight—with Christine and old Toby, of course. We're going to the opera. Afterwards we're having a little party, just the four of us, in one of those private supper rooms at the Capoulade. We're all meeting in the foyer at Covent Garden."

He glanced at his watch.

"Carolyn's probably on her way in, now. Nuisance if this fog gets any worse. By the way, you haven't seen Toby, have you? He's popping in here for a minute before he goes home to put on a boiled shirt and collect Christine."

As we stood talking, I noticed that once or twice Roy put a hand lightly against his breast pocket. But for what Raffles had said in the hansom, I probably should not have noticed the trifling gesture.

As it was, it seemed to me positively to shout aloud the fact that on this night of fog, this perfect night for crime, the lively young diamond merchant indeed was carrying an anniversary gift for his young wife—a gift, undoubtedly, of diamonds.

"There's Toby," Roy said. "Excuse me."

He crossed to Toby Lucas, in the doorway, a burly fellow with a battered, cheerful face rubicund from the cold outside. Toby still wore his outdoor things; he carried a valise, and he greeted Roy with a broad grin, and the brothers-in-law crossed the hall and went upstairs together.

Henge and others drifted away to their engagements, leaving Raffles, Chastayne, and myself at the bar. As we talked, Raffles, I knew, was keeping an eye on the staircase visible through the doorway, watching for Roy Norcott to come down. I, too, kept an unobtrusive eye on the staircase.

After a few minutes, I saw Toby Lucas come down and stride across the hall to the street door. Roy Norcott did not appear. Raffles took out his watch, glanced at it.

"Time we had a bit of dinner, Bunny," he said.

We took our leave of the monocled Chastayne and, as we went upstairs, Raffles said, "Roy's probably in the dining room, but we'd better make sure."

Roy was in the dining room, sure enough.

We took a table but had not yet ordered dinner when Roy tossed down his napkin and, taking up a valise which stood beside his chair, went out, giving us a grin and a wave as he passed.

"We'll give him a minute to get downstairs and collect his outdoor things," Raffles said. "Incidentally, did you notice he had that valise Toby brought? I wonder why."

As we went downstairs, the room with the bar was empty. There was nobody else in the hall as we got our capes and opera hats, but as we went out on the steps we were just in time to see a hansom with Norcott in it go jingling off into the mist.

Luckily, another hansom was dropping a fare. As we took our seats, I was watchful for anyone else trailing along after the hansom ahead, but, during the whole of the journey, I saw nothing to arouse my suspicions.

A glimpse through the fog of vague figures humping sacks and carrying towers of round baskets on their heads, and a clinking of hooves on cobbles, told me that we had entered Covent Garden. Next moment, we pulled up in a crush of carriages under the misty radiance of the Opera House's innumerable gaslamps.

We hurried into the vast foyer. From the open doors to the auditorium came the bedlamite jangling of a large orchestra tuning up.

"There he is," Raffles said.

Following his glance, I felt an instant relief. Roy Norcott was in the act of depositing his hat and cape with the *vestiare*. He lifted his valise to the counter.

And suddenly Raffles's fingers clamped on my arm. I looked at him quickly and was astonished by his expression.

"What's the matter?" I asked.

"We've been unforgivably dull, Bunny!" Raffles said grimly. "Our plan was to stick close to Roy Norcott because he was carrying diamonds. But, dammit, he no longer is carrying them. Toby Lucas has them. We've been following the wrong man!"

I gaped at him. Before I could speak, he drew me sharply to one side. I saw that Roy was coming across the foyer. I thought he was making for us, but his delighted smile was for a girl who had just come in. She was Carolyn, safely arrived from Roehampton.

"Darling!" I heard her say, as Roy squeezed her hands. "But where are Christine and Toby?"

"They'll be along," Roy said. "Fog's delayed Toby, I expect."

"Or a blackjack," Raffles muttered, as the couple moved away. "Come on, Bunny!"

From the brilliance and perfumed warmth of the foyer, we plunged out again into the gloom and chill of the fog. Raffles seized on a stationary hansom, told the cabbie to make the best speed possible to Russell Square.

"That valise, Bunny!" he said, as the horse clattered off with us over the cobbles. "When we saw it had changed hands, we ought to have seen the whole story.

"What kind of surprise would diamonds be to a diamond merchant's wife? None! He went to his friend and brother-in-law Toby . . ."

"Toby?" I said.

"The fur importer," said Raffles. "Roy went to Toby for something choice in furs for Carolyn's anniversary present. And Toby—whose everyday business is furs—would he give his wife

Christine a nice fur as an anniversary surprise? Of course he wouldn't! What he did, quite obviously, was pick out from Roy's stock something choice in diamonds for Christine's anniversary present. And at the club tonight Toby gave Roy the valise with the fur in it, Roy gave Toby the diamonds."

"But, confound it," I said, "how could the Anniversary Thief, not knowing the chaps, possibly guess at this transaction between them?"

"I don't know," Raffles said. "All I know is that this criminal seems to go for jewels. Roy, who carried a fur, has reached the Opera House safely. Toby, who carried diamonds, has not turned up!"

The hatch above our heads opened.

"Russell Square, Guv," said the cabbie.

Raffles told the driver to wait and we made our way forward into the darkness.

Suddenly a stentorian roar of "Cab!" stopped us both in our tracks. A door of a house standing open made a misty oblong of light, against which were silhouetted two figures standing on the porch steps.

"I wish you wouldn't," I heard a girl's voice protesting anxiously. "It's so silly to go to the opera after what's happened, Toby. You ought to be lying down. I'm sure I ought to have sent for a doctor. You've got an enormous lump on your head. You're probably concussed."

"Cab!" roared Toby.

To the girl he said, "My head's been kicked repeatedly by rugger boots, Christine. It's been proved that it's impossible to concuss it. Don't worry, dear. I was knocked cold for a minute, but my head's all right, now—sound as a bell, except that I have to wear my opera hat on one side, because of the lump.

"What makes me boil is your present being pinched, prettiest thing in the whole of Roy's stock—diamond pendant, heart with an arrow through it. Ye gods, when I think of a dirty, sneaking, porch-skulking blackjacking footpad pinching a bloke's anniversary present for his wife. . . . But he's not going to spoil our party with Carolyn and Roy . . ."

Raffles drew me away. We returned quickly to the hansom at the corner, and Raffles, paying the cabbie, freed him to answer Toby's shouts.

"Now, what?" I said. "Your Anniversary Thief is no longer just hypothetical. He's struck, he's grabbed the swag, and he's vanished into the fog. There's no hope of finding him, now."

"I wonder," Raffles murmured.

He lighted a cigarette, inhaled thoughtfully.

"He was lying in wait for Toby. Therefore, he'd guessed somehow of the transaction between Toby and Roy.

"Bunny, I've been thinking about what you said in the hansom coming here. How did he guess—not knowing the chaps? Surely the simplest answer must be that he does know the chaps, knows them well."

My heart jumped. "What are you driving at now?"

"Suppose," Raffles said, "he doesn't just pick his victims from the Marriage Announcement columns of the newspapers. Suppose his information about them is a great deal more personal and detailed than that. Suppose that, in fact, he's a fellow who attends a good many weddings of chaps like Toby and Roy. You catch my drift?"

I stared at him under the wan nimbus of the streetlamp. I recalled the conversation in the club this evening. I felt a sudden, tingling excitement.

"I know what's in your mind," I said. "And it is possible . . ."

"Possible enough," he said, "to make a call on the chap. I know where he lives. Come on, we can walk it quicker than find a cab now. It's not far. He lives just off Bond Street—Oxford Street end. He has a flat."

It took us the best part of thirty minutes in the fog before we were standing on the pavement of a turning off Bond Street, peering up at a set of first-floor windows.

Raffles led the way into the entrance hall of the flats, and up tiled stairs to a tiled landing with a palm and gas jet.

Along to the left, where a second flight of stairs led upward, was a door with a polished nameplate and letter slot and a coir mat outside it. "That's his place," Raffles said.

He reached up, turned out the gas jet. I felt him drop on one knee on the mat, to push up the letter slot and peer through it. "All dark in there," he whispered, straightening up. "It's worth having a prowl round."

As he spoke, he was working on the door with the picklock he always carried. I heard scarcely a sound, yet in a few seconds he had the door open.

He drew me quickly inside, closed the door, relocked it with the picklock. Only then did he strike a match and hold it up.

I saw that we were in a small, well-furnished hall.

Before us, a door stood open. Raffles moved forward to it, holding up the match. Over his shoulder, I saw that the room was a large, comfortable sitting room. Moving forward, Raffles touched the last flicker of the match to one of a pair of gas globes above the mantelpiece. The mantle popped alight.

Raffles moved quickly from picture to picture, lifting each slightly to glance behind it. He found no safe. He paused, looked keenly about the room, then crossed to a tall bookcase to the left of the fireplace. The lower part of it had sliding wooden doors.

Raffles dropped on one knee, slid the doors open, chuckled quietly.

"Here we are, Bunny!"

Looking over his shoulder, I saw a squat, square safe. But suddenly he slid the doors shut and rose smoothly, putting a finger to his lips. We listened. Someone was coming up the tiled stairs—at the run.

Raffles reached up, turned out the gas. Then he thrust me behind the window curtains and followed me.

A key sounded in the lock of the hall door. I heard the door open, slam shut. Footsteps came into the room, a match scraped, a gas mantle popped.

Light showed through the gap at the edge of the curtains. I could see Raffles, on my left and nearer the gap, peering sidelong through it. I could see part of the bookcase to the left of the fireplace. I did not breathe.

I heard the doors which concealed the safe slide open with a bang, and I knew our man must be opening the safe.

Stealthily, Raffles reached upward with both hands. He took a double grip on the red chenille curtain. He waited, peering sideways through the gap at the curtain edge. Suddenly he gave a violent downward yank, ripping the curtain from its rings. He launched himself obliquely forward, falling, curtain and all, on top of the man kneeling at the safe.

Shrouded by the curtain, the man could not see us. Pinned by Raffles's weight, he struggled violently, but the folds of the curtain hampered him and muffled his shouts.

Raffles nodded me urgently toward the other curtain. He did not speak for fear that the man might recognize his voice. I divined Raffles's intention and, whipping up a dagger letter knife from the top of the bookcase, I plunged the knife into the curtain still hanging before the window.

Thankful for the fog shrouding the panes, I ripped the curtain downward, sawed off a strip. I made a slipknot in it, nosed it over the man's flailing ankles, jerked it tight.

I slashed two more strips from the curtain. Raffles slid them under the man, knotted them to pinion his arms. In a minute or so, he was thoroughly wrapped up and trussed in the curtain.

He went on struggling, rolling, squirming about on the carpet as Raffles rose and picked something from the floor, held it up for me to see.

His gray eyes danced.

The object that dangled by a slender chain from his finger was a heart-shaped diamond pendant transfixed by an arrow.

The door of the safe stood open. Squatting beside it, Raffles transferred a number of things to the pocket of his cape. He held up one of them for me to see. Rubies flashed hotly from a little gold bracelet, almost certainly Bill Foster's anniversary gift to his wife Kathy.

Raffles rose. He took a sheet of notepaper from a letter stand on the bookcase. With a pencil he scrawled a few words in capitals on the paper, held it up for me to see: From a Friend.

He tucked it with the diamond pendant into an envelope, flipped the gummed edge along his tongue tip, addressed the envelope to Mr. Toby Lucas, thrust it into his pocket.

Taking another sheet of notepaper, he scrawled again in capitals, and again held the paper up for me to see:

YOU HAVE 24 HOURS TO LEAVE THE COUNTRY. AT MID-NIGHT TOMORROW SCOTLAND YARD WILL BE IN-FORMED OF THE IDENTITY OF THE ANNIVERSARY THIEF—WITH EVIDENCE.

He put the paper into the empty safe. He winked at me, jerked his head at the door. We crossed to it, paused for a moment to look back at the trussed-up monstrosity which was grunting, writhing, bouncing, and heaving about strenuously all over the carpet, knocking over chairs and occasional tables in its indefatigable contortions.

Raffles closed the door on the strange spectacle.

He broke our prudent silence as we emerged into the fog and turned left toward Bond Street.

Chuckling, he said: "Getting himself untangled should keep him busy for half an hour or so, I think. Tomorrow we'll post Bill Foster's bracelet, with another 'From a Friend' note. Toby's pendant we'll deal with right away. The other items from the safe we shall have to think about at our leisure. I doubt whether much can be done about returning them to their rightful owners.

"Now, the opera must be pretty well over. We'll get along to the Capoulade. This sounds like a hansom jingling up now. Don't let the cabbie see your face, Bunny."

I understood this warning when, arriving at Henrietta Street, Raffles stopped the hansom at the corner, tipped the cabbie liberally, gave him the envelope addressed to Toby, and asked him to drop it in at the Capoulade.

The fog was dense along Henrietta Street and, as the hansom rolled off, we followed, walking quickly, keeping it in sight. A hundred yards along the street, it pulled up before the Capoulade.

The cabbie climbed down from his perch, stumped into the restaurant, reappeared, climbed to his perch again, and drove off.

"That's that," said Raffles. "Now for a well-earned supper, Bunny!"

Despite the fog, the Capoulade, a small but popular restaurant, was crowded but we were lucky enough to get a table. I felt lighthearted and, having missed my dinner, quite ravenous. Munching with gusto, I looked round at the animated scene—and a sudden rigor as of lockjaw seized upon me.

Across the room, I had caught the glitter of a monocle. I stared.

"What's the matter?" Raffles asked. I swallowed my mouthful with an effort.

"Chastayne!" I said.

Raffles glanced across at the man-about-town, who, with his usual air of dissipated distinction, was supping with a very pretty woman.

"What about him?" Raffles said.

"What about him?" I said. "That conversation at the club! About his being 'the perennial wedding guest, never the groom,' and about his being a rich man today if he had back all the money he's spent on wedding presents in his time! I thought . . ."

"You thought Chastayne was the man we left trussed up?" Raffles said.

He looked at me curiously.

"We knew that the method of the Anniversary Thief was to get ahead of his man, Bunny, and lie in wait for him.

"When I said he might well be a man who attended a lot of weddings, and who knew Roy and Toby intimately, I certainly thought it possible that he was someone who belonged to the club, and who was with us there tonight.

"But obviously he had to be someone who saw Toby arrive with the valise, saw him go upstairs with Roy, guessed what was going on between them, and therefore left the club before Toby did, so as to be lying in wait for him in his own porch.

"That couldn't possibly have been Chastayne, who stayed talking at the bar with us long after Toby had left.

"My dear old chap, the man who left the club at the right time to lie in wait for Toby, and who certainly attends far more weddings than Chastayne, is Philip Henge, of course—the bow-tied, velvet-jacketed, fashionable photographer with a flat over his shop just off Bond Street."

I finished my supper in a dream. I could not get over my curious misconception.

But toward one o'clock, a rather rewarding thing happened. Up on the gallery landing of the restaurant, the door of one of the private supper rooms opened. The four people who came out were the two pretty, dark-haired, blue-eyed sisters, Christine and Carolyn, and their husbands, Roy and Toby.

All four—including Toby, despite a visible lump on his head —seemed gay and excited. And I noticed that Carolyn, the young diamond merchant's wife, wore a beautiful fur, while there sparkled at the throat of Christine, the young furrier's wife, an exquisite diamond pendant in the shape of a heart transfixed by an arrow.

From the landing, the four caught sight of us. They waved happily.

Raffles rose to his feet, and I followed his example. Together, we raised our glasses to the radiant girls above us.

"Happy Anniversary!" called A. J. Raffles.

The Coffee Queen Affair

"And how are you, Adelphi Brown?" asked Raffles, in his amiable way.

We had dropped in at Coster John's Coffee Room in Fleet Street, hub of the London newspaper world, on a languid and thundery evening.

A hangout of journalists, Coster John's had a sanded floor and dark-paneled walls, and at the moment the girl we had dropped in to pass the time of day with had the place all to herself.

Russet-haired and twenty-one, she was behind the counter, watching the brassbound coffee roaster rotate in aromatic smoke over a blue flame.

She was the daughter of a journalist called Byron Brown, once pretty well known, who had departed this vale of fears and left behind him, as journalists were apt to do, nothing more substantial than a legend, so that Adelphi had had to fend for herself from the time she was seventeen.

"Why, Mr. Raffles and Mr. Manders!" she exclaimed. She was wearing a dress the hue of café-au-lait, with a frilled little cream-colored apron. Her eyes were brown, very candid, and warm. "I haven't seen you for ages!"

"We seldom get down here to the Street of Ink these days, Adelphi," said Raffles, "because our friend Bunny Manders here has to some extent deserted his old profession of journalism."

"I'm sorry to hear that, Mr. Manders," she said, looking at me with reproach.

I felt myself color, for I knew how loyal she was to the profession I had pretty well abandoned in order to live on my wits —or, rather, on those of A. J. Raffles.

"Tell us," he said, as Adelphi began to prepare our coffee in a small copper jug with a long handle, "how are things going with you, Adelphi?"

"You always ask me that in such an earnest way," she said, smiling. "Things are going fine with me, thank you. I do well. Everybody in Fleet Street comes here."

"Because of you," Raffles said.

"Because they respected my father," she corrected. "Now, drink your coffee while it's hot. Here comes some custom."

A couple of journalists walked in. Things had been pretty quiet in the news line of late, and they were putting their heads together about the chances of pumping up some recent jewel robberies—nothing to do with Raffles and myself, unfortunately—into a pained outcry against police laxness.

We yielded the small counter to these conspiratorial newcomers, carried our coffee to a table. Raffles offered me his cigarette case and, as we lighted Sullivans, his gray eyes studied Adelphi Brown.

"You know, Bunny," he said slowly, "if I were enough of a scoundrel to ask a girl to marry such a scoundrel as me, I think I'd long ago have . . ."

He shrugged slightly.

"Oh, well," he said, "it'll be a very lucky man who gets Adelphi Brown. She's the most beautiful, lovable, talented girl currently dispensing coffee in the whole length and breadth of London."

"Oh, come, Raffles," a voice said, "that's a pretty steep claim."

We looked up. A third man who had come in paused at our table. Tall, thirtyish, he was an actor called Alphonse Bird. He had a profile that had been a good deal murmured about by theatergoing ladies, and he carried it as though fully conscious of its fatal elegance.

"Have you seen Prudence Bailey," he demanded, "at the Baghdad Coffee Divan?"

"Never been in the place," Raffles said. "Nevertheless"—he snapped his fingers—"so much for Prudence Bailey."

"I defy you to snap your fingers," the actor said hotly, "once you've seen Prudence."

"Done," Raffles said. "Allow us to drink our coffee in relative peace, and take leave of Adelphi, then we'll come with you to your Baghdad shambles."

In a four-wheeler, the three of us rode through the increasingly oppressive night to Leicester Square.

The Baghdad Coffee Divan was on the ground floor of a building across from the gas-flaring Byzantine splendor of the Alhambra Music Hall. Heavily carpeted and lighted from niches in which stood lamps of the kind neglected by the five foolish virgins, the Baghdad was not my style of coffee house. We had to crouch on tooled leather objects, so-called pouffes, at round, brass-topped tables about a foot high.

"Here she comes," Bird said, arranging his profile to the best effect.

The girl approaching us wore a kind of vaguely oriental costume which, I was obliged to admit to myself, charmingly became her. She was dark-eyed, indisputably lovely, but her tone to Alphonse Bird was distant, even cold, as though she shared my own lack of enthusiasm for the man.

"Good evening, Mr. Bird," she said. "Turkish coffee?"

"Prudence," Bird said reproachfully, "please smile for my friends. Do, Prue!" To my embarrassment, he threw a disgusting, actorish throb into his voice. "Oh, Prue, do! Just to oblige."

She gave Raffles and myself a delightful smile, from which, however, she very justifiably excluded Alphonse. But the actor looked at us complacently as she went off.

"Well?" he said. "There goes the girl whom *I* maintain to be the most beautiful, lovable, talented girl currently dispensing coffee anywhere in London. Raffles, I defy you to snap your fingers at her."

"Nothing could induce me to do so," Raffles said. "But you must grant—"

"What's the pow-wow?" a voice interrupted. "May I intrude?"

The man who joined us was about forty. He wore evening dress and a monocle, and had an air of slightly dissipated distinction. His name was Charles Chastayne.

"My dear fellows," he said, on hearing the subject of the argument, "beyond doubt the most charming girl currently dispensing coffee in London is Mayday Pennington, at the Ottoman Coffee Oasis, upstairs in Glasshouse Street. Look here, we'll just pop round there and settle the whole controversy."

In a four-wheeler, the four of us rode to Glasshouse Street.

From a sunken basin in the center of a tiled floor strewn with rugs, at the Ottoman Coffee Oasis, rose the silvery plume of a small fountain. The place, murmurous with conversation and the rustle of falling water, and set about with potted palms, was cool and lulling.

Chastayne led us to a group of small ottomans arranged about a corner table of Lebanon cedar.

"Here she is," he said, as we sat down, and he caused his monocle to glimmer benignly at the girl who approached with a slight jingling of the bangles on her slender wrists. "Good evening, Mayday," he said. "Sultry evening, isn't it?"

"Yes, I think there's thunder in the air, Mr. Chastayne," she said.

She was a glorious, violet-eyed girl, in attire discreetly suggestive of the harnus of the East, and she looked from one to the other of us with a shy smile. "Egyptian coffee?" she asked.

"Thank you very, very much, Mayday," said Chastayne, and, as she left us, he turned his monocle on us with a glitter of satisfaction. "There, now," he said, "you must concede that that settles the argument."

"By no means," Bird said. "I still maintain that Prudence—"

"Hallo, chaps," a voice boomed. "Having an argument? What's it all about?"

A stocky, exuberant fellow in the middle twenties came leaping and bounding across the rugs to us. He went in for yachting, and had a round face whipped fiery red by exposure to gales, and a foghorn of a voice, which possibly was the reason why he was known to his friends as "Masthead" Maloney.

Told of our difference of opinion, he bellowed with derision.

"Point is," he thundered, "you none of you know what you're talking about. Now, look. Behind the Persian Baths in Jermyn Street, there's a place called the Bosporus Coffee Arcade. There's a girl there who . . . But why talk? Let's grab a growler and you can see Fleur Francis for yourselves."

Unfortunately, utterly bewitching as Fleur Francis proved to be on our arrival at the Bosporus Coffee Arcade, we all continued to cleave to our own opinions. Over coffee, the dispute got pretty heated. Suddenly I noticed that a keen look had come into Raffles's eyes.

"Would you chaps," he said, "care to back your opinions?"

All instantly expressed their eagerness to back their opinions up to fifty pounds.

"But what's the use of talking?" Chastayne said. "In a case like this, it'd be virtually impossible to find an impartial adjudicator."

"How about an outsider—strictly neutral?" said Raffles. "An American for instance?"

We stared at him in sudden silence.

"There's a suitable American in London at the moment," Raffles said. "Young chap. Been cutting quite a social swathe. Designing mammas are fluttered. There have been newspaper paragraphs about him."

"That's right," Chastayne said. "Lee Jordan. College man, but must be a bit odd, as he carries everywhere on his travels a safe that's said to hold his worldly wealth—a bale of bearer bonds, or something of the kind, as big as a haystack."

I felt the pulse throb suddenly in my temples. I guessed instantly that Raffles had been seeking some way to make the acquaintance of the American with the safe, and had spotted in the present controversy a plausible pretext to approach the man.

In a four-wheeler, the five of us were borne at a brisk clip-clop and jingle, under an ominous rumble of thunder, to Half Moon Street, where the American was known to have established himself in service chambers.

"Kindly inform Mr. Jordan," Raffles said to the porter of the chambers, "that a deputation representing the English theater, journalism, and sport, waits on him to beg his adjudication upon a piquant controversy."

The porter repeated the message carefully, and left us. Returning, he said that Mr. Jordan would be happy to receive the deputation, and led the way upstairs.

The instant we filed behind Raffles into a cream-paneled sitting room with red-shaded wall candles, I spotted the safe. Square, quite small, and partially covered by a poncho or some such thing, it stood in a corner.

On the walls of the room, a number of pennants were tacked

up, apparently college trophies. Jordan himself was seated at a piano, which he was playing rather dreamily.

He rose at our entrance. He looked about twenty-three, which was four years younger than Raffles, and a year younger than myself. Wearing a silk dressing gown over evening dress, he was tall, loose-limbed, with a tanned, agreeable face, almost platinum hair, and dreamy blue eyes. He received us in a vague but civil way and, begging us to be seated, gave us a very good brandy indeed.

Raffles explained the purpose of our visit.

Seated on the piano stool, his well-kept hands clasped lightly about one shin, the young American listened with a faraway expression. Then, swiveling gently on the revolving stool, he played a few bars of some haunting Mississippi air, and rose to replenish our snifters.

"I'm flattered and charmed, gentlemen," he said, in a lazy, attractive voice, "that you should have chosen me to adjudicate on the unusual and interesting point you seem to have at issue here. You can rely on me for a conscientious, impersonal judgment. Now, it seems some careful research will be called for, and you won't expect me to come right up with an answer. I'd need, if I'm to get my teeth into the subject, say, a couple of weeks?"

"Excellent," Raffles said. "In that case, I invite the present company to a bachelor dinner, at my place, on the night of—next Saturday week. Mr. Jordan will then announce the name of Adelphi Brown, Prudence Bailey, Mayday Pennington, or Fleur Francis, as that of—in his judgment—the most beautiful, lovable, talented girl currently dispensing coffee in London. To the champion of the girl chosen by Mr. Jordan—let's call her the Coffee Queen —the others will each pay the sum of fifty pounds."

This understood, we all shook the American warmly by the hand, and adjourned the proceedings.

I fully intended to have a private word with Raffles, to veto —on the grounds of Jordan's youth and his accommodating attitude—any designs against the safe. But when we got outside, the storm was breaking. Thunder was detonating overhead and the first fat raindrops were splashing down.

To escape the imminent deluge, we all made a dash in our various directions, Raffles to The Albany, where he had his bachelor chambers, I to my flat in Mount Street, Bird and Chastayne and Maloney to wherever they severally pigged it.

Raffles went north next day, to play cricket against Warwickshire, then Yorkshire, and it was not until Tuesday morning of the following week that I saw him again.

Tanned, silk-hatted, a pearl in his cravat, he turned up at my flat as I was shaving.

"A gorgeous morning, Bunny," he said. "I've come to rout you out for breakfast."

The best breakfast in London was to be had at a certain hotel overlooking Kensington Gardens. Often, on summer mornings when he had no cricket on, Raffles thus would co-opt me for a walk through the park and breakfast at expansive leisure.

Today was heavenly, the trees in full leaf, the flowerbeds blazing in the sunshine. We were strolling along by the Serpentine admiring the swans, when a voice hailed us from Rotten Row, the riding track. We saw Lee Jordan dismounting there from a big bay horse. We walked across the sanded track to him. He was very well turned out for riding, but his dreamy charm seemed marred by an air of worry.

"Say, fellows," he remarked, after a word or two of greeting, "I guess you didn't realize what kind of a poser you were wishing on me. I've been devoting all my time to it. I've had the very real privilege of escorting each of the young ladies on her day off. And if you figure it was a cinch, persuading them to come out with me —why, you just don't know them. It was worth coming three thousand miles to get acquainted with any one of those girls, just by herself. But *four* of them . . ."

I was startled, and rather touched, by the dreamy, troubled way in which he went on to speak of the girls. He had taken

Adelphi to the Tower of London, Prudence to see the sculptures in the British Museum, Mayday to admire the dappled deer in Richmond Park, Fleur on a diverting steamer trip to Margate.

"Man alive," Raffles said, looking at him keenly, "you talk of them as though you're half in love with them."

"Half?" Lee Jordan said. "I'm sure as hell in love. But with which one? I'm taking Adelphi out again tonight, but—I don't know. Which one am I in love with? I've never felt this way before."

He gazed out vaguely over the Serpentine, and shook his head.

"You fellows certainly wished a poser on me," he said. "I'm in trouble, but please don't feel badly. It's just Fate, I guess."

He swung back into the saddle, and we stood watching him ride away dreamily in the flicker of sun and shade under the trees. We looked at each other.

"What the devil d'you make of that?" Raffles said, frowning. "He *is* in trouble, no mistake, and there's no denying it's my doing." We walked on thoughtfully toward breakfast. "Damnation, Bunny," Raffles said, after a while, "assuming his intentions to be honorable, which we've no reason to doubt, suppose he goes and proposes to the wrong girl, what then?"

"How d'you mean?" I said.

"If it were Adelphi," he said, "well and good. We know all about her, and any man who got her would be an enviable man, I don't care who he is or where he comes from. But in all conscience, what do we know about the other three? I freely admit that what stimulated my own interest in Lee Jordan is his wealth, his safe full of bearer bonds or whatever it is. Now, I can't help wondering: how far may Jordan's money have inspired the evident responsiveness to him of Prudence, Mayday, and Fleur?"

"Oh, I don't know," I said uneasily. "I'd say he was pretty attractive to women, money or no money."

"No doubt," Raffles said. "But the thing is, Bunny, for all his air of dreamy worldliness, his extreme youth keeps showing. Dammit, he's not long out of college, and he's in an unfamiliar country. He's in love—perhaps in love with love—and he's frighteningly vulnerable.

"I wish all four girls well, but there's no denying it's my doing that he met them. If he marries one of them, then the least I can do is to ensure, if possible, that it's one who loves him honestly. I can see only one way to ensure that, and that's by setting the girls a simple test of sincerity."

"But how?" I said, mystified.

"He's going out with Adelphi tonight," Raffles said. "It's my chance. Tonight, I'm going to clean out that safe in which he's reputed to carry his worldly wealth, and Lee Jordan will then see which of the girls stands by him when it becomes known, through the police and the newspapers, that he's no longer the rich young American, but flat broke."

He chuckled.

"Don't look at me in that horrified way," he said. "This is one of those instances, Bunny, which enable us to maintain to ourselves, in moments of self-examination, that at least our status in crime is still amateur. This is a crib to be cracked for an altruistic motive. The swag will be returned to Jordan anonymously, intact —no matter how keen our sense of deprivation—as soon as it has served its purpose. Come, now. Let's breakfast. I've things to get moving."

He was in the liveliest spirits. For myself, I was in a fever of funk when I stepped, that evening, from a neat brougham that jingled to a momentary standstill halfway along Constitution Hill. The brougham belonged to Ivor Kern, the receiver we did business with, who had an antique shop in King's Road, Chelsea.

I slipped unobtrusively into Green Park. The summer twilight was deepening to purple. Soon the park gates would close. I was dressed as a valet off duty for an hour to take the air. With a boiled shirt, striped waistcoat, braided trousers, I wore a tweed jacket and bowler hat. Round my waist, under the jacket, was wound a valet's swallowtail coat, and my face and hair had been touched up a bit by Kern.

I sauntered across the grassy knolls of St. James's Park toward the lights shining out from the windows of the clubs along Piccadilly. Of two of the clubs I was myself a member. Never had Raffles and I worked so close to our own doorsteps. I did not like it.

As I neared the rendezvous, which was the great gateway just across from Half Moon Street, a shadow detached itself from a tree trunk and fell in with me.

"All clear," Raffles murmured. He was dressed much as I was. "Jordan went out about six. As I learned this morning, the porter of the chambers locks the outer door about this time and goes to a tavern in Shepherd Market for a bite and a beer. I saw him go out a few minutes ago. It should be plain sailing, Bunny."

Two menservants at ease, we crossed Piccadilly, clip-clopping with theaterbound cabs, and strolled along Half Moon Street to the house where Jordan had his chambers. With a quick glance each way, Raffles poked up the vertical letter slot for a look into the hall, then unlocked the door with a skeleton key.

We slipped inside. Raffles closed the door, led the way up the stairs to the first floor. There was a feeling of people being in the house, but along the carpeted corridor all the doors were closed.

"Right," said Raffles. "Keep watch, Bunny. I'll try not to be long."

At the angle of the staircases stood a pedestal bearing a bust of Seneca. I hid my jacket and bowler behind the pedestal, slipped on the swallowtail coat.

Along the corridor, Raffles already had dealt with the lock of Jordan's quarters and vanished within.

My heart pumping slow and heavy, I lighted a cigarette with unsteady fingers. Loitering like a valet who had stepped out of his master's room for a hasty puff, I peered now along the corridor, now up the stairs to the floor above, now down into the hall toward the front door. All the gaslights were turned low, and a clock in the hall ticked in an uncanny way, now fast, now slow, as though talking to itself.

From the floor above sounded an intermittent booming, which I seemed to know yet could not identify. Interminably, the clock ticked. I crushed out my cigarette nervously on the brow of Seneca, pocketed the end, lighted another.

I sweated. I cursed Raffles for the time he was taking and for all his quixotic works, his very existence.

I started violently as a door slammed, above. Footsteps came thundering down the stairs. Looking up, I glimpsed in the dim light a round, youthful, but fiery red face.

My blood froze. It was Masthead Maloney. The booming I had heard was his resonant voice; he must have been visiting residents in the building. As he bounded down at me, I bowed almost double.

"Evening, my man," he boomed, in his hyperthyroid way.

He went leaping on down the stairs. The street door below closed behind him with a slam that rattled every window in the house.

I felt a touch on my arm. Wringing wet, I spun round. It was Raffles. He grinned, patting his jacket, under which he was hugging something.

"I've got the swag," he said. "Off you go. I'll give you one minute, then follow. See you at Kern's place."

I whipped off the swallowtail coat, tied it round my waist, grabbed from behind the pedestal the jacket and bowler, and, donning them as I went, ran down the stairs. I opened the front door a crack, for a look along the street, then slipped out into the night.

Half an hour later I was safely at Ivor Kern's place drinking a stiff whisky with him in his cluttered sitting room over the antique shop, when Raffles walked in.

He tossed on to the table a black leather satchel secured by a thin brass rod with a small padlock, also brass, at each end.

"That's all there was in the safe," he said. "Bearer bonds, presumably. Seems a rather slim satchel to require a safe to be carried about in. However, Ivor, hold this intact for us. It'll go back, unopened, to Lee Jordan when it has served its purpose."

I still felt uneasy. Of all Raffles's crimes, it was precisely those which he called "amateur," repercussing as they did on human character, which I most misdoubted and feared.

There was nothing in the papers the next day, nothing the following day, Thursday. Friday was the opening day of a match against Somerset, at Lord's Cricket Grounds, and Raffles was playing. I did not go there as we always avoided each other for a few days after pulling a job.

There still was nothing in the papers about the Half Moon Street robbery, and I went to bed with the feeling that some unseen net was closing stealthily, inescapably about me.

Scarcely, it seemed, had I closed my eyes than I was jerked awake by the jangling of my doorbell. I ran into the hall, pulling on my dressing gown, my hair on end.

The bell was leaping up and down frenziedly on its spring. Tremors went through me, uncontrollably. My breath held, I opened the door a crack. On the landing stood Lee Jordan and A. J. Raffles.

"Morning, Bunny," Raffles said, as they came in. "We're wanted."

"Wanted?" My dry lips shaped the word, but no sound came from them.

"Wanted as witnesses," Raffles said, "of the marriage of Adelphi Brown and Lee Jordan at Holborn Registry Office, at eleven-thirty this morning."

I could only stare.

"Lee has to return to the United States urgently," Raffles said, "so he was able to get a special license. He only remembered this morning about witnesses, so he came round to The Albany to rope me in, and we've come to co-opt you."

He took out his half-hunter.

"It's now quarter to nine. Luckily, Somerset are batting today, so I've sent word to Lord's that a substitute must field for me. Now, we've got to do this marriage as right, Bunny, as the hurried circumstances allow. Lee and Adelphi are sailing in the *Teutonic,* boat train leaving at one-thirty.

"Now, then! I shall collect Adelphi and get her to the Registry Office at eleven-thirty. You, Bunny, will stand by Lee and get him braced up and on muster. Right? Good. I'm giving a wedding breakfast for them, at The Albany. So I'm off, now, to see my wine merchant."

I shook hands with Lee and congratulated him. To my surprise, Raffles shook hands with me. I felt a square of paper pressed into my palm. The instant I had closed the door on them, I read the penciled message:

> This makes nonsense of our plan, Bunny. Get round to Half Moon Street quickly. I judge that Lee's had no occasion to open his safe, so *doesn't yet dream* that the satchel's gone. I've got to put it back. Give me time to get to Kern's, collect satchel, return to Half Moon Street. Then, on some pretext, get Lee out of his chambers for *at least fifteen minutes.* I'll be on the watch.

I burned the paper, dressed hastily in wedding finery, and, stopping only to buy a carnation for my lapel, rushed round on foot to Half Moon Street.

Lee's dreaminess had quite fallen from him. He was pacing restlessly up and down. Clothes were scattered all over his sitting room, portmanteaus gaped open.

"I'm not good enough for her," he was muttering. He looked at me in a kind of agony. "I'm telling you, Manders, I'm a no-good son-of-a-gun."

"Now, now," I said, "every bridegroom feels that. Brace up!" Somehow, I got him packed and dressed. All the time, I had one eye on the clock, estimating Raffles's movements, and simultaneously was racking my brains for some pretext—since it was far too early as yet to leave for the Registry Office—to get Lee out of his chambers for fifteen minutes.

The perfect pretext occurred to me as I stepped back for a critical survey of his morning dress. He was wearing a waistcoat of New York cut. I let my glance dwell on it subtly, as though conscious of doubt and despondency about the garment.

"Lee," I said impulsively, "I want to give you a little wedding present. My haberdasher is in Sackville Street, a stone's throw away. No, no, I won't hear a word. Here's your hat."

It took us five minutes to walk to Sackville Street, ten to pick out a decent pearl-gray waistcoat for him, five to walk back. This was five minutes more than Raffles had asked for. Feeling pretty pleased with myself, I was totally unprepared for the sight that met my eyes when Lee and I entered the hall of the chambers.

A uniformed constable was standing there, and two plainclothesmen whom I know by sight as Inspector Kortright and Sergeant Ellis were talking to the porter. I was certain, instantly, that Raffles had been taken. My feet turned to ice. But when the porter murmured something to Kortright, and that big, grim man came toward us, it was Lee whom he addressed.

"Mr. Lee M. Jordan?" he said. "I have to inform you, Mr. Jordan, that I am here to execute a search warrant upon you. We will adjourn to your quarters, please."

I was so taken aback by this that I blurted, "Surely there must be some mistake? Mr. Jordan is getting *married* at eleven-thirty!"

"Your name, sir?" Kortright said to me coldly. And when a note had been taken of it, he said significantly, "I think you'd better come along, too, Mr. Manders."

I felt as though in a trance as we all went upstairs to Lee's sitting room.

"Leaving England, Mr. Jordan?" said Kortright, surveying the packed luggage.

"By the one-thirty boat train for the *Teutonic,*" Lee said. "See here, Inspector, what's going on here?"

"Ever hear of the Knickerbocker Kid, Mr. Jordan?" Kortright said, with a kind of frosty geniality. "No? You surprise me, sir. Because an information has been laid, to the effect that Mr. Lee M. Jordan, temporarily of Half Moon Street, is known to the New York underworld as a jewel thief called the Knickerbocker Kid."

I stood stunned.

"The dogs," Lee Jordan said softly. "Why, those cute dogs!"

He strolled over to the piano and, sitting down on the stool, played a few dreamy arpeggios. Then he swiveled on the stool and linked his hands lightly about one shin. "I came over in the *Cunarder* with some fellows I was in college with, Inspector." He nodded at the pennants which, in the rush of packing, he had omitted to take down from the wall. "We kidded around a whole lot—practical jokes—you know the way it is on a voyage. I guess the score came out on my side, and some of them allowed they aimed to even with me before we all sailed for home." He smiled with dreamy amusement. "This 'information,' now—I take it that it was anonymous?"

"That's as may be," Kortright said.

He looked from the platinum-haired, dreamy young man at the piano to the college pennants on the wall, and he seemed a bit shaken.

"At all events," he said, "in recent weeks we've had a crop of jewel robberies, much played up in the newspapers. Hence this search warrant."

"Go right ahead," said Lee Jordan. He tossed his key ring to Kortright, and smiled. "The Knickerbocker Kid," he murmured, amused. "Why, those cute dogs!"

He turned back to the piano and, still smiling, immersed

himself in the plaintive melodies of the Mississippi delta.

I could not take my eyes from him as the search went on all around me.

"I'm a no-good son-of-a-gun," he had said to me.

What had he meant?

My mind was racing. Suppose he were a jewel thief, suppose his black satchel had contained swag and he knew that the satchel had been taken from his safe, then the poor young devil's present dreamy imperturbability was based on an illusion, for he could not know that I had lured him to the haberdasher's in order to give Raffles a chance to put the satchel *back* into the safe.

Having gone through the luggage, and requested Jordan to move so that they could go over the piano and stool with probes like long knitting needles, Kortright finally brought up the matter I had been dreading.

"This safe here, Mr. Jordan," Kortright said. "I understand it accompanies you on your travels."

"Why, no," Lee said, in his vague way. "I'm all through with it now."

"Open it please," said Kortright.

"Sure," said Lee.

A nightmare inhibition clamped me rigid as, dropping on one knee before the safe, the platinum-haired youth turned the cylinder of the combination back and forth, depressed the lever, and with dreamy confidence pulled open the heavy door.

The safe was empty.

"I reckon," Lee said, "that leaves just my own person."

"Mine too," I croaked, in a voice like a stranger's. "I insist on being searched."

They drew blank with the pair of us, and Kortright took it hard.

"So you're sailing on the *Teutonic* today, Mr. Jordan," he said. "I think you're very, very wise."

With this nasty remark, the unwelcome visitors grudgingly withdrew, and I exclaimed, "Ye gods, look at the time, Lee! We'll be late at the Registry Office."

In the hansom, we said hardly a word. I was wondering what in the world had happened to Raffles and the mysterious black satchel. Toward the dreamy fellow at my side, I felt the constraint imposed by a great enigma: Was he or was he not the Knicker-bocker Kid?

The hansom jingled to a standstill in Gower Street, before the red-brick building of Holborn Registry Office. Window boxes filled with tulips were festive in the sunshine.

I told the cabbie to wait, and with Lee I mounted the steps and passed through glass-paned swing doors into a large, dim hall. A clock there ticked with a hollow, fateful sound. It was two minutes to eleven-thirty. A clerkly man glided up to us, pinching on eyeglasses to consult a paper in his hand.

"Mr. Lee M. Jordan?" he murmured. "Quite so. Special license, I perceive. The Registrar will be ready for you in a few minutes. The lady—h'm, Miss Adelphi Brown—will be here on time, I trust. Be seated, please."

He glided away. Lee Jordan ran a finger round inside his collar. I mopped the palms of my hands. The clock chimed two mellow, throbbing notes. Before the sound had died away in the hush, a hansom jingled to a standstill outside.

Raffles alighted from the hansom. I expected to see him turn to help Adelphi down, but he did not. He was alone. He removed his silk hat as he strode into the hall. His keen face was impassive.

The clerkly man came gliding up. "The lady . . . ?"

"Kindly show us to a room," Raffles said, "where we can talk privately."

Shaking his head worriedly, the clerkly man showed us into a gloomy, shelf-lined room, closed the door on us. Raffles took a Sullivan from his cigarette case, looking with gray, hard eyes at Lee Jordan.

"I am an investigator," Raffles said, "for an insurance company. I have methods of my own, to which the police here find it in their interest to turn a blind eye."

So icily convincing was his tone that I almost believed him myself.

"My attention was drawn to you, Jordan," he went on, "in connection with some recent jewel robberies. I utilized the controversy over the Coffee Queen as a means of making your acquaintance and verifying the existence of your safe. On Tuesday night, when you were out with Adelphi Brown, I cracked that safe and removed the satchel it contained."

All Lee Jordan's dreaminess had fallen from him. He had turned haggard.

"No need to tell you," Raffles said, "what I found in the satchel. Stolen jewelry, wadded in cotton wool. In return for the latitude the police grant me, it was my bounden duty to expose you to them."

"*You* did it?" Jordan muttered. "I wondered who the hell . . ."

"If someone denounced you to the police," Raffles said, "it wasn't me. I held my tongue, Jordan—for one reason only. That reason was Adelphi Brown. Because of her, because of the feeling I have for her, I intend to know, first, if Lee M. Jordan is your real name. I want the truth, and intend to have it."

"It's my real name," Jordan said, "I swear it." He was in torment. "Adelphi," he said. "I knew I ought never to have . . ."

"Second," Raffles said, "what was the idea of traveling around with that safe?"

"It was a stunt I thought up," Lee said. "I knew no one in London. I figured the 'rich young American' who traveled with a safe would be good for paragraphs, attract people to me. Designing mammas—that kind—marks. The safe worked fine, though it was as empty as a last year's pumpkin."

"Indeed," Raffles said dryly. He had been attracted by the safe himself. "It wasn't empty on Tuesday night, Jordan. How was that?"

"I must have been out of my mind," Lee said. "Sure, I knew that safe might attract crooks as well as marks, so naturally I didn't keep my swag in it. But that Tuesday, right after meeting you fellows in the Park, I decided my best bet was to get out of England.

"Just talking to you made me realize, somehow, how mighty tangled up I was over those four girls, and I figured the only thing was to run out on 'em. So I collected the swag from where I had it cached.

"But, come right down to it, I couldn't bring myself to break my date with Adelphi that evening. Just *had* to see her once more! So there I was, I had that satchel of stuff on my hands and no place to put it. So I thought, hell, it'd be okay in the safe, just for the few hours I'd be out. But . . ."

"But it wasn't," Raffles said, even more dryly. "You returned to your chambers to find the satchel gone. Surely, not knowing what repercussions might follow, your instinct must have been to bolt instantly. Why didn't you?"

"I was hamstrung," Lee Jordan said miserably. "That evening with Adelphi—that threw me, that settled it. When I found the satchel gone, I knew I ought to run like a jack rabbit, but I couldn't run without her. I ran *to* her. I ran right around to Coster John's Coffee Room next morning. I swear to you, I meant to tell her the truth about myself and give her my solemn oath that, if she'd have me and come with me, I'd go straight as a gun barrel from then on. But when she looked at me with those brown eyes of hers, as honest as the day . . . Goddamn, I couldn't tell her! I'm a no-good son-of-a-gun. I just took her in my arms."

There was not a sound in the room. Raffles was watching Lee Jordan. Wretchedly, I was remembering what Raffles had said to me about Adelphi: "If I were enough of a scoundrel to ask a girl to marry such a scoundrel as me . . ."

I could not conceive what was going on in his mind. I looked at the floor.

"Jordan," Raffles said slowly, "knowing your incriminating satchel had been taken, it needed a lot of courage for you to stay in London these past few days, the statutory time required by your marriage license—a great deal of courage.

"Now, I *could* see that that stolen property stuff gets to the insurance companies with no questions asked. But in matters of the heart, no man living has the last word. It's always with the woman.

"Jordan, Adelphi is in the hansom outside. She knows nothing whatever of what's happened. Now, you can take your choice. You can go out to her now and tell her the truth about yourself, in which case what follows will be up to Adelphi. Or you can walk away, and sail on the *Teutonic*—alone."

The two crooks looked at each other for a moment, then Lee Jordan said, "Okay."

He turned and walked from the room.

"Bunny," Raffles said to me, quietly, "I saw you get him out of the chambers. I was watching from a porch, along Half Moon Street. I waited a minute or two, then was just going along to hocus my way in past the porter when the police turned up.

"I strolled past the front door. It was open. I paused to light a cigarette. I heard them questioning the porter about Lee Jordan. I walked straight on round to The Albany, picked the padlocks of the satchel, found jewelry in it, and recognized some pieces that an insurance company had described in advertisements. It told me the whole story."

"He's called the Knickerbocker Kid," I whispered.

"Whatever he's called," Raffles said, "let's see what's happening."

We went into the hall.

Outside the glass-paned doors, Lee Jordan was standing hesitant on the steps. The hansom was not drawn up directly before the steps. Adelphi could not have seen him, any more than he could see her. He could walk away if he chose. He went down the steps. Again he hesitated. Then, very slowly, like a man drawn by something stronger than himself, he walked along and mounted into the hansom.

Raffles walked across the hall, pushed open the swing door, beckoned to the cabbie. The man climbed down from his box, came up the steps to us. Raffles gave him half a sovereign.

"They need a few minutes alone," he said. "They've something to discuss."

The cabbie nodded understandingly. "I've seen many a couple in two minds on this here doorstep," he said. "It's a big step, sir —marriage."

"A very big step," Raffles said.

But only he and I knew how big was the step that faced Adelphi Brown.

The clerkly man glided up to us.

"Gentlemen, is there some hitch?" he said, troubled. "The Registrar has already been waiting for some minutes."

"Our compliments to the Registrar," Raffles said, "and we beg his indulgence for a few minutes more. We shall be ready then— or never."

The clerkly man glided away unhappily. Steadily, in the silence, the clock ticked. Raffles looked at the cigarette in his hand. He put the cigarette carefully back into his case.

In the sunshine outside, the hansom stood motionless. Now and then, the harness jingled as the horse stamped.

At last, I saw Lee step out of the hansom. He turned. He gave a hand to Adelphi. Her dress was the hue of café-au-lait and had lace on it. She wore a little round straw hat of the same color, and she carried a small bouquet.

Raffles and I held open the doors for them. They seemed not to see us as they walked past, holding hands very tightly. They seemed not to see anything at all, but I knew that never as long as

I lived should I forget the look in the eyes of Adelphi Brown.

So Raffles, who had not spoken for her because he was a crook, stood witness for her marriage to a crook. I could not guess what irony he might be feeling. There it was, for better or for worse, as the Registrar read out.

I kissed the bride, and she turned to Raffles, and I knew that he kissed her, too, but I did not want to see that and I busied myself signing the book. We followed Adelphi and Lee out into the sunshine.

All Gower Street seemed suddenly to have become jammed with hansoms. More came up with a clip-clop and jingle even as we stared. Fleet Street had got the word, as it usually did.

Out of the hansoms came tumbling what seemed to me most of the journalists in London. They had come to see old Byron Brown's girl, Adelphi, of Coster John's Coffee Room, off on her honeymoon.

Amid the tumult, I saw Raffles take an envelope from his pocket, whisper to Lee. I saw Lee's sudden grin, quite undreamy. He scribbled on the envelope, Raffles returned it to his pocket without looking at it, and Adelphi and Lee ran the gauntlet of cheers and rice showers.

Lee helped Adelphi into the hansom, and Raffles, stepping forward, called, "The wedding breakfast's at The Albany. Gentlemen of the press are welcome."

"Good on you, Raffles!" yelled an Australian cricket correspondent.

In the hansom in which I had come with Lee, Raffles and I were first away after the one carrying the nuptial couple.

"Raffles," I said, as we jingled briskly across Cambridge Circus in the sunshine, "the swag of the ex-Knickerbocker Kid will, I trust, be duly, if anonymously, delivered to the interested insurance companies?"

A glance at his face reassured me. But, after a while, another thought occurred to me, and I leaned from the hansom to look back at the long line of other hansoms jingling along behind us up the whole length of Shaftesbury Avenue.

"All the same," I said, "entertaining this lot is going to cost us a pretty penny. It's just as well we shall win our bet from Bird, Chastayne, and Masthead Maloney."

"Just as well," Raffles said dryly. "Especially as, not knowing how Lee is placed for ready money, and not wanting him to fall into temptation before Adelphi's influence is fully established, I slid a couple of fifty-quid notes into his pocket."

He took out an envelope.

"Now, about that bet, Bunny—I reminded Lee to render his formal judgment. I have it here."

He unfolded the envelope. For some seconds he sat looking at it, his face impassive, then handed the envelope to me.

I read the penciled scrawl: "I hereby adjudge London's Coffee Queen to be Miss Prudence Bailey of the Baghdad Coffee Divan, Leicester Square. Lee M. J. Jordan."

"Prudence?" I said incredulously. "We've got to pay fifty quid apiece to that actor chap Alphonse Bird? But in heaven's name—"

"It's a bit of a shock, Bunny," Raffles agreed. "You can see what's happened. We've tripped up over a single word. The bet stipulated 'the most beautiful, lovable, talented girl *currently* dispensing coffee in London.' But at the time Lee delivered his judgment, Adelphi wasn't currently in the coffee-house business. She'd already resigned!"

Meditatively, he offered me a Sullivan from his cigarette case.

"Well, let's be good losers, Bunny," he said, "and make the most of what we have."

"Have?" I said blankly. "What *have* we?"

"Most of Fleet Street's on our tail," said Raffles, "but only you and I have the whole story of Adelphi, Bunny—and a kiss to remember her by."

An Error in Curfew

As we emerged from the Albert Hall after a concert about eleven o'clock one mild night in London, I was humming to myself a theme from one of the works we had heard.

"What a haunting little air that is, Bunny!" Raffles remarked.

"I've always," I said, "particularly admired that concerto of Dr. Emma Valentine's."

"If I'd known that," said Raffles, "I'd have introduced you to her. She was the old lady who stopped to have a word with me as we were going in."

He glanced across at the line of carriages inching along under the gaslights in the arch of the main entrance.

"There she is now," he said, "but I don't think this would be the best time to introduce you. She's among her own kind."

The old Doctor of Music seemed very small. Her gray, smooth hair was parted in the center. About her frail shoulders she wore a Chinese shawl, and she supported herself on an ebony stick. There was great distinction in her profile, a gentle humor in her smile; and the men, obviously musicians, who were seeing her into her carriage bowed over her hand with a rather touching deference.

223

"She asked me to tea tomorrow—Sunday," Raffles said, as the old composer's carriage drove off toward Kensington High Street and we ourselves walked away in the opposite direction. "I'll take you along with me, Bunny. I'm sure Dr. Emma won't mind. She's living now in a hotel overlooking Kensington Gardens. She lived for many years in a small house she owns just nearby here, but last year a companion who lived with her had to go abroad, and Dr. Emma couldn't stand living in the house without her."

"Very understandable," I said.

"Somebody lent Dr. Emma a furnished flat in The Albany for a few months," he went on. "I had many a talk with her there. She was worried about her house, and her things in it, especially her piano, a concert grand, which she values enormously, as most of her best works were composed on it. She didn't want to sell the house, or let it furnished, because she had the idea that at any moment she might get over what she considers her irrational feeling about her old companion not being there and would be happy to go back to it again. But, as I say, when she left The Albany she went to a hotel, and I gathered, this evening, that she's still there and still has the house problem on her hands."

We were walking past some of the great embassies which faced the Park and, changing the subject, he said, "I see the Imperial Ambassador is entertaining again."

The lofty windows on the first floor of the most imposing of the embassies stood wide open. I glimpsed the faceted sparkle of many chandeliers, heard the lilt of violins.

"The most tireless entertainer in London," Raffles said. "He works like a beaver to try to make some sort of favorable impression on public opinion here because his government's policy is so damned unpopular."

He took a thoughtful pull at his cigarette.

"He's got another junket on, on Monday night. He's staging a sort of private view, at the embassy, of the Imperial collection of jade, which is being sent over on loan—another bid for public opinion, of course—to be exhibited at one of the museums here."

He flicked away his cigarette suddenly.

"Look, Bunny, to return to what we were discussing," he said, "Dr. Emma's house, being unoccupied, is probably going to rack and ruin. In case she should ask my advice about it, as she did last year, it mightn't be a bad idea, as we're in the vicinity, to see what kind of a state it's in. It's only just round the corner here."

The corner we turned, to the right, led us into a dark little square. Off this, we turned again to the right, into a narrow street with only one wan gaslamp at its far end. The street was lined with modest little Regency houses and, pausing before one of them, Raffles said, "This is Dr. Emma's."

"It's really too dark," I said, "to judge what sort of state it's in."

Taking my arm, he drew me up the steps into the porch, and I was astonished to realize that he was going to work in his deft way on the door lock with the instrument he always carried.

"Granted you're a friend of Dr. Emma's," I said uneasily, "but are you sure it's in order for us to look round inside? I don't quite—"

He cut me short by opening the door, pulling me inside. In the pitch darkness, I heard him relock the door. He struck a match and, as he held it shielded in his hands, I saw that we were in a small, white-paneled hall, furnished with tall-backed chairs and a coffer or two, with a carpeted staircase facing us, and a baize-covered door to the left of the stairs.

With growing uneasiness, I followed him to the baize-covered door, which he pushed open. We entered a narrow passage with a bolted door at its end. Raffles shook out the match, moved forward, and I heard him unbolt and open the door. He drew me after him, closing the door behind us.

We were in a small yard or patio, with a wall to either side and a much higher wall facing us. A faint diffusion of light on the far side of the higher wall silhouetted a row of spikes along its top.

Raffles moved across the patio, with me following him. He lifted a garden table, placed it against the wall. Climbing on to the table, he reached up, gripped two of the spikes, pulled himself up, peered over the wall.

As I stared up at him in astonishment, I became aware of the sound of violins from somewhere on the far side of that wall. Instantly, I realized why he had come here. The blood rushed into my head.

Raffles dropped back beside me, brushed off his hands. He chuckled.

"It's just as I thought, Bunny," he said. "The possibility didn't occur to me till we were passing the Imperial Embassy just now, but Dr. Emma's unoccupied house proves to be right at the back of the embassy garden."

I could have struck him.

"I'll have nothing to do with it," I said. "To think of using the house of a great old lady like Dr. Emma Valentine as a means of getting at the Imperial jade—"

"Who said anything about using her house?" said Raffles. "Dammit, Bunny, you know me better than that. I couldn't resist checking that the possibilities were as I suspected, but my curiosity was purely academic. I wouldn't dream of using her house for such a purpose. Come on, we'll go now."

My relief was heartfelt as I followed him back across the patio.

"Mind you," he said, as he turned the handle of the back door, "if this unoccupied house hadn't been Dr. Emma's, I'm not say—"

He broke off sharply. He turned the door handle again.

He said, "The door's bolted."

I went cold.

"Impossible," I breathed. "The house is unoccupied."

"Doors don't bolt themselves," he said.

He stepped back, glanced up at the back of the house, then at the walls to either side.

"I wouldn't have us caught here for a fortune," he whispered. "Over that side wall there, Bunny. Quick!"

There were no spikes on the side wall. We climbed four such walls in succession, moving swiftly and silently, and dodged across four little patios similar to Dr. Emma's. My bellows were pumping when finally we dropped down into the little, dark square, and headed out of it, walking pretty briskly.

I saw that Raffles was keeping a weather eye to our rear and, as we were passing Knightsbridge Barracks, he said, "One thing, anyway—I'm certain we're not followed."

My tension relaxed slightly, but I was still worried.

"What the devil do you make of that bolted door?" I said.

"Offhand," he said, "my guess'd be that somebody was lurking in the house who'd been struck, as I was, by its tactical potentialities in relation to the Imperial jade, and was using the house as an observation post on the embassy. But dammit, that won't wash, Bunny."

"Why not?" I said.

"Because he'd have heard us pass through the house," Raffles said, "and he'd know that, whoever we were, we'd try to come back through it, because there's no other exit from the patio. Why in the name of reason, then, draw attention to his own presence in the house by bolting that door?"

We canvassed various theories, but they were all as porous as a colander, and we parted in a thoughtful mood, Raffles to go to his chambers in The Albany, I to my flat in Mount Street.

Personally, I felt so guilty about having trespassed in Dr. Emma's house at all that I had just as soon have got out of going to tea with her next afternoon, Sunday; but Raffles called for me about half-past three and we walked across the park in the sunshine to Dr. Emma's hotel.

We were conducted upstairs by a pert pageboy, and I was surprised to hear coming from behind the door at which he knocked a hubbub of young feminine voices.

Throwing open the door, the boy announced in a piercing treble, "Mr. Raffles and Mr. Manders, ma'am."

The hubbub ceased abruptly.

The room was flooded with sunshine from tall windows which stood open to a balcony overlooking the Round Pond. Dr. Emma, with her Chinese shawl about her frail shoulders, sat on a settee near the windows. Beside her, on her right, sat a gray-eyed, amber-haired girl with a sensitive face; and on the old lady's left sat a dark, slumbrous-looking girl of Italian appearance.

Sheets of music manuscript were spread on Dr. Emma's lap and littered on the carpet, and leaning over the back of the settee were three other girls, who straightened up at our entrance.

"Buttons," Dr. Emma said to the pageboy, "there's now one more to come. When she arrives, please ask them to send in the tea." Smiling, she held out a hand. "Welcome, Mr. Raffles!"

"Dr. Emma," said Raffles, as he took her hand, "I've ventured to bring a friend with me, a devoted admirer of your work—Bunny Manders."

"I'm delighted to see you here, Mr. Manders," said Dr. Emma. "You must meet my young protégées." With a pleasant gesture, she indicated the girl on her right, saying, "Miss Monday," and then the girl on her left, saying, "Miss Tuesday." Making my bows, I felt a growing bewilderment as she continued, indicating the other three girls, "Miss Wednesday, Miss Thursday—and Miss Friday."

The girls returned our greetings decorously, though it seemed to me they had all they could do to keep their pretty faces straight, for their eyes were dancing with suppressed amusement.

"Really, Mr. Manders," said Dr. Emma, seeing my perplexity, "it's too bad of me to mystify you gentlemen. Please forgive an old woman her little joke. Mr. Raffles, do you recall how patient you were with me at The Albany, when I inflicted on you the tedium of my indecisions about my house and my little bits and pieces there?

"When I met you last night at the Albert Hall, I felt I owed it to you to let you see how shrewdly I've solved at least one of my problems. So I asked you to tea today, and you must regard the way in which I introduced my protégées as a particular privilege, for the names I used are those which we use among ourselves. Isn't that so, Monday?"

The amber-haired Monday girl smiled.

"When we first knew Dr. Emma," she explained to us, "and started coming to tea with her every Sunday, she'd say, when we arrived, 'Ah, here's my Miss Tuesday!'—or whichever of us she happened to be greeting. At first, you see, Dr. Emma remembered each of us best by the day in the week when it was our turn to have the use of her house for the afternoon and evening."

I felt a sudden misgiving.

"The use of her house?" Raffles said, in his easy way.

"Of the piano in her house," said the Italian-looking girl. "Of her concert grand. *Scusi.*"

"As you know, Mr. Raffles," said Dr. Emma placidly, "I was particularly worried about my piano. My fingers don't allow me to play on it nowadays, and pianos, if they aren't to deteriorate, *must* be played on. The problem was solved for me one day when I chanced to be thinking about my young days, when I was a working girl in London, studying theory and composition in my spare time and dreaming of a scholarship in music. I was handicapped by the fact that my resources were inadequate to buy or even hire a piano, and search as I might, I couldn't find in all London a furnished room to live in that had a piano *in* it."

She smiled reminiscently.

"Remembering the shifts and devices to which I was put," she said, "to get my greedy fingers for an hour or two on the keyboard of somebody else's piano, I wondered how girls living in furnished rooms were placed nowadays. So I put in an advertisement, asking if there happened to be any such girl who might care to come and practice on my concert grand in her spare time and prevent it from going to rack and ruin. Mr. Raffles, the results were surprising. So many replies! So many girls! And only one piano!"

She tidied up the sheets of music manuscript on her lap.

"I decided," she said, "that my piano should be played on *every* day, so I chose six girls of musical promise, whose half-days off from their occupations ran from Monday to Saturday. I gave each girl a key to my house, so that she could have the house and piano all to herself, quite undisturbed, for the whole of her afternoon and evening off. My only stipulation, since I didn't want the girls walking home unescorted through the streets at all hours, was that they should pack up their music and lock the house securely behind them not a minute later than ten o'clock."

I was listening in fascination. Vivid in my mind was the mysteriously bolted door. But it had been after *eleven* when Raffles and I had trespassed through the silent house.

"All the girls," said Dr. Emma, "promised me faithfully to observe my ten o'clock curfew. So now, Mr. Raffles, you see how cleverly I've solved the problem of keeping my dear old piano at concert pitch."

"*Eccolo,*" said Miss Tuesday, and all the girls nodded.

I stole a glance at Raffles, but just then a knock sounded on the door and, though I did not clearly catch the name piped in the pageboy's treble, I saw Dr. Emma smile past me at a newcomer.

"Last but not least, my dear," said Dr. Emma. "Buttons, send in the tea now, please. Mr. Raffles, Mr. Manders—Miss Saturday."

I had to force myself to turn and face her. She was a rather small girl, pleasingly formed, trim and self-possessed. She wore a pretty little hat on her smooth, blond head, and was plucking off her gloves, one finger at a time. She inclined her head to Raffles and me, but, as she glanced from one to the other of us, her fingers became suddenly still, and I had an uncomfortable impression that there came into her clear blue eyes a shade of reserve.

"Come and sit down, Saturday, and take off your hat," said Dr. Emma. "Mr. Raffles is an old friend of mine. We were just telling him and Mr. Manders about the little arrangement we all have among ourselves."

"I see," said Miss Saturday. She looked down at her gloves, finished removing them, placed them together. She smoothed them thoughtfully, then suddenly looked up and said, "Dr. Emma, has anybody besides us girls got a key to your house?"

My feet felt rooted to the floor.

"Certainly not, Saturday," said Dr. Emma. "Why do you ask?"

The girl moved forward, sat down in a chair facing the old Doctor of Music, and said, with composure, "I have a confession to make, Dr. Emma. I was practicing your F-sharp Piano Concerto yesterday. It's very difficult, and I was at it solidly from three o'clock on, with just one small break. That was when, as it began to get dark, I stopped to make a cup of tea on the spirit stove and light the piano candles and pull the drawing-room curtains. Then I went on practicing, and I have to admit to you frankly that, when I thought to look at my watch, it was gone eleven."

Raffles took out his cigarette case meditatively.

"I felt very guilty at having broken the solemn promise we all made to you, Dr. Emma," said Miss Saturday. "I closed the piano at once, packed my music case, and blew out the piano candles. I was just about to feel my way across to the drawing-room door when I heard a mutter of men's voices in the porch. The lock of the front door turned and the men came into the hall."

There was a knock at the door and the pageboy came in, carrying a cakestand in each hand, and followed by a waiter pushing a tea trolley. The trolley rattled in the silence. Nobody paid any attention.

"Go on, Saturday," said Dr. Emma, as the door closed.

"The drawing-room door was half open," said the girl who had stayed late. "I saw a flicker of light in the hall as a match was struck. Standing by the piano, I was sort of at an angle to the door, and I saw two huge shadows for a second on the wall of the hall.

And then the men were gone, through the baize-covered door, and out to the back of the house. I heard the back door open and shut."

"You ran out the front door at once, I hope," said Dr. Emma, "and told a policeman?"

The Saturday girl looked down at her gloves, smoothing them. "That's what I have to confess," she said. "I didn't." She looked up. "Dr. Emma, may I ask you something?"

"What is it, Saturday?"

"Because of what I've told you," the girl said, "do you intend to put an end to our using your house and your piano?"

The other girls were as still as statues.

The old lady made a little movement with her hands, resting on the sheets of music.

"What else can I do, Saturday?" she said. "I must have been mad. It never entered my head that there could be danger in one or other of you girls being quite alone in that house, night after night. Of course it must end."

"I knew it," said the Saturday girl. "I knew that would be your very first thought. I knew it as I stood by the piano, in the darkness, in your drawing room, with my heart going thump-thump-thump like mad. I wanted to run out the front door and find a policeman, but I kept thinking that if I hadn't broken my promise and overstayed my time, I'd never have found myself in such a position, and that the moment the police came to you about it, the first thing you would do would be to end the arrangement, and that I'd ruined everything for all six of us. I just stood there. I couldn't move."

Neither could I. It was Raffles and I who had ruined everything.

"Then an idea came into my head," said the Saturday girl. "I thought that perhaps you need never know anything about what had happened, Dr. Emma. I didn't know what the men were doing out at the back, or even whether they'd gone altogether. But they were obviously marauders, who thought the house unoccupied, and the idea came to me that if they tried to come back into the house and found the back door bolted, they'd realize that the house wasn't unoccupied at all, and they'd get as big a shock as I'd had, and they wouldn't be able to get away too fast. So I crept along the passage in the dark and bolted the back door."

The amber-haired Monday girl shuddered.

"I just couldn't have done it," she said. "I'd never have thought of it, even. I don't know how you had the courage."

"It wasn't courage," said Miss Saturday. "It was desperation. When I'd done it, I crept out of the front door, locked it behind me, and ran like a hare, with my music case. And I have to confess, Dr. Emma, that I was determined not to breathe a word to you about the matter."

"Why did you, then?" said Miss Tuesday.

"Because of you," said the Saturday girl. "Because of you five, of course. It dawned on me as I was coming here today, and I've been walking about in Kensington Gardens, thinking about it, which is why I was late for tea. Suppose something like it were to happen when one of *you* was alone in the house? Something worse, perhaps? And I'd said nothing? How would I feel? I realized it was no good, I just *had* to tell Dr. Emma—and all of you. I had just a faint hope that the men might possibly have been friends of Dr. Emma's that she'd lent a key to, but—"

"Suppose we went in twos?" said Miss Monday. "No, that's no good—our half-days off are different." Her sensitive face brightened. "Suppose we each got someone to come and sit with us while we practiced?"

"From two or three in the afternoon till ten at night?" said Miss Friday. "Who could any of us find to do that?"

"It must end," said Dr. Emma. "I ought never to have allowed it in the first place. My dears, I shan't know a moment's peace until you give me those keys back. *Please!*"

She held out her hand. I just could not stand it. I walked to the window and stared out at the Round Pond, freckled with the sails of model yachts in the sunshine. I heard the clink of the keys as the stricken girls relinquished them.

"Dr. Emma," said Raffles slowly, "I wonder if I might make a suggestion? To the police, of course, in view of the length of time that's passed without any notification to them, this would be now pretty much what they call, I believe, a cold trail. It's impossible to argue with your decision to ban your house to these young ladies. The arrangement, as it stood—and as we've seen—was not altogether wise. On the other hand, I wonder if I might, as an old friend, Dr. Emma, look into this whole matter a little further for you? Between us, I feel sure Bunny Manders and I could work out some absolutely ideal way to guarantee the safety of these young ladies at their piano practice."

I turned from the window and looked at him. His eyes were on Dr. Emma. A murmur of gratitude and renewed hope came from the girls. Their eyes were on Dr. Emma, too—all except those of Miss Saturday, who was looking down at her gloves, smoothing them thoughtfully on her knee.

Obviously reluctant to dash the girls' hopes, Dr. Emma agreed, though doubtfully, that Raffles should look into the whole position for her and make his recommendations. So we had tea, now, in a rather less depressed atmosphere than might have been expected.

Raffles and Miss Monday carried their teacups out on to the balcony, where they stood chatting together in the sunshine. I pulled myself together and did my best to be generally agreeable, but a continuing reserve in Miss Saturday's manner discouraged me from making overtures in her direction, and I was intensely relieved when at last Raffles and I were able to get away.

"Damn you, Raffles," I said bitterly, as we walked across the gardens, "I've never felt such a low hound in my life. We've lost those girls a privilege that was priceless to them. What's more, that blond Saturday girl is suspicious of us."

"She has a gnawing doubt about us, certainly," Raffles said.

"She's a most unusual girl, Bunny. I admire her greatly. Not one in a hundred, in her place last night, would have bolted that door. And we reacted to it exactly as she foresaw! I take off my hat to Miss Saturday.

"Again, this afternoon, when she walked into Dr. Emma's tea party, where usually there are no men, and saw two men who might conceivably have cast such shadows as she glimpsed for an instant by matchlight on the wall last night, one could see the little, warning bell ring in her mind. Yes, she has an uneasy, gnawing doubt about us, and we've got to remove it. What's more, we've got to make good my virtual promise to solve the problem that's arisen as a result of the ban Dr. Emma's placed on her house."

"I don't believe anything on earth will make Dr. Emma part with those keys again," I said. "What have you in mind?"

"The Imperial collection of jade," said A. J. Raffles.

I stopped dead. So did he. He took out his watch and glanced at it.

"The girls'll probably be taking their leave of Dr. Emma pretty soon," he said. "I'll see you at Kern's place later this evening, Bunny. I've some arrangements to make there. Meantime, I want to see just where Miss Monday goes when she goes to her furnished room. I need her address."

"Miss Monday's?" I said, mystified.

"Just so," said Raffles. "I enjoyed my chat with her on the balcony. She's a very nice girl. Comes from Colchester."

He turned off down a side path which curved back toward the hotel.

Ivor Kern, the receiver of stolen property with whom we did business, worked under cover of an antique shop in the King's Road, Chelsea. Just after eight o'clock that evening, as I was sitting drinking sherry with Kern in his cluttered, gaslit sitting room over the shop, Raffles came walking in.

"Ivor," he said, "I want you to send one of your minions down to Colchester by an early train in the morning—one that'll get him there fairly soon after the post offices open. I want him to send a telegram to a young lady. I've written her name and address, and the message to be sent, on this piece of paper."

Kern nodded, pocketed the paper.

"Next," said Raffles, helping himself to sherry, "I want six revolvers and plenty of ammunition, some sticks of dynamite with fuses, six masks, a glass-cutter, a big bunch of skeleton keys, six pairs of gloves, and a selection of jemmies and similar house-breaking tools. All must be untraceable, and I want them packed into a valise."

I felt myself go white, but he chuckled and put a friendly hand on my shoulder.

"Don't worry, Bunny," he said. "I put a foot badly wrong last night, and led you into an embarrassing situation. I won't make such a ghastly mistake again. Now, as soon as Ivor's made the preparations I've asked for, we'll take him out to dinner and forget the whole business, and tomorrow morning, Bunny, I'll call for you at your flat."

It was mid-morning when he called, about eleven o'clock, and he invited me to accompany him to a shop in Bond Street. It turned out to be a ladies' shoe shop, and the first person I saw, when we entered, was the amber-haired Monday girl. She was sitting on a little stool, fitting a shoe for a customer. She looked astonished to see us. With a word of apology to the customer, she rose and came to us.

"Miss Monday," said Raffles, as we raised our hats, "we're busy on the little private inquiry entrusted to us by Dr. Emma. There are one or two small questions we'd like to ask you. I can quite see that you're preoccupied at the moment, but could you possibly dine with us this evening?"

"Oh, I'm sorry," she said. "I just can't. Not this evening. My father's wired me that he's coming to London on business and wants me to meet his train at Liverpool Street at seven o'clock. I had the wire half an hour ago. My landlady sent the telegraph boy here with it."

"I see," Raffles said. "Well, fathers must come first, of course." A thought seemed to strike him. "Does your father often come to London on business?"

"Why, no, never," she said. "I can't imagine what it can be about."

Frowning, Raffles took out his cigarette case.

"This may seem an odd request to you," he said slowly, "but might I suggest that you wire your father asking him to confirm, by telegram, that you're to meet him at Liverpool Street at seven this evening? This is a bow at a venture, Miss Monday, but there's just a possibility that there could be a clue here to Miss Saturday's adventure. If you care to write out your telegram now, Manders and I could send it off for you. Now, what time do you finish work today?"

"At six," said Miss Monday, as she scribbled the telegram. "I've traded my half-day off with another girl."

"Then perhaps, if we call for you here at that hour," Raffles said, "you'd let us know the result of your inquiry to your father?"

As we went to the post office to send off Miss Monday's telegram, I demanded of Raffles what the devil his game was, but I got no change out of him. At six o'clock, when Miss Monday came hurrying out of the shop, we were waiting for her.

Her sensitive face was alight with excitement, her eyes were sparkling, and her first breathless words were, "It *wasn't* my father who sent that telegram to me this morning!"

A keen look came into Raffles's eyes.

"Miss Monday," he said, "I'm sure you must know where your friend Miss Saturday lives. Could you accompany us there?"

"Oh, yes," she said eagerly, "but Saturday won't be at home now. She works at a Public Library, and she's on till eight this week."

Raffles hailed a cab and, as the gaslamps began to shine out in the mild twilight, we jingled through the streets to the Public Library, where we found Miss Saturday busy at the desk, issuing books.

We let Miss Monday have a word with her first, and when both girls joined us, in a recess among the bookshelves, Raffles said, "We'd very much like you to come with us to the Imperial Embassy, Miss Saturday. In fact, your presence is absolutely essential, and the matter's urgent. Would you care for me to have a word with the Chief Librarian?"

She gave A. J. Raffles a pretty straight look.

"That won't be necessary," she said coldly. "I'll speak to him myself."

In the cab, with the horse clip-clopping along toward the Imperial Embassy, Miss Monday burst out, "But why? *Why* should someone have sent me that false telegram?"

"It looks very much," said Raffles, "as though whoever's behind all this has picked up a good deal of information about you young ladies who use Dr. Emma's house. He evidently knows that *your* day there is Monday. Today's Monday. So it looks as though he doesn't want you there after seven this evening. He wants you well away at Liverpool Street Station, kicking your heels watching successive trains come in, and Dr. Emma's house quite unoccupied."

"But Monday wouldn't have been at the house tonight, anyway," said Miss Saturday, "because it's all off, and the house is banned to us."

"*We* know that, of course," said Raffles, "but it's obvious that the man who sent this telegram doesn't. How could he?"

Miss Saturday thought it over with her usual composure, and in the look she gave A. J. Raffles, after a minute, I thought I detected a slight change for the better. And her tone was less wanting in trust as she asked, "Why are we going to the Imperial Embassy, Mr. Raffles?"

"To get, I hope, to the bottom of this business, Miss Saturday," Raffles said. "And here we are at the embassy, I think."

The arrival of guests for the private view of the Imperial collection of jade was clearly imminent. All the lights of the embassy shone out into the evening, and the doors to the great hall stood wide open. The white-gloved, knee-breeched footmen on duty at the door looked a bit askance on noting that neither the girls nor Raffles and I were in evening dress.

"We're here," Raffles said, to the footman who barred our way, "on a matter closely touching the safety of the Imperial jade. Here's my card. Take it at once to the relevant official. Hurry, please. It's urgent."

After a brief wait, we were conducted across the brilliant hall to a room in which a rather bleak-faced man in full evening dress, with decorations, rose from behind a desk to greet us. He had Raffles's card in his hand.

"Mr. Raffles—the England cricketer?" he asked.

Raffles admitted it.

"I'll go straight to the point, sir," he said. "No doubt you know the name of Dr. Emma Valentine, and that her house closely neighbors the embassy garden, at the back there?"

The official nodded.

"Dr. Valentine, I'm glad to say, is among the guests we expect here this evening. As to her house, I've often paused, when walking in the embassy garden, to enjoy listening to her at her piano."

"I'm sure these young ladies will appreciate the compliment you pay them," Raffles said, "because it's themselves you've been hearing at Dr. Valentine's piano in recent months."

Briefly, he explained the circumstances, adding, "This young lady will now tell you of an experience she had on the night of Saturday last."

The official's face grew increasingly bleak as he listened to Miss Saturday's story.

"Dr. Emma," said Raffles then, "wished me, as an old friend, to look into the matter for her. It wasn't until this morning, when I learned of something that had happened to this *other* young lady, that I began to have a glimmer of a suspicion." He turned to Miss Monday. "Please tell this gentleman about the telegram."

Breathlessly, Miss Monday told her story.

"You see, sir?" Raffles said. "Tonight is the night of the private view of the Imperial jade. Steps have been taken, by someone unknown, to ensure this young lady's absence from the house. The house is just at the back of the embassy. The inference seemed to my friend Mr. Manders and myself so inescapable that we brought both young ladies here to you without a moment's delay."

The official was on his feet, tugging at the bellpull.

"We are deeply in your debt," he said. "Footman, bring refreshments here. Ladies, gentlemen, I beg you to excuse me. I'll be back in a moment."

He was away a great deal longer than that. As the four of us had a drink, which I at any rate badly needed, we could hear the guests beginning to arrive, and a voice announcing the distinguished names, with their honors.

It must have been half an hour or more before the official returned. He went straight to the tray on the desk and poured himself a stiff whisky.

"My dear Mr. Raffles," he said, "I very much hope that, as in a sense Dr. Valentine's representative, you'll approve the action that's been taken. There really was no time for the formality of a search warrant. The Scotland Yard man on duty here tonight effected an entry just now, in company with a couple of our embassy guards, into Dr. Valentine's house. The house was unoccupied, but the Yard man reports to me that criminals had indeed planted equipment in the house in preparation for a raid on the embassy. A gang of six men, at least, must be involved, as a quick search has revealed a valise, hidden in a kitchen cupboard, containing a veritable arsenal, including half a dozen revolvers, masks, and even dynamite."

I felt sudden sweat in my palms. I knew now where Raffles had gone when he had left me last night.

The official went on, "The Yard man and the guards are now lying in ambush in the house. But the Yard man expects nothing to come of it. He pointed out to me that the men probably have been using the house nightly for the past week or more, planting their stuff there and keeping watch on the embassy. Naturally, they'd have taken note that the young ladies always left the house by ten, so the men themselves would have entered the house nightly at a later hour."

"On the Saturday, then," Raffles said, "when they found the door mysteriously bolted—"

"They'd have guessed at once what had happened," said the official, "that the young Saturday lady must have overstayed her time and been still in the house when they entered. Their problem would then have been to know whether she'd seen them and whether she'd gone to the police about it.

"As the Yard man points out, the men are certainly keeping an eye this evening on Liverpool Street Station. If the young Monday lady shows up there, with no plainclothesmen discreetly in attendance, the criminals will know that the young Saturday lady, for whatever reason, can't have gone to the police, and therefore Dr. Valentine's house can be used as planned. On the other hand, in the Yard man's opinion, the fact that the young Monday lady hasn't shown up at all at Liverpool Street Station, and that it's now past seven and too late for her to do so, will scare the men off completely, because they won't know what the position is."

He poured himself another whisky. He obviously was badly shaken.

"To us here at the embassy," he said, "it's immaterial whether the ambush that's been laid is abortive or not. The point is, a really appalling hold-up, considering the eminence of the guests we have here tonight, has been averted. Believe me, Mr. Raffles, His Excellency and all of us feel profoundly grateful to you."

"If these young ladies," Raffles said, "hadn't chanced to be using that unoccupied house in the evenings, and if this young lady hadn't happened to overstay her time on Saturday—"

"Precisely," said the official. "What would have happened just doesn't bear thinking about. We're deeply indebted to the young ladies."

"They, on the other hand," Raffles said regretfully, "have lost, as a result of what's happened, a privilege they greatly prized."

"Quite so," said the official, "and I'm very sure His Excellency, as an expression of gratitude, will wish to compensate the young ladies in any way he can. I—"

"In point of fact," Raffles said, "the ideal way of ensuring the safety of the young ladies at their piano practice would be for each of them to have a simple little upright piano, which takes up so much less space than a concert grand, in her own room where she lives. If the six young ladies each had her own piano—"

The official looked at him in consternation. "Six pianos?"

"If His Excellency himself," Raffles hinted delicately, "could possibly find the time to be present in person at some modest little ceremony of presentation—"

I saw a sudden gleam come into the official's eyes, a look of calculation. And I guessed instantly the cunning thought which Raffles had planted in the diplomatist's mind. This was a difficult period, internationally; the Imperial Embassy could ill afford to lose a heaven-sent chance of making a sympathetic impression on the British public. With journalists present, a modest little ceremony in the piano salon of some large furnishing store, with the Ambassador making in person a gesture of gratitude and compensation to six pretty girls . . .

The official smiled suddenly, with a bow of agreement.

Miss Monday, sensitive and vulnerable, could not hide her incredulous joy. But I saw that it was Miss Saturday, with her proud little blond head, whom Raffles was watching with a tense anxiety. Delight shone in her eyes for an unguarded moment, but then she regained her customary composure.

"I'm afraid, speaking for myself," she said, in her thoughtful way, "I couldn't possibly accept such an award."

My heart sank. She really was a most difficult girl. But the official, though obviously taken aback for a moment, exerted all his trained charm and diplomacy, and presently succeeded in overcoming her objections.

When we had taken the girls home, and once more were alone in the cab together, I drew a long breath of relief.

"Congratulations, Raffles," I said. "You pulled it off! You've paid our debt to the girls of the banned house."

"Yes," Raffles said. "That's off our minds."

He offered me a Sullivan from his cigarette case.

"But about that collection of jade," he said. "We must give it some further thought—one of these days . . ."

Bo-Peep in the Suburbs

"Well, thanks for the game, Derek," said Raffles.

What had started as a friendly hour or so of poker after dinner had turned into an all-night session, but, as he rose from the table, he looked as fresh and debonair as ever. I did not know how he did it. Daylight was showing round the edges of the curtains and, for myself, I felt a physical and moral ruin.

Derek Fenn, whose guests we were, protested, "Not going already? Stop and have some bacon and eggs. These other chaps'll stay, I'm sure."

The mere thought of bacon and eggs made me feel queasy. But Derek Fenn could afford to be hearty. A large, likable, sandy-haired fellow, he was born lucky. Though still barely thirty, he already had made a mint of money in the hazardous business of West End play production. Everything he touched seemed to turn to gold; it was he who had just skinned us all at poker.

Raffles said, "Not for us, Derek. Look at the time! I'm supposed to be at a committee meeting at Lord's Cricket Ground this morning."

"Well, if you *must* go," said Derek, and, hunting up our outdoor things for us—we were in evening dress—opened his front door.

His house was in a London suburb, and the sun came up as Raffles and I, heading for the station, walked along one pleasant, deserted street after another. A heavy dew sparkled on the lawns before the houses and on the bright flowerbeds.

"It's a joy to get out of doors, Bunny," Raffles remarked. "What a damned silly way to spend a . . ."

He broke off abruptly, gripping my arm, bringing me to a standstill.

"Listen!" he said.

We stood motionless.

For a moment all I could hear was the whistle and chirp of the early birds in the gardens, but then there came drifting to me another voice, another song. Somewhere nearby, among these sleeping houses, a woman's voice was singing, quietly yet clearly:

> "Little Bo-Peep has lost her sheep,
> And doesn't know where to find them . . ."

I whispered to Raffles, "Some young mother singing to her child in the nursery."

All round us the windows of the houses shone blankly in the early sunlight.

Raffles shook his head. "She's outdoors, Bunny—walking—coming closer . . ."

Spellbound, we listened to that lovely voice singing in the sunrise that simple little air:

> "Leave them alone and they'll come home,
> And bring their tails behind them . . ."

The voice died away.

Raffles walked forward to a corner just ahead. I followed him. The street name on the corner was Raynescourt Avenue. We looked along the street. All along it the shadows of trees slanted across from left to right.

The street was empty except for a solitary, slender figure strolling along in the middle of the road. The stroller carried a small suitcase with the bright new labels of a shipping line on it. She passed momentarily into shadow.

As she emerged from it, her hair in the sunlight shone amber. She was glancing up at the windows to either side and, as she wandered along slowly toward us, she began to sing again:

"Little Bo-Peep has lost her sheep,
And doesn't . . ."

She spotted us, standing there in tree shadow at the corner, and her song broke off sharply. She moved quickly to her left, on to the sidewalk on the far side from us. Clearly, she wished to avoid us, and I was embarrassed when Raffles walked across the street and went straight up to her, raising his hat.

"Forgive me," he said, "but I can't resist thanking you for adding an enchanting touch to an enchanted hour of the day."

I saw her color heighten, but she smiled; and at this, I plucked up the courage to walk across and, raising my own hat, say, "May I venture to couple my thanks with my friend's?"

She was in her middle twenties, clean-cut in look and dress, her eyes dark gray, her complexion a golden tan. She seemed confused for a second, as she looked from one to the other of us, then she gave a little laugh.

"I hardly know whether to pass the hat round now in the approved style," she said, "or to explain my real reason for singing in the street. Perhaps I'd better explain, in case you should report to the authorities that a person at large in Raynescourt Avenue seems in need of care and restraint. Absurd as it may sound, I really *have* lost my sheep!"

I gaped at her.

But Raffles, in his easy way, said, "If we can be of any help, please look upon my friend Manders and myself—my name's Raffles—as obedient sheepdogs to any bereft shepherdess."

"I believe you really mean it," she said. "My name's Kate Dover. Thank you for your offer, but I'm afraid you can't help me. My only trouble is that my mother and my little girl are in one of the houses in this street, and I just don't know which house."

"How very tantalizing for you!" Raffles exclaimed.

"Isn't it?" said Kate Dover fervently. "Especially as I haven't seen them for eight whole months. I'm an actress and I've been abroad, touring with a repertory company in South Africa. I left my mother and my six-year-old daughter Drusilla living in rooms in London.

"Just before I sailed for home, from Cape Town, my mother wrote to say that she and Drusilla had moved into some new rooms —in the suburbs.

"She put the new address in her letter, but I stupidly went and lost the letter on the ship. I remember perfectly well the name of the road they've moved to—Raynescourt Avenue. But I've been so used to writing to the old address that for the life of me I can't remember the number of the new one. I just haven't a notion!"

She glanced despairingly along the vacant, tranquil street.

"How enigmatic it looks!" she said. "We disembarked at London docks in the middle of the night, and I rushed straight out here, madly excited, on the very first train. I got here just at daybreak and walked up and down the street, looking at all the numbers, hoping that some bell would ring in my memory. But it just didn't. I was sitting on a seat along there, feeling baffled, when the sun came up. I knew Drusilla would be awake. She always wakes early. You know how children are."

"Certainly," said Raffles, the bachelor.

"The thought that she was behind one of those blankly shining windows," Kate Dover said, "probably sitting up in bed playing with her dolls, and I didn't know *which* window, just drove me crazy. So I thought I'd walk the whole length of the street singing one of the nursery rhymes I sing for her at bedtime when I'm not away working. I hoped she might hear me. If she did, I knew she'd recognize my voice instantly and look out of the window and yell at the top of her voice, 'Mama!' D'you see?"

"Excellent idea," Raffles said. "It deserves to have succeeded. As it hasn't, perhaps more direct methods are called for. Bunny, you take one side of the street, I'll take the other. We'll knock 'em all up, house by house, and ask if they have a Mrs.—— Mrs.——"

He glanced at the girl.

"May I ask the more mundane name of Mrs. Bo-Peep, Senior?"

"My mother's name is Mrs. Belman," said Kate Dover. "But I can't possibly let you do this! My mother would be horrified. She's very conventional. If I were to knock up the whole street at sunrise, in company with two—forgive me—two strange men in evening dress—"

"I see your point," Raffles admitted. "But what d'you propose to do, then?"

"I must just be patient, that's all," said Kate Dover. "I'll sit on that seat under the trees along there until the postman shows up. He's bound to have had letters at some time for my mother and know which house she's living in. Truly, I've only to be patient a bit longer and everything'll be all right. So, please—don't let me keep you."

She so obviously wanted to be left alone, to dwell on the delight of presently finding her mother and her little girl, that really there was nothing we could do except escort her to the seat and there leave her.

The seat was opposite Number 53, an attractive house covered with autumn-red creeper, and with lace-curtained windows, lying back behind a short, yellow-graveled path between two small lawns.

"I don't quite like leaving her with her predicament unresolved, Bunny," Raffles said, as we walked on along Raynescourt Avenue.

"Our evening dress is against us," I said. "We could only embarrass her."

He nodded. We looked back from the end of Raynescourt Avenue. All along it slanted the shadows of the trees, from right to left. There was no sound or movement except those of the birds, as their joyous flittings shook the night's dew from bush and blossom. The windows of the houses were blank with sunshine.

Her hair shining amber, her small suitcase beside her, Kate Dover sat alone on the seat opposite Number 53, the house with the red creeper.

I gave the odd little incident, which happened on a Tuesday, no further thought, except that it occurred to me casually that perhaps the reason Kate Dover's little girl had not heard Kate singing for her might be that the little girl's bedroom was at the back, not front, of whichever house she and her grandmother were living in.

I had a bit of writing on hand, as I still occasionally practiced my ostensible occupation as a freelance journalist; and it was not until Saturday morning that I walked round from my flat in Mount Street to The Albany, where Raffles lived, to see if by any chance he had any money, as I was flat broke after our night at Derek Fenn's.

I found Raffles packing a suitcase. He gave me a rather queer look.

"I've been expecting you round before this, Bunny," he said.

"Didn't you see Wednesday's newspapers, with the story of the attack on Kate Dover after we left her?"

"Attack?" I said incredulously.

Raffles nodded. His keen, tanned face was grim.

"Bunny, I'll never forgive myself for the way we walked off and left her that morning," he said. "I had a queer feeling at the time that we were wrong. I've got all the details now. We left her on that seat, remember? Soon after, it seems, she saw one of the lace curtains move in a downstairs window of the house opposite the seat."

"Number 53," I said, my mouth dry, "house with red creeper."

"Creeper's right," Raffles said. "Kate, thinking someone was up and about in the house, decided to go across and ask whoever was there if they could by any chance put her on to the address in Raynescourt Avenue of a gray-haired lady called Mrs. Belman and a little girl.

"She walked up that yellow-graveled path with her suitcase, knocked on the door. It opened instantly, and a fellow with a handkerchief tied over his face and a revolver in his hand told her to step in, quick. He marched her into the drawing room, tied her up in a chair, stuck a gag in her mouth. It seems he had plenty of cord handy, though it wasn't intended for Kate. It was intended for the man he was waiting to ambush—the postman."

"The postman?" I said. My heart thumped.

"With Kate helpless in the chair," Raffles said, "the fellow stood peering out through the lace curtains. The room was full of sunshine. After a long wait, the postman appeared, with his bag over his shoulder and some packets in his hand.

"He walked up the path, and the fellow with the revolver opened the front door and had *him* in, too, in a flash. He tied and gagged the postman in a chair alongside Kate, took two or three registered postal packets the postman was carrying, slipped out of the house, and was gone like the morning dew."

Raffles took a Sullivan from his cigarette case.

"Pretty neat, Bunny," he said. "The people who live at Number 53 were away. The fellow must have posted a letter to the house, to make sure the postman would call there, then broken in during the hours of darkness to wait for the postman's arrival."

"What in the world must the fellow have thought," I said, "when he suddenly heard that voice outside, singing 'Bo-Peep'?"

"It must have made his skin creep, Bunny," Raffles said. "Peering out, seeing Kate strolling up and down, singing, he must have wondered what on earth she was up to. And then you and I appeared and talked to her and went away, leaving her settled down on that seat exactly opposite. What a problem for him!

"He'd think, of course, that she couldn't fail to see what happened when the postman came to the door, and that she'd raise the alarm before he'd had time to truss up the postman and get the registereds. He must have been at his wit's end to know what to do about her when she played right into his hands by coming across and knocking at the door."

"Is she all right?" I said.

"Fortunately, yes," said Raffles. "In the newspaper story, she was described as 'Kate Dover, aged twenty-six, of Number 34 Raynescourt Avenue.' That's her mother's address, of course—the number Kate couldn't remember. The police soon found Kate's mother and daughter for her.

"It seems that when the postman was missed the police made a house-to-house check over his route, got no reply at Number 53, looked in through the windows, and saw Kate and the postman tied up in there.

"As soon as I read the story, I went out and called at Number 34 to tell Kate how sorry we were that we went off and left her that morning, and to see if there was anything we could do for her—to make up for it. She said there was nothing, but I'm not so sure."

"What do you mean?" I said.

"They're a delightful little family, Bunny," Raffles said, "Kate's mother, Kate herself, her little girl Drusilla. Kate's husband was a young actor called Jack Dover. He lost his life in a theater fire four years ago. Kate's now the sole breadwinner, and that's why she's away so much—she has to take any tour she can get.

"Bunny, she has charm and talent to her fingertips, but at this moment, with her rep tour in South Africa finished, she's 'resting' —out of a job, to put it bluntly, and I could see she's already getting anxious about it. Kate's never had a real chance in her profession, and she deserves one, and you and I are going to see that she gets it. We're going to put money into Derek Fenn's next West End show and make sure Kate gets a part she can make a real impression with."

"Where are we going to get the money?" I said wryly.

"From a man called Leo Pardick, of Number 70 Raynescourt Avenue," said A. J. Raffles.

I stared at him. He crushed out his cigarette in an ashtray.

"I've been pretty busy, these past few days," he said. "I gathered from Kate that the police told her they'd been plagued lately by quite a number of neat little registered-mail robberies, and that they had no doubt the fellow she encountered was one of a gang specializing in such jobs. That, apparently, is the line the police are working on. Bunny, I suspected from the first—and I now *know* —that the truth is different."

He looked at me with the old vivacity dancing in his eyes.

"I learned that Raynescourt Avenue is the last lap of that postman's route," he said. "So between Number 53, where the ambush was set, and Number 72, the last house in the street, the postman had only nineteen houses left to call at.

"Granted that the site of the ambush was dictated by the fact that Number 53 happened to be the house where the people were away, what were the chances that there'd be enough left in the postman's bag, that far on in his round, to make the job worthwhile? Pretty slender, it seemed to me. *Unless,* " said Raffles, "the ambusher had information that some *specific* registered postal packet—one he wanted—was in transit to an address in Raynescourt Avenue between Number 53 and Number 72!"

"In which case," I said quickly, "he'd take anything else that was left in the bag as a blind to what he really was after?"

"Exactly," said Raffles, "and the thought nagged at me. So I looked up the local street directory, with special reference to those last nineteen houses in Raynescourt Avenue. I did it on spec., Bunny, but I struck oil!

"There was a name that rang a faint bell for me—Pardick, tenant of Number 70. I felt sure I'd heard our old friend Ivor Kern mention the name Pardick at some time. Ivor's an encyclopedia of criminal information, as well as a fence, an antique dealer, and a craftsman in woods and metals. I went to see Ivor."

"He knew the name?" I said eagerly.

"He did," said Raffles. "He once fenced some stolen jewelry for a man called Pardick, whose line was working as a commercial traveler, mostly in the north of England, and pulling off jobs on his travels. I took Ivor out to Raynescourt Avenue, and we contrived to get a glimpse of Pardick, of Number 70. Ivor said he's not the same man."

"He's *not?*" I said, taken aback.

"No," said Raffles, "but he's so much like him that Ivor's certain he must be the other Pardick's brother. You see what that suggested? Any jeweler or diamond merchant will tell you that the safest way to send small articles of high value from one place to another is by registered postal packet. How about it, then, if the commercial-traveling Pardick has been systematically pulling off jobs on his travels and, to get the swag quickly off his hands, sending it by registered mail to his highly respectable brother, Leo Pardick, of 70 Raynescourt Avenue? Ninety-nine times in a hundred, it'd be dead safe."

"But last Tuesday morning was that hundredth chance?" I said. "Some interloper was on to the game, had information on the latest posting of a packet, and so staged the ambush for the postman? But why didn't he hold up Leo Pardick himself?"

"Probably because he knew that both Pardicks are as alert as foxes and dangerous as wolves," Raffles said, "compared with a defenseless postman. No, Bunny, it's you and I who're going to tackle Leo Pardick. There's no juice for us in the fellow who ambushed the postman. Let the police chase him. That suits our book very well.

"Later on, of course, when claims come in from the senders of the one or two registereds that were stolen, the police'll wonder why no claim's come in on the packet addressed to Leo Pardick, 70 Raynescourt Avenue. But it'll be too late, then, to get curious. Mr. Pardick's already flitted."

"Flitted?" I said.

"The ambushing of the postman was a red light for him," Raffles said. "It fairly bristled with nasty implications for him. So he's upstaked and changed camp, confusing his trail very skillfully —but not so skillfully that he shook off the bright lad whom Ivor Kern, at my request, put on to watch him."

"You know where Pardick is?" I said.

"Need you ask?" said Raffles. "That gentleman undoubtedly has a lot of accumulated loot salted away somewhere, in highly portable and negotiable form, and we need it—to advance Kate Dover's career. At the present moment, Leo Pardick, with his appearance quite competently altered, and calling himself Thomas Elderfen, is staying at the Embankment Hotel, bottom of Arundel Street, Strand. I think he's waiting there to liaise with his brother, so that they can coordinate their arrangements for extensive—and luxurious—travel abroad."

Raffles chuckled as he resumed the packing of his suitcase.

"I'm now going to see Ivor Kern," he said, "to get the latest situation report. Then I shall be moving, with *my* appearance slightly altered, into the Embankment Hotel, to size up the crib. I want you to keep in close touch with Ivor Kern, Bunny. As soon as I'm ready for you, you'll receive word through him."

He took up his suitcase and, walking out, left me there in his sitting room with my knees and spine feeling like wet tape.

The Embankment Hotel was a solid, respectable old place, a favorite with businessmen from outside London. At five o'clock on the Monday afternoon, a porter carried up my two suitcases to a room on the second floor. One suitcase contained my personal things. The other, which was locked, had been handed to me that afternoon by Ivor Kern.

I did not know what was in it.

My room, which had a lofty bay window draped with lugubrious red chenille curtains, looked out over the Embankment. The sky was thundery, a premature twilight was closing in, rain was sheeting down over the gray river. I lighted a cigarette, my hands unsteady, the match flare and my spectral face reflected in the window. A tug hooted mournfully from the river.

I was standing at the window, smoking nervously, wondering what the devil I was in for, when the quick opening and closing of the door brought me round with a start. It was Raffles. His appearance, like my own—I had registered in a false name—had been slightly but effectively altered.

"Good man, Bunny," he said, "on the dot, as always. I just looked up the room number against your alias in the register. My own room's on the same floor. After a weekend here, I have this whole place and its routine at my fingertips. You brought the suitcase from Ivor? Yes, I see you have. Well done."

He sat down on my bed, lighted a cigarette.

"Now, then," he said. "Here's the situation. Pardick's carrying his swag in a padlocked briefcase. He's so sure of himself, so smugly confident that he's above all suspicion, that he's had the gall to deposit that briefcase full of loot in what he believes to be the most secure place for it—the safe in the hotel manager's office."

"The hotel safe?" I said. "Oh, hell, Raffles! That's more than we bargained for."

"The crib certainly presents a problem, Bunny, as you'll see," he said. "The manager's office, which adjoins the reception desk in the hall, is locked at night, but I've found a means of access to the office and I've made a preliminary examination of the safe. I shall need from one to two clear hours to get that safe open. But there's a joker, Bunny."

"What kind of a joker?" I said, drying my palms on my thighs.

"The time element," said Raffles. "The outer door of the hotel is bolted at midnight. One man—the night porter—remains on duty in the hall. He's ex-Army, tough and competent. He keeps a loaded revolver in the drawer of the reception desk and also has an alarm bell—a frightful clarion—to his hand."

"I don't like this," I said.

"Listen to me," said Raffles. "A low light is left on all night in the manager's office. In the door, exactly opposite the safe, there's a small peephole window through which the night porter takes a glance into the office from time to time. Now, then. A plate of sandwiches and a bottle of beer are left out for the night porter's supper. He has it at about one A.M., if all's quiet. To eat it in comfort, he sits down in one of that row of saddlebag chairs in the hall. He allows himself about twenty minutes."

"And except for that twenty minutes," I said, "he's liable to glance through the peephole, at the safe in the manager's office, at any minute? But you say you need from one to two clear hours to work at the safe. Raffles, this is an impossible crib!"

"I wouldn't say that," said Raffles, "though this teaser of contriving the necessary working time certainly makes the job an exceptionally attractive one.

"There are points in our favor. For one thing, when I found my way of access to the manager's office on Saturday night and, while the night porter was having his supper, cased the job, I found that the room has a fitted carpet. It stretches right to the wainscot. So the safe, set flush against the wall, stands *on* the carpet. The reason for the carpet and underfelt, as I found when I took a look beneath them, is that the floor's parquet but pretty old and worn, with a good many of the blocks none too tightly fitting. So I took a few measurements."

"Measurements?" I said, puzzled.

"For Ivor Kern," said Raffles. "I gave them to him, with my instructions, on Sunday morning. The little job he's done for us is in that suitcase you've just brought. I hope it may solve the working-time problem—which is the crucial obstacle to be overcome in cracking this crib. Now, then, Bunny . . ."

"Yes?" I said.

"Go down and dine," said Raffles. "I'll be down presently. Remember, we don't know each other. While in the dining room, take note of three separate sets of doors—the service doors, at one end; a pair of doors marked banqueting room, at the other end; and the main doorway opening from the hall. Shortly before one A.M., I'll collect you from your room here, and we'll get to work. Go down and dine, now."

I found the big, dignified old dining room overlooking the Thames fairly well filled with out-of-town businessmen, some of whom studied their order books or professional journals as they dined.

I took careful note of the relative position of the doors Raffles had mentioned; and shortly before one A.M., I understood why he had told me to do this. For, by way of a service staircase and a stoneflagged passage which skirted the dark, hot, silent kitchens, we came soundlessly to a swing door—one of the waiter-service doors I had been told to note—and re-entered the dining room.

To the left, the double doors to the hall, where the night porter was on duty, stood ajar. Enough light came through the gap to illumine faintly the dining room and its many tables. To the right was the wide, lofty window bay—and my skin crept as I saw a point of red light moving along, slowly and uncannily, just outside the windows.

Next second, a mournful baying note filled the dining room, and I realized that what I saw was the masthead light of a tugboat passing by on the river.

Quickly, I moved after Raffles to the door marked banqueting room at the far end of the dining room. He set down the suitcase, unlocked the door with a skeleton key, and we stepped into stuffy-smelling darkness.

"Not used once in a blue moon, this room," Raffles whispered. "I'm relocking the door, in case the night porter should happen to try it if he walks round."

From his gloved hand, a ray of light shot across the room, glimmered on the floor of polished parquet, stamped a white circle on a door facing us.

"That door there leads into the manager's office. It's now just on one, Bunny. The night porter should be starting his supper. Tie a handkerchief over your face—as I'm doing. Now, come on."

Again using a skeleton key, he opened the door to the manager's office. As he had warned me, there was a light on in there, not a strong one, but I saw at once the medium-sized safe standing, with a stack of ledgers on it, flush against the wall to the right.

Raffles moved to the left, to a door opposite the safe, glanced through the square peephole window in the door, then whispered to me, "Keep an eye on him."

I took a cautious glance through the peephole into the hall.

The reception desk was just to the right. Facing me across the hall was a row of deep saddlebag chairs with small, brass-topped tables between them. In one of the chairs the night porter was just starting on his beer and sandwiches and the evening paper.

I stole a look at Raffles.

He had lifted the stack of ledgers from on top of the safe, set them on the floor, and now was moving away a heavy chair which stood between the safe and the door of the banqueting room, to the right. Using a footrule and a sharp knife, he made in the fitted, dark red carpet a cut parallel to the safe and about a foot to the left of it. From the corner of that cut, he made another, at right angles, along past the front of the safe to the door of the banqueting room. He then rolled forward the strip of carpet and underfelt he had cut, until the roll was pressed against the side of the safe.

Sweating, I glanced out through the peephole. The night porter's jaws moved rhythmically as he started on his second sandwich.

I looked at Raffles. With a chisel, he was further loosening an already loose parquet block against the side of the safe. He worked out first one block, then a second, adjoining it and further in under the edge of the safe. He unlocked his suitcase, put the two blocks into it, took out a flat tobacco tin.

Over the handkerchief that masked his face, he glanced at me in swift inquiry. I looked through the peephole, nodded reassurance to Raffles. He beckoned me to him, gave me the tin.

"French chalk," he whispered. "When I heave, throw plenty of it well in under the safe."

He took a crowbar from the suitcase. Inserting an end of it in the hole he had made under the safe, he strained upward on the crowbar with all his wiry, hard-trained strength.

I was down on one knee. I saw, in the hole, that the base under the parquet floor was of the kind usually found under parquetry —namely, bitumen on a hard surface.

As Raffles strained upward on the crowbar, the safe, the strip of carpet on which it stood, the roll of carpet pressed against it, tilted to the left. At once, while Raffles held the safe atilt, I threw white powder in thickly on to the dusty parquet floor under the safe. I could hear Raffles's hard breathing.

"Right," he said, in a gasped whisper, and let the safe down gently, silently, to its original position.

He returned the crowbar to the suitcase, stepped to the peephole, glanced out, returned to me. Taking the tin, he scattered

French chalk thickly along the strip of parquet to the door of the banqueting room. He opened that door, scattered more chalk on the threshold and on the parquet floor of that room.

"Now, then," he breathed. "You push. I pull."

He unrolled the strip of carpet, took a good grip on it with his gloved hands, and while he pulled, backing toward the banqueting room, I pushed hard on the safe itself. To my surprise, it moved —reluctantly at first, then more easily; and on the parquet made slippery by the French chalk, the strip of carpet with the safe standing on it tobogganed smoothly along right into the banqueting room.

"Fine," Raffles whispered. "Back to your post!"

In an instant, my heart going like a drum, I was at the peephole. The night porter had still a sandwich and a half left; his beer glass was a third full.

I glanced at Raffles. From his suitcase, he had taken a small roll of carpet. It was of the same dark red, with the same pattern, as the rest of the carpet. It fitted exactly the gap left by the strip he had cut away.

He now took from the suitcase a square panel of wood. It was of the same color as the safe now standing in the banqueting room. He set the panel flat on the new strip of carpet. Then he took from the suitcase two more panels. He fitted them, upright, into slots in the base panel. He then fitted a panel across the top.

I stared, in stupefaction.

Raffles added a wooden door, fitted with a metal lever handle and a combination dial, and there before my eyes was another safe —the twin of the real one now in the banqueting room.

Raffles placed the stack of ledgers on top of the safe he had built, put the heavy chair back where it had been before. He motioned me to join him. I took a last glance through the peephole, at the night porter now coming to the end of his supper, then I nipped after Raffles into the banqueting room. With his skeleton key, he locked the door.

"Well done, Bunny," he whispered. "It's all plain sailing now. You can leave the rest to me. Here in this banqueting room, I can take the rest of the night to open the safe and get Leo Pardick's briefcase. No one's in the least likely to disturb me here. And the night porter can feast his eyes as much as *he* likes, through the peephole, on our prefabricated safe in the manager's office."

"Prefabricated!" I breathed exultantly. "Magnificent, Raffles!"

He chuckled.

"Slip up to your room now, by the way we came," he said. "I'll lock the door to the dining room after you. The manager's an early bird, but if you check out at about six A.M., that'll be well before he goes to his office. The guests here are mostly business-men, with early trains to catch, so there'll be a dozen or more checking out at that hour. I shall be one of 'em, you can count on that!

"Off you go, Bunny. Drop in at The Albany for lunch, and I'll let you know what there is in Leo Pardick's briefcase."

What was in Pardick's briefcase proved to be the richest haul we had made for a long time. We felt it warranted champagne with our lunch. And three days later we went to see Kate Dover, living at 34 Raynescourt Avenue with her mother and her little girl.

On the way, by arrangement, we picked up Derek Fenn at his house.

"Who *is* this person you want me to meet?" asked the brilliant young impresario, as we walked round from his house to Raynes-court Avenue.

"A friend of ours," Raffles said. "I wrote and asked if we could bring you to meet her, and she's very kindly invited the three of us to tea. Better not talk about poker, Derek—Kate's mother is rather conventional, I understand."

Conventional or not, Kate's mother seemed to me a charming

lady; and though children made me feel awkward, as a rule, I was captivated by six-year-old Drusilla, Kate's daughter.

"I wonder," Raffles said to Kate, after tea, "if you would perhaps do something for me? That is," he added, with a sudden air of doubt, "if it wouldn't remind you too painfully of the experience you—and the postman, poor chap—had at Number 53 in this road?"

Kate looked at him thoughtfully for a moment, then she smiled.

"I think I know what you're going to ask," she said. "All right —just to oblige you, Mr. Raffles."

Twilight was closing in, the small sitting room was growing shadowy. But it was the sunrise of that morning just over a week ago that I saw in memory, and the sparkle of the gardens where the joyous flittings of the birds shook the night's dew from leaf and blossom, as Kate sang, very quietly:

> "Little Bo-Peep has lost her sheep,
> And doesn't know where to find them.
> Leave them alone and they'll come home,
> And bring their tails behind them."

As Kate's voice died away, there was a small cry of protest from Drusilla.

"Mama! Darling!" She ran across the room to Kate. "You haven't lost your sheep any more." She pressed her cheek to Kate's and, comfortingly, stroked Kate's hair. "You've *found* us!" said Drusilla triumphantly.

I happened to notice Derek Fenn's expression. Never had I seen such tenderness, such longing, as there was in his eyes as he looked at Kate and Drusilla.

Raffles must have seen it, too. Abruptly, he pressed out his cigarette in an ashtray, rose to his feet.

"I'm afraid," he said, in his easy way, "Manders and I must

be getting along. We have a dinner engagement and have to go all the way back into town. *You,* of course, live quite close by, Derek . . ."

"Yes," said Derek, seizing on the cue hopefully. "I live no distance away at all—just round the corner, practically . . ."

Derek was invited not to hurry, and he sat down again, beaming.

"So much for our plans to advance Kate's career, Bunny," Raffles said dryly, as we walked to the station. "It's more likely, by the look of things, that we've put an end to it. We took Derek there to arouse his professional interest in Kate. But did you see his expression? What we've aroused, unquestionably, is not his professional interest in Kate, the actress, but his personal interest in Kate, the charming young widow. Mark my words, he'll marry her—and nothing'll stop him. He'll get her, all right."

"He's born lucky, that fellow," I said.

"He is, indeed," said Raffles. "And, you know, Bunny, it makes one begin to realize the high personal price you and I pay for the kind of life we live."

"Price?" I said. "What price?"

"Bunny, think of some of the adorable girls we're thrown together with at times living as we do. Yet, because we still have certain lingering instincts of decency, there is an increasing number of reasons why we can never feel free to do what an honest man like Derek Fenn is free to do—that is, ask a fine, straight, lovely person like Kate Dover to share his life."

"An increasing number of reasons," I said, frowning. "What reasons?"

He gave me a strange look.

"The tales behind us, Bunny. . . ."

The Governor of Gibraltar

It so happened that His Excellency the Governor of Gibraltar had been at the same school as A. J. Raffles and I. As an unexpected consequence, I found myself, one bright autumn morning, occupying a corner seat in a First Class compartment of a train about to depart from a London station to connect with the liner *Karroo Star* at Southampton.

Raffles had strolled along the platform to watch for our old friend Ivor Kern, who was to travel with us in the ship. The warmth of the sun shining in through the open door of the compartment was pleasantly relaxing after the bustle of our arrival. It was not every day that we set forth to be the guests of the governor of a Crown colony and, in expansive mood, I felt that the occasion warranted a cigar.

I was just lighting one when a figure came between me and the sun. Glancing up, I saw standing on the platform, looking in at me with eyes of as nearly a true violet as I ever had seen, a girl dressed all in white, with a violet sash. The breeze that stirred lightly the ribbons of the hat in her hand, and toyed attractively with her shining, soft, blue-black hair, added to her appearance of pretty fluster.

"Please," she said breathlessly, "are all the seats taken in here or could you keep me one till the porter brings my luggage?"

"Certainly! Delighted! I'll put something on it," I said, and, springing to my feet, I lifted down Raffles's green baize cricket bag and placed it on a vacant seat.

The girl rewarded me with a slightly distracted smile, turned away, seemed to hesitate, then impulsively turned back.

"Pray excuse me," she said, "but do you know London well? I wonder if you could tell me—I've been here so few weeks, a visitor from Cape Town—if a big shop called Paradix, in Piccadilly, is all *right?* I mean, honest—reliable?"

"As a Londoner myself," I said, "I can confidently reassure you. Paradix of Piccadilly is one of the best of our ladies' dress shops—quite above reproach."

"You greatly relieve my mind," replied the girl. "You see, it's getting so near train time, and they promised faithfully to send a pageboy here to the station this morning with my new dresses that I've bought and paid for. They had to be altered, do you see, and, unfortunately, as there are seven of them, they weren't quite ready when the shop closed yesterday, so they told me to look for their pageboy here, bringing the dresses in bandboxes, and I just haven't seen a sign of any pageboy, and—oh!" She broke off. "Pray excuse me!"

She was gone. I leaned from the doorway to watch her until, a flutter of white and violet in the sunshine, she vanished among the passengers thronging the platform. How very like a girl, I reflected indulgently, to get herself in a fluster about dresses! A quite needless fluster, too, for a firm like Paradix of Piccadilly was, of course, the acme of merchandising honor.

However, after a minute, I spotted the girl returning, and I felt a twinge of anxiety for the good repute of London. For she was accompanied by no pert pageboy flourishing bandboxes, but was alone and walking dejectedly.

"What's this?" I said, with concern, as she approached. "No luck?"

"Oh, the boy's come, sure enough," she said, "but he's so stupid. He won't let me have them. He says there's an additional charge, for the alterations, of nine-pounds-fourteen, and I've nothing left but a silly letter of credit for a hundred pounds, which the purser on the ship will cash for me. But the boy just refuses to come to Southampton with me to get the money there. He says his instructions are to get it here at the station, otherwise he must take the dresses back. I don't know how any boy can *be* so stupid! He doesn't seem to grasp that I shan't have a stitch to wear on the ship!"

I could not help smiling.

"The main thing is," I said, "your bandboxes have arrived. Now, you'll of course permit me to make you a small advance which you can repay to me on the ship. No, no, I won't hear a word! I insist!" I thrilled to the touch of her slim, cool fingers as I stilled her protests by pressing ten sovereigns into her palm. "Now, hurry and catch the boy before he leaves the station," I urged her, "and I'll keep your seat for you."

The deep look she gave me as she hurried off was a promising augury for the coming days at sea. In fact, as I reseated myself and pulled with enhanced relish at my cigar, I wondered if perhaps there might not be a chance of persuading her to break her voyage at Gibraltar. I felt that she was a girl of whom I would like to see more. It might be a good thing, I fancied, to choose the right moment to let fall the information that Raffles and I were to be guests of the Governor.

We were not on intimate terms with His Excellency, as he had been at the school a good many years before our time; but he was a keen cricketer and had followed Raffles's career in that sport with special interest. So that, finding himself sponsoring a Gala Cricket Week in Gibraltar, and deciding—now that the English season was just finished—to invite a few good amateurs to come out and stiffen the Government House side against some strong Army and Navy teams, the first person he had thought of, naturally enough, was Raffles.

In inviting him to come, and to bring someone along with him, the Governor had added, "There's also an important service which you're the very man to carry out for me."

Intrigued by this, Raffles had accepted the invitation, saying he was bringing me. And when Ivor Kern had heard where we were off to, and had expressed his envy, Raffles had said, "By all means desert this shop of yours, Ivor, and come along with us for the trip. We go in the *Karroo Star,* which calls at Gibraltar on its way to Cape Town, and return eight days later in the sister ship, the *Karroo Queen,* which calls at Gibraltar on its way *from* Cape Town."

As I leaned back in my corner seat, admiring the length of my cigar ash, the thought of escorting the girl with violet eyes to Government House garden parties and balls enticed my mind to halcyon daydreams.

"Look at him, Ivor!" said a voice. "Purring away to himself like a cat that's swallowed a canary!" In light raglan overcoat and gray bowler, his keen face tanned, a pearl in his cravat, Raffles stepped into the compartment. "Hallo, what's my cricket bag hogging that seat beside you for, Bunny?"

"I'm reserving the seat for a young lady," I said. "She'll be here in a moment with her luggage and seven bandboxes. Kindly remember that I saw her first."

"The point is well taken," Raffles conceded. "On the other hand, have you noticed that the train's beginning to move?"

Startled, I glanced from the window. It was true. The platform sights were streaming backwards at a quickening tempo. Leaping up, to the ruin of my cigar ash, I thrust out my head into the sunshine. Nowhere along the platform, now rapidly receding, could I see the girl.

"She seems to have missed the train," Raffles remarked.

"She can't have done!" I exclaimed, turning on him. "I just lent her ten pounds."

"Note the *non sequitur,* Ivor," said Raffles. "But tell us, Bunny—what were the circumstances of this accommodation?"

I explained the girl's predicament, so engagingly feminine. And smiles broadened slowly over Raffles's face and the pale, young-old, cynically intelligent face of Ivor Kern, until it seemed to me that they were grinning from ear to ear.

"Oh, my dear chap!" said Raffles.

"What do you imply?" I shouted.

But, with a stab of horrified understanding, I saw all too clearly what their hilarity implied. They thought I had fallen a victim to the wiles of a confidence trickstress! Appalled, I sank back into my seat.

"But a girl like that!" I said. I was reluctant to believe the worst of her; I *could* not believe it. "If you'd only seen her, Raffles! Truly violet eyes, white dress, and—"

"Violet eyes?" He gave me an odd look. "Eyes of a true violet are very rare, Bunny. I knew a girl once—" He broke off, turned to Ivor Kern. "Ivor, do you remember a clandestine client you had, a couple of years ago—something of a nine-day wonder—a fellow the newspapers dubbed 'Jack-of-Diamonds'?"

"Phil Benedict," Kern said. "For about six months he was the most sensational safe-breaker in London. He pulled off job after job, all on diamond merchants of Hatton Garden. I fenced some of the stuff for him. He was a young fellow—year or so younger than you, Raffles. And from much the same kind of background —gentleman bred. Why, I remember making you and him known to each other, in the room over my antique shop."

The receiver smiled cynically.

"He was another pick-and-choose amateur—like you, Raffles.

But he was certainly a nine-day wonder. Then he just faded out, disappeared. I've often puzzled over whatever became of Phil Benedict."

"He was a strange case," Raffles said. "In one respect only was Phil a criminal—he had a kink against Hatton Garden diamond merchants. The odd thing is, his father, who seems to have been a domestic tyrant of the worst possible kind, was a Hatton Garden diamond merchant!"

"I'll be damned," said Kern. "But how did *you* know that?"

"Phil told me himself," Raffles said. "I saw quite a bit of him after that meeting at your place. Bunny here had parted company with me; he was living in that hideous garret near Tattersall's. And I saw quite a bit of Phil. As a matter of fact, I was best man at his wedding.

"That's all that happened to Phil, Ivor—he got married. It seemed to me a rather quaint romance—and a rather touching one. He married a girl called Eugenie; Ginnie, he called her. Her background was—uncommon. There was a kind of essential innocence about Ginnie, a real innocence of heart. Yet, you know, she'd been brought up by a guardian who had the whitest hair, the most frail and patrician face, the most courtly and beguiling manners of any confidence trickster in London. And he'd spared no pains, from her childhood up, in coaching her to one end—to excel in his own profession."

Excited, I opened my mouth to speak, but Raffles's gray eyes quelled me.

"When Ginnie and Phil got married," he said, "each of them took me aside in the vestry to confide to me, privately, that they were determined to go straight and to keep each other straight. Do you know, they were such a charming young couple, and so desperately in love and in earnest, that I'd have staked my life on their sincerity. They went abroad on their honeymoon, and that was the last I saw of them. Ginnie's favorite color was white. Her eyes were the only truly violet eyes I've ever seen."

He looked at me grimly as he took a Sullivan from his cigarette case.

"If Ginnie Benedict is back in England," he said, "working adroit little confidence tricks round the London termini, it's the saddest news I've heard for a long time. What in the world can have happened to that couple?"

I never had seen him so depressed.

We were a silent trio as we sat over our drinks round a table in the Pompeian Saloon of the ship that night. Arms folded, Raffles stared unseeingly at his glass, faintly vibrant to the throb of the engines deep down. I knew what he was brooding about, and so did Ivor Kern. But Kern grew impatient.

"Hang it all, Raffles," he burst out, at last, "all this gloom over a—"

He checked as a figure glided out from behind a potted palm nearby. A white arm reached between us. Slim fingers placed on the table before me a neat, small tower of gold.

"Your money, Mr. Manders," a voice said softly.

I gaped for an instant at the ten sovereigns, then looked up incredulously into eyes deeply violet, with dark, long lashes.

Raffles jumped up. "Ginnie!" he said. "Ginnie! *Why?*"

"May I sit down?" she said.

She took the chair he placed for her, glanced round as though to assure herself that there were no other passengers within earshot.

"I had two reasons for what I did," she said.

"One of them was to find out whether I altogether had lost the—the opportunism, approach, and timing taught to me by my guardian." She glanced at me. "I didn't know your name, Mr. Manders, until I asked your dining-saloon steward just now. But I saw you and Raffles walk on to the platform this morning. Him, of course, I recognized at once. Then he came back alone. I thought that probably he was going to the bookstall and that I'd just have time to—to make the little test of myself that I wanted, *needed,* to make."

She turned to Raffles. Her voice trembled a little, and I realized that her composure was maintained only by an effort.

"My second reason for what I did," she told him, "was to make yet another test—a test of *you.* I thought that Mr. Manders, when he realized he had been victimized, probably would describe to you the—the harpy who had tricked him, and I thought you might guess who she was. I wanted to watch you, see how you took it. I've *been* watching you—on deck this afternoon, in the dining saloon this evening. I've been trying to read from your expression whether the thought that Ginnie Benedict had fallen so far from her high resolves weighed on you at all. I wanted to try to judge —oh, Raffles," she said, with sudden passion, "I wanted to know whether Phil and I really meant anything to you any more!"

Her hands, on the table, were tightly clasped. Raffles's brown hand covered them. And he said gently after a moment, "It was so important, Ginnie?"

"So terribly important," she whispered, and I heard the tremor in her breath as she drew it in, deeply. "Raffles, you know that just once, during that crazy, spendthrift Jack-of-Diamonds period of his life, Phil had a narrow escape from being caught red-handed, and that he knew his face had been seen? Well, that was why, when we went to Rome for our honeymoon, we decided to stay there, stay out of England—for safety.

"Truly, in Rome we went absolutely straight. And it was— hard at times. So few jobs for Phil, as a foreigner, and what there were didn't last long. When our baby, Philippa, was born, Phil said that we simply had to do better for her, somehow. And about four months ago, by sheer luck, a chance of a good job in Cape Town came his way. He jumped at it. He went off there, and was to have sent for us as soon as he was settled in. Instead—he's been arrested!"

"He met a diamond merchant," said Ivor Kern cynically, "and the old kink—"

She turned on him.

"Yes, Mr. Kern, he *did* meet a diamond merchant. Or, rather, he was seen by one. The one from Hatton Garden who knew the face of Jack-of-Diamonds! That's what happened, Mr. Kern. Phil somehow managed to send a letter to me. At this moment, he's in the *Karroo Queen,* the sister ship of this one, being brought back to England by a Scotland Yard man."

The deep throb of the engines seemed to me to grow more audible. The glasses on the table vibrated. The knowledge that our own return bookings were in the *Karroo Queen* burned in my mind. I dared not look at Raffles.

"The moment I had the news," Ginnie went on, "I left Philippa with the Italian family we were lodging with in Rome. I can trust them; they all adore her. I came to England. I booked in this ship as far as Gibraltar, using a false surname. I've booked back in the *Karroo Queen.* I shall be at least *near* Phil for the last stage of his journey to—to ten or fifteen years behind bars. A lifetime! Am I mad to dream of trying to use the—the wiles I was taught? Of using them to try to get Phil, somehow, out of the hands of that Yard man long enough to jump overboard, to swim and swim and swim in the hope that by some miracle a fishing boat will pick him up?"

Raffles said, "Ginnie—"

"Oh, I know," she said. "It *is* mad—quite mad, of course. But when I was sitting in the train there, thinking just such wild thoughts, *you* walked on to the platform. If you knew how my heart leaped! Raffles, Phil's friend, who stood by us at our wedding, and was the one man, the one cracksman, who might conceivably find a way to steal Phil back for me out of his cell in that ship!"

She leaned forward. Her eyes were shining.

"Raffles," she said, almost in a whisper, "what is a prison cell but just another safe? Not with jewels in it, or money—but *a safe with a man in it?*"

The whispered challenge seemed to me to hang on the air, the lamps in the saloon to burn with an increased and hectic brightness. Steadily, the engines throbbed. Raffles took a Sullivan slowly from his cigarette case.

Ivor Kern spoke.

"Ginnie, I'm sorry, but, girl alive," he said, "face the facts! Gibraltar's the last port of call for the ship Phil's in. These ships, when they call there, stay twelve hours, no more. They don't even dock; they lie out in the bay. The cells are certainly below the waterline. With a prisoner of Jack-of-Diamonds's reputation for clever evasions, you can bet your life that that Yard man will have an eye on the door of Phil's cell every minute the ship's at anchor —especially as it's the last port of call, when a prisoner being brought back for trial might be expected to try something desperate. What could Raffles do? He never carries a weapon. He never uses the slightest violence. No, Ginnie, I'm sorry for you, but you've simply got to face it. Jack-of-Diamonds is beyond help, now —he's in the box."

Raffles was looking at the match he had struck. I saw his eyes, with that sudden gray gleam in them that I knew so well, go for an instant to Ivor's face, then return to contemplation of the match flame. A queer half-smile came to his lips. He dipped his cigarette to the last flicker of the flame.

"As to that, Ivor," he murmured, "we shall see!"

The day we passed Cape San Vicente, where the long Atlantic rollers broke in high-flung flashes of white against the rust-red cliffs of Portugal, I was standing beside Ginnie at the promenade-deck rail. Raffles was absent, having taken to spending much time getting himself shown about the nether regions of the ship, and Ivor Kern was playing the pianoforte in the saloon.

I glanced uneasily at Ginnie. She was watching the passing

headland and, such was her faith in Raffles, I knew that at this very moment she was seeing herself and Phil, with their child Philippa, making a safe, fresh start in some distant country. It worried me intensely for in my heart I believed her vision to be a mirage. At that moment, she turned her head and saw me looking at her. She smiled, putting a hand impulsively on mine.

"Have you forgiven me the ten-pound trick, Bunny?" she said.

"Ah, now—Ginnie!" I said. I would have done anything for her.

But Raffles, that night, in the three-berth cabin we shared with Ivor Kern, said, "All that can be done up to the moment, Bunny, has been done. The ships being sister ships, operated by the same company, I now have the geography and routine of both at my fingertips. I know the precise situation of the cells and the strong room, and—"

"The strong room?" In my upper bunk, I raised myself on one elbow to peer down for a better look at him.

"The *Karroo Queen*," he said, "will certainly be carrying South African gold and diamonds. The presence of plunder has a tactical relevance."

He was reclining in his bunk, one hand behind his head. Flicking ash from his cigarette, he glanced across at Kern.

"Tell me again about this man in Gibraltar whom you mentioned, Ivor."

"Osmanazar?" Kern said. "As I told you, I don't know him personally, but I've heard of him, just as he'll have heard of me. We're in the same line of business. He's the biggest handler of stolen property in the Western Mediterranean. He works under cover of an emporium in Gibraltar called Osmanazar's Bazaar. I feel pretty sure he'll let me use some back room in his place to carry out the work you want done."

"So far, so good," Raffles said. "One thing bothers me a bit, because of its total unpredictability. You remember, Bunny? I mean 'the important personal service' which the Governor was good enough to say I was 'the very man' to carry out for him. There's a possible source of complication there. I wonder what the devil His Excellency can want of me?"

The Governor was not at the dock to receive us in person— we had scarcely expected as much—when the tender chugged us ashore next day. In the noonday heat, the multi-hued, flat-roofed houses which nestled in terraces up the precipitous side of the Rock sweltered visibly.

As we set foot on the wharf, a young officer approached us. He wore a pipe-clayed helmet, scarlet tunic, skin-tight bottle-green trousers strapped under the instep, small silver spurs. His hand was outstretched.

"Raffles, welcome!" he exclaimed. "Delighted to see you. You remember me, at school? Yorick Hope-Jenyns. I was in old Motley's house. I got my colors from you in your last year as captain of cricket. And, Manders, old fellow—how *do* you do? This is simply capital! His Excellency has placed you both in my hands. I've good billets for you, and a very full program." He glanced round. "Orderly!"

"Sir?"

While the brawny ranker took charge of our luggage, Raffles presented Hope-Jenyns to Ginnie, using the false surname she was employing, and introduced Ivor Kern as Ginnie's uncle, the much admired connoisseur, of the King's Road, Chelsea.

"Friends met on the ship, Yorick," Raffles explained. "I see you have a carriage here. You could perhaps suggest a suitable hotel for them, on our way to the billets?"

"Delighted," said Hope-Jenyns, with an ardent look at Ginnie.

As we set off at a spanking trot in the high-slung yellow carriage with its red-tasseled white canopy, he continued to look frequently into Ginnie's eyes under the pretense of drawing her attention to such places of interest as the Casemates, the old Water Gate, the Moorish Castle.

"We are now going up Main Street," he presently announced. "Yonder is a shop, Miss Ginnie, where I must advise you always to beat them down if you give them custom—Osmanazar's Bazaar."

Between the throngs of garrison ladies in their bustled summer gowns, twirling parasols languidly as they sauntered by with their escorts in Navy white-and-gold and military scarlet, with here and there a kilt of Highland tartan, I glimpsed, through a doorway hung about with tarbooshes, Moorish slippers, camel harness, children's sailor suits, kimonos, castanets, and bullfighters' hats, the shadowy, enigmatic interior of Osmanazar's Bazaar.

It looked as hot as an oven. And in the gala days that followed I did not envy that ingenious artificer in woods and metals, Ivor Kern, for I knew that the mysterious task Raffles had set him was keeping him occupied for long hours in some shuttered little fly-humming room in Osmanazar's rear regions.

As for me, Raffles told me nothing, as usual.

He and I shared good billets in Bombhouse Lane with some cricketers who included that graceful batsman, the young Jam-Sahib of Kushghir, who had been at school with us. A nonplayer myself, I had no other task but the pleasant one of calling each morning for Ginnie at her hotel to escort her to the matches.

Twice we saw the Governor. Each time, it was on the parched brown cricket ground between the high bastion lined with date palms and the harbor. On the harbor side, the brasswork and white awnings of the dreadnoughts at anchor were dazzling against the background of the bay and the distant white buildings of Algeciras, which looked like a handful of pearls cast down against the parched red hills of Spain.

The first time we saw the Governor was when he looked in at the pavilion for a moment to shake hands with Raffles and myself and bid us welcome.

"Don't forget, Raffles," he said, at parting. "I have an important job for you."

The second time we saw him was later in the week, as he was taking his seat to watch the cricket in company with the Port Admiral. He spotted me, where I stood beside Ginnie's deck chair, and lifted a hand to us graciously.

The cricket went well, Raffles with his deceptive spinners being the mainstay of the Government House bowling, as the Jam-Sahib—always an aesthetic pleasure to watch—was the mainstay of the batting. But we were no nearer knowing what His Excellency had in store for Raffles; and as the golden days passed, and the nights brilliant with balls aboard one or other of the dreadnoughts succeeded each other, I knew he was getting more and more anxious. For each day brought the *Karroo Queen,* with its prisoner, closer to Gibraltar.

Before we knew where we were, the culminating night was upon us, the night of the Governor's Ball.

"And still we don't know what he wants done!" Raffles said grimly.

In full evening dress and opera hats, scarlet-lined capes over our arms, we walked up the narrow Bombhouse Lane and turned left under the bracket lamp at the corner into the raucous uproar of the fleet at liberty in the grog shops of Main Street.

Ginnie was waiting for us in the foyer of her hotel. She was a picture in white, a cape of violet velvet over her arm, her hair raven, her shoulders ivory. The funereal Ivor Kern stood beside her chair.

Raffles dissembled the anxiety I knew he felt, but he was brisk and kept his voice low as he said, "All ready, Ivor?"

"All ready," said the receiver. "The *Karroo Queen's* been reported. She'll be in about midnight. She'll start discharging and taking in cargo as soon as she's anchored. Our box is already down at the cargo sheds. It's consigned as from a Mr. Pascarella to a London firm. Neither exist. The origin of the box will be quite untraceable. It's marked for the strong room and will go out to the ship, in the first cargo lighter, as soon as the anchor's down.

Osmanazar's arranged the other detail, as you asked, and the name of the man concerned is Ibañez. The *Karroo Queen* is due to sail again at noon tomorrow."

"Right," Raffles said. "We shall see you, then, Ivor, a bit before noon tomorrow, when you come out to the ship in the last passenger tender." He turned to the girl. "Now, Ginnie—"

"Yes, Raffles?"

She was keyed to the highest tension. In her shining eyes and quickened breathing was betrayed her excitement at the knowledge of how close now was the ship bearing her young husband, of how few remained the miles of starlit sea that separated them.

"You know your program?" Raffles said. "Tomorrow morning Ivor will take you to La Línea, the Spanish frontier, and put you on the diligence to Algeciras. From there you will take a train to Madrid, go to the address you've been given, and wait there—for Phil. Right? Then, as there may not be time for good-byes later this evening—" He held out his hand. "Ginnie—my dear—godspeed."

She looked at him with her eyes of misted violet. She took his hand in both of hers, carried it to her breast, and pressed her lips to his.

Then we went to the ball.

Only I, who knew so little else, knew the secret anxiety that gnawed at Raffles's mind, the anxiety which made him, under the chandeliers of that glittering ballroom, glance so frequently at the ramrod-backed, white-haired figure of the Governor, in his splendor of scarlet mess jacket and decorations.

The Governor and his lady danced with this guest and with that. There was gaiety in the lilt of the violins. In the arms of the Jam-Sahib, Ginnie waltzed. But I stood by the tall windows, open to the purple night where the palm trees in the grounds were darkly silhouetted against the sky of stars over the wide bay, and I watched Raffles.

He smiled as he talked to his dance partner; he had, seemingly, not a care in the world. But he could not keep his glance long away from the Governor.

It must have been nigh on midnight when, a dance ending, wide doors were flung open by footmen, disclosing in an adjoining room the silver and crystal of long buffet tables. It was the interval. A buzz of chatter arose. There was a drift from the ballroom.

The Governor beckoned to a person here, a person there, and, left as by a receding tide, there remained upon the shining floor a small group composed of the Governor himself, his lady, Ginnie and the Jam-Sahib, Raffles, Hope-Jenyns.

The thumping in my chest grew more sultry. The Governor said something to Hope-Jenyns, and the aide-de-camp went from the room. I had an uncomfortable feeling that I had no business to be here; but, just then, the Governor spotted me. He came across to me, where I stood by the windows, and the whole group followed.

"Ah, Manders, my friend," said the Governor, "you're in this, too, you know. The ladies as a very special privilege, but you fellows by right of having been at the old school." He rubbed his hands together briskly. "Now, where's young Hope-Jenyns? Ah, there you are, Yorick! You have it, I see. Put it on the window seat."

The aide-de-camp placed on the window seat a large box of polished mahogany. That it was in some way connected with the task which the Governor had for Raffles, I could not doubt. My palms were moist. I dreaded what fatal complication this box might prove to be for Raffles's plans. I gritted my teeth as the Governor stroked the box affectionately.

"Any of you guess what this is?" he asked, smiling. "Or why I consider that A. J. Raffles—and Yorick entirely agrees with me —is the very man to trust with this important mission? What, no guesses? Very well!"

He threw back the hinged lid. Within the box, on a lining of white satin, lay a great gold cup.

" 'The Governor's Challenge Cup,' " said His Excellency, reading aloud the engraved legend, " 'Presented to His Old School, by the Governor of Gibraltar, as an Inter-House Cricket Trophy.' Think that's all right? Such a trophy's been needed for a long time. Now, then, Raffles, I'm appointing you my special envoy, to deliver the cup to the school, and read my bit of a speech on my behalf, at the next prize-giving. Give him the script, Yorick. Good. Well, now, Raffles—what do you say?"

With his invincible ease of manner, Raffles said just the right things, in just the right way. And I saw in his eyes not only relief, but a dancing exultation, as he added, "And for the honor, Your Excellency, of acting as your personal envoy, I'm more grateful than you can possibly—"

His voice was drowned by the far-carrying, ominous, deeply baying note of a ship's siren. Ginnie's hands flew to her throat. We all looked from the window—to see, moving in slowly across the dark waters of the bay below, the innumerable lighted portholes of the *Karroo Queen*.

The Governor now suggested that we who were sailing in the ship might have packing to see to and wish to take our leave. Availing ourselves of his thoughtfulness, we escorted Ginnie back to her hotel, then hurried to our billets. Without bothering to change, we strapped up our luggage.

"A wonderful stroke of luck, Bunny!" Raffles exulted, patting the box containing the cup. "The thing I've been dreading most, all along, proves to be the best thing that could possibly have happened. The cup gives us a better excuse than any of the half-dozen I'd invented to go aboard right away.

"More! I had a word with Hope-Jenyns. I told him I wouldn't know a moment's peace till I'd seen the cup safely deposited in the ship's strong room, and he's arranging for us to go out in Government House's own launch. So, instead of in a hired bumboat, we'll be arriving in such style as will put us utterly above suspicion as regards—imminent events. Your bags ready? Good. There's a carriage waiting. Yorick is to meet us at the docks."

So it was that, as a cargo lighter was drawing away from the liner's side an hour later, the stentorian hail of a Navy coxswain rang across the starlit water:

"*Karroo Queen*, ahoy! Government House launch coming alongside!"

Stepping on deck as His Excellency's envoy, in full evening dress, cape and opera hat, a Sullivan between his fingers, Raffles with his air of casual authority dimmed even the magnificence of Hope-Jenyns's scarlet and gold. And the Captain and the Purser, on being apprised of Raffles's requirements, personally conducted us to the strong room to deposit the Governor's box.

Shadows cast by the Purser's safety lantern wheeled about the strong room, with its rows of metal shelves lining reinforced bulkheads. Raffles glanced about him with tolerant interest.

"Quite a Golconda you have here," he remarked indulgently.

"Golconda's right, sir," said the gratified Purser. "In the safe there, South African diamonds. In those small sacks on the shelves, gold dust. As for those small wooden boxes, their weight would astonish you—that's bar gold."

But I could not take my own eyes from a much larger box, a black wooden box which stood in a corner and which I knew must have been brought aboard from the lighter we had seen. For its front was labeled: PORCELAIN AND MANCHU SILK. CONSIGNED BY J. PASCARELLA, GIBRALTAR.

"Well, Yorick," said Raffles, turning to Hope-Jenyns, "I think we'll see you off, and then—if the Purser, when he's secured his treasure chamber here, will be good enough to send us a steward to show us to our cabin—speaking for myself, I shall be very ready to retire to my bunk."

No sooner were we alone in our cabin than his whole manner changed.

"Now, then, Bunny!"

He opened his cricket bag, fished out from among the bats and pads a coil of Manila rope and a collection of curious metal objects attached to a ring.

"Skeleton keys," he said. "What's known to the professional fraternity as 'a large, light bunch.' Ivor got them from Osmanazar for me. What time is it?"

My hands shook so that I scarcely could get out my half-hunter.

"Quarter to two," I said, with parched lips.

"Some time between three and four is the vital hour," Raffles said, "unless Ivor's computations are sadly astray. To be on the safe side, we'll get to action stations as soon as we've changed."

When we had done so, he opened the door a crack, peered out, stepped quickly from the cabin. The alleyway was deserted, dimly lit by the blue glimmer of the safety lamps. About us was the uncanny silence of a ship at anchor, with engines stopped.

Raffles moved with the swift certainty of a man who knew his way. Only twice were there checks in our descent into the depths of the vessel. One with folded arms on a laundry hamper in a break of the companion stairs. The other was when we had to duck into a recess to let the ship's corporal, on his rounds with lantern and truncheon, go past us.

Deeper still in the ship, we stole down an iron ladder into a narrow, faintly blue-lit alleyway. Just to the left was a shallow recess partially stacked with spare lifejackets. Ducking into the recess, we just had room to stand upright, side by side. Obliquely ahead along the alleyway, on the right, were three iron doors with grilles in them, showing them to be cells. Opposite them, from a door standing open, shone a rather stronger, yellowish light.

"The Yard man's observation post," Raffles whispered.

The man was alert. I heard the rustle of a newspaper. I saw a faint curl of smoke from that open door, could even smell pipe tobacco. A glass clinked, and I heard the *glug-glug* of beer poured from a bottle.

The slow thump in my chest measured the minutes. They

stretched to eternity. For what we thus waited I had no notion. It was intensely hot. Perspiration poured from me. I seemed to feel myself crawled over by a legion of nameless itchy things. My eyes glazed. My mind wandered—to be brought back suddenly by Raffles's iron grip on my arm.

I held my breath, listened, heard running footsteps. They came closer, grew louder. Startingly, they came clattering down the iron ladder.

"Sergeant Teemer!" A young ship's officer darted past our recess. "Detective Sergeant Teemer!" he shouted.

A burly man, collarless, in shirtsleeves but wearing braces and a leather belt as well, lumbered out into the alleyway, a revolver clamped in one huge hand.

"Mr. Jackson!" he exclaimed. "What is it? What's wrong?"

"You're wanted at the strong room instantly!" Jackson seemed beside himself with excitement. "Captain's orders! Your prisoner's loose, Sergeant! He's slipped you! They have him cornered, by sheer luck, but he's armed and liable to start shooting any minute. Strong room fast as you can get. Come on, man!"

The detective's jaw fell. He stammered, "Impossible! Slipped me? Armed? Not possible, Mr. Jackson! He's in the middle cell there—asleep."

"Asleep?" roared Jackson. "Damnation, man, ain't I telling you the crafty fox is in the strong room? In among the boodle, his hands right in the perishing till! Purser heard something knocked over in the strong room with a deuce of a clang. He got a lantern, unlocked the door, and strike me, there he was, in hat and cloak, with a revolver in his mitt! Your prisoner, Jack-of-Diamonds— Purser saw his face as clear as day! Purser slammed the door on him before he could shoot and cornered him in there!"

The detective turned and gripped the grille in the door of the middle cell. He shook the door. It stood firm. He twisted his neck to peer in through the grille, but this act got him into his own light, and there was a hint of panic in his voice as he bellowed, "Benedict!"

From the dark cell came nothing but utter silence.

The detective turned upon Jackson a face of unplumbable consternation. "My keys," he said. "I'll get my keys—I'll get my lamp—"

"You'll get damned well hanged," shouted Jackson, "if you muddle about here while Jack-of-Diamonds cuts loose with that gun! He can only have got into the strong room by cutting through one of the bulkheads somehow, and he may come out the same way any second, and come with bullets! Come on, man, come on, come *on!*"

Jackson darted away toward the ladder. The detective remained suspended for a second in a purgatory of demoralized irresolution; then something seemed to break in him and, with a great shout, he went thundering up the ladder after Jackson.

Instantly, Raffles ducked out from the recess. He stepped to the door of the middle cell. The skeleton keys were in his hand. As he went to work on the lock, he called sharply, "Phil?"

At once, a drawn, pale, handsome young face appeared behind the bars of the grille.

"Raffles?" said Phil Benedict. "A. J. Raffles? Ye gods! I heard all that shouting. I listened. Last port of call—I thought Ginnie might have been mad enough to scheme some fantastic attempt. It seemed I was believed to be in the strong room, so I thought I'd better take the cue, and I crouched down behind the door here—out of sight—"

"Thank heaven for your quick wits," Raffles said. "I counted on 'em. The only way of getting you a message telling you to do just what you did was to make *them* shout it to you."

He jerked the door open. Phil Benedict, barefoot, in shirt and trousers, stood there blinking. Raffles thrust the coil of rope into his hand.

"Topside now, Phil," Raffles said, "fast as you can move! Tie this rope to the rail, slide down it so that you enter the water without a splash. Swim straight for the lights of Algeciras on the Spanish side. There's a boat waiting on that bearing. Before you've gone far, it'll pick you up. There's a man called Ibañez in it— Spanish smuggler. He has clothes, disguise, and money for you, and will give you an address in Madrid where you'll find Ginnie waiting. No, don't talk! Hook it! Good-bye forever, Jack-of-Diamonds. *And good luck, Phil!*"

With one swift handshake, Phil was gone, like a wraith, barefoot up the iron ladder, gripping the coil of rope. And by rapid stages, now walking fast along the dim-lit alleyways, now darting aside into brief concealment, Raffles and I regained our cabin. At once, he thrust his head from the open porthole, remained there for what seemed to me many minutes. At last, he turned, a gray gleam in his eyes.

"Clothes off, Bunny, and into our bunks quick! I've dropped the skeleton keys into the water. No suspicion is likely to attach to the Governor's envoy, but we'd better be in our bunks—just in case. Phil's well away, or we'd have heard a boat lowered by now. They're probably still cordoning that strong room, trying to decide whether to chance the odds and open the door."

"In heaven's name," I panted, as I, too, tore off my clothes, "who have they got cornered in there?"

Raffles grinned.

"Not 'who,' Bunny," he said, " 'what'! The nails that apparently secured the lid of the Pascarella box were only nail *heads.* The lid actually was held in place by a thin wire hook on the inside. The wire was treated with an acid, the corrosive action of which was carefully timed by Ivor to within an hour. When the wire snapped, the hinged lid shot back with a devil of a clang. Up popped, on a powerful spring, a dummy figure, cloaked and hatted, with a wax face fashioned in a very tolerable likeness of Phil's, and a dummy revolver jutting from the cloak. Swaying a little on its spring, to the slight movement of the ship at anchor, it must have made quite a poignant impression upon an alarmed and puzzled man seeing it suddenly among the shadows cast by his lantern. Remember Ivor's remark to Ginnie that Jack-of-Diamonds was beyond help now—he was in the box? For some reason, the fruitful thought crossed my mind that some might think it the proper place for a Jack—*in the box!*"

He turned out the light and in the darkness I heard him chuckling.

Yet when, in the sunset light of the following evening, we once more—homeward bound, this time—passed Cape San Vicente, and I stood with Raffles and Ivor Kern at the promenade-deck rail, we were all three strangely silent.

Far inland, beyond the blue mountains of Portugal, lay the arid Spanish plateau. And I knew that somewhere there, alone in a train bound for Madrid, Ginnie with her violet eyes, filled with an infinite anxiety and an infinite hope, must be watching the sunset fading from the sky.

I wondered how it would be for her, in the outcome—for Ginnie, and the husband and the child who were all her little world.

"They'll be all right," Raffles said. It was as though he had read my thought. And he said, "You know, Bunny, unredeemed sinner as I am, and seldom as I delve into such deep matters, there's something about Ginnie Benedict, the ex man-made confidence-trick girl with the innocent heart, which makes me believe that a certain plea will be remembered in her behalf—and, through her, in Phil's."

I glanced at him.

He was gazing thoughtfully across the water at the distant white flashes where the long Atlantic rollers flung high their spray against the red cliffs of the lonely Cape.

"Plea?" I said, puzzled. "What plea?"

" 'Forgive us our trespasses,' " said A. J. Raffles.

The Riddle of Dinah Raffles

In the sunshine of an autumn noonday, a great many carriages with fringed white canopies and clip-clopping horses were jingling to and fro along the palm-lined esplanade which skirted the blue waters of the Bay of Naples.

Among the carriages was one carrying Raffles and myself.

"Too bad you're not sailing with me, Bunny," Raffles said, as he offered me a Sullivan from his cigarette case. "It's still possible, you know, that we could get you a berth in the liner coming in tomorrow. No chance of persuading you to change your mind?"

"None whatever," I said. "I don't mind going along with you on your country house cricket jaunts, but your serious cricket is another matter. Though mind you, I'm very glad you arranged to travel down overland and link up with the rest of the England team here. I wouldn't for worlds have missed this trip down to see you off."

Raffles chuckled.

"Good old Bunny! Well, you know your own mind best. I won't try to press you." He changed the subject. "I wonder what's in this batch of letters?"

288

We had made a pretty leisured journey here from London, and before he left his rooms at The Albany he had arranged for our Naples hotel to be a forwarding address.

The letters had been handed to him as we were coming out of our hotel, and now with a word of apology he took them from his pocket and shuffled through them.

"Bills, mostly," he said, "as usual. I—" He broke off. "Now, here's a coincidence," he said. "A letter from Australia—and I'm on my way there."

He tore open the envelope, took out a thick sheaf of notepaper, unfolded it, glanced at the signature on the bottom page. I could have sworn he paled under his tan. He went back to the beginning, began to read. I was troubled by the curious expression still on his face.

"Bad news?" I asked.

He shook his head.

"The letter's from my sister," he said, "my sister Dinah."

He took a last pull at his cigarette, flicked it out under the canopy.

"I've never told you before that I have a sister, have I? Well, she's now on her way to England. I haven't seen her since one summer vacation when she was ten and I was fourteen and we were both home from boarding schools."

He looked out thoughtfully over the incomparable bay.

"When my father died," he went on, "he left precious little. And he had only one relative, an uncle in Australia, a very good, solid bloke, some kind of country bank inspector, name of W. F. Raffles. It was arranged that what little my father had left should be used to see me through school, and that Dinah should be sent out to Mr. and Mrs. W. F.

"Dinah and I wrote to each other for a while, but then the letters trailed off. W. F. had a little farm, where he ran a few sheep as a hobby. Dinah sounded happy there, and I was happy enough. So, bit by bit, we lost touch."

He took another cigarette from his case.

"Sometimes the thought of Dinah has gnawed at my conscience, Bunny," he said. "I've felt I ought to get in touch with her. But somehow, knowing she was happy, and that any day my own activities might bring me a frightful purler—somehow, I always felt it'd be kinder to let her lead her own life."

"The wheel turns," I said. "Now, she's taken the initiative."

He nodded.

"She's read about my being picked for the M.C.C. team against Australia. See where this letter's addressed? 'C/o M.C.C., Lord's Cricket Ground.' Forwarded from Lord's to The Albany, from The Albany to here. And she says"—he opened the letter again—"she says: 'I see you're in the England side that's coming here. I do congratulate you. What a pity, though, if you've sailed before I arrive. But no matter, I shall be in London when you return. I'm longing to see what you look like now, and to know all about you and your doings.'"

Raffles returned the letter to its envelope.

"Me and my doings!" he said wryly.

"She's evidently not coming specifically to look you up," I commented.

"By no means," he said. "She seems to be coming to England permanently. I gather that Mr. and Mrs. W. F. are both dead, and that Dinah is coming to London to 'try her fortune.' Poor, naïve kid!"

He gazed out unseeingly over the Bay of Naples for a moment. Then, abruptly, he turned to me.

"Bunny, we must go to the shipping office, find out whether Dinah's liner touches here at Naples—and if so, when."

Ten minutes later we were in the shipping office, looking blankly at each other.

"Of all the foul luck!" I said. "Her liner calls here just three days after you'll have sailed."

"To which," he said, "there's only one answer. I don't sail."

I said, "You can't do that, Raffles. You've got to go." Then I added, seeing how distressed he was, "I'll wait for her ship and travel back to England with her, if that would help."

Raffles cheered up at once.

"You'd do that, Bunny?" he said. "It's awfully good of you. And I can't think of anyone better for the job. You're the very man to take her in hand."

"You can rely on me implicitly," I assured him.

"One good thing, anyway," Raffles said. "There's no need for my rooms to stand vacant. You can install her in them very snugly."

The old vivacity danced in his eyes.

"You'll have a Raffles just round the corner at The Albany, after all, Bunny."

"But what a different Raffles!" I said ruefully. "A naïve girl!"

Mid-morning on the third day after Raffles departed, I was on the wharf, looking out at the newly arrived liner at anchor and at the incoming tender puffing shoreward, her decks bright with dresses of summery muslin, many parasols, and masculine straw hats. The tender came alongside and the gangway was run out.

In the sweltering confusion, an awful thought struck me. I had secured a booking with no difficulty; but now, as I watched the cargo slings sway baggage up out of the tender, it occurred to me that Dinah Raffles might have decided to leave the ship here and save herself time by going on to England overland. Many people did this.

I studied the passengers descending the gangway, obviously bent on sightseeing during the few hours the liner would remain here. Raffles had told me that his sister had "oat-colored braids," but apart from that I had no clue to her appearance. Yet now, suddenly, my attention was riveted by a girl who appeared at the head of the gangway.

She was a graceful, gray-eyed girl, cool in a dainty dress. She carried a parasol and long gloves in her hand. I could have imagined her and Raffles together, he a bit the taller; they would have looked well, have complemented each other.

But if she were indeed Dinah, she no longer had braids. Her pretty hair, as I saw when she turned her head to speak to someone behind her, was secured at her nape by a neat little bow of black velvet.

That turning of the head made me certain she was Dinah. The clean-cut profile, the smile, these could have belonged to no one, I felt, but Raffles's sister.

I watched her as, with a hand to her skirts, she started down the gangway, escorted by a sleekly good-looking, dark-haired fellow in his middle thirties wearing a well-cut gray suit.

Motioning the porter carrying my portmanteau to follow me, I began to edge my way through the milling crowd.

While I was doing so, I saw a trio of vividly clad gypsy girls, with jingling tambourines, gather about Dinah as she set foot on the wharf.

With a smile, she let one of the girls draw her aside, clear of the gangway and, poring over her palm, gabble forth some stream of nonsense.

"*Si, si, e vero, signorina, e vero!*" I heard the gypsy girl vociferating, as I drew closer. "One of the protected ones! It is wrote— here in your hand. *Eccolo!* Always I know them—the protected ones! One in a million, signorina. *Vabene,* you'll see one day— you'll remember!"

"I'm sure I shall," I heard Dinah say, and by her voice alone, so cool, friendly, and amused, I should have known her anywhere for a Raffles.

I could not help grinning to myself at the thought that, at that very moment, I, her officially appointed protector, was working my way through the crowd to reach her. But just as I was about to step free, declare myself, and produce the letter of credentials which Raffles had given me, the gray-suited fellow with Dinah tossed the gypsy girl a coin and, putting an arm very familiarly about Dinah's waist, drew her away toward the line of waiting carriages.

The bland possessiveness of the gesture came as a shock to me. I stood staring.

And I heard the man say, "You see, Dinah? One of the protected ones! And did you notice who the girl rolled her eye at when she said it?"

He meant himself, of course; and I was so taken aback that I let them go right by me. It had simply not occurred to either Raffles or me that Dinah, totally inexperienced and for the first time in her life footloose, might have got mixed up with some man in the course of the voyage.

I watched the chap hand Dinah into one of the carriages, and then I went out in the tender to the liner. Having seen my baggage to my cabin, I went straight to the Purser's office in the main deck foyer, where I was lucky enough to get hold of the Assistant Purser.

Oh, yes, he knew Miss Raffles very well. The man who had taken her ashore? He was a Mr. Graham Forbes, of a wealthy English family long settled in the Argentine. It appeared that Forbes had been in Australia studying sheep-farming methods with a view to experimenting with sheep on his Argentine properties.

"Going to England, is he?" I asked.

"Only as far as Lisbon. He gets a ship there for Rio and the River Plate."

"He became acquainted with Miss Raffles on board?" I inquired.

And then, seeing that the Assistant Purser was beginning to look askance at my questions, I took him into my confidence.

"I'm a close friend of Miss Raffles's brother. He's unable to meet her himself and he's appointed me a sort of brother by proxy. Though I don't know her personally yet, I have a responsibility. From what I saw of Forbes's manner to her on the wharf just now, I sensed—well, a possible entanglement."

The Assistant Purser nodded.

"He met her on board here, and made a dead set at her from the start."

He looked at me strangely.

"Seeing how you're placed, Mr. Manders, I'd better be open with you. I may tell you it's just as well you've shown up. Forbes keeps it very dark when he's traveling, but I happen to know he's a married man—got a nice, pretty little señora in the Argentine."

I compressed my lips.

"There's worse to come," the Assistant Purser said grimly. "I was on the River Plate run once. I know all about this Graham Forbes. He's a charmer. He can tell the tale. More than one pretty girl traveling alone—well, I've heard stories. As a matter of fact, I've heard one right in this ship—from a pretty youngster called Mary Moore, down in Third Class."

Frowning, he filled his pipe.

"She came to me one day, aboard here," he said, "and told me she'd noticed that a certain girl who was young and traveling alone —she meant Miss Raffles—seemed to be in danger of losing her head over Forbes.

"Miss Moore told me that she herself had met Forbes some months ago, in a ship going out to Australia. She was going to Australia to get married. Unfortunately, she fell in love with Forbes, and she let him talk her into breaking it off with the man she was going to marry and running off with Forbes, instead. That's his line, Mr. Manders. I know.

"Quite by chance, Mary Moore learned he was already married and had been lying to her. She taxed him with it. When he saw she had his number, he just left her—flat.

"That girl's been badly hurt, Mr. Manders. She had too much pride to go back to the man she'd broken off with. She worked to earn her fare back to England, and she's returning unhappy and virtually penniless."

"Does Forbes know she's in this ship?" I asked.

"He doesn't dream it," said the Assistant Purser. "And Miss Moore didn't dream Forbes was aboard, either, till she happened —from the Third Class deck for'ard—to spot him up on the promenade deck with Miss Raffles. After that, she kept her eyes open, and she saw Forbes and Miss Raffles together so many times that finally she came to me and told me Miss Raffles ought to be warned that Forbes is a bad lot.

"I told Miss Raffles and suggested she have a talk with Mary Moore. Whether she did or not, I don't know. She's still going about with Forbes, so I doubt it. Mr. Manders, it's as well you've shown up, but I don't envy you. You've got a situation on your hands."

Helpfully, he saw to it that I got a place at the same table as Dinah and Forbes in the dining saloon when they returned from their day out. The tables were long ones, seating twenty a side.

Watching the couple at dinner that evening, soon after we sailed, I saw that Forbes monopolized Dinah completely; his jealousy was glaring.

I wanted to get Dinah alone, to introduce myself. But as I watched Forbes escort her from the saloon, it was obvious that I stood a poor hope of getting her alone. So I went to the smoking saloon to write her a note.

A poker school was in session there, with a gray-haired, hardfaced man running in luck by the look of it. I sat down at a table nearby and, calling for writing materials, wrote my note to Dinah, saying I looked forward to a private talk with her as soon as she could make it convenient.

Sealing the note, together with Raffles's letter, into an envelope, I dispatched a steward to hand it to Miss Raffles's cabin steward with instructions to see that she got it as soon as she went below.

I had a few brandies and watched the poker game for a while, then went down to my cabin. I turned up the light to undress, climbed into my bunk, turned the light down to a blue speck in the dark. Lulled by the muted throb of the engines, I soon—despite my perplexities—fell asleep.

How long I slept, or what awakened me, I did not know, but suddenly my eyes were wide open. Through the porthole I could see a scatter of distant stars. I was listening intently.

There was the deep beat of the engines, the hiss and slur of the sliding water, the slight vibration of a tooth glass in its bracket. No other sound.

Tension was beginning to relax in me when a silent, hooded shadow blotted out the porthole and the stars, and remained there —motionless.

My heart gave a great thump.

"Who's there?" I said hoarsely.

I heaved myself up on an elbow, turned up the blue speck of the lamp. The light bloomed, dazzling me. I put up an arm to shade my eyes.

Standing near the foot of the bunk was a figure wearing a hooded cape of deep blue velvet.

"You wanted to talk to me privately?" a voice whispered.

Slim hands reached up to put back the hood. I saw a girl's face, clean-cut as a cameo. Clear gray eyes, dark-lashed, looked at me levelly.

"You're my brother's friend. So I came as soon as I could— Bunny," said Dinah.

I gaped at her. I felt as if I were dreaming. "But, Miss Raffles!" I said. "Dinah! To come here! To my cabin! I didn't mean—"

"Oh, I know," she said. "But where else could we meet privately? There's somebody—a Graham Forbes—I have a reason for not wanting him to know about you. Where else but here could we meet without his getting to hear of it? On ships, everyone gets to hear everything."

"What of it?" I said. "Forbes or no Forbes, you've evidently read your brother's letter; you know I'm his closest friend—"

"Which would be enough," she said, "to make Graham quite wildly jealous. He's like that, Bunny, and I don't want to—upset him."

"Dinah," I said dryly. "I begin to think my dropping on you out of a clear sky must seem an unwelcome complication."

"Oh, don't say that, Bunny," she said, but she gave me an unfathomable look.

I remembered that I was sitting up in my bunk clad only in my nightclothes. I reached out for my smoking jacket and donned it.

"This is hardly the time or place I had in mind for our talk," I said, "but since you've chosen it—won't you sit down?"

"Thank you, Bunny," she said, and, drawing her cape about her, she seated herself on the one small upholstered stool.

Her clear gray eyes met mine. Her brows, a shade darker than her hair, subtly reminded me of Raffles.

"Dinah," I said, "did Raffles make any recommendations in his letter?"

She hesitated. Then she said, "He told me that he would like me to be guided by you in all respects."

"And how do you feel about that, Dinah?" I asked.

"Why, of course, Bunny," she said. "I shall be very happy to be guided by you."

It was my cue to get to grips with the Graham Forbes entanglement. I told her what the Assistant Purser, in view of my status as brother-by-proxy, very properly had seen fit to confide in me about Graham Forbes.

I mentioned the unfortunate Mary Moore and rather cruelly rubbed in the sufferings Forbes's unfortunate wife must endure. I pulled out all the stops.

Dinah, sitting on the stool, chin propped on her palm, never took her eyes off me. I waited for her to speak. Had I seen tears in her eyes, I should have been embarrassed but, taking them to be a sign that I had impressed her, not ungratified.

Instead, gazing at me meditatively, she put a hand to some pocket in the silken lining of her cape and drew out a little gold comfit box. Opening it, disclosing some small squares of Turkish Delight, she offered it to me absently.

"Sweet, Bunny?" she said.

I was dumbfounded. To the very life, it was the gesture with which countless times I had seen A. J. Raffles, when deep in thought and having heard scarcely a word of some theory or protest I had been earnestly advancing, take out his cigarette case and offer me a Sullivan, saying absently, "Smoke, Bunny?"

I shook my head, and Dinah, gazing into space, nibbled meditatively at a piece of Turkish Delight.

"Bunny," she said, at last, "I feel sure there's a great deal in what you say. Perhaps I've been very silly. If I tell you that I shall be happy to be guided by you in principle, and make a clean break from Graham, will you be happy if I handle the detail of it in my own way?"

My spirits rose.

"But of course," I assured her. "After all, the matter's highly personal."

"Then will you please," she said, "promise to behave for the present just as though you don't know me at all? That's just part of the detail, Bunny. In principle, I'm being guided by you."

"In that case," I said, feeling hugely relieved, "I promise willingly."

She gave me a grateful look and, rising, drew up her hood, preparatory to departure.

"What a wonderful talk we've had!" she said. "And we're friends now, aren't we? I'm so glad. Good night, Bunny."

"Good night, Dinah," I said.

She opened the door a crack, peered out along the corridor, smiled at me once, most sweetly, then was gone. I expelled a long breath of relief and satisfaction and, well pleased with the progress I had made, was just leaning back against the pillows when I remembered the disturbing manner in which Dinah had got in touch with me. The belated thought struck me that I ought really to assure myself that she got back safely to her cabin, one never knowing what inebriates from the smoking saloon might be reeling and grimacing about the companionways of a liner at night.

I pulled on my trousers hastily and stepped out into the corridor just in time to see Dinah turn the corner into one of the main corridors running fore and aft. I followed.

The wider corridor, along which Dinah's slim, hooded figure was hurrying, was lighted by dim safety lamps spaced at wide intervals. For'ard, where the corridor opened into a small foyer, I saw her pause to reconnoiter the foyer before crossing it.

Not wishing, if seen, to appear to be dogging her, I, too, paused to reconnoiter the foyer before crossing it. And I saw fall across it a man's shadow, queerly slanted.

I peered up obliquely to my right and saw a man standing on the companion stairs, craning far over the banister to look along the corridor after Dinah. Suddenly he darted down the stairs, across the foyer, and, flattening himself against the wall, watched Dinah round the angle of it.

Some way along the corridor, Dinah opened a cabin door and went in. Instantly, the watcher across the foyer walked forward along the corridor and paused outside Dinah's cabin. He seemed to verify the number on the door, then turned and came walking back to the foyer.

I, too, stepped into the foyer. I was angry and disturbed. I had half a mind to accost and question the man, but I feared it might start an altercation which would involve Dinah in scandal.

I just took a good look at the chap as we passed in the foyer, and gave him a perfunctory, " 'Night."

" 'Night to you," he replied.

He was the lean, gray-haired, hard-looking customer who had been raking in the chips at poker in the smoking saloon. I realized he must have been coming down from a late sitting when he had spotted Dinah. He looked dangerous to me, and I did not like the slight, grim smile on his face.

I returned to my own cabin mystified and uneasy. During the long weeks of the voyage from Australia, Dinah seemed to have become involved not only with one, but with two men. She was beginning to seem something of a riddle to me. What the truth was I could not imagine.

By a bit of luck, the first person I saw when I went on deck early next morning was my friend the Assistant Purser. He was strolling up and down smoking a before-breakfast pipe, and I fell in with him, for I wanted to ask him about the gray-haired poker player.

But before I could do so, and as we reached the for'ard rail and were about to turn to retrace our leisurely steps aft, the Assistant Purser paused.

"There she is," he said. "Girl I told you about, Mr. Manders. Mary Moore."

The deck below was thronged with Third Class saloon passengers. Standing alone by the capstan right up in the bows was a slender, dark-haired girl.

"I'm sorry for that kid," the Assistant Purser said grimly. "Look at her there. Probably thinking of what lies ahead of her at the end of this voyage. No money, no job, a London winter. Pretty different from the prospect she was going out to. Just one little mistake—listening to a smooth charmer like Forbes—and there she is. Not a prospect in the world." He shook his head. "And you can't tell 'em!"

As we turned to retrace our steps aft, the gray-haired poker player stepped out on the deck in front of us. He wore a white pongee suit. He walked across to lean with folded arms on the rail.

"Who's that party?" I muttered.

"Now, there's another," said the Assistant Purser. "His name's Ben Galley. He's a cardsharper. I know it but can't prove it. Heaven knows I've dropped enough hints to passengers not to play with him, but it's a waste of breath. They won't be told, Mr. Manders."

"Have you noticed him show any interest in Miss Raffles?" I asked uneasily.

"Come to think of it," he said, "he tried damned hard to ingratiate himself both with her and with Forbes. Forbes cold-shouldered him, having no interest in anyone but Miss Raffles. What made you ask, Mr. Manders?"

But I nudged him. Dinah and Forbes had come out on deck just ahead. Extraordinary girl! She looked as fresh, as limpid as the morning. She gave the Assistant Purser a reserved, charming smile, but her gray eyes committed upon myself an act of cool oblivion.

That night I was leaning gloomily on the rail of the boat deck when I heard the approach of idling footsteps, and a voice murmured, "One of the protected ones—"

I glanced over my shoulder, to see the shadowy forms of Dinah and Forbes, arm in arm, strolling by.

"Remember, Dinah?" Forbes was saying. "The gypsy girl at Naples? You're alone in the world, my dear. What is there for you in London but disappointment and heartbreak? Confound it, Dinah"—his tone grew ardent, urgent—"why not sail with me from Lisbon? I can make you in sober fact, if you choose, 'one of the protected ones' of this world. I have the means, Dinah, you know it. There's nothing I can't give you."

His lying voice faded as they passed. I was burning with rage, but I had promised Dinah to let her handle the detail of her break with him in her own way, and I was about to step out and beat a retreat when they came again, strolling back past me, and I heard Forbes saying earnestly:

"But of course! What else? Of course I'm talking of marriage—"

"It's impossible, Graham," I heard Dinah say. "It's quite impossible."

"But why, Dinah? Why?"

I waited with relish for her to give it to him straight from the shoulder that she knew very well he already had a wife.

Instead, she said, "Because the real reason I'm going to London, Graham, is—to be married."

I wondered if I had heard aright. I was utterly bewildered.

"Oh," I heard her say, "I know I ought to have told you long ago, Graham—right at the beginning of our—our—what I thought was our mere flirtation. I feel so ashamed now."

"Confound it," Forbes said, "who are you going to marry?" They had paused.

"Does it matter?" she said, rather listlessly. "I call him Bunny."

At this, I wondered if my hearing or merely my reason were deserting me.

"You don't love him," Forbes said violently. "You love me, Dinah, and you're coming with me. Forget London. Forget him—this Bunny—"

"It's not so simple, Graham," she said. "I promised. I gave him my word. He's waiting there in London for me. It's all arranged—"

Suddenly enlightenment flashed upon me. She was making her break. She would not tell him she knew that he was trying to deceive her, that he already had a wife. No, she was punishing him, instead, where it would hurt most, in his jealous possessiveness. There was another man waiting for her . . .

"To hell with him!" Forbes said. "Dinah, send him a cable from Marseilles tomorrow."

"I can't, Graham. It's out of the question. Don't ask me. I owe so much to Bunny. I'm so deeply committed, so much in his debt. My fare to England, my bills in Australia that he arranged for his lawyers to settle up for me. Oh, I can't desert him, Graham. Truly, it's unthinkable. I . . ." They passed from my view—and hearing.

In Marseilles harbor next morning as I shaved, still thinking about this, a knock sounded on my door. A steward entered, handed me a note. I motioned him to wait and, all lathered as I was, tore open the envelope.

The note was from Dinah:

Dear Bunny,
The ship sails again at six this evening. I am so glad to have been guided by you, and I am making a clean break, as you so wisely advise. So as to make it quite irrevocable, I have made up my mind to leave the ship altogether, here at Marseilles.

I think I must have the same feeling as my brother, who says in his letter to me that there are times when he simply doesn't know what he would do without you. For, Bunny—may I count on your escort overland to London? If so, perhaps you would be so very kind as to book a room for me, just for tonight, at the Hotel du Monde here, in the rue de la Canebière, and meet me there some time during the afternoon?

My brother, in his letter, tells me that I can always "confidently count on Bunny"—and indeed, I am doing so.

Your affectionate friend,

Dinah Raffles

This was highly satisfactory to me and, thinking I would scribble her a line to assure her of my compliance with her wishes, I asked the steward, "Is Miss Raffles in her cabin?"

"No, sir," he said. "She went ashore about ten minutes ago."

"Indeed?" I said, surprised. "With her luggage?"

"Oh, no, sir," said the steward. "Just sightseeing. She went with Mr. Forbes."

The day darkened for me. I could see no sense in this. If she had made her break with Forbes, what rhyme or reason was there in waltzing off on another shore excursion with the man?

At all events, there was nothing for it but to pack my traps and go to the Hotel du Monde on the sweltering Canebière, crowded with carriages, thundering drays, and clanging little yellow two-horse tramcars.

I reserved her a room; and, in deference to the conventions, I conveyed my own traps to another hotel nearby.

Here I had a surprise, for, as I entered, I saw a slender, dark-haired girl, pretty but with a worried, preoccupied expression, just turning away from the desk, with a pageboy carrying her valises. I thought I recognized her; and, sure enough, on my signing the register, I saw that the last entry was "Mary Moore—British."

I lunched on bouillabaisse and at two o'clock went to the Hotel du Monde. It looked to me a very average kind of fleabag, but I sat waiting in its dim foyer until well past five.

Then an appalling suspicion began to shape in my mind. Suppose that in the end Dinah had had the reckless folly to yield to Forbes's persuasions? Suppose her note to me had been a trick designed to rid herself of a hampering complication? Suppose her object was to leave me behind?

The idea sent a hot wave of panic over me. I snatched out my watch. I sprang to my feet. It was just on six. Sailing time! At that very moment, the deep siren-boom of a departing liner sounded to me across the flat rooftops of this alien city. I stood there stunned.

Then the bead curtain hanging in the street doorway was swept aside—and Dinah Raffles walked in.

She was followed by a cabman carrying her portmanteaus. In her cool, composed way, Dinah glanced round the foyer. She saw me standing there staring, and she came to me, smiling, and gave me her hand.

"I see my brother was right," she said, "when he told me to count on you. Will you see me to my room, please, Bunny? I have something to say to you."

The porter carried her luggage upstairs, and unlocked the door of Dinah's room.

I was too relieved by her arrival to take issue with her incorrigible disregard of normal convention. I tipped the porter heavily and explained to him that I had news from England to discuss with the lady.

I was embarrassed by the inimitably Gallic look he gave me; but this was Marseilles, and he left us without demur, closing the door behind him.

I turned to Dinah. In the dim, hot room, with its closed shutters, she made a cool and graceful figure, not a hair of her fair head out of place, the tiny black velvet bow neat at her nape.

I moved to throw open the shutters, but she stayed me with a light hand on my arm.

"Not just yet, Bunny," she said, and she smiled. "I've been guided so wonderfully by you, and I've made a clean break just as you advised—but there's a tiny little complication come up. Do you think that presently, just for a few seconds, you could manage to look thoroughly grim and formidable?"

As she asked this surprising question, she was unstrapping one of her portmanteaus. She raised the lid, took out something that jingled.

"When I was a small girl—oh, eleven, twelve, thirteen, Bunny," she said, "I used to go about with my poor old guardian, W. F. Raffles, on his bank-inspecting rounds. It was lonely for him, driving his horse and trap all by himself, so I often went along. Because of the possibility of bushrangers he always went armed— and he carried these things, too. I kept them as a memento of him, for I loved him dearly. I never dreamed they'd come in useful one day."

She turned to me, holding, of all things, a pair of handcuffs. Before I realized what she was about, she snapped one cuff on to my left wrist and the other on to her own right wrist. Lightly but firmly, she steered me to a position behind one of the window curtains.

"There, that's splendid, Bunny," she said. "Don't make a

sound till I give a little twitch on the handcuffs, then just step out, looking grim, and with your right hand in your pocket, and say harshly, 'Right! That's enough!'

"You see? And now I stand with my back to the curtain edge, looking toward the door—like this, you see—and my right hand a bit behind me, so that the handcuff won't be seen. There, now we're just right. All we have to do is wait."

In all my felonious experience with A. J. Raffles, never had I known the like of this with his sister Dinah. The dim, hot room was still. The pulse throbbed a measured beat in my temples.

Suddenly I became aware of footsteps approaching along the landing. Steady, unhurried, somehow sinister, on they came. They stopped. On the door of the room fell three distinct, deliberate knocks.

"*Entrez,*" Dinah called in her clear voice.

I heard the door open slowly, close slowly. I chewed my lip. In the room, silence stretched interminably.

Then a man's flat voice said, "Frightened, Miss Raffles? You look kind of frightened, standing there."

Dinah did not speak, did not stir. A bead of sweat trickled down my face.

"Nothing to say?" said the man. "Beauty and brains and a still tongue? You're a wonder. Honest, I mean it, I really do. Mind if I light a cheroot? I've had sort of a hard day—following Miss Raffles and Mr. Forbes around Marseilles."

I peered down at Dinah's manacled hand. It was perfectly still but tightly clenched, the knuckles white. I heard the scrape of a match, caught a whiff of smoke.

"Did you know," said the man's voice, "that I'd marked Forbes as my meat within a few days of our sailing from Sydney? I reckoned to relieve him of some of his excess funds at poker. Could I get him in a game? Not a hope!

"All he had time for was a slip of a girl with fair hair and a bit of black velvet ribbon in it. Kind of ladylike and elegant. Lady born, in fact. That's what she seemed to me, at any rate. Until I discovered that she'd suddenly taken to slipping down to Third Class, very clandestine, to talk to a girl down there called Mary Moore. Now, what did that mean?"

He chuckled.

"I couldn't find out," he said. "But just last night I had a bit of luck. Spotted you and Forbes right up for'ard on the boat deck. It was nice and dark, and I got close enough to hear a thing or two. Very interesting!

"I heard Forbes begging and imploring you to let him give you fifteen hundred pounds to pay off an indebtedness you reckoned you'd incurred to some man in London—an obligation that, you felt, compelled you to keep a promise to marry him."

A bead of sweat trickled down my face. I realized that Ben Galley must have overheard the continuation of the conversation of which I had heard the beginning.

"Forbes wanted you to run away with him," said Galley. "But no, you felt too bound and beholden to the man in London. Only, somehow, in the end you kind of let Forbes talk you round. Didn't you?

"Only, Ben Galley—Ben was curious to know more about all this. So he followed you and Forbes ashore today. Off you went in a victoria to the Crédit Lyonnais, where he drew fifteen hundred pounds, in hundred-pound notes, on a letter of credit, to square the debt to the would-be bridegroom in London.

"Then off to the Post and Telegraphs and, while he waits in the victoria, in you go—to seal the notes into an official registration envelope and send it off insured, with a line to tell the poor fellow in London he'd lost you.

"But *did* you in fact send off that money? Not you! You came out with that money still in your purse, and off you went with Forbes on a day's sightseeing, with poor Ben Galley following along. Eh?"

He laughed aloud.

"And then what?" he asked. "Why, you got back to the ship, all hot and done up from sightseeing, and you both went down to your cabins for a nice leisurely bath and change before the dinner bugle went. But what happens? Five minutes later, up on deck you come, with a steward carrying your baggage. And you quit the ship for keeps, just as they're getting ready to remove the gangway for sailing."

A tramcar's bell clanged sharply under the window.

"And when he realizes what's happened," said Ben Galley, "he'll keep very, very mum, will the rich irresistible Mr. Forbes, because this is a story he wouldn't like his wife in the Argentine to hear about.

"And so here's Ben, Miss Raffles. When I saw you nip down the gangway, baggage and all, I wasn't far behind, baggage and all. I followed you here. Didn't expect that, did you?"

He was wrong, I knew. Dinah had known.

"I've got a proposition," said Galley. "I can't imagine where in the world you got that 'waiting bridegroom' story, but it has possibilities. With your looks and that fairy tale and my poker, we can make a tidy pile, you and me, traveling the world. In partnership. Me the senior partner and banker. And banker, Miss Raffles! So just fork over the fifteen hundred, for a start. Let's have the money, dear."

Dinah did not stir, did not say a word. My heart thumped. All the time, the light filtering between the slats of the shutters was fading.

"Stubborn?" said Ben Galley. "Clever girl like you?"

Into his voice crept an uglier, a colder note.

"You know better than that, surely—a girl with your gifts. Have you forgotten where you are? Marseilles, my dear! La Canebière, my dear! Do you know their reputation? You've been clever, you've taken risks, but you've maneuvered yourself into kind of a nasty corner. Strange things can happen in Marseilles to young ladies who take risks, Miss Dinah Raffles."

I felt a twitch of the handcuff at my wrist. Instantly, with my right hand jammed forward in my pocket, I stepped out sharply from behind the curtain.

"Right!" I said. "That's enough."

Dinah, looking at Ben Galley, gave a slight shrug and lifted her hand so that he could not fail to see that she was handcuffed to me.

The effect upon Galley was electrifying. He took just one horrified look at the handcuffs, then spun round, yanked open the door, slammed it behind him. The sound of his running footsteps receded rapidly along the landing.

"Bunny!" said Dinah. Her voice shook. "Oh, Bunny! Bunny, you make a wonderful detective. He thinks he talked too much, and he won't stop running for a month."

She was laughing. Yet, in the twilit room, I had an impression that there was a tremor in her mirth. She had outwitted Galley. Without one word, by the simple gesture of lifting her hand so that he saw the handcuffs, she had outwitted him.

Yet I knew intuitively that she had been terrified of the man, for she was only a girl, after all—a young and human girl. And somehow, my unfettered arm was about her slim shoulders, patting them, seeking to comfort her, to soothe her.

"Dinah, my dear—" I was profoundly shaken by what I had heard. "The risks you've run—"

"But I had to, Bunny," she said, "because of the ribbon shop."

"Ribbon shop?" I said blankly.

"Mary Moore's ribbon shop," said Dinah. "You see, I was quite ready to be friends with Graham Forbes at first. I quite liked him. But when the Assistant Purser spoke to me about him, and when I slipped down and talked to Mary and heard how Forbes had lied to her and cheated her, I was furious.

"And I was worried about Mary because she seemed so sort of broken, no heart for anything, and nothing to go to, and no money, and I was afraid of what might become of her.

"So I asked her if she would like to have a little ribbon shop, and she said she would. Well, it seemed to me, Bunny, that the very least Forbes owed her was a little ribbon shop. Don't you agree?"

"Dinah," I said, amazed, "I—"

"But Mary's so proud," said Dinah. "I knew she'd never take the money for it if she thought it came from Forbes. So I just told her I had some business in Marseilles and that, if she'd just go ashore and wait for me at the nearest hotel to the Hotel du Monde, I'd call for her in the evening with my London lawyer, who was meeting me here—I meant you, of course, Bunny—and who'd easily arrange for some money for the ribbon shop, and then we'd all go on to London together by train.

"Bunny, do you think Forbes's fifteen hundred will be enough for a little ribbon shop?"

"Dinah," I said, with a thickness in my throat. "I don't know anything about ribbon shops. But, Dinah, don't you realize? If you had been alone, in Marseilles—with that man Galley."

"But I wasn't alone, Bunny," she said. "I knew I could count on you—my brother's friend! I knew I had you to protect me."

She was so close. I breathed the fern fragrance of her perfume. With my arm about her, my clumsy fingers touched the velvet of the little bow at her nape. The dim light filtering through the slats of the shutters made a pallor of her face. Her eyes shone like stars. Her lips, so close to mine, were smiling.

"One of the protected ones," she whispered. "A gypsy girl called me that, Bunny. And it's so true."

I felt her cool fingers cup my hot cheek for an instant, light as moths.

"So very true, my dear friend—Bunny," she breathed.

Then in a flash, to my bewilderment, she thrust me from her, and from the belt at her waist plucked out the key of the handcuffs. In a moment, she had them unlocked, and was all in a bustle for us to collect Mary and leave Marseilles at once, this very night, on the train for Paris.

Still dazed by what had happened, I went to the door and called the porter to help with the portmanteaus. A minute or so later Dinah and I were on our way to pick up Mary.

Dinah reached across to me in the shadowy interior of the vehicle. She tucked an envelope into my wallet pocket and gave the pocket a little pat.

"Of course, it must be you who produces the money when we've helped Mary find her little ribbon shop," she said. "I want you to be banker, Bunny. I want always to have you to guide me and advise me and think for me and protect me, just as my brother said you would, and as you've already done so wonderfully. And, Bunny . . ."

"Yes, Dinah?" I asked.

We had stopped outside Mary's hotel.

"Do you think that perhaps we'd better not tell my brother anything about all this? He mightn't understand, perhaps."

"Well, now, Dinah," I said slowly, "as to that, do you know —I really think he might!"

74 75 76 77 10 9 8 7 6 5 4 3 2 1

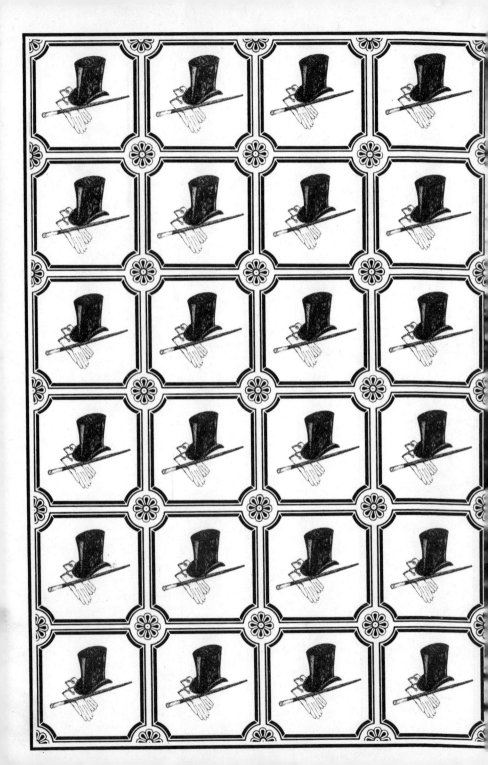